Riot and Retribution

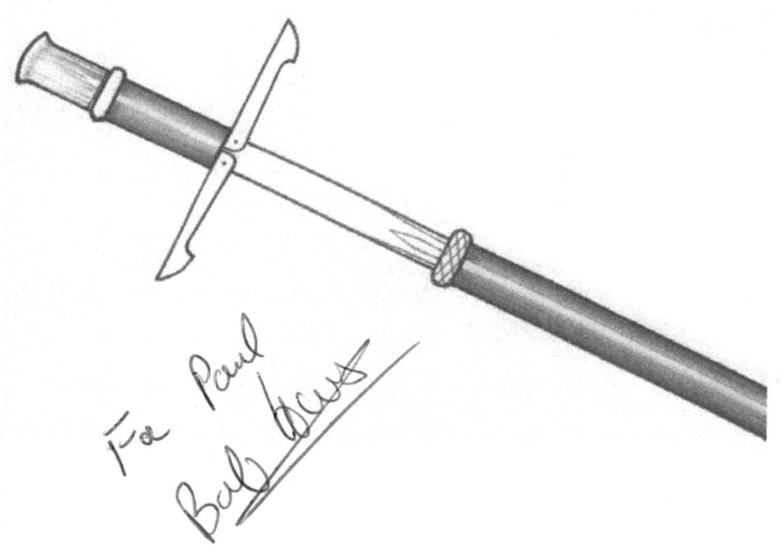

Alex E. Robertson

Best wishes,
Alex.

RIOT AND RETRIBUTION

Published by:

ALPHA Education Press
9010 93 Street NW
Edmonton, Alberta, Canada, T6C 3T4

Cover art created by Ana María Espiñeira Luksić (Viña del Mar, Chile)
Cover layout by Hilary Strickland (Bath, UK)
Swordstick on cover and title page, other illustrations and maps with the assistance of Max Schonbach (Bristol, UK).

The artwork for the brothel scene was inspired by an image in: Hill, Marilynn Wood. Their Sisters' Keepers: Prostitution in New York City, 1830-1870, Berkeley: University of California Press, 1993.

Library and Archives Canada Cataloguing in Publication

Robertson, Alex E., author
Riot and retribution / Alex E. Robertson.

ISBN 978-0-9938764-2-4 (paperback).--ISBN 978-0-9938764-4-8 (hard cover).--ISBN 978-0-9938764-5-5 (ebook)

I. Title.

PS8635.O22835R56 2016 C813'.6 C2015-904648-3
C2015-908220-X

Printed and bound by CPI Group (UK) Ltd, Croydon, CR0 4YY

Contents

Cast of principal characters

London

Nathaniel Parry	gentleman, occasionally employed as a government agent
Caradoc	his dog, a Welsh terrier
Lord Melbourne	Home Secretary in Earl Grey's Whig government
Lord Palmerston	Foreign Secretary
Richard Percy	Home Office administrator
John Drake	Foreign Office employee
Charlotte Drake	his wife
Elizabeth Drake	his daughter

Bath

Dr Charles Parry	physician
Emma Parry	his wife
Raphael Vere	owner of the New Bank
Mathilda Vere	his wife
Roderick Wilson	senior clerk at the New Bank
Janie Wilson	his wife
Henry Blake	clerk at the New Bank
Anna Grant	his fiancée and also a governess
Captain Oliver Peterson	retired sea captain
Lydia Peterson	his wife
Emma Peterson	his second daughter
Maddie and Ginette	his twin teenage daughters
Diarmuid Casey	a political agent
Colette Montrechet	a courtesan
Martha Spence	landlady of Walcot Street
Thomas Spence	her father-in-law
Matthew Spence	her son, a sailor
Mary Spence	her daughter-in-law
Johnty Spence	her grandson

Mr Bishop	landlord of the White Hart Inn
Frederick Tooson	barman
Tobias Caudle	potboy
Arthur Jamieson and Robert Turner	printers
Captain Charles Wilkins	textile mill owner and captain of the yeomanry
Neville Fairfield and James Cruttwell	members of the yeoman cavalry
Joshua Shadwell	owner of the Green Park brothel
Rosie Shadwell	his wife
Jabez and Billy	his bodyguards and enforcers
Barbara and Abigail	child prostitutes
Frances	child procured for sale
Mordecai and Declan	bargees, occasionally employed by Shadwell

Outlying villages

Howard Dill	gentleman of Norton St Philip
Mrs Danby	Mathilda Vere's mother

Bristol

Edwin Ravenswood	ship owner, exporter and a principal investor in the New Bank
Amanda Ravenswood	his wife
Eli Trevellis	captain of Ravenswood's clipper, the *Blue Dragon*
Cornelius Fu Lee	guest from China at Ravenswood's residence
Mr Kizhe	business associate from China

Prologue

Evening: 29th September, 1831.
Cantina Buenavista, Puerto de la Cruz, Tenerife.

They were almost ready to set sail for Bristol, twelve months after they had left for the China seas. The crew of the *Mathilda* had spent the last three days taking on supplies, patching the torn main-sail and recuperating after the long haul round the African coast. The shabby cantina had been full to bursting since half past seven that evening, when all the crew, bar the last dog watch, had been let loose on their final shore leave. A hiss of expectation coursed through the crowd as a velveteen curtain was pulled aside and a young woman and two men stepped out into the light.

Isabella snatched up two handfuls of her polka-dot frilled skirt, arched her neck, and slowly lifted her sculpted head framed in coiled black plaits. Flashing fire from her eyes, in one swift move she hitched the hem above her knees as the men howled a welcome. Slowly at first, but then gaining speed, her neat narrow feet in the old black shoes began to tap. Juan, sweating into his shirt in the heat of the bar, clapped in syncopation as the metal tips rang on the flag floor and Miguel closed his eyes, lifting his harsh voice in a chanting cry. Faster she stamped, faster, her fingers clicking, her arms moving in the sinuous rhythms of the Andalusian back streets she had left behind.

The sailors were transfixed, the front row brought literally to its knees, largely on the insistence of the men behind. All worshipped at the shrine and competed for a better view: especially of her miraculous bosom which heaved with the drama of the dance over a tight-laced red bodice; but also to see more of her satin skin, glowing like warm honey in the lamp-light, her slicked-back oiled hair glossy as a sea-bird fresh from a dive. Their battered spirits drank in the sight of her, and revived.

"Fine woman that," said a philosophical drinker at the bar, without taking his eyes from the show. "I'd take 'er home for two pins but I can't see 'er fittin' into the general way of things in Compton Dando."

"Too wild you'd be thinkin'?"

"Exac'ly."

Away from the bar and the dance floor, other women plied a different trade. At a table by the stone stairway a fist flashed and landed square in the slack jaw of a sailor, sending him sprawling back in his chair, but leaving a smiling girl in a yellow frock still perching on his knee.

"Come wi'me mi'dear," said Elijah taking a tight grip on her arm and hauling her off the limp sailor. "He can't hold his drink."

From a dark corner, Matthew watched the scene unfold over the dregs of his wine and his empty plate. He disliked Elijah Berry, a swaggering bully of a man, and was annoyed to see his petty victory. He rose silently and began to edge away. His head had ached too much to join the banter at the bar and he was still nursing a maimed hand, roughly bandaged to protect the two cauterised stumps. They were all he had left of the two middle fingers on his right hand after a clumsy accident in the main-mast rigging. He cursed as he stumbled over the threshold, hoping it was the drink and not the other problem, the recurrent fever which had plagued him since they had made their last landfall in the Gulf of Guinea. He made his way out into the sultry night, passing more overheated cantinas disgorging ragged bursts of music, the buzz of talk, and disordered crashes from erupting fights.

"Too many men, not enough women," he muttered to himself, catching sight of two sailors who had struck lucky and were following a raven haired trollop into a back room. She glanced behind her, swaying her hips, trailing her fringed shawl, lazily amused as they capered after her. One was just a boy, with a reckless grin and high hopes.

A bawling chorus blasted out from the next open door.

"Farewell and adieu, to you fair Spanish la-hey-dies!
Farewell and adieu to you Ladies of Spain.
For we've received orders to sail for Old England
And perhaps we shall never more see you again!"

He passed the fish-wives' deserted stalls and the squat black fort of San Felipe, walked unsteadily along the harbour-side and headed for the quay where the *Mathilda* swayed on the tide. Exhausted, he sat on the low wall and looked back. High above the small knot of the town and towering above the island was El Teide. It had bare scree slopes like the mountains of the moon, and its snowcap glinted cruelly in the starlight. He had thought to climb it, at least to the snow line. It was not to be. He rose and picked his way over the ropes and lobster pots to the ship. Once back on board he took the companionway to the lower deck and the safety of his hammock. He rolled in, gasping down shallow breaths in the close dark.

As his heart steadied, the familiar sounds of the night washed back into his consciousness: the chirrup of the crickets from the shrubs by the harbour wall, the whine of low flying insects, the creak of settling timbers, distant voices and snatches of song from the bars. He sank into a confused sleep and his body started to pump out the familiar round of symptoms: violent heats, shivers and drenching sweats, followed by creeping chill and shooting needles of pain in his limbs. Dark thoughts tormented his muddled head: dreams of the voyage, the Indian opium shipments to China, and the secret cargo, hidden in a cabin all the way from Bristol to disappear one night after they docked in the Gulf of Tonkin. The cargo had not rested easy. Young voices had set up keening cries night after night in the early months of the voyage. He had heard their punishments and the mewling after. He woke with a shudder, groped in his pocket for the pellet of opium he had saved for the night and bit into it. As he waited for the deadening rush of peace he prayed for his safe return home, to Bath and his Mary. It would happen: touch wood. He stretched out his good hand to the comforting timbers of the hull.

Early evening: 30th September, 1831.
Brooks's Club, St James's St, London.

William Lamb, also known as Lord Melbourne, and since the spectacular collapse of the Tory party, the nation's Home Secretary, shoved out his legs to full stretch and arched his back against the comfortable support of the leather armchair. He held himself taut momentarily, before subsiding, hands clasped behind his head. He eyed the side table at his right hand: a plate bearing a solitary biscuit in a sea of crumbs, an empty glass and a drained crystal decanter standing easy by a three branched silver candelabra. This last was lavishly engraved with glimmering festoons, positively awash with them, as he was himself, with the vintage port.

Melbourne was pleased with himself, pleased to be with his own coterie in his club, pleased to be isolated from the harsh world that caterwauled indistinctly behind its sheltering walls. He relished his image as a champion of liberality and sturdy independence, as did most Whigs. More than this, or perhaps because of it, he and his party were eminently better fitted to run the country than the Hanoverian monarchs who squatted on the throne.

"What was said about Johnny Russell's people?" he mused, "just a little greater than God?"

Melbourne gave a brief neigh of suppressed laughter. His people, irreverent and swaggering, inbred and adulterous, were the only ones capable of reforming the country whilst keeping the reins firmly held in their own aristocratic hands. They were in power on a reform ticket, and had to deliver votes, at least to the middle classes. The so-called "coach of reform" had lurched into motion and was now careering wildly into the unknown. It needed a strong driver, holding both reins and whip in his hands. A new government, a new turnip-headed king in the person of William IV, ripe in years, keen for action and simply in need of a steer: a new decade.

Melbourne's bubble of enthusiasm suddenly deflated, pierced by the unpleasant memory that 1830 had ushered in a vicious revival of revolution in Europe and that the Whig reform programme, supposedly bringing a fair voice to the people, was specifically designed to avoid any suggestion of democracy. Melbourne grimaced as he contemplated the next few months, during which the government would have to achieve this miracle, less of a coach drive perhaps than a tightrope walk over a yawning abyss leading directly to hell. Passion, sound and fury were not in Melbourne's repertoire, and all were being traded wholesale by the many warring factions. He preferred to cultivate the image of the dilettante, the man of many parts, effortlessly achieving his purposes with no perceptible effort being expended. He always liked to think of himself as the classic eighteenth century man of reason: civilised, languid, cynical. He turned his mouth down in distaste at the prospect of the trials ahead.

However, just one more problem needed to be addressed that day, and it could be dispatched in the club. This was a happy thought, as the atmosphere in all departments of Whitehall was becoming increasingly hysterical. He sighed at a mental image of Wellington in the Lords' lobby the previous week, puce and glowering at the prospect of giving a few middle class men a vote, hoarsely demanding "the sharpening of swords" for the onslaught to follow when, presumably, the ravening masses would rise and overthrow all that was decent. Whether the people proved to be revolting or not, it was certain that intelligence must be improved in order to forestall any plots which might be hatching. Wellington was certainly right in another of his mutterings, that when planning a campaign one must always be able to see what is on the other side of the hill.

With great reluctance, Melbourne acknowledged his need for more accurate information. Every large town needed efficient government servants of some description to support the work of the Justices of the Peace. These servants needed to keep their ears to the ground to detect the first whispers of trouble.

All major industrial centres had been discussed the previous week, mainly through liaison with the local magistrates, as had the eastern agricultural areas, but decisions needed to be made about intelligence from the south-west. To his surprise, this area was proving to be something of a hot-bed of trouble. Fortunately, the matter seemed to be in hand, and this evening the formalities of engagement would be completed. Lord Palmerston, the Foreign Secretary, fellow club member and Melbourne's unofficial brother-in-law would materialise, bringing with him a solution in the shape of an experienced official from his department. Palmerston had other business to deal with concerning the port of Bristol and had suggested that his man could oversee both foreign and domestic intelligence interests from there.

Palmerston's long-standing affair with Melbourne's sister

Emily, conducted with barely the minimum of discretion, was tolerated by her husband Lord Cowper and also by her brother. Melbourne admired Emily unreservedly, despite her being devilish beyond permission, and he liked Palmerston all the more for the connection. At the prospect of the endlessly energetic Pam wading in to solve the remaining problems, Melbourne allowed his mind to stray from those pressing and ugly matters. He detested the concept of surveillance, as did all right thinking Englishmen. Damned shabby occupation for a gentleman in his view: smacked of Continental deceit, but, needs must. Britain stood on the edge of a political precipice with threats to law and order not only from the middle and respectable lower classes, all of whom could rise if the voting was not widened, but also from the terrifying mobs, the residue of society lurking beneath. Misplaced radical agitation could cause them to rise from the depths, an unstoppable tide of scum discrediting the acceptable classes who supported change. His thoughts depressed him and he sighed windily.

"But the port was excellent," he declared, cheering up. "Oh yes.... uncommon excellent." He rolled his tongue over his front teeth and smacked his lips. "Damned fine. Deuced good."

The heavy door opened silently to admit Chislett, Melbourne's favourite club servant.

"Mi'lord, Lord Palmerston's coach has arrived."

"Excellent," said Melbourne, rubbing his hands. "Two non-members will be accompanying him Chislett, so show them all into the Strangers' Room."

Melbourne quit his usual seat and strolled across the hall to the only room in the club where he could deal with the man that Palmerston was bringing to him. He stationed himself in the most comfortable chair with his back to the St James's Street window. The dying rays of the autumn sun shafted through it, ready to do splendid service by illuminating the rest of the party to a detailed scrutiny, whilst leaving him inscrutably shaded. As he smiled indulgently to himself he heard the confused sounds of a party entering the hall. In a moment Chislett ushered them in.

"Mi'Lord: Lord Palmerston, Mr Percy and Mr Drake."

Percy and Drake bowed, murmuring, "Mi'lord", obsequiously from the doorway, whereas Palmerston swaggered in, blared a greeting and flung himself into the seat opposite Melbourne. He exuded confidence from the shock of wiry badger-hair on his head to the tip of his mud-bespattered boots. He was flushed and wind-burned from the exertions of two day's hunting, a picture of rude health. He settled expansively into his chair, eyes darting round the room. Tall and spare, Richard Percy, a recent addition to Melbourne's secretariat, stood awkwardly. He was fishing in his bag to locate paper, ink bottle and pen, pausing to rake his hand through his lank dark hair, sweeping it out of his eyes, then to adjust his gold-rimmed glasses which were in danger of slipping off the end of his nose. John Drake had deftly manoeuvred himself into position for taking the seat to Melbourne's immediate left, which was nearest to the drinks table. He could slide into it effortlessly when the noble lord deigned to invite the commoners to be seated.

However, Melbourne was not occupied with the furthering of Drake or Percy's comfort, but was focused on his own material well being. "More port Chis-lett," he drawled. "Taylor's 1811 mark you, and snap to it. Then away you go. I want this room free from servants until further notice".

"Yes mi'lord," said Chislett blandly. He bowed, retreated and silently closed the door.

"Good evening gentlemen." Melbourne indicated seats for the two guests by sweeping his arm vaguely round the available chairs, the sketchy gesture lifting his rear modestly from his seat, which was as much of a formal greeting as he was inclined to give. Percy sat economically, setting up his writing materials, whilst Drake took his place as he did everything, to maximise comfort for himself. He settled his stocky body into the luxurious depths of the seat, smoothed his reddish-brown beard, narrowed his eyes and prepared to enjoy this unusual opportunity to study two of the most powerful men in the kingdom at close quarters. Chislett glided in with a silver tray bearing more port, and glasses, which he made a move to fill.

"Light the candles first Chislett", ordered Palmerston, ruthlessly sabotaging the carefully staged *mise en scène*. "Let the dog see the rabbit. What!" He continued briskly. "Now then Melbourne, I hear there was renewed rumpus in your place yesterday afternoon. How's the Bill?"

The Reform Bill, the only Bill, and as Lord Brougham repeated endlessly, "nothing but the Bill", was everyone's obsession. It was the first test of fire for the Whigs since ousting the Tories, who had had their marching orders purely because Wellington would not accept any change of any kind in the voting system. Since June the Tory majority in the House of Lords had been in the process of bellowing down the second version of the Bill, a furore outside the hearing of Palmerston whose Irish title kept him in the gladiatorial pen that was the House of Commons.

Melbourne smirked. "The Iron Duke is not enjoying his rustication from office Pam. He is leading the roar to devour our offering, despite our handsome majority in your place and the hateful prospect of the masses rising to murder us all in our beds if we fail."

Secretary Percy had organised himself sufficiently to perfect his attitude of readiness, sharpened pen in hand.

"Damn it Percy! What the hell do you think you are doing?" said Melbourne with unusual vim. Percy blenched and began to shovel his belongings away even more smartly than he had taken them out. "You don't take notes in the Club for God's sake man. You are here to listen and then to take yourself off and do your scribbling back in Downing Street. And what the devil were you going to write anyway? That the people terrify the government? What would happen if such sentiments were read? No, no, no! Wait and listen. You will hear news of a contract if all proceeds well. You will draw it up in your office."

"I am sorry my Lord," blustered Percy, nettled to be criticised in front of Drake. "I misunderstood."

Melbourne's focus of concern had already moved on from Percy who was ignored. He turned again to Palmerston.

"Now Pam," continued Melbourne, "the matter in hand. As you know I am in need of a small number of experienced gentlemen to take themselves off to principal towns during this present period of instability. Apart from the reports from our magistrates we need other streams of information from experienced people who know what they are looking for. We will not entertain free-lance, *agents provocateurs,* ours will be government servants adept at working in the field. Northern, central and eastern centres we seem to have settled, we must conclude with the south-west where I gather you have an interest." He gestured to Drake. "This gentleman is your protégé I take it?"

"Yes indeed, my protégé," beamed Palmerston fruitily. "This is Mr John Drake. Done sterling service in France for the Foreign Office during the recent revolution and before. Three years was it?"

Drake nodded in agreement and began energetically, "Yes mi'lord I was…"

"Son-in-law of Fitzroy. Placed you in the Office under Canning, didn't he Drake? South-west man originally. Some family down Bristol way haven't you? He's the best man for your needs Melbourne, and for mine."

Drake abandoned his efforts to enlarge on his experiences as he was, at long last, motioned to help himself from the drinks tray by Melbourne.

Drake appeared to be giving rapt attention to the noble lords, but had taken to covertly lusting after the distinguished 1811 residing in the port decanter. He reached reverently for his glass, paused to savour the heady nose and sank a generous swig which coursed through him to his very toes. He shivered with greedy delight, cast his eyes round like a ferret and ran his finger round the inside of his shirt collar, a habit betraying his excitement. Drake inspected the decor of the room minutely: brown and green leather, burgundy drapes. Struggling not to grin at the sheer glory of it all, yet intoxicated by his good fortune, he breathed in the heady scents of rich tobacco and a complex bouquet of wines and spirits, which seemed to have seeped into the fabric of the room. He scanned the silver on the side tables and mantelpiece and tried to read the titles on the oil portraits and sporting scenes. This was his first visit, as Brooks's Club was far beyond his social circle and pocket. Key lair of the Whig party since the early days of the old King George III and with shadowy links to the Hell Fire Club and its motto: "Do what thou wilt", the Club exerted an irresistible charm, enhanced by its fearsome reputation for extracting fortunes at the gaming tables as tribute from its elite members. Drake decided, then and there, that he would do almost anything to be part of this tribe: this solid-gold, hall-marked gang of cronies. He wanted it so much that it started to hurt. It was a gnawing emptiness in his belly that soured his enjoyment of the moment and also his considerable successes to date. His hand strayed to his neck again, but his smile was controlled, fixed. Would the Strangers' Room be the furthest he ever got? Surely not, it would make him all of a piece with disappointed money lenders hunting down aristocratic debtors or the doomed Candidates who waited to see if they had survived the Club elections and been deemed fit for membership.

From dull and respectable middle-class origins in the wholesale of textiles, Drake Senior, originally from Frome, had carved out a formidable empire of outlets in South London which had financed the launching of young Drake in the lowest ranks of London society. His ascent had been assured by a brilliant marriage to Charlotte, who at thirty-eight was his senior by two years and had been a mature bride at thirty-two when they tied the knot. Charlotte was a moderately attractive and aggressively stylish woman, sharp-witted and sharp-tongued enough to cut herself, and everyone in earshot when the mood took her. The prospect of marrying into her family and tapping the connections of her influential father far outweighed the periodic discomforts of living both with her and also their small, sulky daughter who was a diminutive replica of her mother. A job in the Foreign Office had enabled Drake to rise meteorically. He had secured a placement in Paris and smoothly transferred to serve the Whigs in the new ministry of 1830. The aching greed that motivated Drake coupled with his questionable morals made him a ruthless and calculating asset to the office. Deceitful, foxy, self-seeking: eyes flicking around the room, assessing, coveting, he wondered what his first move should be to secure membership for himself. On first impressions he gauged Melbourne to be cleverer and more brutal than he pretended to be, not a first choice then as his lever for breaking into the upper-layer of society. He was definitely better off staying in Palmerston's pocket. "Lord Cupid" was bluffer, louder, easier to read.

Palmerston continued: "He could work for you at the Home Office whilst keeping me abreast of affairs. I have a need to deploy some of my staff domestically as our Indian opium trade with China is under increasing threat. The Chinese Emperor has taken against it even more strenuously than before and the authorities in Canton are aiming for the utter destruction of our interest, which is immense. Instead of the 200 chests per year we managed a decade ago we are selling in excess of 20,000, but the amounts impounded are growing weekly as a direct result of this new found zeal." Palmerston thrust out his lower lip in annoyance at the thought of hordes of Chinese officials swarming over British shipping.

"Do I minute that mi'lord when I return to the Office?"

"Certainly not." Palmerston shot an irritated glance at Percy. "Where was I? Ah yes, I need accurate intelligence on the nature of Chinese attacks on our shipping: methods, numbers and so forth. Some vessels are avoiding the usual harbour at Lintin in the Pearl River estuary. I want to know more about these people at the sharp end, off-record. Official channels are not rooting out the truth." Palmerston kicked the edge of the table moodily, showering the floor with a dusting of dried mud. "There are some businessmen, especially in Bristol, who have been most helpful in facilitating the trade and eluding Chinese attentions. We need to know them rather better. I already have a very useful man there. Drake is well aware of him."

Drake arranged his smile into a new one which he hoped looked totally aware, capable and suave, disguising the fact that he had no idea to whom Palmerston referred. He succeeded in appearing sly, but as he was ignored by his superiors all he achieved was to reinforce Percy's dislike of him, which had been festering since the ride in Palmerston's coach from Whitehall. To Percy's disgust Drake had bragged and toadied to the noble lord throughout the journey, forcing him, Percy, to while away the time inventing fiendishly inappropriate acts of revenge.

"The Emperor will not succeed. We will not allow it." Palmerston narrowed his eyes, a capacity for cruelty was there, again, which none but Percy observed.

"The Chinese will buy our opium with their precious silver," Palmerston declared with a bleak finality. "We will obtain their tea, their porcelain, their brocade and their silk, and the trade will not drain our silver reserves. No, by God it will not," he concluded with a flourish, swigging down his port and slamming the glass down on the tray.

"No indeed," replied Melbourne. "By Gad no. But my urgent concerns, mi'dear fellow, are to nail down radical trouble makers in London, Birmingham, Bristol and all points of the compass. With respect, foreign affairs must take a back seat for now. We must improve our grip on the towns subtly, without the cavalry stampeding all over the show. Reform must go through calmly and to our recipe. Unappetising as it may be, we must bring in the middle classes and separate them from the mobs. The French learned the hard way. Remember 1789." He wagged a warning forefinger and then proceeded to stab the table with it rhythmically for additional emphasis.

"Divide and rule. It must be achieved but it will be as close run as Waterloo, mark my words! The whole land is ready to explode. We must not light the fuses gentlemen, but douse them. Quench them. 'Tis all we can safely do."

Melbourne had ceased to beat time on the table and wiped his brow. The silk handkerchief was already damp, as his brow had taken to perspiring freely as the port did its work in the confines of the closed room. The sea of problems, which had temporarily receded, had returned in fresh waves of torment. "The riots on the land have not yet subsided despite spirited action on the part of the magistrates. Labourers still think they will lose their jobs because of the damned threshing machines. Not that there is much grain to thresh given the poor harvest. Hunger has made them even more furious. Now townsmen are agitating for the vote, uniting the classes against law and order. It could bring us down Pam – bring all to hell! We must bring calm. Naturally the damned French with their Citizen King are giving quite the wrong example."

"A very different situation there if I may…"

"You may not Drake", interjected Palmerston, pouring another port for himself. Fortunately, Melbourne had subsided into silence, exhausted by his uncharacteristic outburst, so did not need to be coaxed down from his high horse. Palmerston continued: "What you will do is go to Bristol for Lord Melbourne, and for me, relay intelligence on the status of the region and make yourself known to the local party men, principal business men, bankers and so forth. You will be briefed, and liaise with our existing contact. If, of course, you are in agreement Melbourne?"

Melbourne, working hard to regain his indolent pose and, pretending to be giving his full attention to recharging his glass, managed a lazy nod in Palmerston's direction.

"Excellent, we agree then. You will also liaise with a junior associate who will assist you. Station yourself in Bristol and we will send him to Bath as the radicals seem to be making the old watering-hole into something of a stronghold. I gather the place is often full of foreigners. Anyway, spas are notorious hell-holes, attract all the refuse of the lower classes who prey on the visitors. Based there he can range over Somerset and Wiltshire cloth towns, if required, and report to you."

Melbourne swilled the port around his mouth thoughtfully. He stared briefly at Drake and caught sight of a ragged scar snaking up above the neckcloth and collar, to reach behind the ear. Drake seemed to sense the scrutiny and ran his finger furtively round the back of his neck.

"Nervous tic," thought Melbourne. "Not really surprising. Wonder if someone tried to slit his throat?"

He could well understand that someone might have been keen to achieve this, as he heartily abhorred greedy middle-class upstarts of Drake's stamp. He also disliked the task Drake had been asked to do. As the Tories had had enormous problems in the past with *agents provocateurs* making false claims to increase their pay, it was a key point of Whig policy to distance government from enthusiastic spying. They chose instead to depend on communications from local magistrates. This was vital for morale, as without London style police forces the provinces depended on the goodwill of the local gentry to ensure the rule of law and they were notoriously resentful of interference from London. The army was a brutally blunt instrument, which he would use only as the very last resort. It was time to play a useful card, ameliorate the influence of Drake and ensure that Palmerston did not conjour up another of his men to act as Drake's assistant.

"We will select remaining personnel for this mission only from agents experienced in foreign affairs and they will be paid a regular salary with no bonus payments. On this understanding my office will finance the venture. As for Drake's assistant, I suggest young Parry. His father, Owen Parry, worked for Castlereagh and Canning for years, took his son with him to

France in the late '20s. Died there, poor fellow, son stayed and made himself useful. You said foreigners at spas didn't you? He's good with foreign languages, speaks them like a damned native. Do you know him Drake?"

Drake had heard some stories of Parry senior, who by all accounts was a high-flying, daring and charismatic Welsh charmer who had given distinguished service. He hated him, or rather the thought of him, since they had not met.

"No my lord", he replied blandly, "though his father's name has been mentioned occasionally in the office."

Percy shot a withering glance at Drake, everyone with even the smallest connection to the Foreign Office had heard of Owen Parry, a thorough gentleman and therefore as unlike Drake as the proverbial chalk was to cheese.

"Now Percy," said Melbourne, "you will take yourself off shortly and conclude the necessary paperwork. Just repeat what you have gathered."

Percy answered primly. "Mr Drake to Bristol. Mr Parry to Bath with the remit to visit other towns in Somerset and Wiltshire. All agreed on the authority of Lords Melbourne and Palmerston. Mr Parry to report to Mr Drake. Both to be paid and retained by Home Office. Purpose: intelligence gathering on radical groups and the progress of business contacts with China." Percy's port was untouched, and was destined to remain so.

"Capital," Melbourne rallied at the conclusion of business and rubbed his hands together briskly. "No delay, no delay. Start tomorrow Drake. Take up residence in Bristol, for the foreseeable. Good to meet you. Back to the office with you Percy, there's a good fellow."

Drake and Percy rose as a Greek chorus and bowed briefly. "Thank-you , mi'lords. Good evening."

To Melbourne's surprise, Palmerston also leapt to his feet. His keen hearing had picked up the beginnings of a familiar ragged cheer from the gaming rooms above. He moved swiftly to the door to alert a Club servant that the guests were to be seen out. “Indeed, good evening gentlemen. Well done Drake. Thank you Percy.”

He shot his frilled cuffs in anticipation. “Fancy a hand of whist Melbourne? And if I’m not mistaken the book on next Saturday’s match is not yet closed! I fancy the Northern Giant to lay out the Growler in precisely four rounds!” The twin prospects of cards and gambling on his favourite sport of bare-knuckle prize fighting energised Palmerston. He nipped out of the door smartly, breaking into his self-satisfied, metallic chortle, which echoed up the stairwell as he trotted up to join the growing hubbub at the tables. Melbourne hauled himself out of his chair and loped off to follow. Pam’s ferocious card play would probably fleece him, again, before the night was through. This he understood: this he loved. Ignoring the muffled cries and peals of obscene laughter from the street which pierced the falling quiet of the emptying room, he turned into the hall and ambled towards the stairs.

Chapter 1

10 pm: 5th October, 1831, the City of Bath.

The grand Banqueting Room of Bath Guildhall was still full to overflowing, with all seats taken and many latecomers standing at the sides of the rows of chairs. Chandeliers smoked blearily in the fug of the overheated room. Vast royal portraits gazed mutely from the walls. The Reform Meeting was entering its third hour and was still commanding the attention of the audience, made up mainly of respectable middle-class men and their wives, be-feathered hats nodding and waving as they craned their necks to gain better views. A dais supported the table of speakers, most of whom were leaning back in their seats, exhausted after taking their turns to address the eager, and now also saddle-sore crowd. The glories of the Banqueting Room did not extend to comfortable seats, and many listeners writhed periodically in discomfort whilst maintaining, at great personal cost, expressions of engrossed attention.

An outsider was delivering the penultimate speech. A gentleman of interest because of his London contacts: Mr Diarmuid Casey was reputed to be a friend of Daniel O'Connell, was widely acquainted with Whig members and a regular terror of the reform circuit. Catholic Emancipation had been gained with spectacular success in 1829, catapulting O'Connell into Westminster as the member for County Clare. The very mention of his name now scattered the gold dust of success on those he associated with. This particular associate was a tall, loose-limbed and jaunty Irishman, his pale face lit by wild green eyes, his worn frock coat enlivened by a loudly striped rose and cream waistcoat. Words tumbled from his lips in a melodious stream: justice, decency, the rights of man, the voice of the people and the voice of God. He slipped in the unacceptable phantom of democracy so cleverly, so fleetingly, that most of the assembly did not register that they had actually heard it. What they did hear was fulsome support for the Bill and devotion to the Whig cause and the "£10 householders" who would gain the vote. When he spoke of the people surely he meant them? Their ripples of applause punctuated his beguilement of their ears and eyes, and Diarmuid smiled.

Standing by the door half-way down the left side of the room, scanning the assembly meticulously through the smoky whirlpool of heads, searching and gauging them, a tall, dark-haired man, still wearing his dusty travelling cloak, relaxed slowly against the door jamb, resting his aching back. He balanced part of his weight on the swordstick he held in his right hand and smothered a yawn. The mail-coach journey from London had been the nine-hour marathon courtesy of the Pickwick coach company, perhaps it would have been better to settle for an overnight stop. He and his fellow passengers had been more than ready for a longer break at the Crown in Reading, but it was not to be. The half-dozen inside passengers had time only to unpack themselves stiffly from their narrow seats, creak to the coaching inn, quaff a noggin and wolf a few biscuits purchased from the enterprising Mr Huntley's girls, who could be relied upon to bustle across the road from the bakery as soon as any coach came to a halt. Then it had been up and away.

He suddenly smiled broadly and tapped his stick at the memory, attracting glares from those sitting nearest. Diarmuid Casey's theme did not require grins or taps as he was in the grave early stages of generating wholesale condemnation of the beastly Tory opposition. Nathaniel Parry coughed quickly, disguised the unseemly smile and allowed his mind to wander.

Summoned by Lord Melbourne's Office last week and briefed on his mission, he had spent the intervening days preparing to quit his London rooms for a lengthy stay in the West Country. Not an unpleasant prospect. He remembered many childhood visits, in happier times when with his father, and on one faded, dream-like occasion with his late mother, he had visited family connections in Bath. He remembered Dr Caleb Parry's house as a boisterous and luxurious haven of delights, full of music and laughter. Later, in his teens, there had just been himself and his father seeing Charles, Caleb's eldest son and successor to the famous medical practice. He liked Bath's antique charms; the bowl of hill-sides; the rolling Mendips beyond and further still, the lure of the salt-caked coasts of Devon and Cornwall. He was a Romantic and it all seemed dashed Romantic to him. His cashmere stock, turquoise and tied in a draped Byronic knot, advertised his sensibilities. There was nothing starchy about Nathaniel, unless occasion demanded.

His thoughts returned abruptly to his journey. Caradoc had been a volatile traveller over the later stages. His constant companion and friend for over two years, Caradoc was a wiry black and tan Welsh terrier who normally travelled without complaint, but after Reading he had taken exception to a new passenger's basket, which proved to house a live chicken. In one mighty leap, after a brief warning spell of throaty growls, Caradoc had dived into the dame's basket, dragged out the fowl and shaken it like a rat over the other five passengers in a riot of feathers, cackling, snarling and trampling. All terriers are tenacious hunters and to ignore a bird in such close proximity would have been a dereliction of duty. Strangely, the bird had survived to complete its journey to Bath, banished top-side to the cheap seats. Meanwhile, money had changed hands and Nathaniel had bid the stout dame a courteous farewell when they alighted at the White Hart. But she had not forgiven Caradoc, who for his part had treated her with the lofty disdain quite proper from one of the oldest breeds in the land. Nathaniel and Caradoc had time only to ditch their travelling trunk at the Hart and find the venue for the night's meeting. Despite the White Hart's comfortable attractions, or probably because of them, intelligence would not be so readily gained at that address. He needed to shift to a more rowdy and possibly republican roost before the night was over. Caradoc, though politically minded and a champion of liberal independence, had been left outside, guarding the Guildhall, lying low by the railings which fenced "the area", the deep drop affording light to the lower floors. Caradoc's signature behaviours: excessive barking and digging, would be calmed, the former as he knew he was on duty, and the latter as there was no earth. Nothing else would have prevented excavation to an epic depth.

Nathaniel became excessively hot as the evening progressed, and clearly he was not the only one. Fans were being employed briskly by the old and young bonnets in the audience. He enjoyed looking at women, and his practised eye had selected a good half-dozen strikingly pretty ones, a couple disarmingly so, amongst the expected majority of the plain, the dull and the dutiful. This was a bonus, as lengthy and late reform meetings seeking to win votes for middle-class men did not often draw many beauties. It was predominantly a male gathering, and the lines of chairs were filled with them in their dark frock coats, with beaver top-hats held damply on laps, lace cuffs and heavily ringed hands on stick handles.

Rank after rank, with the women between like gaudy birds, pale faces shone and the air had grown foetid with the press of humanity: powdered women, whiskered men, the odd one with an eye-patch covering brutal military wounds. Suddenly, he found himself gazing at someone altogether different. Close to the back, at the end of a row, poised and oddly calm in the restlessness of the crowd, not deigning to add to the regular flurries of applause but watchful, impassive, was a foreigner, a man from the Far East. He seemed about Nathaniel's own age and build, twenty-six and muscular, but he was dressed more soberly. His garb was of severe black, which, apart from a gleaming white, unruffled shirt, was entirely unrelieved. It was some years since, in France with his father and before the latest revolution, that Nathaniel had met with a man from Cathay. He had been a businessman, a stuffed shirt loyal to the Emperor with no words of his own. This man did not have the appearance of a diplomat. A prolonged surge of applause greeted the end of the speech and Nathaniel was briefly distracted, flicking his eyes to the dais in response. When he looked back, the stranger was looking directly at him. Nathaniel felt a frisson of energy as they held each others' eyes for a silent second before both swivelled away, feigning neutral glances over the company. A dangerous customer, thought Nathaniel, allowing his eyes to remain on the dais where a short, earnest man was begging their attention.

"I am sorry, Ladies and Gentlemen. So sorry to inform you, that Mr Crisp has been delayed." Subdued groans and a wave of chatter broke from the audience. The little man raised his voice quaveringly. "But he will be with us within the quarter-hour to conclude our meeting." He wrung his hands in anxiety and continued, "I beg you to take advantage of the break and perhaps take the opportunity to walk in the lobbies and meeting rooms adjacent whilst we await his arrival."

Before he had finished speaking scores of chairs scraped in unison and hundreds of legs stretched to the rustle of silk and brocade, voices rose with the tide of reformers, as they made their way to the exits. Nathaniel glanced back quickly, but the foreign gentleman had gone. In the next instant, as Nathaniel had been by a side-door, he was borne away by the crowd to the landing and into the first meeting room on the right. Once there he billeted himself by the window, shot it open and breathed in a deep lung-full of the sharp autumnal air. Fire-smoke, horses and a clatter of traffic rose from the street. He leaned out and spied Caradoc foraging in a cart whilst the carter paused to halloo a greeting across the road to a man standing outside the Greyhound. Nathaniel quickly dodged back behind the curtain before he was in turn spotted and unleashed a barrage of barking. He turned to be confronted by a friendly, beaming giant.

"Mr Nathaniel Parry?"

"I am sir, the very same," Nathaniel bowed briefly.

"Well now! How do! It had to be you young Parry. So glad to receive your letter my boy and have you back in Bath. Spotted you earlier idling by the door, spitting image of your father. How the devil are you and why aren't you staying with me?" Bluff and tall as a tree, Dr Charles Parry in full evening-dress had cleaved a path through the throng, trailing a quartet of followers and pumped Nathaniel's hand in hearty welcome. "Damned sorry about your father, fine man. Quite understand your wishes for a quiet funeral, hope you received our condolences in time. Impressive to hear that you worked with him in France. Well done sir! Now let me introduce you to my friends: Mr Raphael Vere and Mrs Vere, Mr Nathaniel Parry, a relative we have seen far too little of over the last few years."

Sixty and sleekly immaculate, Raphael Vere shook hands and inclined his head in greeting. Nathaniel's powerful grip surprised him and he stared directly, fascinated by the travel-stained young man who looked at odds with the surprising credentials recited by Charles. Piercing blue eyes met Vere, but they were not challenging, they twinkled with amusement, so Vere assessed him as an affable young sprig, worth cultivating in honour of the Parry connection which still wielded great power in Bath society. Nathaniel recognised Vere's wife, who apparently was called Tilly, as he had spotted her earlier as one of the more beautiful bonnets of Bath. She was of an age with Nathaniel and greeted him shyly, leaving her delicate white hand in his for just a moment longer than was necessary. She was a vision in peach silk, pearl trimmed and topped by a misty waterfall of blonde curls, sumptuously corkscrewed, caught up behind in a pearl clip and floating in glimmering clouds around her face and shoulders.

"Any member of the Parry family is warmly welcome in Bath," boomed Raphael Vere, "Dr Parry and his esteemed late father are widely acknowledged as the most distinguished medical men this city has ever seen."

Charles Parry bowed at this. "Thank you my friend, though I am as yet merely following in the footsteps. You remember father don't you Nathaniel?

"Of course. Also your famous brother, how is William? Or should I call him Edward, does he still prefer his second name?"

"He's well thank you, exceedingly well, and he's still Edward to us! Commissioner of Agriculture in New South Wales. Australia bi'Gad!" exclaimed Charles.

"Sir Edward," chimed Vere unctuously. "Knighted these last two years. You did know? The Parry Sound in the Arctic should now be the Sir William Edward Parry Sound. Who would have thought we would have a Bath man recognised as one of the greatest explorers of all time!" Vere preened in the reflected glory and smiled conspiratorially with Dr Parry.

"I'm afraid I was in France in '29. My father's illness." Nathaniel had a nightmare vision of his father, sinking with a sweating fever in the heat of Paris: the chaos of the impending collapse of Charles X's government, the stench of the river, his sense of utter despair.

"Let me introduce you to Mr Vere's companions Nathaniel," interrupted Charles smoothly.

"Delighted to meet you, Mr and Mrs Vere," said Nathaniel, turning from them to the other couple in their cluster, which was now almost unduly intimate as the surge of people from the Banqueting Room had forced them, hugger-mugger, into the corner, backed-up to the window. He recognised the man as typical of the retired officer class, hawk-eyed, craggy faced and direct, with none of Vere's urbanity, which Nathaniel found refreshing. Severely clad in clothes of a cut more at home during the French Wars, Peterson was decidedly boots, not shoes.

"This is Captain Oliver Peterson, with his daughter Miss Emma Peterson."

"Captain Peterson, Miss Peterson, good evening."

As he studied the worthy Captain's face, Nathaniel conjured up an image of his own father in the last days, reminiscing from his sick bed about his missions. He recalled a long story of derring-do off West Africa, an Atlantic voyage on a frigate, captained by one Oliver Peterson. The mission had been hard, with scant success, but sweetened by the wisdom and companionship of this man.

"Captain Peterson! Former Captain of the *Renowned*? Hunted slavers in '14?

"I did, forsooth!" replied Peterson warmly. "As Dr Parry observed, I should have known you immediately. You are indeed so like Owen. I remember your dear father with great affection. A man of exceptional daring and skill: a thorough patriot. Yes, an honour to serve with him." The Captain shook Nathaniel's hand with both of his. "Visit us in Marlborough Buildings my boy. My wife will be delighted to meet you. We would all be delighted, wouldn't we Em?"

Nathaniel took the hand of the willowy young woman at Peterson's side. She had not caught his eye earlier, but he now saw that she was attractive enough, but eccentrically dressed to his eyes, which were used to London fashion. Like her father she shunned the extravagances of the *beau monde*. She favoured an Empire style reminiscent of the early 1800s. It was still common to see poorer women decked out in the simple high-waisted gowns of thirty years ago, but rare to see it amongst the middle-class. As she stepped away from her father he saw she was unusually tall, towering over the petite Tilly Vere, and had coppery-red hair caught in a thick plait, and topped with just the narrowest of jewelled bands.

"Good evening, Mr Parry," she said, quietly, hiding to perfection the embarrassing confusion she felt to be confronted with this man. He was unsettlingly, insupportably attractive and she was shocked by the response she felt as she looked into his eyes. She felt her heart miss a beat and a flush rise to her cheeks. She dropped her head and looked away. The merest suspicion of her interest in the visitor would be spotted by her doting father and instantly communicated at home where it would unleash a tirade of questions from Mama. Emma would be doomed to dwell in a misery of embarrassment for Mr Parry's entire stay in Bath.

At twenty-four years of age, it had been made very clear to her that she needed to marry. Her tiresome elder sister Celia had settled triumphantly near Cirencester with her farmer. Brother Robert was in the navy and out of range, so, like the tall poppy that she was, Em presented the next target for Mrs Peterson. The twins were still trilling round the house like overgrown sparrows and provided no alternative distraction whatsoever. Burying herself in books and needlework was not all she expected to do in life, but it suited for now, and there was a degree of freedom. She loved empty afternoons which she was at liberty to fill with strolls and lectures and visiting. Evenings were leavened by seasonal balls and soirees, and of late by attending endless reform meetings with her father, whom she adored. A latent thirst for knowledge had been awakened and politics was becoming an absorbing interest for her: another thing to keep well hidden from Mama. She arranged her face as a study of engaged politeness and concentrated on the conversation.

Captain Peterson was continuing his monopolisation of the visitor: "Did your father speak much of our adventures on the *Renowned*? Rum times, close calls, but what comradeship! Ever mention my officers Grant and Tomlinson? Eh? You think so! Splendid. Your father became fast friends with them both. Grant's girl Anna is here in Bath, Great friend of Em's. Poor

Grant's dead though. Did you know of it? Damned'st thing. Went to bed. Never woke up! But here's the coincidence, Tomlinson's nephew fetched up here too and became the gentleman friend of Anna. Isn't that so Em?" He beamed at his daughter and, sensing her reluctance to speak, continued. "So you have also worked for the government, Mr Parry?"

"Yes Captain, I had that honour in France," replied Nathaniel neutrally. "Now I am here to renew my family connections, to rest and sample the famous waters."

Charles Parry suddenly turned and peered over the crowd as he became aware of a new sound from the Banqueting Room, an unwelcome cacophony of hoarse, accusatory shouts, scuffling feet and the unmistakable crashes of over-turned chairs. "Perhaps it might be politic to withdraw without the edification of Mr Crisp's speech. It was not perhaps the wisest of choices to feature that gentleman so late in the evening."

Worried glances were exchanged between Vere and Peterson, who needed to consider the ladies. Mr Crisp the radical hatter had been a controversial choice in any case, and his other commitments had compounded the situation by necessitating a late appearance. It sounded as though a Tory welcome was brewing to greet him.

Raphael Vere took control. "I propose that you all join me in the Pump Room tomorrow morning at ten o'clock where we can continue our conversation in greater comfort. Captain Peterson and I had planned to meet and I would esteem it an honour for the Parry family to join us."

Growing sounds of chaos from the meeting and the drowning calls of the convenor for calm demanded a hasty decision.

"Delighted," concurred Dr Parry hurriedly.

"I look forward to it," smiled Nathaniel.

Moving swiftly to the staircase, Mr Vere and Captain Peterson chaperoned their ladies past the crowds now overflowing from the Banqueting Room and the two Parrys followed closely as rear-guard.

"So Nathaniel, we meet tomorrow at the Pump Room. You are sure you won't come home with me? My carriage is waiting. Mrs P will be delighted to have you, ample room and all that." Charles beamed, avuncular, gracious, casting a friendly arm round Nathaniel's shoulders. It was churlish to refuse, but it had to be done.

"Perhaps in a few days Charles? Just need to be in my lodgings for a while and conclude some business."

"If you are sure?"

They swept through the double doors and out onto the street, whereupon a wiry black and brown missile launched itself, yapping, into Nathaniel's arms.

"Steady as you go Caradoc," he warned, as the flailing paws deposited a number of muddy prints on the arm of Dr Parry's best evening coat.

"Down sir!" Caradoc was dumped unceremoniously on the pavement. "Sorry about that Charles, he is overexcited. Wanted to come to the meeting. See you tomorrow."

Nathaniel and Caradoc sauntered across the High Street as Dr Charles Parry raised a bemused hand in farewell, flicked absentmindedly at the fouled sleeve and then waved his coachman over from where he hovered in the doorway of the Greyhound.

The noisy crowd leaving the Guildhall filled High Street and the Market Place in a trice and Nathaniel and Caradoc disappeared from view. They skirted the corner of Cheap Street, dodging groups of gentry, carriages and horses, and small ragged knots of beggars, which fluttered and swooped like coveys of bats in the dark corners. Nathaniel walked briskly now, using his swordstick swagger perfected in London and Paris to open a way through seething crowds. Caradoc trotted on his left, acting as out-rigger, strengthening their flank, shooting steely glares and warning yaps. They made their way through Abbey Churchyard, past the Great Pump Room and under the colonnade to emerge into Stall Street, which they crossed to enter the bustling White Hart Inn. Even at this hour, the inn blazed with light and beer-fuelled gusts of noise broke intermittently from the lower rooms. A patchwork of guest-bedroom lights shone from the upper floors and shadowy figures could be picked out in some windows, looking out on the West Door of the Abbey which reared up, enormous against the night sky, the twin lines of stone angels frozen on their ladders in the long climb to heaven. The eponymous White Hart in the form of a handsome statue stood alert above the main door, antlers raised, gazing not to the church but to the dark trees on Beechen Cliff which framed the city boundaries to the south. Nathaniel ducked into the narrow passageway of the inn, dodging the press of visitors spilling out of the doorways of the rooms to left and right. Coffee room, coach office, snugs with leaping fires: he wound his way through to the principal bar, behind which stood a dapper and magnificently moustachioed barman, with a bearing both peremptory and military. He was polishing glasses and whipping the room to order: directing potboys and barmaids, chafing regulars and greeting newcomers.

"Mr Parry! Your pleasure sir?" He was quick to spot Nathaniel as he shouldered a path through the throng to the bar.

"Brandy and hot water if you please, and one of your excellent cold pies. Beef and oyster? Small beer for my companion and a succulent bone if one can be found."

Nathaniel winked at Caradoc who was already reclining comfortably by the fire, emitting a low, appreciative growl.

"Straight away sir!" Ceasing to polish the gleaming rummer the barman called behind him, "Tobias, Tobias!" and at once a young potboy trotted obligingly into the bar from the kitchen corridor. He was clad in a long white apron, liberally smeared with gravy at the hip, oversized boots, battered leather breeches and a scarlet waistcoat, the hand-me-down rig of a Hart postillion. He smiled broadly, blankly, eyes searching for advantage, skin tight over the cheekbones, greasy blonde hair anchored behind the ears and arms loose by his sides.

"Yes sir!"

"Beef and oyster pie for the gentleman and a bone for his terrier. Double-up, double-up!"

Nathaniel settled by the wall at the end of the bar to survey the ebb and flow of customers as he waited. Blasts of heat and clattering came from the kitchen corridor to mingle steamily with the sporadic guffaws and hum of chatter. A tired barmaid poured foaming beer from the jug by the barrels behind the bar. Nathaniel appraised her swiftly, sore red hands, damp apron, somewhat drab and dishevelled but the kerchief crossed over her breast was clean and white and she had a gentleness of carriage and expression. Her movements were considered and her smile was surprisingly sweet. Nevertheless, he reflected, glancing at the flushed, bristling face of the barman as he bellowed additional orders over his shoulder to the kitchen, she would be lucky to keep her place. The other maids were blowsy, defiantly wearing their demure White Hart dresses off the shoulder: dash and fire, crowing laughs.

"Have you decided if you will be wanting a room Mr Parry?" enquired the barman as he poured the brandy and a bowl of beer for Caradoc. "I can offer one for tonight but every last one's taken tomorrow."

Nathaniel smiled, taking his plate from Tobias, who had shot from the kitchen corridor at a half-run with the plate of pie and a bone which he had thrown to Caradoc. "No thank you, I have business elsewhere in town. But I would appreciate the help of a man to handle my trunk and play the link-boy. Can you spare one for a couple of hours?"

Scenting the prospect of easy money, Tobias puffed himself out and drew himself up to what he imagined was the strength and height needed for the trunk handling Nathaniel had in mind. "Sir, Oiy could help Mr Parry sir!" He looked steadily at Nathaniel in silent entreaty, it had been a particularly long day and he had two hours remaining of his usual shift. Spending half an hour pushing a wheelbarrow in the fresh air and selling information to a toff from London was too good an opportunity to miss.

"This boy will do very well if he can be spared," said Nathaniel, amused.

"Tobias, ask leave of Mr Bishop. He's in the office." The barman turned to Nathaniel. "He's hired to you for two shillings sir," he said warily, mentally pocketing one shilling. "Including the loan of a barrow."

The tired barmaid quietly set down Nathaniel's steaming glass then brought over the bowl of beer and a hunk of fatty meat she had snatched from a discarded plate on the bar. She knelt by Caradoc to give him his supper, run her hand over his wiry fleece and smooth his head.

"He likes you," said Nathaniel, "It's a mark of high favour as Caradoc isn't generally keen on new acquaintances."

She smiled, her sweet face alight. "I do love dogs sir. 'Specially unusual ones like him with 'is beard so grand and 'is coat so curly," she laughed softly in delight, scratching Caradoc's ears as he amiably set about his supper.

Tobias pushed through the crowds to stand by Nathaniel, twisting his apron, breathing hard. He had been obliged to scour the stable-yard to track down the proprietor, Mr Bishop, who was dealing with the ostlers and had not wanted to listen.

"Oiy can 'elp you sir. Mr Bishop gives me leave to bring y'r trunk out and see you to y'r lodgings."

"Well done young man. I'll see you by the front door in half an hour."

Tobias fled back to the kitchens, reckoning how much of his shilling he would have to share with the cook.

"I guess you know this city well ma'am," said Nathaniel quietly to the young woman who still crouched by Caradoc, muttering endearments. "I need to find myself some liberal conversation tonight. Can you recommend a tavern with rooms? I've just been to the Guildhall meeting and fancy hearing some more reforming talk."

"Well sir," she said, screwing up her nose in concentration and rocking back on her heels. "I take it you will be wanting a respectable tavern. You'll do well to stay in the upper-town."

"Oh yes," he answered gravely. "Respectable if you please."

"Try the George and Dragon in Walcot Street. There's a regular school of reformers there most evenings and there's clean rooms. If any's to be had at all that is."

In half an hour Nathaniel found himself following in the footsteps of Tobias, who was trundling his belongings in the borrowed wheel-barrow. He wrapped his travel cloak around him more tightly, as a searching wind got up and chased skeletal leaves down Union Street. Caradoc trotted alongside Tobias, guarding the trunk by darting at the piles of ordure in the gutter and challenging passing coaches, shadowy cats and stray dogs. The crowds were thinning, but regular policemen on night-watch passed by, swinging their lanterns and making a show of keeping a look-out for trouble.

Tobias seemed impervious to the cold and kept up a stream of chatter. Like a hound on the scent he could almost smell money. More stories, more laughs, more knowledge. Like the new paper said: "Knowledge is power". Tobias clung to that: it was inspirational. He had listened to the men in the Dragon reading aloud from the new paper which had materialised like a call to arms that very summer. *The Poor Man's Guardian* it was called, selling at one penny, though it was illegal to be caught selling it. Even now, so the men said in the Dragon, Mr Hetherington the editor was jailed in London because his paper was cheap enough for the ordinary people to read and he dared to publish without the government stamp.

Any critical talk of politics was seen as sedition, and it was full of such talk, and full of heady dreams for all poor men. Dreams of voting, of being heard, of having a better life, a fair day's pay for a hard day's work which would fund a decent life: a respectable life with rooms of your own, a place to live in like a proper person. Tobias slept at the back of the stables at the Hart. He was usually grubby, uncomfortable and cold, but his new and temporary kitchen job had at last brought him the steady fuel of scraps which banished hunger. From his craven state of powerlessness and want, Tobias was looking up and wanted to rise. Nathaniel glanced over the thin back, bent over now and stretching the stitches on the patched shirt as Tobias plied himself to his task. The gentle slope caused him to falter, the banter dried up and his breath came in sharp gasps.

"How old are you Tobias?" enquired Nathaniel gently.

"Twelve sir. Oiy know this city like the back of mi 'and. Worked at York House Oiy did last year. Oiy seen the Duchess and Princess Victoria an' all."

"I think you should walk ahead now. Make sure we have a clear path." Nathaniel took the handles of the barrow and pushed Tobias forward. "Go ahead with Caradoc."

The boy stumbled forward. "You sure sir? Thank'ee sir. Oi'm goin' to take you along the Borough Walls and up Northgate to Walcot. The Dragon ain't far. You're wantin' the Dragon ain't you? Mary, Mrs Spence, you know, the barmaid you talked to, she said it was where you'd 'ear some reform talk. She lives in Walcot Street and knows the taverns. Not that she's a drinker mind. She lives with her 'usband's mother, she's a great Methodist is old Mrs Spence. She be not that pleased with Mary workin' at the Hart."

As they made their way up Walcot Street the pavements became more crowded again, warehouses, small manufactories, houses and taverns jostled the street, the black backs of the houses on the Paragon terrace climbed up, mountainous, ahead and to their left, and snatches of music floated into the night from open doors. The George and Dragon was a well appointed tavern, full of drinkers and disputes which grew in volume as they approached the front door. Tobias stayed outside with the trunk and Caradoc took up a perch on top of it whilst Nathaniel made his way in. A hubbub greeted him, coming from the right hand parlour where a hoarse voice was struggling to read to the company from a newspaper, above a growing tide of barracking from his listeners. Nathaniel passed by swiftly to the main bar.

"Do you have a room for tonight?" he enquired, raising his voice above the row from the parlour to attract the sweating barman.

"Just tonight sir," said the barman hurriedly dispatching potboys with ale jugs. "Will that interest you?"

"Seems this city is expecting a landslide of visitors tomorrow landlord!"

"Season's in full swing by next month and preparations are a-foot, but we have market-men here regular. 'Course what with all this Re-form lark we've extra public meetings and assemblies and grand balls and the like. Reform groups are laying on all sorts of entertainments left and right."

"You are a keen reformer then?"

"Keen businessman sir. We likes a bustle in Bath but big crowds are rarer than in the old days. Then we was thronged and jam-packed with the quality. My old father came here fifty years ago to run a tavern and he saw the falling off when the French wars started and damned Boney put paid to the rollickin' times. Glad to see that villain get the beatin' he deserved."

The night was sliding away and Nathaniel was acutely aware that he needed to attach himself to the voluble reform crew in the parlour if he was to earn his keep. He hired the room without further a-do and went out with the waiter who had been charged with taking up his trunk. The urchin Tobias also needed to be paid off. Tobias accepted Nathaniel's florin gratefully but was loath to lose his new patron and made a pitch for more business. "Oiy don't start 'til breakfast tomorrow sir and Oi'm not workin' all the day. Do you need showing 'round town? Oi knows a lot," he faltered at the last, wilting under Nathaniel's steady gaze.

"I thought you had a regular job at the Hart."

"Oi do 'elp out when they're busy in the kitchen," he said, rubbing his face to stave off the leaden fatigue which rolled over him in waves. “Joseph’s laid-up wi’ a broke leg and Oi’ve a few hours a day ’til ’e’s on ’is feet.”

Nathaniel took pity, again. Small boys were famously good at watching and noticing, Tobias might just come in useful.

“Tomorrow before breakfast then young man. Keep your ears open for lodgings for me. Somewhere along this street would suit.”

“Yes sir,” Tobias nodded his head and turned back towards the centre of town, smiling to himself in weary triumph.

Nathaniel, with Caradoc at his heels, plunged back into the Dragon and ran lightly upstairs, following the waiter and his trunk. The dark staircase wound upwards to the first floor, where they took their temporary possession of a room directly above the front parlour. Wasting no more time, he flung his cloak and stick on the bed as Caradoc stretched himself out in anticipation on the rug, watching the waiter light the fire which was lying, ready-made, and sprang obediently to life, “Right, you’re off duty,” he said ruffling Caradoc’s head, “catch a wink of sleep. I’m for a back-seat below.” Nathaniel ushered the waiter out, locked the room and made straight for the reformers. He slipped in to take a place in the shadows by the door, well away from the roaring fire which, unlike the dainty casket in his room, was a heroic affair whose tongues of heat were roasting those near it. A couple of dozen men were jammed into the bar, artisans, small proprietors, all with hats off and eyes alight with notions of the rights of man, fuelled by beer, but also with the intoxication of being in a world on the edge of change. The press of bodies and agitation of the men had generated a sour stench, partially masked by the fumes of drink and greasy smells of roasting meat from the main bar.

The reader, a stout middle-aged artisan, clad in the customary fustian jacket and drab breeches, was rubbing his perspiring forehead with an outsize paisley patterned handkerchief.

“Wait now lads. We’ll ’ave it again to get the sense of it.”

“Sense is clear Arthur. The *Guardian’s* givin’ us warning. Just like Mr Hunt did and none o’ us listened. The Bill should be demandin’ votes for all us men, not just them as pays high rates. £10 householders be damned! Who ’mongst us has the pleasure of payin’ £10 in rates?” said a thick-set man, balding and angry, who snatched the paper and waved it in accusation round the table.

“Oiy ’ave,” piped up a man by the door, “Oiy pays over £10 and so do other businessmen ’ere. Got to start somewheres Robert. Them as pays ’ighly should get a vote first. We need to see ’ow it goes, and folk in small ’ouses can be brought in later.”

“Why,” shouted Robert Turner, flinging the paper down so hard it slid away from him over the blackened, beer-ringed oak table. “It wasn’t what was to ’appen. Tom Paine said it in our father’s time. ‘Nat-chu-ral roights’ we ’ave. We’re not criminals. We`re working men who makes this country run. We does the workin’ and the fightin’ when fightin’s to be done. We pays taxes. Like the Yankees said, no taxation without representation. Universal suffrage is what we’ve a-been after since they Frenchey wars ended in ’15. Why shouldn’t Oiy vote ’cos moiy ’ouse is rated at £6. An’ why shouldn’t a man vote just ’cos ’e lives in his father’s ’ouse? ”

“Ye ’ave representation and ye’ll ’ave more when us £10 ’ouseholders vote.”

“I want to vote mi’self!”

“Ye talks like a blackguard republican! Don’t go a-quotin’ Yankees to me! His Majisty ain’t been crowned more ’an a few month and ye’re a mouthin’ republican sentimints!”

“Now lads, easy now. No one’s a mouthin’ loike a Yankee as I ’ear,” blustered Arthur Jamieson, regaining control of the *Guardian*, and carefully, respectfully, smoothing it down over the table top. “Bob Turner sit down, Oiy knows ye’ll support the Bill and ye’re a patriot through an’ through.” He smiled encouragingly at Robert who took a steady pull at his drink and sighed, deflated.

"I'm not sayin' as I want to see the Bill fail," said Robert, sad and disgruntled. "Tis a mighty thing to make any change. I know it."

"An' it's not just votes is it?" Arthur continued. "They great cities 'aven't even got Members of Parliament of their own as they weren't built in the old days when seats were give out by King John."

"'E never give out no seats," shouted an irritable voice behind Arthur whose owner was trapped too close to the fire.

"Well 'oo did?"

The dispute rambled into historical speculation. Most paused to swig their beer and some decided it was time to call for more. Pints of cider seemed the best solution to the imponderable questions raised, but Arthur, weary from his stint as chairman called for gin and beer: it was "the dog's nose" and nothing else would do.

Bedford's Billiard Rooms, Milsom Street, Bath.

At about this time, as Nathaniel was thinking how much he had missed the soft burr of the Somerset accent and deciding that his first Bath reformers were far less dangerous than many he had heard in London, a well-fed and fashionably dressed gentleman, fifty, superficially handsome and somewhat the worse for drink, was lolling back in his usual chair in Bedford's Billiard Rooms, Milsom Street. He watched the play with unseeing eyes, indifferent for once as he had bigger business on his mind.

Despite the hour the usual crowd of local businessmen and military types was still out in force: half-pay officers, old generals from the Indian Army, Captains and Commanders, spirit soaked, wreathed in tobacco clouds and intent on the games as they crowded round the baize tables. The evening at the gaming rooms had been longer than he had anticipated, which was not usually a problem, quite the reverse in fact, but his wife Janie had been particularly unpleasant and pressing about the time of his return. Was it already midnight? He heaved a sigh and squinted at his pocket watch. It was indeed midnight. Not ten o'clock, when he should have been leaving Bedford's, according to Janie. He swilled back the remnants of his brandy and attempted to banish the vision of that sharp little face which awaited him in the bedroom, hideous mob-cap pulled unattractively over her hair, which would be bristling with papers, thin fingers grasping the sheets in a paroxysm of silent rage which would be given full voice as he inched the door open.

Better to sleep in the dressing-room. He nodded bitterly to himself. Janie had been spoiled as a child in India, waited on hand and foot and indulged by her fond mama. No matter how many servants they employed, it never seemed to be enough to make her content in Bath. He had worked steadily through her inheritance, which, with his miserly pay, barely sufficed to allow him a few gentlemen's pleasures. His credit was still good at Bedford's: just. His wine-merchant too was supplying the essentials: just. He took a considered pinch from his silver snuff box and inhaled deeply, steadying his breathing.

Roderick Wilson did not dwell on his current financial short-comings, instead he dreamed of the future, a rosy future coming ever closer to make a glorious present. Tonight's negotiations should improve his position no-end. What a stroke of luck! He was about to apply just the right amount of pressure to extract a tidy settlement, and who knows what it might lead to? He gazed unseeing as the final frames of the night were played out. Final bets were taken. Waiters lounged, sleepy in the corners. He cared not a fig for the play, but dreamed instead of money, and position, and the irresistible Coco, his exquisite Colette. As French tarts went she was superior in every sense. With his new riches he could install her in some rooms of her own, prevent her from entertaining other clients. He had never really liked that aspect of their relationship. He wanted a mistress, all to himself.

"Mr Wilson," an urgent voice at his elbow, "Mr Wilson, your chairmen are here."

Roderick smiled, immensely gratified. "Yes Jones, thank you." He heaved himself out of the chair, took the proffered caped greatcoat, his hat and gloves, and rolled out into the cold air. Occasional gas lamps illuminated the footpath of Bath's principal shopping street. Pools of light relieved the dark and candles and lamps shone from upper windows. Standing in the shadow by the wall were two burly chairmen, swathed with shawls against the growing cold and wind.

"Mr Wilson sir? Gentleman you want to do business with sent a note earlier saying as you were to come to a meeting."

"That's correct," Wilson had been delighted to receive a message from the barman at Bedford's earlier that evening. He had been waiting for his man to make a move for the last few days and now, at last, a private meeting. No names needed of course, this was a delicate matter. They would meet, settle, and then see how things progressed over the next few months. Wilson climbed into the sedan chair and one of the chairmen closed the door behind him. He felt the chair lift as the men seized the poles, fore and aft, and moved off smartly. Curtains had been pulled over the windows and it was snug. He covered his legs with the rug and sensed they were setting a cracking pace, downhill in the direction of the river. This was surprising as his man lived in the upper-town. But naturally, he could never have a meeting such as this at his home. Perhaps they were to go to the office? Wilson tried to lift the curtains but found they were secured at the sides, not so unusual in the cold weather. Chairmen were having to make special efforts to ensure comfort now that flys were licensed to operate as hackney cabs in the city. Many chairmen claimed they were ruined, but hundreds of them still operated, lumbering up and down the hills of Bath, into the houses if necessary to convey their passengers right to their own bedsides.

The steps of the chairmen had accelerated to a half-run,

jogging over the cobbles, always downhill. Wilson tried the window to see if he could lift it behind the curtain. Screwed shut. He tried the door. Locked. Through his drink be-fuddled wits pin-pricks of anxiety began to stimulate concern.

"Stop!" he called. "Stop now I say!" Their steps thudded onwards. Wilson began to beat in the door. "Confound it I demand to see our route! Stop!"

The chair came to a sudden halt and landed heavily on the ground. The door clicked unlocked and grasping hands reached into the chair, dragging Roderick Wilson out into darkness. Before he had time to call out, before he could take a breath, a cosh whistled through the air and slammed a sickening blow onto his head. Wilson's body, limp as rag, collapsed back into the chair. His slack legs were folded and shovelled in. The door was slammed and locked, the dark figures took up the poles and headed to the river. More cautiously now, down to the lower-town they stole, by the Hetling Pump House, far past the fashionable quarters to the maze of courts and faded terraces broken up to serve as either lodging houses at three pence a night or as squalid dens for prostitutes, beggars and thieves. Past warehouses they hurried, past stables, leather-works and corn-factors to the quay.

The chairmen idled as they approached the river, downstream from the Old Bridge was the ideal spot. Lower down river from the Broad and Narrow Quays, the wall petered out and was replaced by sewage outfalls and marsh grasses, middens and overhanging trees. Floating bodies in Bath often fetched up at such a berth after the wretched suicides had flung themselves from the bridge or slid into the shallows and waded into the green-blackness of the Avon. Just the spot for their burden. Orders had been clear. This was the night that Wilson was going to end it all. He just needed to be shown the way. They found a quiet place in the dark shadow of the corn-factor's warehouse.

"Thank God for that. Bastard was 'eavy."

“Quiet. Get ’im out.” Wolfish eyes gleamed above the shawl wrapped round the lean, bearded face.

His fellow conspirator, broader, stolid and with an ill grace, clicked open the lock, swung the catch and made to pull the body out, but was flung backwards to roll in the filth of the quay. A frenzied figure, bloodied and desperate, broke free and set up a terrified howl, partly blinded by the force of the blow which had stunned him but not rendered him insensible for quite long enough, Wilson took off in a wild career. He stumbled past the first assailant who was scrambling drunkenly to his feet, slithering on the slick cobbles, trying to gain a purchase sufficient for him to charge after Wilson and smother his cries. The other man was on Wilson’s tail, pausing only to pick up a stone and hurl it after his prey. The wounded man zigzagged like a hare before the pack, two sets of running steps now pounding on his trail. His breath came in tearing gasps and his strangled yells died as he struggled, but failed, to give voice to a coherent cry. His lungs seemed to be collapsing, his legs failing to move faster. Faster, faster: he willed his aching body to move and instinctively headed for shelter. He cornered sharply as an alley loomed to his right. He fled down it and crashed into a door, it gave way and he fell into a silent workshop, colliding with a bench and scattering a hail of tools as he burst through, tripping and stumbling into the pitch-dark. He turned to look behind and almost at once the grey of the doorway was darkened by the shapes of the two men. Wilson gasped in terror as they advanced on him. His arms raked the bench behind him, grasping for tools, throwing them in mad desperation at the advancing figures. All but one from the shower of missiles fell helplessly, but a screw driver made contact with one of the heads of the chairmen and gouged a runnel down his face. Bellowing in rage and pain the injured man narrowed the gap in seconds and flew at Wilson, raining blows on him and beating aside arms raised feebly in defence. He caught his victim round the waist, hauled him up and flung him across the bench, into the wall. Wilson’s body twitched as it landed on a tool rack and then moved no more.

"Ye've skewered 'im Mordecai. 'E's stuck through the 'eart on an awl. Ye crazed bugger. 'E was meant to have done 'imself in an' now 'e's stabbed!"

Mordecai glowered, stood hesitant for a moment, then from force of habit leant over the body and ran his hands over the pockets.

"Leave it!" pleaded Declan. "The watch might think the stab was from some junk in the river and 'e's a suicide, not done over in a robbin' clear and simple! Safer for us for sure! Let's get 'im away." He patted Mordecai uncertainly on the shoulder and moved to the door.

Mordecai paused, ready to pull back, but the diamond in Wilson's ring glinted in the moonlight. He wrenched it from the fingers, flabby now, inhuman, pocketed the ring and braced himself to lift Wilson's body from the spike. He grunted with effort as he flung the dead weight over his shoulder and turned to leave.

"Not a word more, matey. Not one soddin' word."

With a glare of murderous intent, Declan was silenced and Mordecai led the way out. The two conspirators paused in the doorway to check the night and saw only a pair of homeless dogs, snuffling over the refuse by the warehouse. Eddies of laughter and music broke distantly from some of the taverns on Narrow Quay and Avon Street but all else was still. They made their way swiftly to the edge of the river wall, and Mordecai let the body down into the greasy flow, kicking it free from the wrack of leaves and detritus by the margin to float freely along the edge of the river. They picked up the poles of the chair and slunk off towards Green Park. Once in the mews they located the correct shed and surreptitiously replaced the unlicensed chair which they had temporarily stolen earlier that evening from a bankrupted chairman, victim of the flashy horse drawn flys which had poached his regulars.

The Bath Road

By three o'clock, in the dead centre of that autumn night, a lone horseman picked his way along the turnpike road from Bath to Bristol. The night in Bath had been unrewarding in terms of intelligence gained on the party he was meant to be stalking, but revealing in many other ways. His orders had revealed that his new employer, the Bristol trader Mr Edwin Ravenswood, was a subtle one, an intricate planner, relentless in his pursuit of his purpose: utterly ruthless. This he could understand, in view of the business they were in. The journey to Bristol had started at the end of the previous year when he and his men had joined the crew of Ravenswood's ship, the *Blue Dragon*, in the harbour south of Canton. He had sailed to Bristol and delivered the sealed boxes of currency and bullion, as expected, and had spent the months of the *Blue Dragon's* refit serving Ravenswood before the return to China. The service had been singularly instructive.

He glanced up as a distant light caught his eye. He was nearing a toll house and had no inclination to rouse the keeper to pay his dues. The night's journey was close to its end, as his destination was his employer's home which was acting as his own temporary residence. Arno's Tower, Mr Ravenswood's new manor-house in Arno's Vale, was a short gallop over the field and through the wood, beyond the other mansions of the *nouveau riche* which had sprung up on the outskirts of Bristol by the old medieval village of Brislington and now overshadowed its own modest manor.

He gathered his horse for the leap and soared over the hedge, disappearing from the road and setting his course for the distant Ravenswood mansion. Soon tiny lights glinted into view like shards of glass and the tower stood dark in relief against the stars. He picked up the broadening path, cantered along it for half a mile, called out to the watchman to pull the gates back and swung his horse down the drive to the pillared entrance. The protruding stone tower, crowned by crocheted spires, was pierced by arches and flanked by stone griffins as high as a man, illuminated from below by gas jets, which also shone out from stone and iron settings below the yawning mouths of gargoyles, which shot from all the crowded battlements and turrets of his employer's Gothic fantasy. The Chinese guest, the mysterious stranger who had caught the eye of Nathaniel Parry in the Guildhall meeting a few hours before, leapt from his horse and surrendered the reins to a stable-boy who had appeared as Ravenswood's servants always did: unbidden, discreet, attentive.

"Cornelius!" called a deep, resonant voice from the hallway as he climbed the steps and entered the open doors. "A fruitful night I trust?"

"Interesting sir, but not as fruitful as we wished," replied Cornelius Lee. "Our quarry was not at his usual pursuits but retired home quietly after a political meeting. I will attend his gaming club on the next high stakes evening and proceed with our original plan." He bowed briefly. "And now sir, if you have no further instructions I will retire."

Edwin Ravenswood fixed his newest employee with a searing stare, taking in the powerful physique and cat-like calm of the undoubtedly dangerous Mr Lee. Ravenswood smiled his cold, dead smile and inclined his fine dark head. "Yes, Cornelius, goodnight. I await an important guest so instructions can wait for tomorrow."

Cornelius moved gracefully to the huge winding staircase which coiled round the central tower of the house like a serpent, connecting its arcaded floors and culminating in a high dome of stained-glass, blind now, with not even the wan light of the moon to light it and shower the stairs with colour. He moved silently onto the second floor landing, opened and closed his bedroom door firmly and stood silently on the open landing, watching the hall below. Within ten minutes his patience was rewarded as the rush of carriage wheels on gravel sounded in the drive. Confused footfalls, carriage doors: Ravenswood's greetings followed and Cornelius stole forward to the edge of the arcade, concealing himself behind a pillar.

"Honoured sir," Ravenswood sounded reverential. "A pleasure: a great pleasure to welcome you to my home."

Cornelius registered the unusual level of deference, the desire to please. It boded nothing but ill.

"My servants will take your luggage to your suite. Your valet will have the adjoining room. Would you care for refreshment?"

Cornelius leaned forward just enough to catch sight of the guest, one sighting being ample, he did not wait to hear an answer but melted back into the shadows and soundlessly entered his own room and comparative safety. He took off his hat and riding coat, his boots, waistcoat and jacket, laid them out precisely and sat, cross-legged, before the open window, looking far away, over the tree tops to the stars. He breathed deeply and placed his hands on his knees. The newcomer was important indeed, a man whose face he had come to know over the last few hard years, a man known by repute to all those who sailed the high seas on the dangerous side of the law. This man was feared by all who even suspected one iota of his capabilities, of his brutality and of his capacity for calculated cruelty. He was the emissary of the Count and seemed untouchable, operating on a level beyond reach. He was Kizhe.

"Kee-jay," repeated Cornelius to himself: in Russian it meant "others". "How many others? How many guises and stratagems of destruction stemmed from his fertile brain? How many deaths had he conjured to gain his fortune and that of his shadowy master? This man, this important man, the Mongolian-Russian who held the Count's steel chains of power which linked the Russian Empire, China and all the East. Their reach was long, through the opium fields of India and Afghanistan, through the brothels and harems of the Levant and the governments between. And now Kizhe is here."

As an optimist, Cornelius Lee had no option but to consider

the new advantages of his position. As a realist he moved swiftly on to the latent threats and dwelt on them until the first fingers of dawn crept over the sky, and he had no considerations left.

Chapter 2

Dawn: 6th October, 1831.
The George and Dragon, Walcot Street, Bath.

"Thank you, that's all I need."

The pert chambermaid had to accept that no more services could be rendered or tips cajoled from the handsome guest, so she gave up, made a sketchy curtsey and flounced off along the landing. Caradoc took the opportunity to slink out behind her in search of some exercise and breakfast, whilst Nathaniel padded over to investigate the washstand in the dark corner, which leaned askew against the oak panelled wall. Earlier the maid had laboured up the stairs with a steaming jug of hot water which now waited, cooling, by its matching porcelain basin. Both were elegantly restrained, Dresden style, but had seen better days.

He poured a generous measure, sluiced his face and rubbed it dry on the linen towel, before shivering involuntarily and wrapping his dressing gown closer to combat a sharp and persistent draught that had set up through the ill-fitting window as the morning wind rose. It was not surprising that the chambermaid found him unusually attractive: he cut a dashing figure in his Damascus silk-velvet robe, intricately patterned in rich chestnut-brown, tawny-gold, maroon and deep sea-green. It had been his father's, a souvenir of a mission to Turkey when Owen had been in the entourage of the envoy to the Sublime Porte. The provenance appealed strongly to Nathaniel's taste for the exotic, and without doubt, Lord Byron would have approved of it.

He took a seat at the table by the fire, which was slowly flickering into life after being rattled up by the maid when she had returned to deliver his breakfast. He surveyed the spartan fare of beer and bread which sat, uninspiring, before him, and sighed, inwardly declaring that the morning should not pass without him sampling Bath's famed sugar buns, and maybe the local brioche, "a Sally Lunn". All could be washed down by something tasty, maybe creamy hot chocolate or a tiny strong coffee. With those delectable thoughts he could almost smell Paris. Sparely built, powerful, and with a martial passion for exercise, he was usually hungry and it seemed a very long time since the pie at the Hart. Nathaniel yawned, ran his hands through his tangle of black hair and moved to the window to get a clear view of the street below as it came to life.

The Corn Market was opposite and a few men were hovering in the street by the doors. Horse-drawn carts rattled by with milk-churns and cheeses, mountains of vegetables for the daily provisions market and straw for the livery stables. A scavenger's cart moved, noxiously, away from the beasts' pens by the market stalls, the men chivvying each other, clumsily struggling to quit the street before the watch spotted them. He looked higher to the undulating line of green hills that bounded the city, broken by the valley of the Avon. To the east lay London and the new rooms in Lambeth which had recently become his home, to the west, the port of Bristol and a pressing engagement with one John Drake. He heard some heavy movements above as other guests started to rise.

Nathaniel stirred himself to find clean clothes and repack his trunk. He crossed the room and knelt on the floor to raise the heavy lid and survey his belongings. He deliberated on his movements for the day. New lodgings must be had, and preferably nearby, as Walcot Street seemed a canny billet, stationed as it was between the upper and lower towns. He would visit a few more taverns to gauge the mood in the city, tap Dr Charles Parry and his circle, the amiable Captain Peterson and the voluble Mr Vere. That should suffice to allow a scratch report to be made to Drake on the 8th of the month in his lodgings in Clifton: a rendezvous arranged when they had met in London. The Home Office briefing by one of Lord Melbourne's staff, a Mr Percy, was quickly done as it required him merely to report on attitudes to reform and the level of threat to law and order. The posting had been complicated by Drake's involvement and his additional instructions. He was to be stationed in Bristol and was charged with the task of negotiating with an entrepreneur involved in the shipment of opium from India to China.

That Britain illegally shipped considerable amounts of opium was common knowledge. India provided a ready source and the East India Company had been a major player for years. What was new was that the Emperor of China had started to apply a more effective embargo and his men were busily impounding British ships and cargoes. It seemed that Drake's man in Bristol was adept at maintaining his trade, flouting the Company's monopoly, and evading the attentions of the Chinese navy. The Foreign Office was keen to know the secret of his success, or at least to assist him in continuing to achieve it. Drake had outlined the importance of his own role and the necessity for Nathaniel supporting him hand and foot, which Percy had not made much of. Drake had also spoken, at length, of his service in France and Nathaniel had idly studied the edge of a wound on his neck which itself spoke of action, but Drake had seemed uncommunicative when Nathaniel raised the names of his old contacts in the diplomatic service at the court of Charles X. He shrugged at the memory. No doubt he would learn more of the doings of Mr John Drake at their Bristol meeting.

Mechanically, Nathaniel continued unpacking: linen, stacks of shirts and jumbles of coloured waistcoats, coats and neck-cloths, his mind left free to speculate on what might be learned in Bristol. Opium was a necessary drug for everyone, from fractious babies in their cradles to the dying on their deathbeds. It brought them all the same blessed tide of sleep. Some fell victim, and craved it to distraction, as the Chinese seemed to be doing in increasing numbers. They had joined the opium eaters. He thought of Coleridge and De Quincey, both of whom had let it eat their lives away. Opium, it seemed to him, was like most things in life, two great opposites, neither existing without the other: Good and Bad, God and the Devil, Heaven and Hell. Both part of the whole: both ever present. He checked his own leather-cased bottles of medical supplies, especially the Kendal Black Drop, his Lancashire cure-all. It contained at least double the strength of laudanum in ordinary doses with the best Turkey opium, saffron, cloves, spirit and acetic acid. Nathaniel had never allowed servants to prepare his travelling case; his life could depend upon it. Not that he put all his trust in medicaments. As Byron said, "Always laugh when you can, it is cheap medicine." He smiled at the memory, it was cheap and it did no harm.

This particular trunk was his father's sea-chest, a sturdy oak carcase with metal bonds, still faintly painted with the family name "Parry". It was a relic from Owen's first voyage to the Levant in the early stages of the French wars, when he was a young man new to the service of his country. In the base, and also in the lid, there were hidden compartments, Nathaniel moved the lining and pressed the lever in the corner of the trunk to raise the base. Snug in the felt lining lay his makila, the Basque walking stick, which had been the companion of both Parrys on walks in wild places, or places where use of the customary swordstick was unwise. Less of a gentleman's accoutrement than his favourite silver-headed stick, it was a shepherd's staff, cut in the living wood of the medlar tree that had seen great service as his quarter-staff and bludgeon. He lifted it out, running his hands over the rich wood, and, grasping the pommel, slid it off to reveal a deadly, glinting spike. Sharp as a spear and deadly, it could run a man through. He examined the point minutely, and, satisfied, replaced the pommel and returned the stick to its place in the base of the trunk. He quickly repacked his belongings, layering them with the grey stems of brittle lavender that still released the faint aromatic scent of summer.

He was distracted by the unmistakable sound of a terrier scurrying along the landing, followed by the unruly steps of a child's boots. He closed the trunk and rose to open the door.

"Ha! Caradoc, in you rascal! How-do young Tobias! What news?"

"Good mornin' sir. Oiy got plenty!"

"Well sit down to tell the tale, and you can eat my breakfast if you want it," said Nathaniel, throwing himself on the bed and dislodging Caradoc who had already buried into the mound of blankets.

"Thank you sir," said Tobias, dragging the chair tight up to the table and falling on the bread and beer. "Good news is," he spluttered, mouth full, "Oiy got you a grand lodgin' in this very street. When Oiy got back to the Hart last night Mary was still there and Oiy told her as you were only in the Dragon a night and needed to stay longer. She straight away upped and said you was welcome to ask old Mrs Spence, her 'usband's mother that is, as y're now after private lodgings and not a tavern. She had taken a likin' to you sir and said you should walk down with me now, afore she leaves for work, and ask Mrs Spence yourself."

"Excellent, and I sense there's more."

Tobias swallowed hard and then paused for effect. "Body of a gentleman 'as bin found in the river!" he said conspiratorially.

"Scavengers saw 'im a-floatin' 'ead down and he's been laid out in the Duke of York on Narrow Quay for to be inspected."

Nathaniel had had the misfortune of seeing a number of dead

bodies, gentlemen and others, and was not as moved as Tobias had hoped.

"Do you get many accidents here, or suicides?"

"Accidents are mainly kids fallin' in sir. Suicides is norm'ly poor folk."

"Any idea who he was?"

"No sir. But the city police are investigatin'."

Nathaniel nodded sagely, but knew exactly how effective that was likely to be. London's new metropolitan force of "Peelers", set up a couple of years ago by the formidable Sir Robert Peel had yet to be spread throughout the country. Some parish police forces were aping the smart uniforms and rigorous systems of the Peelers, but most still dithered on with night watchmen and patchy day patrols. Not one provincial city had yet got a force to coordinate detection of crime over all its parishes. There was unlikely to be much progress made with that particular investigation.

"Good work Tobias. If you've finished with the breakfast, hop off downstairs and I'll meet you in ten minutes."

Nathaniel, forsaking his travel cloak with an eye to the morning rendezvous in the Great Pump Room, turned out in shiny shoes, a worsted frock coat, white ruffled shirt and plain white trousers, burgundy waistcoat and a high beaver-hat, Anglesey style. He and Caradoc followed Tobias up Walcot Street to the beginning of the sharp rise in the road that led to London Street. On the left was a terrace of neat houses in the customary cream-coloured Bath limestone, designed to the customary strict classical proportions decreed when the city was rebuilt as a temple to modernity. For over a hundred years gracious Palladianism had been the only style for Bath, terrace after faultless terrace, making it difficult for visitors to figure out exactly where they were, unless of course they stumbled onto one of the great crescents or the uniquely odd King's Circus. Mrs Spence's house was in a short terrace which proved to be the exception to this rule as all the houses sported pretty Venetian windows. Tobias hammered on the door knocker and Mary answered quickly, less tired now and more comely, but with the same gentle grace Nathaniel had noticed when she served at the Hart.

"Good morning to you sir. Tobias gave you my message! Come in and welcome. Mother!" she called upstairs and bid them walk ahead of her to a bright kitchen at the rear of the house. A large fireplace and cooking range took up most of the far wall, and, sat before the grate in a rocking chair, was a very old man. He lifted his rheumy eyes to the visitors and wheezed a greeting, slapping his hands on the arms of the chair.

"Ha-ha! Ye come forward young men. Come forward I say. But mind the Johnty now! Don't go a-tramplin' the babe though 'ee do get sore underfoot. Come, come!"

Nathaniel and Tobias picked their way, as bidden, over a small child who was managing to maintain an unsteady sitting position whilst occupying himself by exploring a wooden clothes peg. As they moved to take in turn the shaky hand thrust out to them from the folds of the old man's woollen blanket, Mary joined them in the kitchen with a powerful looking woman of about sixty years of age.

"Mr Parry may I introduce you to Mrs Spence my husband's mother, my husband being at sea."

"Good morning madam," said Nathaniel, smoothly and with a bow. "Nathaniel Parry at your service. I gather that I might be so fortunate as to rent rooms here. I am visiting town this month and have some business to complete."

Martha Spence was a commanding woman, dressed in severe high-necked black, strong, big-boned and of late much given to Methodism. Widowed after her husband's death in the winter of 1808 on the retreat to Corunna she looked after her sweet and simple daughter-in-law, the grandson, as yet too small to be indicating if he was to be an adventurer like his father or another little "weak and wan" like Mary, and also the ancient father in-law Mr Spence Senior. Old Tom, normally as cussed as you please did patchy service as baby-minder and vegetable peeler. She eked out her modest income from prudent investments but additional income in the shape of paying guests was vital to keep the family afloat, and the best room and dressing room on the first floor needed a new tenant. Such thoughts prevented her from ousting the truculent looking terrier out of hand and shooing the urchin Tobias Caudle out of her kitchen. If she had told him once it was twenty times about the state of his boots.

She smiled tightly. "Follow me sir."

By the time Nathaniel came back downstairs, deal clinched, money having changed hands and praise having been lavished on the plain and spotless rooms above, other relationships had moved on significantly. Mary had provided Caradoc with a bowl of Tom's beer and plate of hardtack biscuit which he was enjoying whilst listening to the old man talking about hunting dogs and permitting the Johnty to tap him rhythmically with the clothes peg. Mary and Tobias were by the doorway, anxious to leave for work.

"Madam, many thanks, I will return later with my belongings. Now Tobias direct me to the nearest reputable stables. I need to hire a horse."

"That'll be Mr Tasker's Livery sir, Pulteney Mews. Oiy'll point the way as we walks to the Hart," said Tobias, eyeing Mrs Spence suspiciously and hoping she would let him leave without a rebuke. He was cultivating a powerful image of efficiency with Mr Parry and could do without an ear-wigging.

Caradoc, swallowing the remainder of the biscuit, capered after the party.

"Good morning to you Madam, Mr Spence," said Nathaniel.

"Good morning to you," said Martha as she followed them to the front gate. "And you Tobias Caudle," she declared as she slammed the gate shut and glared at the spotless foot scraper. "You can stay at the door if you turns up with boots as caked as that again, ye young besom."

Nathaniel and Caradoc spent a pleasant few hours on the canal path, hacking from Bath to the village of Bathampton and the fields beyond. Tobias had directed them to a well run and busy stable where a fine pale gold stallion had been hired. He proved to be mettlesome and Nathaniel enjoyed the challenge in the freedom of the morning. Dew glistened on the hedgerows, and sprays of the last ripe blackberries shone lustrously as the sun found its way through the morning mist. They galloped along the dusty path, scattering drifts of leaves and the last glowing chestnuts loosed from their green-spiked armour bounced from the pounding hooves. Rabbits thumped away at his approach and the air was alive with bird song. Caradoc ran extra miles circling the fields, chasing the rabbits, hares and once, most unfortunately for him, a sheepdog who proved to be masterfully proprietorial. Shortly after nine they reined in again at the stables, returned the horse to livery and hastily transferred Nathaniel's trunk from the Dragon to the rooms at Mrs Spence's. Caradoc showed no enthusiasm for the tryst at the Pump Room and Old Mr Spence permitted him to lie at his feet by the fire.

Just before ten o'clock as planned, Nathaniel entered the Great Pump Room in Abbey Church Yard and looked about him for a sighting of last night's Guildhall party. The room was grand, and broadly as he remembered it from a previous visit, though the brocade was a tad more tired and the company a good deal more mixed. Middle-aged dames marshalling compliant husbands with gawky daughters in tow had increased in numbers. They were predatory, scenting fresh males to harvest in their drag-nets as potential bridegrooms for the girls and fortunate connections for the families. Musicians played discreetly, providing an atmosphere both cultured and festive. Brutal economic necessities were played out, fastidiously, to Mozart.

The rush of the mineral water and the clink of glasses dispatched by the Pumper could also be heard from his alcove overlooking the medieval King's Bath and knots of people chatted in standing groups or sitting together. Vast glittering chandeliers caught the morning sun and reflected rainbows on the company below. There was constant movement as newcomers arrived and competed to attach themselves to the most fashionable group. Others freshly disentangled from unwise choices milled around the room, eyes darting to find a happier landing. The commanding height of Dr Charles Parry enabled Nathaniel to steer himself to his company with ease. Charles was again free of "Mrs P", who Nathaniel remembered was averse to crowds, but was talking hard to Captain Peterson who stood with a lady and the young woman he recognised as Emma Peterson. There was another gentleman in the group: a small barrel of a man, with a comical smile and bright flush on his cheeks, the latter possibly generated by his unfeasibly tight high collar.

The barrage of introductions and greetings provided the information that Captain Peterson was accompanied by his wife as well as his daughter, and that the rotund party was a Mr Howard Dill who, like Captain Peterson, had business with Mr Vere that morning. Both remarked that it was unusual for that gentleman to be late.

"If you recall Nathaniel, you met him and Mrs Vere last night. He is the proprietor of the New Bank," explained Dr Parry. "He is a shrewd businessman and no mistake. Profits and investments are soaring."

"Yes, yes," added Mr Dill delightedly, his bushy eyebrows leaping above his tiny glasses. "I have known him for years and it has been perfectly astonishing to see the growth of his banking interests of late. I gather you are only here temporarily Mr Parry, so perhaps we will be unable to persuade you to invest in the city!"

"Yes Mr Dill," said Nathaniel. "I am here for a few weeks, enjoying a break from London."

"Tired of London, tired of life!" breezed Charles Parry. "Johnson could not have been further from the truth. You may be tempted to spend longer here Nathaniel. You will be invigorated man! Fresh air, fine waters, and family ties. Mrs P says you are to come to dinner tomorrow, no excuses!"

"With pleasure," murmured Nathaniel.

"And don't forget new acquaintances!" said Captain Peterson. "You are also welcome to dine with us at your convenience, perhaps next week?"

Mrs Peterson had been prepared for this, as her husband had regaled the family over breakfast, at considerable length, with tales of his exploits in the company of this young man's father. It would be distinctly more diverting to listen to such tales in the company of the young gentleman himself, so she had encouraged the offer of an invitation. Annoyingly, although she had met Mr Parry the previous evening, Emma had been non-committal, but that was hardly unusual where young men were concerned. Lydia Peterson glared covertly at her daughter, willing her to look up and smile. Had all those years of expenditure on governesses and tutors been totally wasted? Failing to animate Emma, she beamed encouragement to Nathaniel and was not disappointed.

"Thank you sir, and thanks to you madam, most kind."

Nathaniel liked the Captain and looked forward to the dinner. Madam seemed friendly, but he was amused to notice that Miss Peterson avoided his eye.

"You're deuced lucky to be in a health resort. As are we all," said Dr Parry portentously. "You will no doubt have heard the latest on the spread of the new fever, the cholera morbus?"

"How is it different from our present fevers pray?" asked Captain Peterson. "We have enough of them already to know them fore and aft I would have thought."

"Ah" said Dr Parry, warming to his theme, "this is very different I can assure you. This "Pest from Bengal" is a swifter killer than we are used to. Seems to spread like any other fever through foul airs or contact with sufferers, if you will pardon the mention of such indelicate matters ladies."

"I read about this in the paper, Dr Parry," said Emma

Peterson, her face suddenly alight with interest. “It is almost at our door is it not, having ravaged the Far East and Europe? There was some recommendation to prepare brandy and rhubarb for sufferers and to keep them warm, but there was also talk of confining victims and their families to their homes with a sign telling of the sickness painted on their door. Wasn’t that done in the fourteenth century in the time of the Black Death! Haven’t we moved on? The symptoms are different from that plague, but seem almost as frightful. The violent sickness and clawing of the hands and feet, the discolouration of the bodies…”

“That’s quite enough Emma,” interrupted her mother firmly, placing a warning hand on her daughter’s arm. “I certainly do not wish to hear of such abominations: especially in the forenoon. Dr Parry, perhaps you could expand on the value of our mineral waters in the pursuit of health? Our visitor is perhaps not fully aware of the signal values of the Bath waters for all types of indisposition.”

Emma blushed with frustration, as she had particularly wanted to hear Dr Parry’s views on the impending epidemic. She tossed her head moodily and looked away, only to catch Nathaniel’s amused smile as she did so. She almost laughed aloud, for he winked at her, so quickly, so shamelessly, and, as he had intended, only she saw it. It was so utterly unexpected, so disarming: shockingly delightful and discomfiting in equal measures. She froze in the struggle to compose her features and wondered if she had imagined it.

Fortunately for her, Mr and Mrs Vere arrived at that very moment and Raphael Vere immediately monopolised the conversation. Vere, no longer the complacent burgess, was harassed and anxious. His wife Tilly, resplendent in a sapphire-blue hat and coat with the most exuberant sleeves yet seen in the Great Pump Room, seemed exasperated.

“Good morning ladies, gentlemen,” said Vere unhappily. “Do forgive our lateness, it has been occasioned by a most perplexing occurrence. Nay, worrying I have to say. I received news from the bank this morning that my manager Mr Wilson had not arrived to open for business, an unparalleled occurrence. I went myself to admit the clerks and when Mr Wilson's assistant checked his desk and the safe, he discovered that a considerable amount of money, cash and bonds and various papers had disappeared." He paused to catch his breath. "There was no forced entry," as he added this last, his heavy features sagged at the inevitable construction which might put upon it. "I have known Wilson for over ten years. I cannot believe he might have knowledge of such depredations. Excellent man. Though I have worried about him over the last few months." Vere left his worries undefined.

Whilst partly listening to the fluttering of well-mannered concern generated by this disclosure, Nathaniel privately recollected Tobias's tale of the body in the river and decided to dig more deeply, but was obliged to wait for the opportunity. Thoroughly tired of the conundrum of Wilson, Tilly Vere had set up a fluting monologue on the coldness of the wind, moving inconsequentially on to the impending season of events and in particular the inclusion of various reform soirees, for which, apparently, she could not wait. Under cover of the polite responses to Mrs Vere, Nathaniel saw his chance to move in and have a quiet word with her husband.

"Mr Vere, could I ask you, what worries did you have about such a trusted employee? Forgive me for enquiring but I have some experience of investigations and might be able to offer advice."

"Yes indeed Mr Parry, most kind. Charles has often spoken to me of the impressive successes achieved by you and your father." He paused to ensure the company was well occupied and lowered his voice. "I am sorry to say that Mr Wilson has of late been indulging his habit of gambling to a more significant degree than his means allowed. I must admit he had approached me for help over the last few weeks. I did as much as I could, as a friend. But also as a friend I had to council him to change his company and seek entertainment elsewhere. I pray that he has not taken dire steps to resolve a personal dilemma."

The aside had been noted by Captain Peterson and Dr Parry, who were less than absorbed by the consideration of the soirees that continued to divert the ladies and the jovial Mr Dill.

"Well," said the Captain brusquely, "no doubt all will be resolved speedily. Did any of your employees shed further light on the problem?"

"Mr Henry Blake, Wilson's assistant, is still helping police with their enquiries."

"Henry Blake," said Captain Peterson with renewed interest, "Commander Tomlinson's nephew! Excellent young man, excellent family."

"Ah yes," said Vere, with lukewarm enthusiasm, "young Blake is at present explaining his whereabouts last night. He attended the same gaming rooms as Wilson you know."

Captain Peterson bristled at the slur but was prevented from making a rejoinder by Dr Parry.

"Can't think of a red-blooded male in Bath who hasn't attended gaming rooms! What! Let's hope your Mr Wilson makes an appearance and solves the mysteries before the end of the morning! Now Nathaniel you are determined to remain in lodgings by the river I take it?"

"Yes Charles, for a few days, but I look forward to dining with you tomorrow at Sion Hill."

A burst of joyous laughter distracted the party and they turned to see a bevy of young women swirl into the room surrounding a rakish young man with a brazen mop of red hair and a rose and cream striped waistcoat, who was delivering what appeared to be a rattling good tale. A circling rearguard was formed by a group of mamas and papas, anxious chaperones poised to pluck their charges away.

"Isn't that the speaker from last night," said Howard Dill, craning his neck for a better view, "Good Lord, he seems to be a regular Pied Piper for the young women!"

"Diarmuid Casey," said Dr Parry. "He spoke well, and seems to be unwilling to stop!"

"Introduce me Raphael," demanded Tilly Vere, pulling at Vere's arm and flashing her brilliant smile. She added mendaciously to strengthen her case, "I so enjoyed his speech and have a mind to ask him some questions."

"Certainly my dear," said Vere wearily. "Do excuse us."

From force of habit, Emma Peterson avoided glancing at the captivating Mr Casey and kept her eyes resolutely lowered. Her mother despaired of her and focused on preventing Nathaniel from evading the dinner invitation.

"Well Mr Parry, perhaps you will visit us in Marlborough Buildings and we can arrange a dinner?" said Mrs Peterson.

"By all means," said Nathaniel. "I bid you good morning ladies, gentlemen."

He made his escape and skirted the excited group surrounding Diarmuid Casey. The Irishman was playing up to them with consummate skill and they were drinking in his charm wholesale. But perhaps not all were so easily entranced. As Nathaniel passed by he caught sight of a striking dark-haired woman with an almond shaped face of exquisite beauty. She was dressed in spring-green and had a small corsage of delicate white flowers on her lapel. Smiling archly, not so much at Mr Casey but at the rest of the girls, she posed, holding his arm: cat-like, enigmatic, one bold dark eyebrow raised in quizzical amusement. There's a minx, thought Nathaniel, as he strode out through the doors to Abbey Church Yard and threaded his way through the gathering crowds to the Hart.

A number of enquires needed to be pursued in the afternoon and a little local knowledge would help him start. The Hart was settling down after the recent arrival of a coach, guests had disappeared upstairs or into coffee rooms, parlours or dining-rooms, orders had been barked out and from the kitchen came the answering clatter of pots. Horses, foamed and steaming after ten miles hard labour, were being led to stables by the scarlet-coated grooms. Nathaniel made his way to a familiar seat. The burly barman recognised him immediately, settled him down with a mug of local cider and provided all he needed to know to draw up a plan of attack.

He would start at the York House in the upper town, inn of choice for many London coaches and the venue favoured, as he had already been told and sensed was doomed to be told daily, by the Duchess of Kent and her daughter the heiress-apparent Princess Victoria. The Chequers in Rivers Street was a haunt of chairmen so should give an insight into the attitudes of a disgruntled sector of Bath's workers. The lower town seemed a mixture of the respectable and the reprobate. He decided to tackle a couple in Avon Street, though a disguise would be required by the sound of it if he were to escape rough-handling. The Duke of York on the Quay also seemed a good bet for scurrilous news, he remembered it from Tobias's tale that morning. Surprisingly, the Crosskeys seemed to have a notorious reputation and it was just a few steps from where they were talking, across the High Street in the shadow of the Abbey. That would also do for a start.

"Thank you sir," said Nathaniel, finishing noting the venues in his pocketbook. "There is one other question I have. Where can a man find some fencing practice in the city?"

The barman drew himself up to his full and not inconsiderable height. "You sir, 'ave come to exactly the right place to find out about sword play! I am assumin' you have been in the military?"

"I have served with the army," said Nathaniel cautiously.

"Apart from regular annual trainin', quite regular a group from the North Somerset Yeoman Cavalry meet on Captain Wilkins' land at Twiverton. Real gentleman is Captain Wilkins, he owns a factory there and encourages any gentleman who owns a sword and is keen to keep their hand in. You never know with times as they are. The damned Frenchies a-winding up the

Belgians, and the Poles hammer and tongs at the Ruskies. Not to mention the I-talians!" His moustache bristled vigorously, ready for anything. "You can catch the Captain here. Bath Yeomen use this inn as their headquarters for meetings."

"Thank you for the information," said Nathaniel shaking the barman's hand. "Most helpful."

"You are welcome," said the barman. "Frederick Tooson at your service sir."

As Nathaniel prepared to leave, Tobias loped out from the kitchen corridor at his usual half-run, bearing steaming plates of roast beef, which he delivered before doubling back to Nathaniel.

"Find a good 'orse sir? Do you need any more 'elp?"

"Not specifically young man. But I'll tell you what you can do." He lowered his voice conspiratorially, "Now keep this quiet, but I might spend more time in this town and I need to know if it's safe. See if you can find out where the people live in this city who tend to make up the mobs when there's trouble. Do you know what I mean? Who would be likely to cause the magistrates to read the Riot Act?"

"Oh yes sir. Oiy knows what y're after. Crowds that go a-breaking windows at election nights or go amok at the weekends when they're in drink?"

"Exactly."

"There 'aint no secret 'bout that Mr Parry. Over the river in the Holloway and the Dolemeads and all the lower town round Avon Street and Milk Street 'as most packs of troublemakers. H'immigrants and such as well. When mi ma was alive we lived down by there in Little Corn Street, Little 'Ell it's sometimes called sir. Oiy still knows some o' they lads there."

"Have a chat with them, see how things lie Tobias," said Nathaniel, pressing a half-crown into the boy's hand. "Lot of unrest at the present time with the next reform vote coming in a few days."

"To be honest sir, Oiy don't really know exac'ly what this

new re-form vote is about. Oiy thought being as 'e's in charge and 'e wants reform, Lord Grey would tell all they parliament men what to do and they'd jump to it. But Oiy'll tell you if Oiy 'ear anything of int'rest."

"Tobias, can you read?"

"No sir, Oiy ain't never bin to school."

"Not even Sunday School to learn your letters?"

"Mother didn't hold with religion sir," muttered Tobias, his eyes slewing away in embarrassment. "Anyways, she said you had to have shoes and clean clothes to be let in, and that was not always so for me sir."

"But you know the reform of parliament will give the vote to more men who deserve it don't you?" Tobias encouraged him with a nod so Nathaniel continued. "It has to pass three readings and discussion and voting in the House of Commons, then the same in the House of Lords to become law. The Lords are the sticking point. They do not want more voters."

"Lord Grey's a lord though and he wants it."

"Yes but the majority of the peers are against him."

"Oiy can't read but Oiy can listen," said Tobias, inspired to raise his head. "Mr Turner in the Dragon reads from the new paper to everyone. The poor man's paper says all men 'oo work 'ard and are true Britons deserve to vote. It made you feel you could be something, you could be somebody." Suddenly his face lost its animation, "But them at the top never want others to 'ave anythin' do they sir? They're a-feared for their power."

Nathaniel looked closely at the boy, whip thin, the same patched shirt hidden by the over-sized scarlet waistcoat borrowed from the hook in the kitchen, the borrowed flapping boots, the same tired and grimy trousers reaching his mid-calf. Impulsively he drew a ten shilling note from his pocket.

"Tobias, buy some clean clothes and shoes. There is a dealer I saw in Walcot Street where you can get a second-hand suit complete." The boy looked uncertain. "I can't have you working for me looking like that," said Nathaniel sternly. "And Mrs

Spence will bar you from reporting to me in my rooms if you haven't better boots to change to when you're not wearing Joseph's."

"Oiy'll be loike a new pin sir," said Tobias, his lip quivering. Before the tears fell he managed a lop-sided smile, then dodged back down the kitchen corridor.

The Peterson Residence, Marlborough Buildings, Bath.

After lunch the customary dull quiet descended on the Peterson residence in Marlborough Buildings. Emma sat in the sitting-room sewing a new pelisse in lavender grey, killing time until her friend arrived, whilst the sound of her twin sisters enduring their French lesson wafted down from the schoolroom. Ginette and Maddy were identical, thirteen years of age and given to private jokes, explosive bursts of giggling and general tiresomeness. It was a relief for the whole household when they were brought to order by Mademoiselle Junot. Emma's elder sister Celia had been relatively good company until she made her great match with her farmer. Now short bouts of socialising with the lovebirds went an extremely long way.

Emma continued to run a neat seam down the shimmering fabric, mulling over the surprising events of the morning. Skimming over memories of the usual gossipy small talk that characterised sessions in the Pump Room with her parents, she let her mind return to the most interesting fact. Mr Nathaniel Parry was probably the nicest looking man she had ever seen. Not probably, definitely. The mere thought of him was enough to, what had Anna said that was so funny? Enough to "come over all unnecessary". That was it. She smiled at the memory, but was instantly downcast at the thought of the gruesome embarrassment that awaited her at next week's dinner. Her mother would sense her interest, sniff it out like a pointer and worry it to death, frightening off the outrageously handsome Mr Parry and humiliating her as she did so.

She stabbed her needle into the seam balefully, how ridiculous life was sometimes. Then she felt ashamed and conjured up visions of dead cholera victims piled in blackened, twisted stacks. Her thoughts veered away to drift back to last night's meeting and the impassioned pleas for change. What was the point? Were the mighty Lords in London listening? All would be clear in, she thought carefully, in two days. Just two days: then the vote. There could be MPs for the new industrial towns and cities and ordinary middle-class gentlemen voting in every constituency. It couldn't be wrong, surely? There were other things she was slowly coming to think were not wrong either. Some people spoke of women having a vote as well. No-one at the meeting did though. First things first, she could see that. But if this change went through, who knew where it would end? She breathed deeply, it seemed unimaginable but maybe one day she could take any job she chose, not just governessing like Anna who had little choice, but perhaps a man's job, like a solicitor, or a doctor. How dearly she would love to do that! She could have her own money. She would not be obliged to get married. But then she remembered Mr Parry.

She was interrupted by distant sounds at the front door and Anna's voice in the hall. At last, her visitor. Anna Grant's afternoon off was an oasis in the week. Her childhood friend and boon companion of the years in Portsmouth, when both their fathers were at sea, now worked in St James's Square. It was not five minutes walk away. They had taken to spending an hour or two together once a week, the only time she had Anna to herself now she was engaged to Mr Blake.

Emma rose to greet her friend, but her welcome froze on her lips.

"Anna what on earth is the matter!"

Tear-stained and pale, Anna fled to her side and grasped her hands.

"Oh Em we've got to help Henry. The most awful thing has happened."

"Sit down Anna. Give me your bonnet." Emma rang for the maid, pulled up another chair and held her friend's hands tightly.

She dispatched the maid as soon as she appeared. "Bring some tea Enid. Now, Anna, slowly, from the start."

"Henry and I did something wrong last night Em," agonised Anna, her plump face a picture of misery. "No, not too wrong," she said, catching Emma's stunned expression. "Well I didn't think it would be so. I asked him in to take a glass of wine with me at my employer's house. The family's out until later today. I was left to look after the baby and Henry and I thought it would be a good opportunity to have some time together alone." She screwed up her face in pain at the recollection. "Oh Em when they find out I'll lose my job."

"But why should they Anna?" said Emma briskly. "You are hardly going to confess."

"Henry is in Grove Street police station Emma. Last night money and bonds and papers disappeared from the office he shares with Mr Wilson and," she continued with a sob, "Oh Emma! Mr Wilson has been found murdered. He was found in the Avon and he had been stabbed. In the back!"

"Murdered! I'd heard he was missing. Mr Vere told us at the Pump Room this morning. Are you sure? Anyway what could possibly connect Henry with this?"

"He will not tell them where he was last night Em! But much worse. Oh so much worse. His rooms have been searched, all the employees have had searches, but some of the missing bonds have been found in his! There is no possible explanation. What can we do? What can we do? There was even talk he might have killed poor Mr Wilson! Never, never, Em. Not Henry!"

Anna gave herself up to sustained sobbing and succeeded in creating sufficient noise to summon Captain and Mrs Peterson from their housekeeping conference in the study.

"Good Lord, Anna," exclaimed the Captain. "What on earth is going on?"

"Sit down Oliver," said his wife, pouring the neglected tea.

"Again Anna please."

Anna subsided. She sniffed and hiccoughed her way through the woeful tale for a second time.

"How do you know this?" enquired Captain Peterson.

"Mr Vere was so kind as to send a message. Henry had asked him to let me know and I have been to Grove Street. I have told him he must say where he was last night. He says he won't, but even if he does it won't be enough will it! It doesn't explain the bonds." Her lower lip began to tremble afresh and her eyes swam.

"Right young lady," said the Captain firmly, rising to pass her the discarded bonnet. "You will return with me now to Grove Street. We will speak with Henry together. We will then go to your employers' home to await their return. You will explain what you did last night and I will plead your cause. Let us simplify this toil, one step at a time."

"Father I will come with you," said Emma, glancing at the miserable Anna.

"Yes," said the Captain, not relishing the prospect of walking the streets of Bath alone with a weeping female. "Capital idea Em. We'll be back as soon as possible Lydia."

As they left, Mrs Peterson poured herself a cup of tea, reflecting on the fact that fiancés were not always an asset. It offered some comfort. She pondered how best to inform Mrs Grant of the misfortunes of her daughter, such a pity, and he had seemed such a nice young man.

Arno's Tower, Arno's Vale, near Bristol.

As the Petersons escorted Anna Grant back into town, a private coach drawn by four perfectly matched greys made its way past Totterdown and the last tollhouse of the City of Bristol on the Bristol-Bath road. As it entered Arno's Vale it took a sharp right down a newly metalled road towards the woods. Amanda Ravenswood had made herself extremely comfortable, her feet in their shining patent slippers thrust up on the opposite seat under a fur rug and her hands folded inside the capacious muff which dangled from a silk cord round her neck. She wore a large hat with fur trim, rather excessive for early October, but it had to be done. It was the first of its kind, direct from Paris for the new season. Her mission that afternoon had been satisfactorily completed and it had included impressing Mrs Lottie Drake, the London matron, and also her husband who was apparently of exceeding importance, working directly for Lords Melbourne and Palmerston. To Amanda, used to the commanding and chilling presence of her husband Edwin, Drake had appeared banal and nondescript: not imposing enough to impress with his ferrety-foxy face, his smug complacency. She had made a normal lady's afternoon call on Mrs Drake and had also been rewarded by an introduction to the husband. She had plenty to relay to Edwin on her return home. He would undoubtedly make short work of Mr Drake when they met, whatever his purpose with him might be.

Amanda had the low cunning to realise that it would be of no advantage to her ever to pry into her husband's business. She lived in awe of his power, his rage and his subtle cruelty which marked every aspect of their lives together, even the most intimate. She shivered at the thought of him, even now after two years of marriage he was a fascinating stranger: perilous, potentially deadly. She smiled parting her red lips over strangely pointed, dazzling white eye-teeth. Not features to attract the average man. Edwin Ravenswood was far from average. It had been interesting to see that Lottie Drake was also far from a dull London matron. The Drakes had taken pleasant and fashionable rooms in Clifton. They were well situated in Cornwallis Crescent, on the slopes above Hotwells. After initial pleasantries, John Drake had taken them out for tea to the Bazaar. They had provided a head-turning performance for the provincial *beau monde*. Amanda and Lottie had sat opposite each other like two birds of paradise squaring up for battle: two brilliant egg-timers of style, broadest leg o' mutton sleeves competing, vast skirts billowing below and tiny waists between. She had had the better of it. Mr Drake was to dine with Edwin to discuss their business and she was to meet again with Lottie, who offered not only a clothes-horse duel in extravagance, but also the most deliciously spiteful conversation to be had in Bristol.

The coach pulled up in a flurry of gravel at the forbidding griffin-flanked entrance to Arno's Tower, the Ravenswood mansion. Footmen sprang to let down the steps and Amanda descended haughtily, dispensing her habitual cold glare to the servants, striding up the steps to the echoing stone hall. Her hat and muff were dropped into the hands of waiting maids and she made directly for Edwin's study.

"Mi'lady," the footman caught up with her and bowed low. "Mr Ravenswood is in the Oriental Salon, with his guests. They have only just returned from a tour of the wharf."

His guests from the Far East were clearly still in residence. Amanda glowered as she walked down the west-wing corridor to Edwin's *pièce de résistance*. Of course he had to show it off to them. To impress? To dare them to criticise? Edwin enjoyed living dangerously and she knew instinctively that the two guests were providing much dangerous enjoyment.

But how long would he live to savour it?

She knocked briskly and entered. The salon glowed in the low light of the afternoon sun. Here were Edwin's laquered screens, his paintings and ceramics, his carved dragons, his erotic prints, his weapons of exquisite workmanship and deadly intent. Suits of Eastern armour with winged shoulder-banners and barred masks, swords curved, long, short, sheathed and bare, winking evilly from wall hooks and cradled in ebony stands. Edwin sat on a high-backed chair facing the two men. Cornelius Lee, young and feline, sat as usual, quite still, serenely watchful. Last night's arrival, a Mr Kizhe, was older, more squat, more massively powerful with seamed skin and the eyes of a snake, mesmerising, poised to seize its prey.

"Well my dear," said Ravenswood, with an unspoken warning in his voice. "I'm sure you have plenty to do. I hope you enjoyed your afternoon with the Drakes."

"Yes Edwin. I think Mrs Drake and I had much in common and Mr Drake sends his compliments and looks forward to your meeting."

"You have much in common?" remarked Edwin unpleasantly. "How surprising. I look forward to meeting Mrs Drake at some point."

"Would you like dinner at six?" said Amanda, keen to leave the room which had quickly become oppressive: the suffocating, brooding silence generated by the two men made her deeply uneasy. Her usual barbed exchanges with Edwin were impossible: she did not dare.

"No my dear," said Ravenswood his dead eyes smiling in pleasure at her discomfiture. "Eight. We are going out to shoot."

After an hour bagging Ravenswood's ducks the three men made their way from the water meadow across the parkland immediately surrounding the house and approached the wood. They were accompanied by two of Ravenswood's men with a pair of gundogs, extra ammunition and guns. Edwin Ravenswood and Kizhe walked ahead and Cornelius Lee followed, still in black, unlike the others who had donned elaborate shooting gear. He was also different in that he carried a bow slung across his back and a quiver at his hip. As they reached the outskirts of the wood Ravenswood's henchmen were dispatched to the tree line to act as beaters if required, which also kept them out of earshot.

"I prefer to introduce serious business in the open air when away from home, and in alien territory," said Kizhe watching Ravenswood narrowly, then shifting his gaze to the henchmen who were dipping out of sight and into the trees. "So let us take the opportunity and be brief. The Count has been pleased with your success in keeping the supply lines of opium open to the major Chinese cities and with his continued support that side of the business should continue to prosper. The meeting with your Mr Drake will secure the collaboration with the British government and therefore with the indispensable British navy." He cocked his gun as he spoke and caught a hare as it bounded from cover, the dogs scattered as they vied to retrieve it. "What we need to develop is the new business line that has been developing so well under your guidance Mr Ravenswood. We will have a new triangular trade all of our own my friend." His deep-set eyes glinted at the studied reference to the foundation of Ravenswood's wealth. Edwin's family had grown fabulously rich on the bounty of the infamous triangular slave trade which shipped out of Bristol bound for Africa. British guns, gewgaws and cheap metal goods had been exchanged for African slaves, which were in turn sold on as human cargo to the steamy plantations of the New World to finance the purchase of rum, sugar, coffee and cotton. The abolition of the trade in 1807 had brought little in the way of protest from Bristol slavers, as by then Liverpool had long eclipsed them in the trade, and families like the Ravenswoods had invested wisely in West Indian estates and diversified into less controversial goods.

"It is fortunate indeed," continued Kizhe, "that the British authorities are so dependent on maintaining the opium sales to balance their trade with China. You British do so like your Chinese silks, your brocade," he laughed unpleasantly, "and of course your tea! Which you drink so barbarously. And you Mr Ravenswood, your Chinese art is so important to you, yes?"

Ravenswood stood silently, indulging his guest.

"However, it is the cargo we have found to replace the British pots and pans and mirrors that the Count's interest is now focused upon. We do not need pots and pans and mirrors Mr Ravenswood."

"Sir, there is no problem of supply. Let us speak plainly I have the greatest interest in increasing our supply of the females your customers need. I have two chosen for delivery to fulfil the requirement of the Count. They will sail with the *Blue Dragon* which is completing its refit and will be delivered to the usual harbour."

"The Count wants a continuous supply of children Mr Ravenswood. He has clients with particular tastes in East Africa and the Levant, as well as India and the Far East. I have an urgent order not just for the two ten year olds but also for two small English girls, fair and under three years of age. They stay on board when the next opium shipment is collected in India, then go overland from the Chinese port to be transferred to the customer on the Russian border. Do not fail." He paused, taking aim as a string of birds broke from the woods. The gun roared and a black shape and fluttering feathers cascaded from the sky: the dogs, slavering with flying tongues and pounding feet strove to outrun each other and catch it as it fell.

"I have a supplier Mr Kizhe," said Ravenswood calmly. "The needs of the Count's customers will be met."

"They need to be prepared before delivery," said Kizhe, fixing Ravenswood with a steely glare. "Ensure they are compliant."

"It will be done," said Ravenswood shortly and moved to the attack. "Bristol has a long and formidable record in the business of, shall we call it 'white slavery' Mr Kizhe. For over a thousand years we have been past masters in the trade. Do not think our African blackbirds were our only commodity."

As Kizhe raised his next gun in response to a bird rising from the edge of the wood, Cornelius Lee drew an arrow which he loosed to spear it, silently, before Kizhe had levelled his barrel.

"Ah, ha. The ancient arts are alive and well in Somerset I see," said Kizhe appreciatively.

"I like to keep in practice," said Cornelius.

"It is well that you are here Mr Lee," said Kizhe. "The Count particularly wanted a Chinese courier for the next voyage, not just to check prices with the opium broker but more particularly, to deliver the other goods. I hope I have made clear that it is of the utmost importance that the delivery is made. The customer is a valued colleague of the Count."

Suddenly, a shout went up from one of the men in the wood and a dark figure broke from the trees, encumbered with a bulging bag and trailing a snare, running haphazardly left and right, clearly with the aim of evading shots from the pursuing men and from the hill. Without pausing, Kizhe raised his gun and shot, the distant figure crumpled, fell and rolled to a stop, his bag bouncing down the slope, disgorging a pair of rabbits, bloodied, necks askew.

"Damned poacher," said Ravenswood laconically. "Good shot Mr Kizhe."

Cornelius was already sprinting down the rise to the twitching body. It had been a head shot, a lethal and brutal choice entirely typical of the marksman. The man lay in agonised death throes, half his face blown away to leave a morass of blood and bone, too shocked to cry out, too wounded to rise again. Cornelius knelt and slid his knife mercifully between the man's ribs. He rose and made his way back to the shooting party.

Ravenswood had already called his men over. "Take the body to the lime-pit and the game to the kitchens," he ordered. "Gentlemen, time to change for dinner."

Later that night, Cornelius Lee changed from his evening wear into a close fitting silk jacket with mandarin collar, wide ankle-length pants with room to move and flat black leather pumps, all black as pitch. He limbered up briefly: head, arms, legs, then slowly raised each leg in turn above his head, holding it, holding it, heel turned out to land a blow. He then stood straight and motionless for a heartbeat, turned a standing somersault, landed silent as a panther and slipped out of the window to bound over the balcony and disappear into the night. He stole away like a wraith over the park, vaulted the wall, ran lightly down the metalled drive and passed like a shadow towards the Bath Road. He skirted the grounds of Mount Pleasant, the copper baron's mansion, which until the building of Arno's Towers had been the grandest pile in the Vale. He trod softly in the darkness past the Neo-Gothic archway, past the black bulk of the stables and laundry, brutally built of copper slag and dubbed "The Devil's Cathedral".

"How little they seem to know of devilry here," he thought to himself. He recollected the cruel head shot delivered by Kizhe, the man's shabby clothes, the painful thinness of the flesh under his hand as he steadied the body for a quick release. If that is the Cathedral, Arno's Tower is the gilded throne of the Devil. He chose a narrow path through the undergrowth and sprinted on to his favourite spot: St Anne's-in-the-Wood. He had learned of the old holy well from his reading before he arrived in Bristol and it appealed to him. Long neglected and surrounded by derelict buildings, he had chosen it for his temple. He halted in a dell suffused with moonlight, silent but for the soft sounds of night creatures: the downy beat of owl's wings, the snuffling of hedgehogs, the distant bark of a fox. Here he began his regime, breathing deeply. He bowed his head in the silence of the night and prayed. The Taoism of his childhood had left Cornelius Lee with a residual spirituality. He took comfort through his prayers to the cleansing wind in the trees, to the shafts of moonlight, to the dappled shade and the black well by the ruined wall. The crumbling foundations were all that remained of the proud medieval shrine, visited by kings and made holy by the whispered prayers of the anchorites. He prayed to St Anne, wherever she was, whoever she might have been.

Chapter 3

7th October, 1831, Walcot Street, Bath.

Martha Spence ran a tight ship. By first light she was a-bustle: fires were ablaze and water boiled briskly in the kitchen kettles. Old Tom had been rooted out of his malodorous alcove bed. His chamber-pot empty and rinsed, he had been cleansed, freshly wrapped and anchored into his chair for the day. Mary had been roused to scour the Johnty, soak his napkin and any offending bedding, and lay the breakfast table. The crackle of the fire; the clatter of pots, pans, purposeful feet and busy hands; squeaky chirrups from the Johnty; Mary's soft murmurings and Tom's squeezebox cackling floated up the stairs and through the cracks of the door to Nathaniel's room, and all were overlaid by a mighty blast from the Church Militant.

"Forth in Thy Name, O Lord, I go!" Martha belted out, mercilessly, from the garden.

"My daily labour to pursue.

Thee, only Thee resolved to know," she paused to rustle up more wooden pegs from an apron pocket and finish attaching the flapping wet washing to the line.

"In all I think, or speak, or do."

She smiled, eyes glinting and slightly breathless, watching the steam rise from the sheets and dissipate like a ghost at cockcrow into the cold steel-blue of the October morning. She breathed deeply and gave voice: "Thee may I set at my right hand!"

Nathaniel had taken cover at the first trump, sliding under the blankets for defence, whilst Caradoc had leapt to attention. He had one ear cocked, the other sagging below the vertical and had set up a deafening volley of yapping, energetically trampling his master in time to the fusillade. Driven from bed, Nathaniel pulled on the silk Damascus gown, ejected Caradoc to find the garden and made for the window to inspect the day. He dragged back the central curtain to expose the graceful arched Venetian window and the room flooded with light. Bright and sharp, the sun was rising over Bathwick, lighting up the cream stone of the terraces and the thousand chimneys, dispelling the mists which clung to the treetops. "Keats weather," said Nathaniel out loud. "Autumn and the sun conspiring: 'how to load and bless with fruit, the vines that round the thatch-eaves run.'"

"Are you awake, Mr Parry? Are you alone?" asked Mary, tapping hesitantly at the door. "I've brought your water and breakfast up, sir."

Nathaniel prepared himself for a day on the town, perhaps a canter along the river path, perhaps over the hills and far away. He was in high good humour and, having recovered from the rude awakening, felt inspired enough to attempt a tune as he dressed. He did not select Charles Wesley, but lined up uncompromisingly with his Welsh forbears and struck up his favourite version of *Men of Harlech*:

Da-di-da, di-da-de dadee. Da-da-da-da-da-da da-dee,"

even managing to break into full song for the finale:

"There I mid the swords thick gleaming, Cymru follow me!"

Sadly, this promised to be a day of limited sword-play. He made a mental note to take up the suggestions of Frederick Tooson, the barman in the Hart, for some practice with the local yeomanry. He took his swordstick from the corner, drew it and bent over to inspect it, which brought another vivid memory of his father and the hours they had spent pouring over his heavily wrought eastern blades. He swung the slender sword in a perfect circle, lunged once, then ten times more with the right hand. He swapped hands and lunged twenty times with his left before temporarily sheathing the blade. He took out one of his shabby disguises, a threadbare and rusty frock coat, and hung it on the door, man height. Standing still before it, he tamed his breathing, sank to a stance and in a moment drew the sword to lunge precisely.

Heart. Draw back, re-sheath. Throat. Draw back, re-sheath. Again, again, again. Reluctantly, he put it away and resigned himself to a day of comparative idleness. The only fixture was the dinner with Charles at Summerhill, his Sion Hill mansion. This left the morning and afternoon for recreation and a brief check through his report for Drake, with whom he would spend the next couple of days. In terms of location, Clifton offered some interest, though there was potential for tedium in the meetings with Drake himself. In any event, there was no deferment possible. The Lords' decision on the Bill had yet to be made, so his current surveillance assignment must bide its time. He dawdled over his bread and coffee, reflecting on yesterday's trawl through Bath's inns, taverns, beer-shops and markets. It was as well that he had taken the precaution of disguise for the lower town venues, or he would have attracted unwelcome attention. It had definitely been a makila day: the stout walking stick had proved extremely useful for forging a path through groups of toughs and fending off stray dogs. To his chagrin, Caradoc had been left behind. His appearance was too distinctive and his demeanour of yesterday afternoon had been too combative for covert operations.

Although one of the daintiest cities in England, Bath still offered plenty in the way of villainous alleys, middens, rooting pigs, dead horses, cats and dogs whose bloated bodies wallowed, grotesque and putrid on the lazy flow of the Avon. The river to the west of the old bridge had presented the appearance of an open sewer, with small birds picking their way across it dry-foot from one island of floating detritus to the next. The populace in the lower town had varied between the respectable and the dubiously employed, the desperate, the indigent poor and the clearly criminal. On the quays, raddled prostitutes lurked in door-ways by evil smelling courts. Coarse and blowsy in the harsh light of day, softening as the gaslights were lit and night fell, they turned on their wily charms:

"Buy me a glass o' beer sir?"

Thin waif-like girls, still comely but with old faces, had their feral lines wiped by the dark. Chameleon-like they turned into the "nightingales" and "nymphs" of the lower town, ready to part eager men from their purses. So much, so predictable, he had heard nothing to alarm the powers in London. Enthusiasm for reform was general and was even expressed with some vim in the local Tory newspaper *The Bath Chronicle*, which he had read whilst consuming an unusually fine joint of roast lamb in the Full Moon, the haunt of men of commerce by the river. Support for the Whig government, loyal addresses to the King and an atmosphere of excited anticipation seemed to characterise the whole city: for now.

He made his way to the kitchen, planning to round up Caradoc and bid good day to his hosts before taking a turn on the Parades. That was, after all, what one was meant to do in Bath with the famed season poised to take off. He would stroll in the rarefied air of the upper town and watch the world go by, as it in turn watched him. There had been some pretty sights already. As he jogged down the stairs his mind wandered over his new acquaintances of eligible age: the mild, lovely and work-worn Mary, the earnest Miss Peterson turned out like the Empress Josephine in her house-coat, the ravishing Mrs Vere, the bunch of beauties in the Pump Room, especially the bold almond-faced vixen hanging on the arm of the Irishman. She had looked particularly fine. It was good to have time to think of such things.

"Good day Mr Spence," he said, loudly and slowly as he thrust his head round the door. "Is Mrs Spence here? I will bid her good day before I leave."

Tom looked up from his rug cocoon.

"Ha ha! Come ye over young man! Come over and take a seat along o' me for five minutes." He beckoned erratically. Nathaniel hesitated, then pulled up a chair, preparing to do his duty.

"What tales young man? What has Bath brought thee so far?"

"I spent time in the Pump Room yesterday. A very fine building sir."

"Not all day ye didn't! What else?" demanded Tom, hungry for news, fixing his indeterminate and watery gaze in the vicinity of Nathaniel's shoulder, where the white light of the morning sun shone from the windowpanes and glossed the white wall behind him to a nimbus of light.

Good naturedly, Nathaniel allowed Tom the sport of extracting information from him whilst he manufactured the persona of a well-to-do London gentleman unused to these parts, a martyr to recreation and novelty, anxious as to the likelihood of riot and revolt in these unsettled times. He felt he pulled it off rather well. Tom grew confidential.

"Don't ye be a worritin' y'self sir," he said dismissively. "When great Lords like Grey and Russell are a-wantin' reform, and the ordinary folk are a-wantin' it, and the middlin' folk are a-wantin' it. They's likely to get it! If it be worth 'aving," he muttered, then shot his head out, tortoise-like, and fixed Nathaniel with a glare in the very image of Coleridge's Ancient Mariner. Nathaniel struggled, but failed, to keep a straight face and block the lines bubbling up in his memory: "He holds him with his glittering eye …..The Mariner hath his will…"

Tom continued: "You were but a child in '15 when the people were a-cryin' out for reform. Then it were different. All the Lords were agin' it and reformers were grievously beaten down. Why, Mr Hunt 'imself spoke 'ere in '17. Oiy 'eard 'im. Though it were difficult to get near for the damned cavalry. Dragoons packed round 'im tight as peas in a pod. All they wild talkers like Richard Carlile and they crazed Spenceans, them re-publicans, they got government to take fright they did. With their ve-hement talk and a-flyin' o' the Frenchey flag and a-wearin' they damned red caps. It frightened grand folk." He paused to gather a rasping breath, "Spenceans be all dead now young sir. Wildest of our re-formers now claims they just wants votes for £10 men. £10 bi'God!"

Nathaniel smiled encouragingly, watching, fascinated, as Tom seemed to sink deeper into the wreckage of his long life. Bizarrely, the claw-like hands which emerged from the rug were mechanically knitting a blanket square, the clacking needles marked time and provided a semblance of animation as he struggled to marshal his memory. "When Oiy were strong and workin', before Oiy went to sea, most men 'ad a copy of Tom Paine, we thought 'e talked sense. *Common Sense* he wrote mind! Wrote it for the Yankees he did. And *The Rights of Man*! Lord we did think we knew the road. But then…but then…". Tom shook his head and screwed up his aged features to re-order his thoughts. His face became a mask of taut wrinkled lines as he inwardly struggled to banish the ghouls swirling to the surface of memory: a fiendish mask of Robespierre, the shadow of the guillotine's blade, headless corpses, the shells of men returning from interminable war. "They Frenchies did for reform they did," he growled. "Now we think we 'ave another chance." He gave a wheezy chuckle which collapsed into hacking, tumultuous coughing.

"This is not France, Mr Spence. It will be different this time," said Nathaniel, bending to retrieve the ball of wool as it rolled across the spotless scrubbed floorboards, to snatch it from possible destruction in the jaws of Caradoc who had returned to lounge by the fire, and also from the porridge smeared fist of the

Johnty, who was in his customary position, wobbling by Tom's feet with his sturdy legs thrust out before him. "The Bill is through the Commons with a strong Whig majority. This has never happened before. It could be the start of slow and peaceful change which will in the end bring the suffrage to all men." He inspected Tom closely and felt oddly ashamed as he delivered the platitudes to the old man. Mrs Spence had said Old Tom was over ninety years old. For him the firebrands of the 1790s were wild young men and those days of antique horror seemed more real than 1831.

"Reform brings riots and rebellions which loose wild beasts in men," said the old man sonorously. "Critters you never knew existed in the quiet days. 'Twas ever the same! Mi' old grandf'er told me tales. He was alive in old Noll Cromwell's day! Noll 'e knew the danger of they Levellers and he finished them. But we must 'ave reform. No fear of the wild beasts should stop us."

He sighed and smiled wanly: "'Ave ye heard of the Lollards young man? Do'ee know of they far off days when the poor English all rose up and they said: "When Adam delved and Eve span who was then the gentleman?" Well now we do 'ave gentry, I thinks us all should 'ave a chance to be gentrified. But us 'aven't. They gentry is all going to get the vote, as is the shopkeepers, the middle folk. What chance will the lower sort of people 'ave then to improve they selves? Do ye think the Whigs 'ave forgotten the mistake they made in cheerin' they Frenchies in '89? They is twice shy now sir. Twice shy. They will keep down the common man."

Nathaniel listened in silence, confronting an image of his own early youth, his devoted love for the libertarian Romantics which lingered still. But mad Shelley had drowned and dashing Lord Byron in his Albanian rig had been knocked out by disease as soon as he raised his head for Greek independence. They lived for reform, for change, poetical hearts on their sleeves for the common man. Did they really know what wild beasts their dreams unleashed? He thought of Shelley, standing by the scaffold as the Pentrich conspirators dangled in '17. Shelley famously had no pity for the ringleader, Jeremiah Brandreth, incited by a government spy to raise the Midlands in the name of the people. Shelley, recalled Nathaniel, had written primly that he had no sympathy for Brandreth, as he had killed a man. Then off went Percy with his Mary, off to Italy to sail to his reckless death, so sure he could manage the rising wind. But he couldn't.

A rapid knocking roused them from their thoughts and summoned Martha to the front door from her washing. She came into the kitchen, still rubbing her hands dry on her apron. "Gentleman to see you Mr Parry. I've shown him into the parlour." She shot a suspicious glance at Tom, but he had subsided into his rug and was knitting peacefully.

Nathaniel followed Martha into the front room, which was sepulchrally cold after the warmth of the kitchen. Standing in front of the window, arms behind his back, legs astride, as if in full command of the fore-deck, was Captain Peterson.

"Sir! Good morning to you. How may I be of service?" said Nathaniel smoothly, though his spirits were marginally dampened as he suspected that the worthy Captain had been dispatched by his wife to entrap him into agreeing to an early dinner rendezvous, chez Peterson.

"Mr Parry, I am sorry to disturb you, but I have come to request your help." Captain Peterson swayed back and forth, uncomfortable in the confines of the small room and with the urgency of his errand. "This is not on my own account, but for the sake of two young persons embroiled, I am sorry to say, in a criminal investigation. These two are related to old comrades of mine, both known to your father. Henry Blake is nephew to Commander Tomlinson and Miss Anna Grant's late father also served with me. To be blunt, you know of criminal matters and of London ways of detection. I fear a gross miscarriage of justice could occur. Nay, is occurring! I have little faith in the powers of the local authorities and desire to lay the facts before you to learn your opinion."

"Do sit down sir. I am at your disposal."

The grim discovery of the stab wound in Roderick Wilson's back, the investigation of Henry Blake, the discovery of the bank's property in his rooms and his subsequent incarceration pending trial were communicated to Nathaniel swiftly and sparely.

"Blake was a young fool, Mr Parry. He spent the evening in question with his fiancée, Miss Anna Grant, at her place of employment, in the absence of her employers or any other chaperone, and was loathe to admit as much when questioned. This has been rectified." Oliver Peterson frowned at the memory of the strained interview at the residence in St James's Square. "Rumours of his connections with the late Mr Wilson and gaming establishments have surfaced. Fanciful theories have emerged of either some joint nefarious scheme of robbery cooked up between Wilson and young Blake which ended in murderous dispute, or that Blake chose to intercept Wilson after he had committed a crime and made off with the proceeds." Captain Peterson's kindly face puckered with lines of anxiety. "Miss Grant, who is a close friend of my daughter, came to our home with this sorry tale and sought her advice. I had to intervene! Our connection is close sir. Since the death of her poor father I see myself as in some respect *in loco parentis*. Her mother remains in Portsmouth and her position here was taken partly as I might keep an eye on her. I am fond of both of them Mr Parry and am convinced of Henry's innocence. Could you possibly review the case? Perhaps you might see guilt where biased eyes such as ours cannot, or more hopefully, see a way to exonerate the boy? I have already spoken with Mr Vere the proprietor of the New Bank. He fully supports the idea of my request and insists that your fees and any expenses will be paid in full by the bank."

Nathaniel mentally shelved his plans for the day.

"Not my usual type of enquiry sir, but it will be a pleasure to offer whatever help I can. As you must know, my father held you and your officers in the highest regard. I know what he would have done in my place."

They shook hands and made some preliminary plans. Captain Peterson offered to escort Nathaniel to the Paragon to meet with the widow Wilson. They had some social acquaintance through the Captain's dealings with the New Bank, where he was poised to make considerable further investment in the near future. This might ease a difficult interview. Nathaniel opted to visit the unfortunate Henry Blake at Grove Street police station alone, catching him that afternoon before his inevitable removal to Shepton Mallet Gaol. Having been introduced to Mr Vere, he could deliver his card to the Vere residence in Lansdown Crescent later that day, and if possible meet with him, before the dinner engagement with Charles.

They made good progress down Walcot Street towards the centre of the city, Caradoc loping behind, and took a sharp right turn up a narrow run of stone steps connecting the street with the main road to London, along which the houses of the Paragon were ranged. The Wilson residence was part of that impeccable Palladian terrace and easily found.

"Caradoc, guard duty sir!" commanded Nathaniel as he pulled the doorbell.

A pallid maid answered the door and ushered the two men into a restrained and elegant drawing-room. Paintings of Indian landscapes dominated the walls, gold framed but not lavishly embellished, and the fire was well shielded by a screen discreetly decorated with dried flower arrangements beneath glass. The piano was closed and a clock ticked, loudly, on the mantelpiece. Mrs Janie Wilson had once had a fragile, desiccated attraction, which had withered under the duress of life with her husband. The face turned up to them in weary greeting was sallow with a peevish mouth. It was as if the life had been slowly dried out of her, like the captive flowers on the fire-screen. She sat ramrod straight in a black gown, wrapped in a once exotic but now faded fringed shawl with worn tassels, which she ceaselessly wound around her dry fingers. They were seated and partaking of morning coffee before the subject of the murder was broached.

"So, Mrs Wilson," the Captain began, "Mr Parry, who is well versed in matters of investigation and has worked for the government in London and abroad, has consented to investigate the untimely demise of your husband. Mr Vere has engaged him officially."

"Abroad you say? Have you been to India Mr Parry?" she said. "Happy days I spent there as a child, and as a young woman before my marriage."

"I have not had that pleasure as yet madam."

She pointed listlessly at a large painting of a grand mansion in the English style, surrounded by palms. "My home sir. And those portraits, my dear parents. I will be candid with you sir. My late husband Roderick Wilson squandered my dowry and was frequently away from home indulging his penchant for gaming. I was not wholly surprised to learn that he had met with a misfortune, in the lowest part of the town. No doubt you noticed the lack of a footman in this establishment?" her voice quavered and almost disappeared. "The shame of it."

"So Madam, you are able to bear up at this time of your loss with," Nathaniel paused, inspecting the tight little face, the hard stare, "with equanimity?"

Could she possibly have the contacts and determination to have had him murdered?

"Our family life has not been as happy as I would have wished Mr Parry," she said coldly. "My husband had a mistress, a French doxy. I do not wish to discuss that further. Forgive me."

"Do you suspect that your late husband was involved with dangerous characters madam? Or that those he mixed with might have involved him in criminal activity?" enquired Captain Peterson gently.

"He was an attractive man Captain, he made friends easily and enjoyed the pleasures of life. I really could not say where his conscience would have drawn a line. However, I have seen gaming slips and receipts from all the principal gaming establishments in the town scattered in his dressing room. Mr Bedford's Rooms in Milsom Street were a favorite haunt of Roderick's, but so also were Lock's and Hall's."

Nathaniel rose to leave: "Mrs Wilson I would appreciate the opportunity to see Mr Wilson's room if I may and to make some other enquiries here in your house, perhaps I may speak with your servants?"

"Not today Mr Parry. I am awaiting instructions from the magistrate concerning searches by the local police. You may do so later. Also, you are welcome to attend the funeral. It will be at the Abbey on the 11th of this month and afterwards, here."

Mrs Wilson drew the interview to a close and Nathaniel and Captain Peterson found themselves returned to the pavement.

"Austere woman Mr Parry," said the Captain ruefully, "evenings round the fire would have been long for Wilson. Dashed long. Not excusin' the blighter, but, well, dashed long."

Nathaniel smiled, despite his annoyance at losing the opportunity to search Wilson's house. "Damned bad luck I'm in Bristol for a couple of days. Trail will be cold here. However, I will bid you good day sir. This afternoon I will see young Blake and Mr Vere as we discussed and I'll see what I can suggest." He whistled up Caradoc, who had been inspecting the railed area leading to the Wilson's kitchen, and strode off towards Milsom Street.

By early afternoon Nathaniel was stationed at his usual seat in the Hart. The visit to Grove Street police station had proved to be precisely as Captain Peterson had predicted. A woebegone Henry Blake had been by turns despairing, indignant and desperate, pleading for any assistance possible if it were to save his neck. He appeared to be a callow youth, devoted to Anna Grant, a young woman who was also a featherhead of the first order to think she could entertain a young man in her employer's home and successfully evade detection. It appeared that there had been at least three other servants at home that evening who had spied on the governess's assignation and could vouch for the presence of her fiancé. Henry Blake was unable to explain the appearance of the incriminating bonds, cash and papers at his rooms and he claimed he was a model citizen with few outstanding debts, which, Nathaniel decided, he could verify at least to some extent. However, the depth and breadth of Blake's greed would also need to be known to ascertain whether he was capable of committing the desperate deeds. Nathaniel prodded his dish of West Country faggots with a moody fork. They were rapidly becoming as cold as Wilson's trail and he was pleased to be distracted by a familiar voice.

"Mr Parry, Oiy gat somethin' to tell you!"

The accents of Tobias Caudle were instantly recognisable, and as Nathaniel turned to greet him he was pleasantly surprised to see that the ten shillings had been wisely invested. Polished boots, gaiters and brown trousers were topped off by a clean white shirt, neckcloth and striped waistcoat. There were also signs of him having had his head under the pump to complete the transformation.

"My word young man!" exclaimed Nathaniel whistling appreciatively. "Smart as paint!"

Tobias glowed with pride. "Oiy got two shirts now sir. Mary said she'll wash 'em for me if Oiy'll keep mi face clean."

"Well, what news you young popinjay!"

"Well," said Tobias sidling closer, "Oiy did speak to the boys in Little 'Ell like you asked. Two of 'em 'eard a racket on the night that gentleman went in the river. Lot of runnin' an' roarin' an' that. They was up in a loft lookin' down on the Quay and saw two hefty lookin' men handlin' a body down to the river. One did 'ave a bleedin' face. They passed under a lamp sir and could be seen clear. And that's not half of it," he added clandestinely, "mi friend Tom was in the Duke of York an' 'eard talk of a break-in at the leather-dressers in Hucklebridge Court that same night. The workbench was all over blood sir!

Leatherman wouldn't tell no police or watch though, a-course."

"Well done Tobias," said Nathaniel, reflecting that Henry Blake could in no way be described as "hefty".

"Tobias!" bawled the barman. "Plates a-waiting, front parlour. Double-up, double-up!" Nathaniel slipped a sixpence into Tobias's hand as the boy took off and was about to whistle up Caradoc when he was hailed by the barman Tooson.

"Mr Parry! Are you still after some fencing practice sir?"

"I most certainly am!" said Nathaniel.

"If you'll step along to the coffee room you'll find Captain Wilkins himself. He's meeting with some of his officers but I asked him if he would break off to talk with you and he said he would."

Frederick Tooson's expectant gaze was unmistakable. Nathaniel pressed a shilling into his hand and made his way to the coffee room, ducking the beams as he went.

In the comfortable saloon, Captain Wilkins was sitting at a private table tucked into the corner, talking earnestly with two men. All three had the familiar military bearing, were sharply dressed and purposeful, the coffee remained untouched.

"Captain Wilkins? Sir, may I introduce myself. I am Nathaniel Parry, a visitor staying locally for a few weeks. The barman suggested you had been kind enough to offer a few moments of your time to discuss fencing training. Though I suspect it is not entirely convenient now?"

Captain Wilkins looked up, though clearly privileged and blessed with a massive frame, he was lean and had an exhausted air about him. Nathaniel remembered he was a substantial mill-owner, reputedly employing over a thousand operatives, men, women and children, and treating them all with unusual patronage. Such philanthropy would have been dispensed at substantial personal cost, creating a bed of nails for his profits in the trade depression.

"Do sit down and join us Mr Parry, Bath is not such a large city that I had not heard of you. Dr Charles Parry is an acquaintance of mine and I know he was looking forward to your arrival. I am afraid my fellow officers and I have urgent business but can certainly spare a few moments. May I introduce Mr Cruttwell and Mr Fairfield. We use this hotel as our headquarters for the Bath Troop of the North Somerset Yeomanry and have some tactics to discuss." Nathaniel warmed to this brusque man, his searching eyes, his controlled, elegant bearing.

"Apart from occasional training with the men, a few of us have taken to fencing once a month privately at the tennis court in Morford Street. The 10th falls next Monday and it's our next meeting. If you come there at five o'clock in the afternoon we will be delighted to see you. You will bring your own weapon I take it?"

"I will be delighted to do so," said Nathaniel enthusiastically. "If you don't mind I'll bring this." Lifting his stick, he drew the concealed blade a hand's breadth from the hilt and the quillons sprang out to form a slender guard. The metal blade gleamed wickedly even in the dark corner, the burnished cutting edge curiously patterned and with a cold blue sheen.

"Be it on your own head to fence with such a flimsy weapon," said Fairfield dourly.

"But that's a rare edge you have there," said Mr Cruttwell, leaning over to catch another glance as Nathaniel slid the blade away. "I haven't seen such strange markings before."

"It isn't English," said Nathaniel tersely, cutting the enquiry short. "I'm sorry to have interrupted your planning gentlemen."

Captain Wilkins smiled wearily. "Contingencies sir, contingencies. The Lords' response to the Bill is imminent and they have a Tory majority. We need to be ready."

"Do you expect trouble here?"

The Captain looked grimly at Nathaniel, "We have no idea what to expect sir. But the blades are sharpened."

Nathaniel rose. "I bid you good-day gentlemen. Until next Monday then." After brief bows were exchanged Nathaniel made his way out.

Caradoc spotted him, pausing only long enough to dispatch the abandoned faggots, and padded out at his heels. They made their way to Mrs Spence's *via* the livery in Pulteney Mews where Nathaniel hired a post-chaise for the trip to Bristol, haggled over the pair of greys and then detoured round Sydney Gardens to take the air before making their way home to Walcot Street. Charles had invited him to dine at an unfashionably early hour, so a late afternoon visit to the Vere residence *en route* to Sion Hill would fit nicely. Nathaniel took care over his appearance, remembering the lingering touch of the beautiful Mrs Vere's fingers on his hand at the Guildhall that first night. She was a susceptible and pretty woman, and it never did any harm to make an ally. He laughed to himself as he ran a brush through his unruly hair, dodging his head left and right, trying to find a part of the mirror free from the leprous spotting of age. No doubt continual provision of the good life would keep the pretty filly trotting by the side of Raphael Vere. Sixtyish and running very slightly to fat, Vere was comfortable, indulged and self-satisfied, no doubt all of a dither at the scandal rocking his bank and willing to shower money on anyone likely to make it go away. He tied his turquoise neckcloth in his favoured Byronic draped knot, chose the turquoise, green and white silk waistcoat, keeping the trousers and coat to black. Cloak, top-hat and for the upper town, the swordstick: he was ready.

The walk to the top of Walcot followed by the climb up Guinea Lane was a sharp pull, with even Caradoc slowing to a walk. They issued forth onto Lansdown and soon turned to take a breather. The view had grown to a grand vista. As always, far away above the Abbey Tower and lining the horizon, were the green woods. Below that forest rim, the Bath stone of the sinuous parades and terraces now glowed honey-warm in the late sun. His eyes, scanning the distant trees, stopped to admire the Prior Park mansion which stood out amongst the green of Widcombe, pedimented and columned, its landscaped gardens rolling down the slopes. He turned abruptly on his heel and continued the climb, soon rounding the bend to Lansdown Crescent and following its curve to the Vere residence. He jangled the bell-pull and turned to view Palmer's perfect pastoral vision. There in the midst of the urban crescent was nature. Sheep grazed by the railings and down the steep drop of rough grass to the descending curtains of terraces. At once more domestic and graceful than the Royal Crescent, Nathaniel reflected firstly that Vere had done extremely well for himself, and secondly that he could live there himself with very great pleasure indeed.

"Good afternoon sir." A powdered footman opened the door and unbent himself just sufficiently to usher Nathaniel into a spacious hall with a black and white chequered marble floor and white classical statues standing sentinel along the walls. The curving stairway wound its way up and ahead stretched a long, echoing corridor.

"Mr Parry! Upon my word I am delighted to see you!" Raphael Vere appeared at the first landing and accosted Nathaniel from there. "Bring him up, Tanner. Drawing room."

"Could my dog go to the garden Mr Vere?"

"Oh bring him up! Do!" Tilly Vere had joined her husband, her eyes shining in delighted welcome. "He can join us can't he, Raph? Tanner bring tea."

They settled in a bright pink and green room on the front of the house, with a sumptuous view, batteries of beeswax candles already lit and a fire in the hearth. A harp, pianoforte and violin were in evidence, but no sheet music could be seen. Tilly busied herself initially with dispensing the tea and feeding the rapacious and shameless Caradoc with pastries. He lounged, most lordly, by her feet and occupied her whilst Vere unburdened himself, at great length, of his miseries.

"So you see Mr Parry, it is imperative that justice is served. I am saddened by the implication that two of my employees might have been involved in some desperate scheme to rob the bank but I will not shrink from the publicity. Blake must pay the ultimate penalty." In the over-heated room he was sweating and wiped his brow. "Such a blow to think that Wilson would deceive me. I had tried to help him as you know Mr Parry but he was sinking ever deeper into the mire of debt. His addiction to gaming had run out of control. I hope Captain Peterson has informed you that your expenses will be met if you could spare the time to look over this matter. It would be a comfort to know that an experienced investigator was involved." Raphael Vere smiled encouragingly.

"Oh yes Mr Parry," said Tilly Vere. "Such a comfort to know you are helping us. But first, do tell us of the work you have done in London. We hear that you have travelled for the government all over Britain and abroad. It sounds so exciting doesn't it Raphie?" She gazed enraptured, turning her shining blue eyes on him and beaming. The low autumn sun lit her cascade of blonde curls and glittered on the pink diamonds of her jewellery. Chosen to match the upholstery, thought Nathaniel idly but appreciatively. She did not seem to require an immediate answer to her question, but continued to enlarge on the excitements of travel. She moved closer, a rustle of silk as she leaned towards him, enabling Nathaniel to be fully aware of her: her skin, creamy and flawless, the rise and fall of her breasts, her scent, intoxicating and honey-sweet. She was a rare beauty, lusciously vibrant: expensively and fashionably dressed as she had been when he first saw her at the Guildhall. For the afternoon she played the Van Dyke courtesan: vast slashed sleeves, a neckline plunging precipitously, edged in foaming lace.

He suddenly became aware that she had stopped talking and expected an answer. He struggled to haul his thoughts back on track.

"Yes Mrs Vere, travel is a great adventure. It has been a privilege to work in Paris and elsewhere in Europe. Though the travel was not for pleasure alone, wars and revolution do bring their discomforts. I have also been to America, where I have some interests."

A distant peal on the doorbell intervened and presently Nathaniel was surprised to find Mrs Janie Wilson ushered in to join them. The widow was duly greeted, seated and furnished with tea and pastries.

"Mrs Wilson has kindly consented to dine with us this evening and we hope she will stay until tomorrow," said Tilly, stroking Mrs Wilson's arm sympathetically. "So important to be looked after at this terrible time."

Janie Wilson smiled tartly, delighted that the invitation could be accepted on the basis that she was alone and required "looking after", though the idea of the vacuous Tilly caring for her was ludicrous. She wrapped herself more tightly in her shawl, despite the heat of the room and edged away from the attentions of Tilly.

"Madam," said Nathaniel. "I was disappointed not to be able to investigate at your home this morning. A sight of Mr Wilson's room and belongings will materially assist my enquiries," he paused as her frown deepened.

"Oh I'm sure there is plenty time for that Mr Parry," said Vere quickly. "You were to allow the police in weren't you Mrs Wilson, then Mr Parry could perhaps visit?"

"Yes, we had already agreed that," she said pettishly.

"But if Mr Parry knows all about investigating couldn't he go now whilst Mrs Wilson is resting here? The police will not be searching now will they?" said Tilly.

"Mathilda," said Vere warningly, "I suggest that you do not attempt to direct operations. Mrs Wilson and Mr Parry have come to an agreement." Nathaniel was interested to see how swiftly the pose of doting husband dissolved. Vere switched in an instant from swain to elderly father, or even, an unpleasant speculation, grandfather. How old had Tilly been when they married?

"Yes indeed," said Nathaniel, glancing at the clock on the mantelpiece. "And if you will excuse me I have an engagement and should take my leave. Thank you for seeing me. I will be in Bristol for two days but will resume my enquiries when I return."

Nathaniel left the trio to their early dinner and struck off up the hill at a lively pace, looking forward to his rendezvous with Charles.

"What do you make of that then Caradoc?" he said as they rustled through the leaves. Caradoc, unconcerned, barely glanced behind him, over-full with pastries and over-heated, he had enjoyed the attention, felt he had played his part, but was pleased to be out. Nathaniel strode on in silence, not entirely sure what he made of it either, and willingly shelved the matter for what should turn out to be a rather pleasant evening of family gossip and a little business in the form of taking the political pulse of a select group of Bath society.

The Shadwell's Residence, Green Park Buildings West, Bath.

Whilst Nathaniel and the gentlemen round Charles's table at Summerhill House settled into their third bottle of claret and the moon rose white over a low bruise of purple clouds, Rosie Shadwell closed and locked the door of her front parlour in Green Park West and took a strongbox from a cupboard by the chimney breast. With a lithe, cat-like grace she swung the heavy box onto the table and sat down to work. Deftly she unlocked it and began to count the wads of notes and slithering mounds of sovereigns, dividing them into a dozen small piles, four larger ones, and two others of far greater size. Her coppery hair caught the light from the candles and the bright fire, her green ear-rings rattled as she worked and her eyes shone as they always did when she was counting the week's takings.

The room was well appointed, the paintings, sensual and erotic, were in ornate gold frames, the furnishings were opulent, decadent. Madam Shadwell, tightly corseted and casually robed in emerald silk took out a tiny pair of gold spectacles and a notebook. She began to enter the sums in her neat, practised hand, and from the upper rooms, a faint chorus of sounds could just be heard. From the drawing room above her came a lazy buzz of chatter, three female voices, the clink of tea cups and snatches of a tune played idly on the pianoforte. Higher, from one front bedroom came the crack of Mitzi's whip, applied to good effect judging by the groans of pleasure extracted from a plump, white customer trussed naked at her feet. Next door the sounds were fainter still, restricted by the silken gag over the mouth of a hirsute customer shackled to the bed, the rhythmic creak dictated by the spirited attentions of Letty. Volcanic wrestling instigated more conventionally by Clari brought a more erratic cacophony of crashes and bangs from her apartment. The final and higher pitched thread of sound came from the attics. One room was decorated as it always had been, as a nursery. There a customer dangled a girl of thirteen on his knee whilst he sang nursery rhymes in a warbling falsetto. He pawed her restlessly whilst she gazed mutely forward, counting the stripes on the wallpaper.

A soft knock on the front door. Rosie carefully placed her spectacles and pen on the table, moved swiftly to the door, unlocked, then locked it behind her and slipped the key on its long chain into her pocket. Her face assumed a fixed smile, she smoothed her robe over her hips, pulled the neckline lower and opened the door. A sedan chair was quietly spirited into the hall for the customer to emerge, entirely discreetly, in the very confines of this most orderly of disorderly houses.

"Good evening sir. What a pleasure it is to see you again, Josephine has been asking after you and is so excited you have made time to visit us this evening."

If the customer had not been cosseted by Rosie, relieved of his coat, ushered upstairs to meet the girls and plied with drink, he might have wandered down the corridor, out to the back door and down the steps into the cold garden. Down the shadowed path, by the rose bushes and arbours, past benches and dark trees he would at length have reached a two storey building at the rear of the property. This was a coach house which still housed a coach, horses, stable boys and Shadwell's two guards, who could be found standing at the foot of the steps holding bludgeons. On the upper floor was Joshua Shadwell's office, and in that apartment the owner was engaged in conversation with two men. They had upon them the smell of the streets, though their garments were not poor. They sat facing Joshua across his desk, both wary, but one more truculent than the other and sporting a deep, partially healed cut down one side of his face. Joshua himself, as was his wont, had his top drawer open as he spoke, displaying his pair of pistols, ready primed. He was dressed, as usual for business, in sober grey, with immaculate white linen and neckcloth and midnight blue satin waistcoat.

"You have partly redeemed yourselves after the unfortunate skewering of the suicide," he said darkly, his brown eyes glinting dangerously under his heavy brows. "As you know your original fee was reduced to three-quarters of that agreed because of the unfortunate consequences. The placing of the goods in the Kingsmead rooms was done well, most fitting. But placing tackle in rooms when you already have the key provided by me, the obliging landlord, does not exactly make you bloody master criminals. Now does it?"

Joshua was always at his most dangerous when he appeared reasonable. Mordecai and Declan took care not to meet his eye.

"To earn the missing one quarter you had hoped for, my client needs you to be busy tonight. You will go to the Paragon and enter on the quiet," he passed a small piece of paper with a number written on it. "This house. No bloody other. Do a thorough search for papers referring to any business affairs in Bristol or anything looking business-like that you don't understand. Take whatever else you want in the way of general burglary which is what this is meant to be. Come back here to exchange said goods for payment. Let the dust settle. Make it mid-week."

"Will it be an empty house you're a-sending us to then Joshua?" said Declan, anxious, his beady eyes narrowed.

"It is empty tonight, guaranteed." Joshua smiled unpleasantly. "Now about our other business, where the real money lies."

Mordecai sat up straighter, licking his lips. "What've we got on the next sailing?" his voice was harsh, his teeth exposed, yellowed and sharp.

"We have a small but important cargo for a special customer in the Far East. There will be two kids under three years and two of about ten years old to go in your barge as usual to Parker's Wharf on Redcliffe Back. Your contact is Eli Trevellis who is the captain of the *Blue Dragon*. You will pass on the goods tomorrow."

"Where exactly are they now?" asked Declan.

"The two older ones are in the Avon Street stew, drugged and quiet. The others will be purchased tomorrow and moved directly. The deal's going through with their mother, there's no father. Mother's got nine other brats and can't make enough on any game to keep 'em without charity, and anyway, she has no likin' to being known by the authorities. She needs more money for herself and her habits."

"We want no trouble with 'em on the barge," said Mordecai glowering. "Last lot needed more dosing before we made Bristol and we had to knock 'em out."

"Don't you ever mark 'em Mordecai," threatened Joshua, pointing a finger accusingly, "or it will be the last mark you make so help me God."

Mordecai shifted restlessly in his seat, fingers itching to seize Shadwell by the throat and squeeze the life out of him.

"Right-o Mr Shadwell," said Declan. "We will go directly. Come on Mordecai now." He pulled at Mordecai's arm urgently. "We'll be off sure we will."

Mordecai slammed his chair against the table swearing under his breath and made his way out behind Declan. Joshua glared after them and rose to watch his men escort them out of the coach house, through the back gate and onto the path leading to the river.

"Bloody amateurs."

The fact that they ran a regular and entirely legal barge service between Bath and Bristol had initially recommended them to him. His most recent commissions had stretched them to their limits, and if he had not been pressurised himself he would never have risked asking them. He cursed fluently: cursed himself for being beholden to anybody and for trusting anybody, and he cursed his block-headed, cack-handed bargees who had claimed so bravely they were expert murderers. "I should have them do what they do best," he muttered to himself.

Over the last five years they had managed to convey unwanted girls from his brothels in Bath to Bristol for shipment to the lucrative overseas market. The game had become increasingly dangerous over the last two years as ever younger girls had been demanded, girls from the gentry too. Kidnapped girls, and infants, had been shipped with increased regularity. He had a bad feeling about it. Regular tastes he understood, but not this. Rosie never took under twelve's to keep in their houses. No point breaking more laws than necessary. He took one pistol from the drawer and closed it before locking up and heading for the house.

"Goodnight boys," he said to the men as he passed by them and emerged from the dark into the pool of light by the door.

"Goodnight sir."

He walked back to the house slowly, pausing only to check the upper windows. All seemed in order, as usual the lights in Clari's room were on and would continue to be so until dawn. As he reflected that there were worse places to live than a high class knocking shop, a cold wind rose spitting dead leaves into the air and rattling the creeper on the walls. He shivered and hurried on down the path, taking the steps two at a time to make the door and pass into the warmth of the house.

8th October, 1831, Walcot Street.

Nathaniel had a late start the next day. The evening had extended into the night and it had been almost dawn when he returned down Lansdown Hill to Walcot. Talk had ranged comfortably over Bath doings including Charles's new society for creating work for the poor, family news and other trifles until the ladies left the table. It had then quickly descended into national politics, law and order and the inexorable onward march of the cholera. Charles expected it any day now. They had talked up medieval spectres of the Black Death and then banished them with a good dose of inconsequential ribaldry and yet more claret. He reluctantly heaved himself out of bed to prepare for the trip to Bristol to visit Drake. He pulled on his robe and brought in the water and breakfast left some hours earlier by Mary, plodded to the washstand and table, then opened the window to clear his head. A peal of bells rolled over the town from near Southgate: mournful, funereal. He called down to a passing gentleman.

"Sir, why the muffled peal? Who's died?"

The man looked up sadly. "The hopes of the people sir. They are dead. The papers are out with black mourning edges, most shops are shut and St James's is sounding the peal. The Lords rejected the Bill yesterday and London is in a roar. Yesterday's editions have just arrived and the news is all over the city. It's a black day sir, but they'll not get away with it. The people will not stand it. There will be retribution!" His anger animating him, he flushed in confusion, raised his hat and moved off.

In a low mood, Nathaniel left peremptorily with a small bag and Caradoc, to collect the hired post-chaise in Pulteney Mews. He mounted the nearside horse of the pair, bundled Caradoc into the coach and rode postillion for the twelve mile drive to Bristol.

The Drake family's rooms, Cornwallis Crescent, Clifton, Bristol.

By the time he arrived in Clifton and found Cornwallis Crescent he was in better spirits. Footmen sprang out to deal with the post-chaise, the horses and Caradoc, whilst Nathaniel was shown to a grand drawing room to meet John Drake.

"You have found some magnificent rooms here Mr Drake," he said, smiling and eyeing Drake closely, trying to decide why he had taken such an instant dislike to the man.

"Yes," said Drake cautiously. "Need to maintain the image of the service Parry. Also my family are here, so bachelor accommodation is out of the question."

"Are they enjoying their stay?"

Drake reflected for a few moments. Lottie was now enjoying herself immensely, fraternising and competing with Mrs Ravenswood. Drake had encouraged this to further his relationship with Mr Edwin Ravenswood who was proving to be an even better contact than hoped, and definitely one he wanted to keep away from the dashing Mr Parry.

"Who would not be enjoying a few weeks at Clifton Spa? The village has plenty of diversions for the ladies. The waters can be taken and there are ample assemblies and private soirees," he said, airily waving them away with a languid hand. "It's not London, but it serves for a season."

They spent a few dutiful hours discussing Nathaniel's report on Bath and his contacts, omitting the full details of the murder enquiry but including his intention to pursue leads in Bristol. This was followed by Drake presenting his views on Bristol, omitting his burgeoning friendship with the suave and monied Ravenswood. Drake mentioned obliquely that Lord Palmerston's hopes for developing contacts with local ship-owners on the Far East run would be fulfilled, and pontificated on the value of the same for some time, until Nathaniel became restless and encouraged Drake to agree to a walk. Once out of the house, they strode purposefully and in silence up the steep streets to the

Downs. A few groups of gentry were taking the air and animals grazed peacefully. Rabbits hopped and the Downs rolled away to the distant line of trees. They passed a ruined mill and Drake exchanged a few words with its owner, an engaging man, bespattered in paint and plaster.

"He's leased it from the Merchant Venturers," said Drake, more relaxed and less annoying. "He's making a studio and a camera obscura. I come up here each day to see how he is doing. It was an old snuff mill, burned down years ago. Great project."

They continued along the crest of the Downs and then made a small descent to where the grass was interrupted by a stretch of broken ground and piles of stones.

"This," said Drake excitedly, "is the start of a suspension bridge which will link the two sides of the Gorge. A young engineer has faced down Thomas Telford himself and carried the laurels in the competition just this year. He's called Brunel. He'll be about your age."

"French is he?" asked Nathaniel, interested.

"Father is. You must know of him. He's the Thames Tunnel engineer."

The tide was out and far below broad mud banks shelved steeply to the brown flow of the Avon. They looked circumspectly, cautiously craning their necks over the sides of the gorge which was cruelly rocky with stunted trees clinging to toe-holds on the sheer sides.

"St Vincent's Rocks," said Drake, keen to share his newly learned knowledge. "There's still a hermit's cave in the cliff side."

Away from work and the jockeying for position, the ceaseless self-seeking and greed, Drake seemed a more interesting man, a better man. Two sides to everyone Nathaniel reflected: both part of the whole.

In a rush of good nature, Drake decided to extend the walk to take advantage of the day. They descended the steep incline from Clifton and pushed on to the centre of town. They made their way to the wharves at the foot of the red cliffs for a session in the Ostrich where they consumed a large quantity of local cider before making their way round the pub to a back yard to treat themselves to the spectacle of bare-knuckle boxing.

“Lord Palmerston would appreciate this,” shouted Drake animatedly. “Great sporting man is Lord Cupid you know!”

“So I hear,” said Nathaniel.

“Do you box, Mr Drake?”

“Not personally,” said Drake.

“Sword-play?”

“Not now.”

Drake’s hand strayed to his collar and his finger instinctively ran along the side of the ragged scar. His head swimming from the flagon of cider, his mind raced back unbidden to Paris in ’25. The yells of the crowd receded. He could hear again the terrifying whistle of his opponent’s blade as it sliced the air to land with bone-jarring force on his feeble guard. He re-lived the desperation of being driven back, his spine crashing on the stone wall. He felt the hot breath on his face as their blades locked and the screeching ringing by his ear as his opponent pulled his sword free for the final flurry. He had sagged to the ground, spent and craven beneath the renewed fury of strokes when the shots rang out. He had survived: his second, as treacherous as himself, had brought two primed pistols. Not the most gentlemanly end to a duel of honour. His challenger and his second lay in seeping pools of blood whilst his own man had spirited him away.

When they returned to Cornwallis Crescent, Nathaniel had a pang of remorse to see the indignities to which Caradoc had been subjected in his absence. The child Lizzie, a small and imperious termagant, had attached ribbons to him and a doll’s coat. The sturdy beast was tolerating it in view of her years, though an older torturer would have been fought off long before. The evening passed slowly. The abrasive Lottie had returned from town and encouraged Lizzie to recite poetry before dinner. She herself provided a musical interlude on the pianoforte after the lengthy meal and Nathaniel had retired early. He was mildly surprised the next day to find that Drake was occupied with an afternoon and dinner engagement with Mr Ravenswood, which would limit their final meeting to the morning. He was clearly not to be invited to the session with the ship owner, as Drake was of the opinion that Palmerston's business could be discharged very well without him.

"I will take myself off to the docks this afternoon," said Nathaniel over breakfast. "I'll dress for the occasion and have a look at the vessels, just to familiarise myself with the traders. Where does Mr Ravenswood keep his ships?"

"King's Wharf, down the Floating Harbour at Redcliffe," said Drake, pausing in his assault on the toast and raspberry preserve. He smothered his reluctance and added: "His next ship for the east is the *Blue Dragon*. You can't miss it. It's a clipper. Raked masts and ends sharp as a rapier, built for speed. It's got a carved dragon as a figurehead with Bristol blue glass eyes. But I wouldn't poke around too much Parry," he said patronisingly. "He's got some Chinese crew this year. They don't take kindly to strangers and you'd better look out for yourself pretty generally around the docks."

"Thanks for the advice," said Nathaniel.

That evening, in the darkening twilight, a dishevelled man and his dog made their way along Marsh Street, side-stepping the refuse and beggars, eyeing the inns and beer-shops. Gales of laughter and singing blew out of the bars, Irish fiddles scraped tunes and the stamp of dancers' feet beat time. It was a rackety quarter of the docks, brimming with sailors, immigrants, itinerants, swindlers, murderers and thieves. Nathaniel wound his scarf higher and pulled his hat lower. The latest additions to his wardrobe, acquired from a local pawn shop, stank of the previous owner. Caradoc had growled a protest, but the rank odours of Marsh Street soon eclipsed both the smell and his early objections. In truth, anything was preferable to being sought out for entertainment by Miss Lizzie in Cornwallis Crescent. They sidled into a rowdy tavern called the Three Sugar Loaves. The swinging sign sporting a painting of three white conical loaves was a common sight in the city where sugar refining still boomed on the back of the West Indian molasses trade. He had seen other taverns with the same name, but none was so brutishly unappealing.

The air was stifling, a miasma of beer and spirits overlaid with the smoke of a hundred tobacco pipes and the rancid puffs from the fire sulking under a pile of vegetable peelings. Nathaniel bought brandy and water and edged his way past the crowd at the bar, past the fiddlers and a pair of raucous quarrelling whores, being egged-on to settle their differences with a fight by the growing crowd that seethed around them. Through a low doorway he saw a quieter room and made for it. Men were hunched over shove ha'penny boards, some played cards, some chess. Backgammon held a bunch of punters by the fire but away in a corner alcove he spotted a small, intense group of Chinese sailors making preparations to play a different game. He stood by the fire, warming his hands, listening and watching. He recognised Mandarin, but the accents were strong and the men made few comments as they settled.

Their approach to the game was reverent and controlled. The two players bowed gravely, this was a game the like of which he had never seen played before, and would not again until the century was old. But he knew of it. He recalled his father's gentle voice spinning a web of mysterious tales from his travels: battles, swordplay, dragons, emperors and the subtle game of stones. As he rubbed his hands before the flames, he watched covertly from the corner of his eye. A cloth had been laid on the table, marked out with nineteen lines in both the horizontal and the vertical. Two piles of counters were emptied from leather pouches: white stones of clam shell and the others small rounds of black slate. The older player took a place with his back to the wall and the white shells were pushed towards him. The younger took the slate pieces, held the first one between his index and middle fingers, and placed it, carefully, on an intersection of the lines in the upper right hand corner. The atmosphere was calm, yet with underlying tension, the rowdy guffaws and shrieks of the bar faded into insignificance with the muted slides of the ha'pennies, the shuffle of cards and jests of the other players around them.

Nathaniel felt impelled to draw nearer. As the players silently took turns to place their stones, they contested the territory provided by the squares. Pieces were sacrificed, taken prisoner, territories ebbed and flowed but inexorably the older man playing white gained the advantage. Nathaniel watched as the game unfolded, leaning on the chimneypiece, entranced. Quarter hours had grown to an hour when he became aware that he was being watched. There was a still figure at the far end of the bench whose eyes were upon him and he sensed that they had been so for some time. He turned to look directly into the eyes of a man of about his own age, powerfully built. He was the man he had seen at the Guildhall on his first night in Bath. Again, dressed entirely in black, even his shirt now covered by a dark scarf, he bowed slightly, acknowledging Nathaniel. He was recognised, despite the stinking rags from the pawnbroker, despite the passage of days. Another memory flashed unbidden, the stories of black-clad mercenary soldiers in feudal Japan: the ninja, murderous, secret, invincible. Nathaniel made a bold move and took a seat by the spectators. Within another quarter of an hour the game ended with the victory of the older man. Surprisingly, no money changed hands, but the players bowed to each other, aware of the other's skills, the younger man bending significantly lower than the elder.

"You know the game?" inquired the man in black, moving closer to sit by Nathaniel and speaking with only the slightest trace of a foreign accent.

Nathaniel hesitated momentarily, then decided on a degree of honesty, as he still felt the same latent energy and danger in this man he had sensed on first sighting him. "My father travelled in the East before his death a few years ago. He explained this game to me, but I had never seen it played. I take it this is by way of a travelling set. Is it not conventionally played on a wooden board? And am I correct in suggesting that it is strategic rather than tactical in the sense that chess is a tactical contest?"

"Yes. The game is called Wei Ch'i, and was invented in China thousands of years ago. It is an art of encirclement in which strength and final victory depend on the highest levels of strategic competence. The man who played white is a master. His tenacity allowed him to achieve ultimate hegemony in the field. You noticed, I know, as I was watching you. You admire such tenacity?" He smiled. "Perhaps we should be introduced? I am Cornelius Fu Lee. I am here on a business trip and I'm sailing for the east shortly. These men are from the ship's crew. We're probably the only Chinese in Bristol. I have not seen one other despite the so-called Cathay Wharf I found by Redcliffe church."

"I do admire tenacity sir, and here I saw strategic calculation of the highest order. I am Nathaniel Parry. Like you I am on business here, visiting a colleague, but intend to return to Bath shortly and stay for a few weeks. I am visiting my family and I have rooms there. I recognise you Mr Lee, and I know you recognised me. We attended the same political meeting at the Bath Guildhall."

Cornelius Lee smiled: "*Touché*."

Nathaniel decided to ignore Drake's advice. "The main shipper to the east from here is Mr Edwin Ravenswood. I believe his *Blue Dragon* is preparing to sail. So I suspect he is your employer. He seems to be making an excellent trade in opium whilst others are falling foul of the Emperor's searches."

Cornelius Lee stared impassively at Nathaniel. "You are well informed Mr Parry. What might your business be?"

"I am an associate of Mr John Drake."

Cornelius nodded. "As I expected. And tonight he dines with Mr Ravenswood. We both have the evening off my friend."

Nathaniel glanced over the now completed game. The two players were discussing the match, re-setting the early positions, the master explaining some weaknesses in black's opening play. Cornelius followed his gaze, "You see how the master teaches his opponent? Next time, perhaps, his game will improve and white will have a bigger challenge. Both will improve as a result. Even though they are opponents, by cooperating they each achieve a higher objective."

Nathaniel eyed Cornelius speculatively for a moment. "May I buy you some refreshment Mr Lee?" They made their way to the bar.

"Brandy?"

They sat facing each other over the steaming pewter mugs of brandy and hot water.

"To successful trade," said Nathaniel, raising his mug.

"To success, Mr Parry." Cornelius continued, "The opium trade to China is of great importance to England is it not?"

"Of the greatest importance," answered Nathaniel. "It is essential if we are to balance our trade there."

Cornelius reflected without speaking, then looked directly at Nathaniel, holding his gaze and seeming to look into his very soul. "You seem to appreciate the subtleties of Wei Ch'i Mr Parry. We consider that it is a reflection of life, and is a game of harmony and balance. In your opium trade, do you operate a moral balance or just an economic one?"

"In what sense?"

"A balance of the greater evils: the relative threat to Chinese lives and the danger of degeneracy through opium addiction versus your reluctance to spend your silver?

"Men have free will Mr Lee. Opium is not seen as an illegal substance in England, in fact it is a principal medicament. Taken as laudanum here, the poor call it their "penn'orth of elevation". And why not? It kills pain, improves health and raises their spirits. God knows that many of them need that. There's little joy for the poor in any land. "

Cornelius continued, unmoved. "Foreign sales to opium dens are illegal in China. Did you know that nine in every ten young men in coastal areas are now addicted to opium? There is no harmony in such a condition."

A silence grew between them. Cornelius Lee might well be a danger to the trade that the British government was at such pains to promote. Nathaniel looked at the face opposite him, which was closed, unreadable.

"Are you playing devil's advocate Mr Lee?"

"All games are potentially deadly Mr Parry. I like to be on the side of the light rather than the dark."

Nathaniel, perplexed and making a move to leave, suddenly noticed that Caradoc had stretched himself out on the floor by Cornelius Lee and, most uncharacteristically, slept with his head on Lee's feet.

"My dog likes you Mr Lee. It is rare for him to lower his guard and trust a stranger."

"We are no longer strangers."

He held out his hand to Nathaniel, who grasped it and was surprised to find the hand he shook to be extremely hard, yet heavily calloused only on the knuckles, not the palms. The hands of a fighter he thought: no businessman and certainly from his demeanour, no sailor.

"Goodbye Mr Lee."

"Mr Parry. Until we meet again."

Chapter 4

Mid-morning: 10th October, 1831.
Cornwallis Crescent, Clifton, Bristol.

Nathaniel's leave-taking of the Drakes was pleasant enough. He had breakfasted leisurely, and was pleased that Caradoc had been spared a return bout of annoyance from the infant Lizzie, who was tormenting her governess by the time they started work on the ham and kidneys. Lottie had also finished at the table and swept off to a morning assembly where she would meet Amanda Ravenswood. His hired post-chaise and pair had been well groomed in the stables to the rear of Cornwallis Crescent and the horses were stamping to be off by the time he made his way to them with Caradoc and Drake. Nathaniel threw in his bag and hoisted Caradoc onto the seat.

"Thank you for your hospitality Mr Drake. Shall we travel to London together on Friday?"

"I don't think so Parry," said Drake. "I don't want to be tied to a set time. I'll see you in Percy's office at Whitehall on Monday the 17th for the meeting, as planned."

Drake waved Nathaniel off courteously enough, well pleased to have that particular player off the field and safely returned to the pavilion, to be dealt with in due course. He turned on his heel and marched out of the stable yard, but instead of returning to the house made for the Downs. The evening with Ravenswood had raised possibilities, some of them alarming. He felt a cold sweat break out on his skin as the autumn wind raced up from the Severn and cut through the fine material of his coat. He needed thinking time.

Back to Bath

The road to Bath was well metalled: efficiently turn-piked along its entire length and thick with every category of traffic. Nathaniel set up a cracking pace, stretching the hired chaise to its limits. He entertained himself weaving round the wagons and the trails of pack horses, racing a mail-coach and a couple of young bloods in gigs. Caradoc bounced like a cork beside Nathaniel on the driver's seat and yapped relentlessly, pouring scorn on the lesser canines racing their wheels as they passed farms and villages and be-rating collectors at turnpike cottages. Even after they had returned the steaming horses and filthy chaise and walked back to the rooms in Walcot Street, dusty, spattered with mud and aching in every muscle, they were both in triumphant high spirits. Caradoc flung himself at Tom's feet by the fire whilst Nathaniel managed to persuade Martha to undertake the lengthy business of boiling up water for an unusual mid-day wash in his room. He climbed the stairs and settled to write a report for Lord Melbourne. He and Drake had planned to return to London for a meeting with Melbourne and Palmerston to acquaint the noble lords with the progress of events, but on the personal front he needed to return briefly to his rooms in Lambeth. He stripped off his stained travel clothes, donned the Damascus robe and assembled his writing equipment. He hauled his travelling desk out of the trunk and balanced it on the bed, arranging himself behind it on piled up pillows, cross-legged like a Caliph. His meeting with Cornelius Fu Lee had intrigued and concerned him. He took out his knife and sharpened his pen. Cornelius could usefully stay out of the report.

Nathaniel had felt disturbed since the previous night in the snug at the Three Sugar Loaves and was assailed by nagging doubts. He had never before questioned the ultimate morality of the opium trade. Why should he? It was a normal assumption that all men's choices could lead to good or evil. That was the nature of free will. Damn it, milk could kill a man and often did, most town water could be lethal, especially for strangers. Opium was a precious commodity, and it could drive the most brilliant to craven beggary and madness. He dipped his pen in the ink-pot and began to write his report, carefully, in his immaculate script. The sound of the soft repetitive scratching of the pen on the paper filled the silence of the room. He covered a side, sanded it, and blew away the excess. As he paused, a vision of Coleridge flickered before his inner eye. *Kubla Khan* would never have been written without opium. He recited aloud:

"In Xanadu did Kubla Khan
A stately pleasure-dome decree:
Where Alph, the sacred river, ran
Through caverns measureless to man
Down to a sunless sea."

He loved those lines: they were the zenith of Romanticism. He repeated them slowly, relishing them, and then, as it seemed for the first time, he was alive to their overwhelming threat, the sinister horror eclipsing the beauty.

"But oh! that deep romantic chasm which slanted
Down the green hill athwart a cedar cover!
A savage place! as holy and enchanted
As e'er beneath a waning moon was haunted
By woman wailing for her demon lover!"

Coleridge's brilliance and his physical miseries were part of his family's mythology. Charles Parry and his late brother Fred had been friends of the famous poet and his father had treated him in the grips of his addiction. On the way to speak in Bristol in 1813, Coleridge had rested in Bath, and got no further than the Greyhound in High Street, where Caleb Parry had attended him. Coleridge had been sunk in torment, his pains tearing him like a caged leopard devours its prey: his sanity, his precious "I-ship" slipping away. Slipping away, thought Nathaniel uncomfortably, on the "sunless sea", through the yawning abyss. He saw again the grave face of Cornelius, heard his voice, low and relentless, relating the sorry tale of destitution and misery. He conjured up to mind an image of desperate and degenerate youth in China, coastal towns laid waste by the relentless march of British trade: a trade he was employed to further by masters who required him to see Cornelius Lee as an enemy; a dangerous one. He grinned wryly as he finished his report. There was no doubt that Cornelius was dangerous, but he was finding it hard to see him as an enemy.

By half past four that afternoon, with swordstick jauntily employed and setting a brisk pace, he was striding up Walcot Street towards the London Road, Caradoc frisking at his heels. It had been too long since he exercised his sword and he looked forward keenly to the session at Captain Wilkins's fencing club. He had had a gloomy conversation with Mr Tasker and the grooms at the livery when he returned the post-chaise. It had reminded him of the frustrated rage of the people at the Lords' rejection of the Bill and Old Tom's mutterings about the "wild beasts loosed" had followed him out of the house. Perhaps it was more than exercise he would be needing. They climbed the steep hill of Guinea Lane and crossed Lansdown to make their way to Morford Street and the Tennis Court which accommodated the gentlemen and their fencing. Nathaniel settled Caradoc at the door and sought out Captain Wilkins to make himself known.

Wilkins was with his friends, the morose Fairfield and a corpulent, jovial man who looked familiar. All three were busy, clad in white shirts and breeches with stiffened padded waistcoats, limbering up as effectively as their respective constitutions allowed. It was a lofty room, well suited to purpose, with the nets stowed and half a dozen other teams of gentlemen in separate groups, un-sheathing weapons, fixing blunting tips to their points, laughing, excited.

"Welcome Mr Parry!" said Captain Wilkins, striding over and wringing Nathaniel by the hand. "Stand on no ceremony! We form up in fours and you will be occupied directly as Mr Cruttwell is delayed. May I present Mr Howard Dill, the fourth member of our usual quartet."

"Good day sirs," said Nathaniel. "Mr Dill, I recollect I have had the pleasure of meeting you last week, in the Pump Room. You were with my relative, Doctor Parry."

"Capital!" declared Dill, his circular glasses both flashing white as they caught the light. "What a memory Mr Parry! Indeed we did meet exactly as you say!"

"I see you have brought your weapon of choice," said Fairfield dismissively. "We fight with duelling swords first tonight sir. Whole-body target: tip to score. I see you are determined to fight with a thin cross-guard lacking even a knuckle-bow to protect your hand. We cannot be expected to make allowances."

"I can assure you sir that I do not seek allowances of any kind."

Nathaniel's mouth offered a friendly smile but his eyes did not. He threw his cloak to the wall, grasped the silver hilt of his stick and unsheathed the sword, a weapon previously admired by the absent Cruttwell and dismissed out of hand by Fairfield. The Japanese tempered blade flickered grey-blue in the light, along the rolling curves of the water-mark and on its shimmering edge. He fixed a false tip to the end of the sword, stepped back lightly, placed the hollow cane aside, and swung the weapon one-handed in a tight circle, flicking it over his wrist, catching it smoothly. "Shall we begin?"

"Very well," said Captain Wilkins with a sudden snort of

laughter, "Champing at the bit what! Fairfield, first bout with Parry here."

Mr Dill passed his wire-mesh mask to Nathaniel then moved aside, surprisingly briskly, to stand by the Captain who directed the combatants to starting positions.

Nathaniel raked his left hand through his hair, clearing his eyes, then slid the mask over his face.

"*En garde*."

Fairfield, also masked and ready, shifted on his feet, settling his weight on the back foot.

"*Prêt*."

Wilkins lowered his hand simultaneously with the verbal signal to start.

"*Allez*!"

The fencers dropped into strong stances and circled warily. They feinted again and again. Tap, tap, tap, sword met sword: weighing each other's potential, quartering the floor, feeling the responses. Padding, slow moves forward, then "*appel*" – stamp, stamp – startle, circle again: wary, waiting; biding their time.

Fairfield suddenly sensed an opening and made a mighty lunge followed up with a barrage of blistering attacks. Nathaniel, true to his name was swift with the parry, deflecting, weaving away. His economy of movement astonished the watching pair, Dill chuckled in appreciation.

"*In quartata* and *passata-sotto*! Princely Mr Parry. Princely!"

Fairfield breathed hard, sweat starting to run on his face. Nathaniel had turned and ducked and dodged away, he had been led a dance. A shameful one. He gathered his strength and attacked with renewed ferocity. The clash of blades rang and rang again. Clanging, faster, feet slithered and stamped. Back and forth: back and forth.

Nathaniel sensed his opponent was tiring and delayed, delayed, delayed. Then as Fairfield roared in like a bull with a hefty lunge, Nathaniel's characteristic mercurial parry was followed up instantaneously with a devastating riposte. He deftly switched sword hands as he turned and threw his opponent off balance. Fairfield staggered backwards in disarray: one, two, three, four, five blows, and on the last theatrically disarmed, his sword flew from his hand to skitter across the floor and crash to the wall.

"Bravo!" cheered Dill and Wilkins.

"Bad luck Fairfield."

Neville Fairfield held out his hand, blowing hard, trembling with the after-shock, but he was a soldier, able to swallow his pride.

"Pleasure to spar with you Mr Parry."

"And I with you sir."

Nathaniel's initiation over, the atmosphere lost its charge of aggression and the evening unwound happily enough. The rotund Dill survived, his dignity intact, and even acquitted himself well in some of the competitions. They paired up for alternate bouts, accommodating Cruttwell when he arrived and moving on to sabres. By the end of the evening, sweating and garrulous, they begged turns with Nathaniel's blade.

"The balance is rare," panted Wilkins as he returned it after he finished sparring with Nathaniel, who in turn handed back a borrowed sabre. "Very different from anything I've used before."

"The blade is Japanese, specially made for my father. He brought it back from the Orient and had it dressed in England. I have had cause to be grateful to it," said Nathaniel examining it carefully, "and I still follow my father's advice to train with both hands. Sorry if it surprised you Mr Fairfield." He smiled, meeting Fairfield's eyes and was rewarded with a rueful grin. Fairfield steered the conversation onto more neutral ground.

"Where did you learn to fence?"

"With my father, but also in London. I was fortunate enough to attend Master Domenico Angelo's club, the "School of Arms" in the Haymarket. It moved just last year to St James's Street, but it is still the same, and the best. The founder's traditions live on to the third generation. Old Mr Henry instructed me, and Mr Henry the Younger. He still works at the club when he has time but he's busy training the army."

"Impressive," said Fairfield. "But if I were you Parry I would keep up the practice. Times are dangerous. There's to be a reform demonstration in this city on Thursday this week. Thousands will be mustered and we just don't know what will happen. All the magistrates are under starter's orders to read the Riot Act at the first signs of trouble."

"Towns may soon be even unhealthier places than they already are," interjected Howard Dill with undue relish. "I myself, Mr Parry, live in a charming village, just seven miles from Bath. I invite you, nay, I entreat you to visit me!"

"Why thank you very much," said Nathaniel, non-committal.

"I live in Norton St Philip," persisted Dill. "My cook is on leave. Compassionate you know. Aged aunt is ill, needs seeing to, so I'm taking lunch daily in the George Inn. Join me one day sir! Soon!"

Nathaniel could not resist the infectious cheer of the little man.

"Many thanks Mr Dill. It is a kind offer."

The club broke up before eight p.m. and the gentlemen dispersed. Most made their separate ways home, but Nathaniel was restless after the sword-play, his body still coursing with energy, generating a ravenous hunger. He tracked down Caradoc who had taken to excavating a neighbouring garden.

"Report here Caradoc "instanter" if you have any interest in beef and beer!"

The terrier cleared the wall, dragging wisps of vegetation behind him, and skidded to a halt at Nathaniel's feet, yapping, head to the side, one ear raised high.

"Yes, beef and beer sir!" said Nathaniel. "We shall track them down."

He gave Caradoc an affectionate pat and they bowled down the hill to town. They made their way past the darkened windows of Martha Spence's house in Walcot and continued until they arrived at the George and Dragon, where Nathaniel had spent his first night in Bath. As before, heated political dispute was raging in the front parlour and after ordering a pint of porter, a saucer of small beer, and a beef and oyster pie with two plates, they joined it.

Roderick Wilson's funeral service in Bath Abbey was held the next day and was well attended, as were all functions that were held in that hub of society. The Abbey was attended daily as an arena for public promenade: gossip and show. Funerals added a frisson of gothic melancholy, morbidly exciting for visitors and locals alike. The black-clad congregation filled the nave below the soaring Perpendicular Gothic tracery that created "The Lantern of the West": their low whispers swashing like an incoming tide round its walls. The Abbey walls had been pierced so thoroughly they provided a better original for the saying "more glass than wall" than Hardwick Hall itself. The great Abbey windows shone, their muted rainbows of stained glass lit by the lowering afternoon sun and their shafts of light catching the multitude of settling dust motes.

The mourners had taken their places in small groups in the half-hour before the arrival of the coffin and Nathaniel had come early, placing himself at the back of the church to gain a better view of the company. Raphael Vere and Tilly had come in ostentatiously. She managed to shoot him a sly smile, unbeknown to her husband, before clattering along the pew, her jewellery tinkling as she went, her whispered asides sounding just too loudly to pass unnoticed. Captain Peterson, Mrs Peterson and the three girls had taken their places discreetly. The twins made a pretty picture as they fluttered in, identical in every aspect and turned out in lilac with black ribbons. Emma Peterson had ignored him on entry but he had noticed a blush on her cheek. She had a dignity and elegant beauty which he observed idly for a while. Miss Peterson reminded him of a roe deer, chestnut brown and glowing, hesitant and fragile, ready to run. But then he remembered her from the morning in the Pump Room: feisty, clever, and admonished by her mama for her unseemly interest in the cholera. His eyes wandered away to roam over the massed ranks of Wilson's associates: gentlemen of business, of his clubs, customers from the bank and representatives of the assorted social hierarchies of the city with their wives and families. He saw Charles and Mrs Parry at the front, Charles's massive bulk towering over the other mourners. They caught each other's eye and nodded.

Behind him the main doors opened and a cold draught brought a blast of autumn into the church. He turned as the organ struck up a funeral march and watched the coffin borne aloft down the central aisle, followed by the veiled, crabbed figure of Janie Wilson and assorted distant relatives. Most eyes followed them as they trooped dolefully towards the altar, but Nathaniel paused to watch the ushers as they began to close the heavy doors. A slim figure clad in shimmering black silk slipped in between the robed Abbey servants and took a place opposite to him, on the back pew to the left of the nave.

The service wore on, predictably. They listened, they prayed, they stood, they sang, they sat, they listened, they stood, they sang. Towards the end, Nathaniel noticed a slight movement to his left, the woman on the back row raised her veil to dab at her eyes, and he was rewarded by a sighting of a familiar almond shaped face, creamy skin and cat-like eyes: a little paler in the face, a little redder in the eyes, sadder but unmistakable. It was the minxy girl from the Pump Room who had dangled on the arm of the Irish politician. She felt his curious stare and met his eyes boldly before dropping the veil into place and turning to look resolutely ahead. He decided to question her as they left. It was too good an opportunity to miss and for the remaining half-hour he looked forward to a useful exchange with the most entrancing woman he had yet seen in Bath. Gathering intelligence on Wilson had never seemed quite so engaging. But he was doomed to disappointment. As he watched the coffin disappear through the doors on its way to the waiting coach, and prepared to make his move, his arm was grasped by Mrs Charles Parry. She had made her way, clandestinely, down the south aisle in the closing minutes of the service.

"Nathaniel," she scolded, tightening her grip on his arm and turning him to her.

"You really should have come up to sit with Charles and me! You shall now accompany us to Mrs Wilson's reception at the Paragon. The carriage is in Orange Grove and we can catch up on all your news of your friends in Bristol! Come on, no delays!"

As they made their way out through the great doors, he glanced to the opposite pew and was in no way surprised to see that it was empty.

They were decanted at the Paragon by Charles's servants, and made their way to the drawing room on the first floor. The apartment became crowded and hot very quickly. Small groups formed and extended their elbows to carve out standing space for themselves as they juggled glasses and plates which were constantly replenished by a footman and two maids.

"Is that Tanner, Mr Vere's footman," asked Nathaniel covertly of Captain Peterson as they sank a welcome goblet of wine by the open window.

"Vere's paid for the whole affair and lent a couple of servants to wait on. Damned decent of him," said the Captain.

Nathaniel pondered this. "Last week I called in on the Veres, as we'd planned, after I saw young Henry. Mrs Wilson arrived at Lansdown Crescent for dinner. Vere seems to be keeping a very kindly eye on her."

"Typical of the man, as you see. By the way, have you seen Wilson's rooms yet?"

"No, I was rather hoping to remedy that shortly."

"You've heard of the robbery? No? The very night you saw Mrs Wilson at the Vere's this house was broken into. Wilson's dressing room was ransacked by the sound of it, quite a bit is missing."

"Damn. I should have insisted on a search last week. Our killers are evidently closer and less casual than might have been the case. All good evidence to help clear Henry Blake, but we need something more concrete."

"Killers? Plural? Where did you learn that Parry?"

"Local source," replied Nathaniel.

Further discussion was impossible as the Veres and the rest of the Peterson family broke from the crowd in a cluster to join Nathaniel and the Captain.

"Mr Parry, at last I meet with you again!" Mrs Peterson fixed him with a look that brooked no argument. "We do hope you can come to us for dinner on Thursday, Thursday 13th yes?"

"With pleasure," said Nathaniel graciously.

"Mr Parry, Papa said you live in London!" piped a small Peterson female.

"How exciting!" bizarrely, two identical pipes sounded.

Nathaniel was forced to laugh out loud as the other twin chimed into the conversation. Her voice was identical to her sister's, as was her intonation, and her clothes, and her wide-eyes, and the precise angle of the set of her dainty jib. They giggled in unison, identically.

"Ladies. It has its excitements, as has every city including your own! I have not had the pleasure of being introduced to you and fear I shall disgrace myself by confusing your identities!"

"I'm Maddy and I'm the oldest by five minutes."

"And I am Ginette."

"Now I will never make a mistake," said Nathaniel seriously, whilst surreptitiously noting that Maddy's efforts to pluck her eyebrows had shortened her left brow just enough to create a difference from her sister's. That should be enough to give him the edge over them for the next couple of weeks.

Pink with embarrassment, and keeping to the outskirts of the circus entertainment provided by her sisters, Emma hoped that the exchange with the dashing Mr Parry would end before she betrayed herself. She still found him too attractive to look at if there was any danger of him meeting her glance.

"Miss Peterson, how very nice to see you again, though under sad circumstances. I assume you knew Mr Wilson quite well."

"Oh, yes, I mean, no, I did not know him very well," she stammered, looking reluctantly into the amused gaze of Nathaniel. "Father knew him better than I did Mr Parry. But it is nice to see you again."

"Stupid! Why did you say that?" she said to herself as she clenched her hands tight on the black reticule she found she was holding before her like a buckler in battle. She lowered it instantly.

"Your mother has been kind enough to invite me to dinner on Thursday. I do hope that you will be at home that evening." Nathaniel smiled at her broadly. "We will have more opportunity to talk."

"I look forward to it," said Emma, willing herself to relax and hoping that the pounding of her heart was not noticeable through her gown.

"Though how could it not be?" said the inner voice of reason.

It was not necessary to dwell on the possibility that she might look as though she were having a heart attack, as she found herself elbowed aside. Tilly Vere leaned into their conversation, disentangling herself from her husband's arm as he continued to talk animatedly to Captain Peterson.

"So pleased to see you again Mr Parry," she said breathily, looking up at him with her shining, limpid eyes through fluttering lashes. "Tell me all about your visit to Bristol."

Emma looked down, affronted to see a drift of Tilly's blonde curls resting on her own arm. She discreetly brushed the tendrils away and forced herself to listen attentively, and with grudging admiration, as the accomplished flirt displayed a master class in teasing and coaxing, plying her wares, soliciting Nathaniel's smile, all within reach of her husband's neglected arm.

The arrival of the widow curtailed the conversations and changed the dynamics of the group. To avoid the necessity of repeating well-worn condolences, Mrs Charles Parry launched into a monologue on the short-comings of the forthcoming season and held forth powerfully, engaging the Veres and Petersons *in toto*. Briefly, Nathaniel found he had Janie Wilson to himself.

"I was sorry to hear of the robbery Mrs Wilson. Although there is little chance of finding any clues I am still hoping for your permission to conduct a search."

"Certainly Mr Parry, you may do it now. I care not," said Janie Wilson, with an acid smile. She lowered her voice to a conspiratorial rasp. "Though it is amongst the low-lifes and bawds of this city that I recommend you pursue your investigations. You could not fail to notice the creature sitting by the door opposite from you in the Abbey! How she had the audacity to attend I cannot imagine."

"The young woman who arrived late?"

"The very same. I saw her on the way out. Colette Montrechet is the French baggage I told you of. Known to my husband in every sense of the word and no doubt hoping for money. She shall not have a penny. Though who knows when the estate will be settled. This house was robbed last Friday, and the thieves rifled Roderick's papers. I know he had been redrafting his will. His solicitor was awaiting it but fortunately does not have a copy of the new version which might just have rewarded the trollop for her services. We shall have to wait and see."

Janie Wilson seemed entirely unaware that she had not only informed Nathaniel of a motive for murder on the part of the mistress, but also managed to place herself prominently amongst the possible suspects.

"So sorry to hear of the burglary Mrs Wilson, but if you will permit me I would still like to see your husband's belongings."

"Then do so now." She beckoned a maid over from where she fidgeted by the door. "Show Mr Parry to my husband's dressing room."

The search proved fruitless, as expected. He rejoined the Petersons and the Veres and drew off the men for a private word out of earshot of the rest of the party.

"Mr Vere, I have conducted a search here but as you will know there has been a robbery and the trail is cold. However, the good news is that it seems increasingly likely that Mr Wilson was killed by two men, one of whom sustained a face wound during the assault. I believe your employee Henry Blake to be innocent and I strongly suspect the incriminating papers were planted in his rooms. I am following a lead at present which could provide witness evidence to identify the perpetrators."

Raphael Vere flushed red.

"Mr Parry, this is remarkable!" he gasped. "Who gave you that information might I ask? I sense a reward in the offing!"

Nathaniel observed his excitement with interest. Perhaps Mr Vere knew more of Wilson's foibles and their possible effect on his business than he admitted.

"I'm afraid it is too early to discuss that, but you could help me with another aspect of Mr Wilson's affairs. Were you aware that he might have been preparing a second will? Did he ask you to act as witness perhaps?"

Raphael Vere seemed surprised, but also more collected. "No, certainly not."

"No matter," said Nathaniel. "I will present the facts when my investigation is complete. A few days should suffice."

Raphael Vere bowed and moved back to Tilly, allowing Nathaniel to manage a private word with the Captain.

"I think an interview with Wilson's mistress would be useful. Apparently he had a liaison with a Miss Montrechet. I am persuaded she was the woman accompanying the young Irish politician when we met in the Pump Room."

"Yes, that's Diarmuid Casey, he has rooms in Queen Square, in the house on the corner of Gay Street. You could have a word with him first rather than seek her out. Better form don't you think?"

Nathaniel decided to leave Caradoc where he had left him before attending the funeral, stretched out before Mrs Spence's fire by Old Tom's feet. He made his way thoughtfully down Milsom Street, determining to visit Queen Square and present his card at Casey's rooms. He was picking his way past the exquisite shops decked with a profusion of clothes, shawls and every toy an inventive and commercial mind could design, avoiding dogs on leads and women's parcels, ballooning from the arms of their beaus, when he heard a shout and caught sight of a familiar face.

"Mr Parry!" bawled Tobias a second time from across the road. He was waving from a large shop-front opposite and was partially obscured by bristling scaffolding and advertisements for its grand opening the following month. "Mr Parry! Wait for me sir!"

Tobias skipped between the carriages and jumped the dung piles to present himself at Nathaniel's side.

"Oiy gat some intelligence sir," he said confidentially. "Oiy saw a man with a scarred face, fresh wound an' all on one o' they Bristol barges late last Friday. Might be the man mi boys from Little 'Ell saw the night Mr Wilson got murdered."

"There's probably a few bargees fit that description Tobias," said Nathaniel.

"Maybe," said Tobias, thinking hard to ensure he did not miss a tip. "But it's somethin' ain't it? And Oi'm still askin' mi boys to keep an eye out for you sir, riverside and up-town. Some do crossing sweeping up 'ere."

“Not very successfully,” said Nathaniel eyeing the mole hills of dung.

“Well I’d better be off then,” said Tobias disconsolately. “I’m deliverin’ a message to Mr Jolly.”

Nathaniel took pity on him.

“You’ve done well Tobias. Keep sharp. And don’t say too much to the boys from Little Hell. They may serve two masters.”

Nathaniel pressed sixpence into his hand and Tobias dodged back across Milsom Street, ducking under the scaffolding to disappear into the dark interior. Nathaniel made his way via Quiet Street to Queen Square and the temporary residence of Mr Diarmuid Casey.

The concierge instructed a maid to see Nathaniel upstairs to Mr Casey’s rooms. He was ushered into a small entrance hall as she disappeared with his card. He glanced around, swiftly appraising. It was dingy, paint peeling, but with a riotous bunch of dahlias firing the side-table with colour and the scent of autumn. The tired rented rooms were lit up by their presence: short-lived, evanescent. They reminded him of his first sighting of Casey, the fiery speaker in the Guildhall, and the second sighting, when he was surrounded by the swarm of girls, the satin gad-flies of the Pump Room, drinking him in, a wild draught of Ireland. A dark brown velvet curtain swept aside with a clatter of brass rings, and Diarmuid Casey presented himself with a bow.

“Well hello Mr Parry! Welcome. Come in sir.”

Nathaniel could not have been more pleased to do so, for as he entered the room he was greeted by the mocking, smiling, feline eyes of Miss Montrechet. She was reclining on the brown velvet chaise longue, dangling elegant ankles and dainty feet, evidently recovering from her mourning by consuming substantial glasses of Casey’s spirits.

“Sit down here sir directly and make yourself at home!” Diarmuid Casey beckoned him over, placed a glass in readiness and offered him a comfortable seat by the fire. "Let me revive you before you launch into your business. And let me introduce you to my friend, Miss Colette Montrechet."

Nathaniel took her outstretched hand briefly, then settled into an armchair opposite Diarmuid.

"I am delighted to meet you both as it is with both of you that my business lies. I am investigating the death of Mr Roderick Wilson on behalf of his employer Mr Vere."

"Are you now," she said, putting her head to one side and narrowing her eyes, sharpening her features. "And you are here, hot-foot from the Paragon I suspect? Your poor head bursting with venomous details of my affair with poor Roderick? Did the formidable black widow poison you with her bite?"

She laughed softly, and continued, her voice melodious and surprisingly sweet: with just a breath of her native France remaining, lifting it in an entrancing lilt.

"Poor silly man!" she raised her shoulders and pouted. "He deserved her, but he didn't deserve to die. He was so excited the night before his death. Ooh, la, la, was he excited! He said he was to become rich. He said his ship was coming in. Which would have meant that mine too was likely to make a safe haven!"

"Will you be taking a dram of my *uisce beatha* Mr Parry? From the oldest source of whiskey in all of Ireland."

As Diarmuid poured a generous measure into a heavy, fluted tumbler, Nathaniel noticed that the bottle was only half-full, its wrappings discarded on the floor. A few remaining slices of seed cake sagged awry on a plate, which itself balanced uncertainly on a pile of papers spilling from the side table.

"'Tis from Ulster. Established well over two hundred years, but the distillery is smart as paint, built in my father's days."

The three of them raised their glasses which glinted tawny gold before the warmth of the leaping fire.

"A *votre santé* Mr Parry. And since we're sharing a drink you can call me Coco."

Bold, self-possessed, yet wary, she challenged him, still in her black gown, but with a rose pink shawl draped over her slim shoulders, softening the light on her skin.

"*Slainte*" said Dairmuid gravely. "To freedom, Mr Parry, and you can call me Diarmuid since we're sharing a drink."

"Thank you both for your hospitality," said Nathaniel slowly, weighing their mood, watching the sly smiles exchanged between them and savouring his drink before he continued.

"I have no doubt that Roderick Wilson was murdered by someone other than Henry Blake who has been arrested on suspicion of the deed. Papers and money were probably planted in his rooms and Wilson's papers have been stolen. Mrs Wilson certainly bore her husband ill-will. The marriage cannot have been entirely happy," he glanced at Coco, waiting for reactions. "Perhaps she had the capacity to plot his murder?"

Nathaniel left the question in the air and continued to watch Coco. Almost as likely as Janie to have profited by the death if the second will materialised, and with contacts amongst the low life of the city, she could have played more than a small part.

"Janie Wilson is a lady Mr Parry," said Coco, chiding him. "Do you know nothing of Bath ladies of a certain age? Possibly the slow drip of poison over months or years, but certainly not a contract for killing! This is not Naples!"

Nathaniel smiled, "Mr Wilson probably left you something in his will Miss Montrechet."

She shrugged. "Possible but unlikely. I doubt there was much to leave!"

Nathaniel tried again. "Mr Wilson's employer, the generous Mr Vere, certainly has the welfare of Mrs Wilson at heart and perhaps seeks to preserve her reputation." Outside a coach creaked by, wheels clattering and harnesses jingling, inside the fire settled with a crack, sending sparks racing up the chimney, but Nathaniel got nothing in reply. He turned to Coco and tried a different tack.

"What do you know of Roderick Wilson's recent good luck

and his relationship with his employer?"

"Roderick was always generous," said Coco, draining her glass and automatically refilling it. "But he had started talking of setting me up in an apartment at his expense. That was new. He still gambled, but I don't think he had won substantially. As to Raphael Vere, I suggest you speak to Howard Dill. You were with him at the Pump Room last week. Little fat man. Sweet man." She yawned, briefly displaying perfect white teeth.

"I do know him," acknowledged Nathaniel. "I spoke to him last night. Why might he be helpful?"

"He is one of the original depositors in the New Bank. He knew Vere's first wife and her husband who started the bank in the first place. Visit him. Do you know where he lives?"

"The village of Norton St Philip I believe."

"Lovely house," said Coco, as she suddenly sat up on the chaise longue and dusted the seed cake crumbs from her lap. "Diarmuid, you rascal, you've let me drink too much whiskey. I must go. I'm on duty with a new gentleman tonight. I need my beauty sleep." She eyed Nathaniel closely, studying his reaction.

"Good afternoon Miss Montrechet," he said, standing and bowing.

"Good afternoon, Mr Parry." She looked at him, offering a challenge and repeated slowly, "Good afternoon, Nathaniel. You're very handsome. Find out who killed Roderick and come and see us again."

She gathered her shawl about her, drained the remainder of her whiskey, and kissed Diarmuid who took her arm and led her to the door. She paused as she passed Nathaniel, and in one graceful movement, gently shook off Diarmuid and slid her arms round Nathaniel's neck to hold him close, brushing her lips slowly against each of his cheeks. She pressed her warm, supple body against him, her soft breasts against his chest, staying just long enough for him to breathe in her perfume. A surprise: the clean fresh scent of lavender, not the heady spice of a tart. He felt it a matter of some congratulation that he had not wrapped his arms around her to enjoy more of the same, but had managed to sit down and remind himself she was a whore. He finished his tumbler of whiskey before Diarmuid returned after seeing Coco out.

"She has rooms upstairs. Gorgeous creature! We've been friends for years," he said breezily as he refilled their glasses. "Poor thing was upset when old Wilson passed. She is too soft-hearted for her own good so she is."

"Have you both lived in Bath long?"

"She's been here a couple of years, but I've just fetched-up for the season to do the rounds with reform speeches in this corner of the south-west. I'm in Mr Daniel O'Connell's connection and hoping for a seat at the next election." His green eyes flashed in delight and he flung off his jacket to reveal a none too clean shirt and the same striped waistcoat he had sported when Nathaniel first saw him. "There's a new world round the corner Mr Parry. Nathaniel is it? Yes for sure," he screwed up his eyes to focus on Nathaniel's card which lay on the side table. "The freeing of the Catholic Church in '29 opened the flood gates. All Danny's doing mark you! By God the man's a saint. The Liberator he is to us all."

He raised his glass solemnly and rose for a toast, "To the sainted Daniel O'Connell. God bless him!"

Nathaniel raised his glass. "To Mr O'Connell! Good health!"

"That's the spirit!"

"You think the Bill will pass soon?"

"Got to. Got to happen," said Diarmuid, sitting forward, the picture of boyish energy, gripping his glass, his thick thatch of chestnut-red hair on end like an unruly ploughed field. "You know the trades are rising this Thursday do you?"

"I heard there was to be a march," said Nathaniel. "Do you sense trouble?"

"Who knows!" Diarmuid's eyes gleamed, relishing the possibility.

"Is Miss Montrechet a reformer?"

Diarmuid roared with laughter and slapped his thigh. "Coco! She hasn't a political bone in her body! Her family lost everything in the Revolution. Grandparents were murdered in 1790, everything confiscated, so her father was ruined. He muddled along, got married, made a life of sorts but got killed in a riding accident in '19. Coco was about ten. Her mother just faded away, dead in a year. Coco wasn't the fading type! She lived on the streets and survived. By God did she survive! She was a grand courtesan in Paris when I met her. We met up again in Ireland, in Dublin. She'd followed some fella there but it didn't work out well. Couldn't be more pleased to see her here. I rolled into the Pump Room a few weeks back and there she was. She'd been fairly steady with Wilson, but had a couple of other customers. Mr Howard Dill being one of them. She found me rooms here, she's just upstairs and here we are!"

Diarmuid drained the last of the bottle of whiskey into their tumblers.

"Why don't we make our way out for a bite to eat? I have a powerful hunger!" he declared.

"Why not," said Nathaniel. "Whilst we are about it, could we make our way to Wilson's sporting haunts? I have a mind to find out a little more of his reputation."

"No sooner said than done!" declared Diarmuid, leaping to his feet and grabbing his coat. "'Twill be a famous evening. I feel it in my bones!"

The next morning Nathaniel picked his way on his hired horse through the steep valley of Limpley Stoke. Caradoc darted in and out of the deep drifts of leaves, worrying sleepy mice out of their nests and taking detours to dig ferociously in promising holes by the road side. The trees were alive with a rustling wind and snatches of bird song, the straggling flight of a migrating flock marked the wide blue above as one undulating black arrow. Startled deer lifted their heads by the tree line in answer to Caradoc's yaps and the drone of a late bee zipped by the horse's head causing him to start and stumble on the stony way.

"Easy, easy now boy."

Nathaniel swung himself out of the saddle as the horse laboured up the steep rise and tramped along beside him as they climbed above Monkton Combe, heading out on the Frome road for Hinton Charterhouse, the last village before Norton St Philip.

Only a slight headache remained above his left eye, which was surprisingly lucky considering the long evening spent with Diarmuid Casey. They had started in Bedford's Billiard Rooms in Milsom Street, Wilson's premier haunt, and had quickly established that, although a heavy gambler, Wilson had redeemed the larger part of his debts and had left there on the night of his murder in good spirits. He was collected by chairmen commissioned by a gentleman he wished to meet, but there the story had dried up. The waiter seemed to think the chair was a private one, as he recollected no licence plate and the men were not familiar. They had made their way via the Hiscox Rooms in New Bond Street, where Wilson was partial to a flutter on backgammon, and thence to Lock's in Union Street. They had then supped magnificently in the Hart before concluding the night's investigations in Kingston Buildings at Hall's. The story had been the same at every port of call. Wilson was not in precipitous debt, was unlikely to have been slain because of his habits and had been well pleased with himself in the week before his untimely death. The small hours had found him back at Diarmuid's rooms, where his genial host had produced a fiddle and proceeded to play like a demon, coaxing his guest to roar his way through an hour of Irish drinking songs followed by a voluntary of every favourite Welsh ballad he could muster. He had returned to Walcot Street in the dead of night, crept in through the kitchen window, ousted an outraged Caradoc from his bed and slept the sleep of the just. He had slept through the dawn rousing of the household, catching only Martha's final offering of the morning. At the signal, "We plough the fields and scatter, the good seed on the land," he quit the bed and made ready for his rural expedition.

He had managed to leave by mid-morning and had been spared rigorous questioning from Martha as she was fully occupied in exclaiming with Tom over a communication from Mary's seafaring husband. An a.m. start had been vital in order to negotiate the hire of a horse and arrive in Norton St Philip in time to catch Howard Dill at his lunchtime stall in the George. Nathaniel had made excellent time on the quiet roads, the most time consuming obstacle had proved to be an unreasonably large flock of sheep in Hinton, herded at a snail's pace by an elderly sheepdog. Despite this he managed to rein in shortly after noon and hand over his horse to one of the George's stable boys. He made his way through the flagged medieval courtyard to a wood-panelled dining room at the front of the inn where it was an easy matter to locate his quarry. Howard Dill sat behind a robust portion of pie and a pewter mug of cider, smiling beatifically and watching the smoke rise against the metal fire-back to lose itself in the cavernous chimney.

"Mr Dill, I hoped to find you here. May I join you?"

"Well, if it isn't Mr Parry! Delighted, delighted my dear fellow! Sit down, let me order your lunch directly." He shouted to the barman, "Here my man, I have a guest! In fact," said Dill cheerfully, "two guests. I spy a thirsty terrier."

The innkeeper made his way smartly to the table with a bowl of water for Caradoc and took the extra orders.

Nathaniel had seated himself by Howard Dill on a high backed oak settle, which kept out most of the draughts, and looked round the room. The lime-washed walls were grimed brown with generations of pipes and fires and the worn tapestries rose gently with the warm currents of air from the fire and periodic cold blasts as the door opened to let in new customers. The room smelled of forests, of wet wool and dogs, smoke, beer and spirits overlaid with the sweat of working men. Four or five huddles of customers now populated the room. Prosperous farmers were talking pay in low voices with their labourers, who were bare-headed and clumsy in their work-worn linen smocks and gaiters, the dogs sleeping in the dark by their feet below the tables.

"It was a good ride, but I'm weary after it I must confess," said Nathaniel, relaxing into the worn velvet cushions stacked against the wooden back of the settle. "This is an intriguing place."

"It was built for the monks long ago. Did you ride through Hinton Charterhouse and see the ruins? It was a Carthusian Priory founded in the thirteenth-century. This was the monks' wool-store. It did duty as an inn for the wool fairs after the monks were disbanded at the Dissolution and it wasn't all plain sailing afterwards, it's had a bloody history. Monmouth's rebels used it for their trysts in the seventeenth-century and Hanging Judge Jefferies tried them here and hung them high on the green for their taking of the liberty!"

"You're well versed in local history sir!"

"I'm a single man. I have no family to fill my time," said Howard Dill, a broad smile belying the melancholy of his words.

"You're happy here?" enquired Nathaniel.

"As a bug in a rug sir!"

They ate in companiable silence, draining their cider, pushing back their plates and stretching out their feet under the trestle table towards the fire. The resident dog, a vast German boarhound, lumbered over and rested his black muzzle on Howard Dill's shoulder, lent over to mop up some scraps of meat from the plates and moved on. Caradoc, worn out by the morning's run, slumbered unopposed in the inglenook amongst the logs.

"A digestif Mr Parry?"

"What do you suggest?"

"We must make a gesture to the Carthusians," said Howard Dill gravely. "The Green Chartreuse if you please sir!" he shouted to the innkeeper.

"The distillation of hundreds of years of holy skill Mr Parry!

One hundred and thirty varieties of herbs and plants suffuse this blessed liquor. It is a medicament of the highest order."

They raised the tiny glasses of bright green liquid to the light.

"Your very good health!" declared Howard Dill.

"And yours sir. *Slainte*!"

"Ah, ha! *Slainte* is it! You have spent a merry evening or more in the company of the estimable reformer, Mr Casey I presume!" said Howard Dill, his spectacles flashing their characteristic opaque blankness in the light of the fire.

"Indeed," said Nathaniel, watching his host closely. "I spent yesterday evening in his company. And I met Miss Montrechet in his rooms before we took ourselves off into town."

"Oh! The delectable Coco! Nathaniel, may I call you Nathaniel? Good. She is a joy sir! But one to be rationed," he screwed up his face in concentration, "to be taken with care. Very like the Green Chartreuse. I avail myself of her charms on occasions. High days and holidays my boy. Unlike the egregious Wilson. Burned at the flame you know. Wanted to fund her entire as his mistress. A doomed venture, but he never found that out. God rest his soul!"

"Coco said you knew a great deal about Mr Raphael Vere, who is employing me to investigate Wilson's death."

Dill's good-natured face clouded. "Raphael Vere is a very wealthy man, despite some calamitous losses sustained in the early canal boom. He has tight dealings with some shippers in Bristol which must have been his salvation. One investor in particular is the key to the bank's new investments. He's called Edwin Ravenswood and he is an exporter, operates out of King's Wharf on the Eastern run. He has a town house in Redcliffe Parade overlooking his vessels. Vere is busy with him on a new project in which Captain Peterson and I might become more closely involved. A new vessel is needed."

He sank into thought, his cherubic mouth for once turned down, his jowls sagged giving a fleeting vision of Howard as an old man. The drowsy warmth of the parlour and the kindly effect of the pie and drinks loosened his tongue further.

"Strictly in confidence!" He glanced round for prying eyes and ears, and satisfied that the other customers were absorbed in their own affairs, continued in a low voice, inclining his head towards Nathaniel.

"He married a lady well known to my family. Mrs Patience Meredith, the widow of Elijah Meredith who founded the New Bank. Patience was five and twenty years older than Vere when they wed. They seemed happy enough, but the year after she died in '18, Vere married Tilly. Fourteen years of age and pretty as a picture, not that she isn't still. They travelled abroad for a time to quieten the scandal, living on the proceeds of Elijah's bank. Her mama was responsible for the match, bundled poor Tilly off as soon as she could. Last of six girls you see and the mama tired of the courting game. She sealed a bargain with the first to offer. Always did like them young did Vere."

"But his wife was by far his senior?"

"Patience was seventy-two when she died but she could have made her century. I do not believe she died naturally!"

Nathaniel pressed his advantage.

"I understand. But what about today? What do you think he is capable of Mr Dill?"

The desolation in Howard's face gave eloquent answer.

The Shadwell's Residence, Green Park Buildings West, Bath.

As night fell in Bath, all was not well at the Shadwell's residence in Green Park West. A casual observer would have noticed nothing, as the house presented its usual respectable face to the street: fresh paint and clean stonework; foot scraper standing to attention, footpath neatly swept and the deep area behind the railings scrupulously free of leaves; chimneys smoking busily. But Madam Shadwell was not on duty in the front parlour and her door stood ajar. Up the elegant staircase on the first floor, the formal rooms were ablaze with flattering candle-light. Snatches of conversation, the clink of glasses, giggles, and the deeper bass voices of two happy customers could be heard floating through the door to the landing. Higher still, on the second floor, the application of Mitzi's lash could be heard distantly from her bedroom. The other doors were also firmly closed, muffling the sounds of pleasure. But higher still, up the winding, narrow stair to the attics and nursery, a different sound. Rosie Shadwell bent over a thin child who squatted, bare-legged over a bowl of water, dyed red with blood which flowed from jagged cuts on her lower body. The girl held a cloth to her face, which had also been laid open by a savage blow. She moaned, rocking back and forth to comfort herself.

"In the name of God Babs, how did it come to this?" said Rosie as she rinsed the girl's legs which were already purpling with bruises. "You look like you've been run over with a coach wheel!"

"I feel like it," Barbara muttered indistinctly, but raised a lop-sided grin.

"What did he hit you with?"

"His hands Ma'am. He had such rings on him. He's ripped my skin all over."

"So I see."

"'E came in like a thunder cloud. Normally all very nice, 'Where's my baby girl?' and all that. Not today Ma'am, he was cruel to me, mocking. Said I was too old and hardened. I should be on the streets." Her eyes welled with tears, "You wont let me go Mrs Shadwell will you? I can serve the men like the rest of the girls. I'm nearly fourteen. I'm not a child now! Per'aps someone else should do the nursery?"

"You will do nothing for at least a week 'til you heal up," said Rosie briskly. "Then we'll see."

She sat on the edge of the bed and looked Barbara firmly in the eye, holding her hands, "We don't hold with customers damaging girls in this house, you know that. But this particular customer is a very important man Babs. Do you know who he is?"

"I know he is a banker, he told me once." She hesitated, "Pardon me for repeatin' it, but he said that he controls Mr Shadwell's investments and holds the future of this house in his hands!"

"Enough Babs. Don't repeat it again. Now hold these wet cloths on the wounds. I'll send Josie up with some honey to dab on when they stop bleeding and she'll bring you fresh towels." She stood and wrapped her robe around herself, tying the sash tightly. "She'll bring up a drink for you. Make sure you get it down, then get some sleep. There'll be no one else in here tonight."

"Thanks Mrs Shadwell."

As the door closed, Barbara's white face crumbled. She covered her mouth with the soaked cloth, rolled over on the bed in a ball and was still. Rosie Shadwell closed the door and descended the stairs slowly, her face livid with rage. The lost earnings would be extracted from that particular customer, in full, with interest. She paused at the landing window and looked down the dark garden. Past the arbours and lawns the lights in Joshua's office above the coach house winked through the trees. She would discuss the matter with him later. He would know what to do. As she turned to make her way back to the parlour, two men came silently through the back gate and made their way to the stable stairs.

Joshua sat opposite the customer in question, letting the waves of abuse break over him and waiting for the blustering storm of anger to wear itself out. He glanced at his clock on the mantle-shelf, it was almost an hour since he had dispatched his men to sort out a spot of trouble in one of his Avon Street brothels. They should be back soon, he reasoned, breaking the heads of that class of customer was not a lengthy or elegant business. And, as it was mid-week, before the night was out,

Mordecai and Declan would also be round to be paid. He would not be alone for much longer.

"And then," roared Vere, "in front of Captain Peterson, Parry talked about having evidence. Evidence! From witnesses mark you Shadwell! Witness evidence that your incompetent moronic assassins were seen killing Wilson. Not only did the suicide turn into murder but the perpetrators were seen, one wounded on his face which makes him a marked man for months to come. If Parry links your men to you, the consequences will be catastrophic!"

"For us both," said Joshua quietly.

"So what do you intend to do about it?" hissed Raphael Vere, his plump cheeks trembling. He gripped the edge of the table and rose to his feet, challenging Joshua Shadwell.

Joshua lent back in his chair, sliding open his drawer to catch the comforting sight of his pistols. Vere was not normally a man of violence, not at first hand, not at his own hands, but tonight he was almost deranged. The findings of the investigator from London had alarmed him and he was now realising the foolish stupidity of his clumsy tangle with Wilson.

"Sit down Raphael," he said, with a steely calm. "Keep a clear head. You've made mistakes already through hastiness. If you hadn't been so desperate keen to have little girls you wouldn't have exposed yourself to blackmail. But accepting you are, desperate keen that is, you should have kept your activities off your own doorstep. Letting a likely character such as Wilson be with you when you were both well gone in your cups, and letting him in your house amongst your papers when you were both the worse for wear were serious errors. My men tried to get rid of him for you, quietly. There were complications. Death can be complicated. And now we have a different problem. Our associate in Bristol will not look kindly on any public unpleasantness. He needs absolute efficiency. Absolute confidence."

Vere's face hardened, becoming mulish. "Do you think I am

not aware of that? Why do you think Wilson had to go? I want this to stop here. I want them dead," he growled. "Both of those clowns. I want all evidence gone. Do you understand, Shadwell!" Vere's voice suddenly rose to a crescendo as he lurched across the table to grasp Joshua by the lapels. But Joshua saw him coming, leaned back, snatched a pistol out of the drawer and levelled it at Vere.

"Sit down!" he roared. "Don't you ever try to touch me! Calm down damn you Vere! Pull yourself together!"

As Vere pulled back, transfixed by the sight of the pistol, the door burst open to reveal the dark bulk of Mordecai Fletcher, eyes blood-shot with fury.

"You want it to end do you?" he shouted hoarsely, striding across the floor and launching himself at Vere. "It will end, you bastard!" He wrapped both hands round Vere's throat and they crashed to the ground. Declan had been on the stairs behind Mordecai as they had first listened in mute incomprehension to the ravings of Vere, demanding their deaths. He raced to pull Mordecai off his victim, as Joshua also ran to the struggling men, pistol reversed to provide a butt with which to rain down blows indiscriminately on them both.

"Stop! Stop you bloody fool! Take his collar Declan, pull him off!"

In the rolling, roaring melee Declan was flung off like a nine-pin. He pitched heavily into Shadwell and scattered the flaring candlesticks, papers, quills and ink from the desk. At the same time the pistol discharged a thunderous retort and plume of smoke. Three men staggered to their feet, but Mordecai Fletcher, face frozen in a snarl of fury, lay in a widening pool of blood as treacherous flames from the fallen candles licked up the curtain linings, firing the window with a lurid light. In that one moment of silence Declan fled. He made it through the door, slid down the stairs, flew across the flags of the coach house and paused swaying at the entrance. Hearing the voices of Joshua's two men at the gate, he threw himself behind the shrubs and into the shadows. Raised voices in the office above and the flicker of rising flames in the window drew the men in to investigate, which gave Declan a chance. He made it to the gate as they entered the coach house, calling for their master, and tore off down the black lane to the quay. Heart beating fit to burst from his chest he hammered on, zigzagging through the courts, making for his barge, but as he neared it, he shied away.

"Safety in numbers. God help me!"

He slowed to get his breath, sat shivering on the ground, back pressed to the Corn Factor's wall, then stood, unsteadily, and made his way to the Full Moon. He slid into the packed bar with the other bargees, bought a drink, voice shaking, and pushed his way to a seat by the fire. In his world, there was only one authority higher than Mr Shadwell. He would rouse his horse and leave for Bristol that night.

Chapter 5

Mid-day: 13th October, 1831.
The White Hart, Stall Street, Bath.

Nathaniel sat over a steaming plate of ham and potatoes, warming his hands. He had excised the prime knuckle-bone from the platter and given it to Caradoc, who was at his usual post amongst the logs in the inglenook of the fireplace. The dog also had his customary saucer of small beer, but Nathaniel had taken brandy and hot water, downing much of it on the spot in answer to the growing chill. During the high winds of the previous night, the trees had shed many of their leaves, which lay in sodden piles of brown and maroon, inert and slimy in the sharp, dank air. His short walk down Walcot had been a cold one. The early touch of winter had bitten through his travelling cloak and into his bones and he had been glad to arrive at the Hart. The bar was over-crowded, dark, and hot as a cauldron, with men bulked out in caped greatcoats fortifying themselves for the afternoon and booming politics into the foetid air. Aping the regular demonstrations in London and the large industrial towns, this afternoon would see the liberal-minded in Bath take to the streets in support of the Reform Bill and Nathaniel was duty bound to watch them at it. The plan was for the demonstrators to convene in Queen Square by one p.m. then march in good order with bands and banners to Sydney Hotel, where the doyens of Bath's reform world would greet them from the hustings on the front lawn. General Palmer the liberal representative of the city would be the main speaker, with Captain Mainwaring acting as Chairman. There was support from an assortment of imported speakers, including Diarmuid Casey, who were to add their own loyal addresses to the King and promote Bath's petition in support of the Bill. Many speeches would be made, songs sung and loyal declarations made before a peaceful conclusion: if all went according to plan. But the spectre of riot hovered, and, just in case it managed to land as it had already done in the Midlands, he needed to secure a reasonable vantage point in Pulteney Street.

The Whig lords in London were on a knife edge, as they needed mass agitations to alarm the Tory lords into accepting the Bill, but those demonstrations must fall short of uncontrollable riots which may lead to revolt. It was a fine and uncomfortable balance. The last thing they wanted was a united working class roused to a mob and demanding the Bill as a stepping stone to universal suffrage: the vote for all men, the Holy Grail of democratic reformers and anathema to the Whigs. It was a dangerous game, as the people, potentially the new Leviathan of power, might just rise in defiance of Commons, Lords and Crown alike to demand individual rights for all men. The gaol at Derby had been attacked earlier that very week and the castle at Nottingham was all but razed to the ground. Nathaniel comforted himself with the fact that both disturbances had been quenched fairly briskly by a deployment of troops. He glanced round the parlour. There did not seem to be any good reason for denying the franchise to any of the men assembled there, though some would fall short of owning a house of the required annual value of £10. He speculated as he watched them feeding, drinking, wearing out the arguments they had been rehearsing since the end of the French Wars. Should all male householders vote?

What about the slum owners, should they lose the vote if they neglected their property? He watched the potboys about their business. Should they vote? They owned nothing, many flitting from rented room to rented room with no responsibilities. Many were illiterate and could not read a ballot paper. Some could not follow a simple line of argument. Surely they could not seriously expect the vote to make its way down to them?

Since June, well before the Lords' rejection of the second version of the Bill, the meetings of massed thousands had started. Hetherington's *Poor Man's Guardian* had acted as a unifying organ for the movement in the capital: enthusing, cajoling, marshalling. Henry Hetherington himself was a founder member of the new National Union of the Working Classes, which revived old fears of united labour. Nathaniel had caught up with the mood in the George and Dragon on Monday night. Excitement had been high, as had been expectations for the success of the demonstrations. But what would success bring? He frowned at the prospect and dug into his mound of potatoes.

Most of the men, waiting now in the cold in Queen Square, not lunching in the Hart, would still be denied a vote. Many houses in the lower town were worth only a half of the value pegged for access to the franchise. Lord Grey himself, Prime Minister and the champion of the Bill, wanted reform only in order to preserve. The rich and powerful would continue to rule, Bill or no Bill. So how long would it be before even the most law-abiding amongst liberals realised that polite protest stood for nought and their patient hopes for gradual, continued improvement were doomed? His mind returned to France and the collapse of Charles X and his cronies. The supposedly bloodless revolt had inflicted three days of mayhem on Paris, enough to remind the locals of the terrors of 1793. The British seemed to have forgotten 1649 and the execution of their king, forgotten the Civil War had happened at all, or at least the government hoped they had.

But on Monday night, aflame with desire for change, Robert

Turner had spoken of 300,000 at a meeting last week in London. The whole of the army would be dwarfed by such a force if called to meet it. The language was also changing. Turner had read out from the penny booklet of the National Union, quoting the *Rights of Man*, describing law as the expression of public will and resistance being a sacred duty if that will be violated. More than this, he read Hetherington's invocation of Lord Nelson's message before Trafalgar: "England expects every man will do his duty". Perhaps "England" meant the workers and the populace was becoming battle ready? Whatever the upshot today in Bath, he knew Monday's meeting in London would be a fraught one. He checked the long-case clock in the corner: he needed to leave within the quarter hour to make his tryst with Robert Turner and Arthur Jamieson, the lynch-pins of the political club at the George and Dragon.

He continued to chew steadily on the ham, suddenly becoming aware that he was making little head-way, despite having been working on it for some considerable time. Perhaps Tobias had had a hand in it in his capacity as trainee cook. He shielded his plate from the elbows of boisterous customers jostling for attention and observed Frederick Tooson at his usual post behind the bar working up a glistening sweat, toiling to meet the unaccustomed demand. Potboys and barmaids were weaving through the press of customers, delivering precipitously stacked plates of food, foaming jugs of ale and sloping tankards to the tables. Nathaniel managed to catch Mary's eye as she passed, laden with four piled platters, and gave her a smile of encouragement. She paused briefly on her way back to the kitchen, fishing a piece of fatty meat from her pocket as she did so.

"There you be Caradoc. You sha'n't go hungry," she smiled, throwing it to Caradoc's lair by the fire. He caught it and gulped it down.

"Glutton," said Nathaniel. "You spoil him, Mary."

"Sir I'm that happy! A little bite o' fat will make the dear creature happy too! All I can think on is my Matthew returning." Her face had lost its strained melancholy and was alight with joy. "Just a few more days. Probably. I keep telling the Johnty that Daddy's coming home!"

A flicker of anxiety crossed her face, after over a year away, to be so near, yet still at the mercy of the seas and fickle, bitter misfortune. Her stomach turned over, the familiar bucking sensation of terror and imminent loss.

"It's wonderful news, Mary," said Nathaniel. "It's put a spring in Martha's step too."

"She dotes on him sir. He's her only son; even though she's none too pleased he's chosen the sea. Anyway, she'll be glad of more help in the house."

"I hope she would ask me, Mary, if her need was urgent."

"Oh sir you're a paying guest, she couldn't. But Old Tom is getting heavier to lift as he's losing what strength he has left in his limbs. We need regular aid. I will think of something. Do not consider what I said sir, I spoke out of turn."

"Could you ask Tobias to come over to me when he can?"

"I surely will sir."

An unusual presence materialised behind the bar in the shape of the landlord, the brooding and magisterial Mr Bishop.

"Now Frederick," he admonished the barman, whose strident moustaches had escaped their waxing in the heat and the hairs stood out at angles like a bristled hedgehog. "We should've anticipated the rush today with the march imminent. We are almost dry of cider and the cellar-man's damned near ruptured with the number of barrels he's raised. Send a boy to the brewery to place an extra order. Delivery this afternoon mind or we'll lose the business."

"Yes sir Mr Bishop," said Frederick, as his employer marched down the steps to do battle with the remaining barrel.

"Tobias!"

Tobias Caudle hallooed an indistinct reply and broke cover from the corridor, scudding to a halt by Frederick and winking to

Nathaniel. "Speak to you later Mr Parry sir!"

Once Tobias had been dispatched to the brewery Frederick took advantage of a lull in the orders.

"Could go either way today sir. Mark my words," he said gravely. "Captain Wilkins and his men are equal to anything, but between the two of us, the rest of the Somerset Militia's a joke. Laughing stock they are!" He leaned conspiratorially over the bar. "Trained in the Sydney Gardens over the summer they did, you never saw anything like it, no not in all your born days! 'Specially if you was in the military." Nathaniel smiled encouragingly.

"Plough boys most of 'em," scoffed the barman. "Their gear's just left-overs from the Frenchey Wars! Guns'd prob'ly blow up and maim the lads before they'd shoot accurate at the angry man! Laughed out of the Gardens they was! By the by, did you enjoy your session with the Captain's fencing club?"

"Capital evening," replied Nathaniel. "Thank you for putting me on to it."

As Frederick seemed inclined to swop confidences, he decided to fish for more. "I also met a Mr Howard Dill again yesterday. We lunched together. Very pleasant gentleman. Do you know of him?"

"I should think so sir. Mr Dill's family were regular merchant princes in Bristol. Slavers y'know. Not that we talk so loud on that subject these days. Wealthy gentleman he is still. A lion in Bath society sir. Notwithstanding his mild appearance if you take my meaning." He gathered together some of the empty tankards which had grown like a forest on the bar as they talked. "Not exactly a benefactor here though, not like the Captain who's a saint! His workers have good wages and get treated every Whit to a fair and a feed. It's a red letter day on the Twiverton calendar I can tell you. And it's well known his youngest workers get off very lightly. You know, under nines. The Short Time fellas are always shouting about them little 'uns. Well they do no more than about six hours a day. It's a regular holiday compared with field work. There's nothing a damned Factory Act can do to better the Captain's regimen I can tell you! Anyway, the government will give the Short Time agitation short shrift. Ha! Short shrift, not short time! That's what they'll get. Whigs have their hands full with the Reform Bill. There'll be no interfering in a man's independence in his own business. Not in our life times at any rate!"

Having put the world to rights to his immense satisfaction, Frederick Tooson puffed out his cheeks and deigned to raise an eyebrow to invite an order from the most insistent of the customers who were densely packed and parched, behind the new and flourishing growth of empty tankards on the bar.

Nathaniel whistled for Caradoc and they made their way out into Stall Street. A brittle, watery sun had broken through the flying clouds, lighting the tops of the buildings and sharpening the shadows. The wind whipped at his cloak and threw the leaves up in squalls. He could hear the multitude as he reached the Upper Borough Walls. The crowd had swelled to fill Queen Square to overflowing and it took some time to locate the printers' delegation where Robert Turner and Arthur Jamieson had said they would be. There were dozens of silk trade banners, riding a man's height above the mass of heads and hats, and flags on poles flapping and cracking in the fitful gusts of wind. Robert, assisted by a puffing Arthur, was struggling to anchor one of the wooden supports of the printers' banner into a leather holster which dangled from a lanyard round his neck.

"Easy Arthur now. Easy! This damned thing'll do me a mischief if it slips. Got a mind o' its own!"

"There you be. Safely stowed."

"Thank God for that. You all roight wit' other end Eddie?"

"Ooh arr," grunted his fellow bearer. "Oiy got 'er 'oisted perfect 'ere!"

The banner was a veritable sail of silk bearing the lavishly embroidered arms of the Printers' Union. It was more usually aired on church walking days and there was some anxiety about it getting wet. Eddie had a bolt of cloth over his shoulder to fling over the banner if the heavens opened, as they seemed poised to do.

"What a crowd!" exclaimed Nathaniel. "You must be pleased with the turn out."

They looked about them, triumphantly. The square was solidly packed with a mass of respectable humanity. Men, and even a few women, all in their best clothes thronged together, talking loudly and excitedly, eyes bright with visions of victory. Who could withstand such numbers? Such a show replicated in all the principal towns of the land must alter the minds of the Lords and win the day, or so it seemed. From Nathaniel's vantage point he could see that the printers were matched by the waving banners of the cabinet makers, plasterers, masons and sawyers, with other trades out of full sight on the other side of the square. Placards bobbed above the heads of the crowd ranging in sentiment from the loyal: "Long live the King!" to the more combative; "We are all agreed" and "The Bill and Nothing Else!"; to the extravagantly inflammatory call of the American rebels; "No taxation without representation."

"Will the authorities let the tax claim stand do you think?" asked Nathaniel.

"They want no trouble," said Robert Turner gleefully. "We own the town today!"

A few constables stood in groups round the outskirts of the crowd, but did indeed seem to be in as good a humour as the marchers, and not a dragoon in sight.

As Nathaniel swept Caradoc up from the ground and tucked him under his arm to avoid him being trampled, he caught sight of a rare scuffle. A group of the notorious "boys of the town" had entered the square from Barton Street and were jostling a group of marchers.

"Ye young demon!" bawled a man, dropping his placard and seizing the nearest boy. "Pick my pocket would you!"

"Wasn't me. Search me! Search me!" The urchin pulled out

his torn pockets as the constables closed in, grasping him and the collars of any other boys within reach. As a body, all the marchers in the area rounded on the scene and made grabs for ears, arms, necks, or rags, whatever came closest to hand.

"Search them all!" roared the victim. "This scallywag will have passed on my wallet to another. We're wise to you, ye young devils."

Blows and cuffs were liberally administered and in moments the wallet was recovered from the floor and the boys where shooed away.

"See what I mean," laughed Robert. "Even them varmints can be tamed when we all act together!"

Nathaniel noticed Tobias on the corner of the square, exchanging rapid words with the boys as they made off for the lower town. Nathaniel made his excuses and caught up with him.

"Oh 'ello Mr Parry," said Tobias. "They're some of mi'boys from Little 'Ell."

"So I see. Mind you don't get too fond of their company Tobias. You seem to be doing well at the Hart."

"I am sir," he smiled. "I got a proper room in the stables now and I'm doing more in the kitchens."

"Yes," said Nathaniel, "I thought you might be. Now what can you tell me about the chances of a riot?"

"There'll be no trouble today sir. All town's calm as a mill pond. See, there's no soldiers and no magistrates. You don't need to worry. The lads just wanted to see what the crowd might 'ave to offer, so to speak."

A mighty blast on trumpets, massed shrieking from the fifes and the booming of bass drums interrupted them.

"Look Tobias, the procession is moving off. I think I'll follow them. It looks safe enough."

Tobias peered at Nathaniel through his straggling fringe and smiled knowingly.

"You're not really frightened at all are you sir?"

Nathaniel flicked him a sixpence, dropped the wriggling

Caradoc to make shift as best he could and merged with the thousands as they followed the drums towards Pulteney Street. Cheers and waves from the windows round the square drew his eyes upwards. Most windows were filled with the smiling faces of elegantly dressed ladies and children, safe above the maelstrom of the crowd and enjoying the spectacle.

"The Bill the whole Bill and nothing but the Bill," bawled a young boy amongst a clutch of infants leaning from a first floor window-sill. He followed up with a delighted shriek of laughter and was promptly dragged in by a governess. Nathaniel waved back to the other children and then sought out the windows of the corner house. Diarmuid's apartment was dark as he expected, but above it, a bonus, Coco in a rose silk dressing gown, her dark hair flowing over her shoulders, a glass in her hand. He waved wildly, surprised by how pleased he was to see her. She blew him a kiss and raised her glass as he was swept on by the crowd.

Nathaniel found himself exhilarated by the experience of marching with so many, the tread of thousands reverberating on the ground, the calls and the snatches of song lifting their hearts and the crush threatening at times to lift him off his feet. He felt the mighty power of the people and tried again the sound of phrase that had come to him so forcibly, the new Leviathan. But it was not a despotic beast on today's showing. It was a creature entirely benign and the atmosphere of good-humoured carnival persisted. As they made their stately progress down Bridge Street towards the broad concourse of Great Pulteney, he raised his head to look to the distant hustings and flags in front of the Sydney Hotel. All before it was now a solid river of reformers. It was unlikely that he would be able to get close enough to hear the speeches and decided it was better to rescue Caradoc, take him home and then approach the hotel from Bathwick Street, short-circuiting the crowd. He caught sight of his dog, whistled him over and scooped him up, so he could make his way back to Walcot against the flow, keeping close to the buildings.

He managed to double back to High Street relatively quickly

and hurried down Walcot Street, setting Caradoc free to run ahead. They passed the deserted George and Dragon, the silent markets and shops, many closed in honour of the demonstration and some, like the premises of James Crisp the hatter, festooned with reform banners urging solidarity. As they closed in on their lodgings, he caught sight of the figure of a woman pacing back and forth in great consternation. Caradoc evidently recognised her and raced over, yapping a greeting. She turned quickly, startled, and bent to pat the dog. Looking up anxiously she saw Nathaniel, called out in relief and rushed to him.

"Oh Mr Parry I am so pleased to see you! I knew you had rooms somewhere hereabouts but had no idea where. I must speak with you. I left Tanner waiting outside the dressmaker's."

The young woman had a veil over her bonnet which fell to her shoulders, obscuring her face, but the voice, the loose bun of golden curls at her neck and the richness of her apparel left him in no doubt as to the identity of his visitor.

"Mrs Vere, follow me, my rooms are here."

He ushered her before him to Martha's front door, observing her distress, betrayed by her trembling hands and stiff back. This was a Tilly he was unfamiliar with. No longer the beautiful, selfish wife with her habitual air of entitlement, but more like a younger sister: gauche, vulnerable and afraid. Nathaniel let them in and they paused in the narrow hall, shutting out the street, creating a moment of proximity and intimate silence, which was instantly to be broken. From behind the door at the end of the passage sounded a high reedy voice, raised in song, and accompanied by an erratic beating of metal percussion on the flag floor.

"We'll rant and we'll roar,
Like true British sailors,
We'll range and we'll roam,
O'er all the salt seas,
Until we strike soundings.....

No, no young Johnty! Thou shalt not beat thy great grand'fer with that ladle! Ye besom!"

Caradoc raised his tail high and trotted straight for the door, pawing it open and making a bee-line for the ancient man and infant by the fire. Tilly Vere stood uncertainly in the dark hall and Nathaniel strode before her to the kitchen.

"Hello Mr Spence. Is Mrs Spence at home?"

"She be out in the back garden sir but will be in directly! Bring in your guest, the Johnty and me could do with a diversion!"

Nathaniel sensed the reluctance of Tilly and spared her that.

"That is a kind offer, but I will speak with Mrs Vere in the parlour if I may, as she has urgent business. Please tell Mrs Spence. Tea would be very welcome if she would be so kind as to make some."

"A truer word was never spoke," said Tom. "Oiy would welcome it like a brother mi'self. Powerful thirsty work conversin' with this young sprig 'ere."

Johnty had occupied himself with a close scrutiny of Caradoc who had appropriated the ladle and was worrying it.

"Just a'fore ye go to be closeted in the parlour," said Tom slyly. "What news of the march? There's been a mighty throng of folk a'goin' down the street this morning."

"It is going very well," said Nathaniel, as he followed Tilly into the front room. "Very good humoured."

"It'll come to nought then!" called Tom after them triumphantly.

Tilly settled herself in a high backed mahogany chair by an occasional table which was draped in a red crushed-velvet cloth and supported two porcelain figures: a coy shepherdess and her shepherd. Tilly slowly lifted her veil to reveal a face grotesquely changed. It was distended down the right side, swollen and reddened, with the bloated and bruised eye-socket closed up like that of a new-born pup.

"Good God what happened to you?"

Tilly's open eye swam with tears and she held the edge of the veil over her injuries, ashamed.

"My husband struck me. As you see, not just once but repeatedly. Mr Parry I am so afraid."

Unannounced by any audible footfall, the door fell open. Tilly struggled and failed to pull the veil back over her face, her hands coming to a premature halt under the silent scrutiny of Martha who stood, framed, in the door-way.

Nathaniel sprang to his feet and introduced the women.

"Mrs Vere, " said Martha, scrutinising the damage to Tilly's face, "as you are seated in my parlour may I ask what has happened to you?"

"I have had a fall madam," blustered Tilly. "Mr Parry is engaged on business for my husband and I need to speak with him privately."

"You may speak in comfort here madam," said Martha stiffly. "I will bring tea and cake for you directly. Mr Parry I hear that was your wish?"

"Very kind of you Mrs Spence," said Nathaniel.

All three of them knew that Martha had to chaperone the meeting. Propriety, religious duty and her unconquerable curiosity made it entirely unavoidable. Nathaniel had to buy time.

"Mrs Vere is feeling unwell and has had no lunch. Perhaps we might also have some cold meat and bread?"

Martha silently accepted the deal and withdrew.

"She will probably give us ten minutes," he smiled encouragingly as the door closed behind Martha.

"Mr Parry! Oh, Nathaniel! Raphael has hurt me in so many ways. I will never trust him again and I'm not staying! I must leave him!" She moved swiftly to the seat next to Nathaniel and seized his hands in hers. "I've known it now for over a year but I guessed it before. My God, I thought I could change him!" her voice broke to a sob: she breathed deeply and continued. "I don't know how to say this. He's not normal, he likes little girls, children. Not women. He married me when I was fourteen years old, but still looked a child. For some time he has baited me," she struggled to articulate the bitterness of her defeat, the first encountered in what had been a singularly charmed life. "He said I had lost my bloom, my freshness!" Unable to resist, she instinctively attempted to flutter her eyelids and gaze into his eyes. The effort caused her to wince in pain. It was pitiful and he felt a stab of sorrow for her, the beautiful, girlish wife, whose existence was valued only for her beauty and whose real self, whose mind and soul, counted for absolutely nothing to anyone.

She continued in a monotone, as though once started, as in a confessional, she must not stop. "He stayed out at nights, sometimes all night. I know he has been with others. Harlots. I could smell them on his clothes. Last night he came in very late and in a wild mood. He was so cruel. That is when he started to mistreat me, he hurt me, abused me." She shook her head, shivering, repulsed by the memory. "Afterwards, in his sleep he was raving, cursing. He called out, 'Babs, Babs, my lovely girl!' I woke him and asked him – who was this Babs? He was in a fury. He struck me about my face with his hand, and beat me with his belt. I will never allow him to do that again but I can't fight him. I'll run away. He was talking to our footman Tanner about business in Bristol tomorrow. Help me Nathaniel!" Tears ran in rivulets down her cheeks and her hands shook convulsively in his.

"Tilly be calm. Listen to me. I agree, you are in danger, but running away won't solve this. You need to extricate yourself more carefully and be able to live a reasonable life without him. It is possible that the law might accomplish this for you. I have been told that your husband's first wife may have died in suspicious circumstances. Keep still and listen! Furthermore, I have a suspicion that he knows more of the murder of Roderick Wilson than he has admitted. At this moment, a young man is in gaol and might suffer the ultimate penalty for that murder, which he did not commit and in which your husband might have been involved. It is vital for many people's sake that we find out the truth. Now, do you know of any reason for your husband wanting Mr Wilson dead?"

Tilly steadied her breathing, thought for a moment and then began.

"Roderick Wilson was an employee and also of late a boon companion of his. They frequented the same gambling clubs and billiard rooms. Probably brothels as well for all I know. One night at the end of last month they had been out very late and came back together to our house. They carried on drinking in Raphael's dressing room and Mr Wilson stayed the night there. When Raphael went to dress the next morning there was a furious argument. I think truly he had forgotten that Mr Wilson was there, he never usually allows anyone else to spend time there alone. Mr Wilson was baiting him over something he had seen. I know Raphael keeps things secretly in there, but usually under lock and key. Tanner supervises the maids as they clean there and the housekeeper doesn't have a key."

"I want you to try to gain access to that dressing room. See what you can find. Anything that Wilson might have seen which would give him a hold over your husband. Anything to tie him to brothels: or to young girls. I am also interested in your husband's relationship with a Bristol ship owner called Edwin Ravenswood. What exactly do you know of that man and their business dealings?"

Tilly moved closer. He tightened his grip on her hands.

"Nathaniel," she breathed. "I know a lot about Mr Ravenswood and I will search the room, but I am so frightened. Please look after me. I am not a poor woman. I think you find me attractive." She kept her good side towards him and leaned in to rest her head in his shoulder. He found their entwined hands pressed between her bosom and his chest as Tilly moved in even closer. Salvation came in the worthy shape of Martha and the tea tray, which struck the door insistently demanding entry. Nathaniel was on his feet in an instant to let her in and Tilly jumped up in confusion, turning her back on the room and studying the view from the window to explain her move from her visitor's seat. Martha bustled round arranging high backed chairs, placing the dishes and cups on the table.

"Now Mrs Vere perhaps you would like to pour whilst I bring the rest?"

Tilly abandoned the veil and set about the task.

Cold lamb and red currant jelly, bread, tea and a cake had been presented, the cake centre-stage.

"This is from a special batch, You are welcome to try it." said Martha proudly. "My son will be home soon and this is one of the plum and treacle cakes he is powerfully fond of."

They worked silently through a preliminary plate-full of meat under Martha's watchful eye. She continued, "He will sail into Bristol any day now!"

They continued to eat in the silence, smiling in encouragement for Martha to fill the void.

"He's on the *Mathilda*."

"That's my ship!" announced Tilly, suddenly animated. "Mr Ravenswood named it for me! My husband's bank has financed a number of Mr Ravenswood's voyages. His shipping company is an important customer and his vessels are an investment for the New Bank." Tilly looked meaningfully at Nathaniel.

"He sails for Mr Ravenswood then Mrs Spence?" said Nathaniel.

"I think so," said Martha. "Yes, I think he did mention that. But it is so long since he went on the voyage." Her face softened and sagged, the sharp features relaxing into a network of wrinkles, and her eyes crinkled with love. "Thank the Lord he will be back soon! At least it's not a warship, just trade you know. Just the seas to combat. No more Bonapartes just yet! God rest his soul but Boney was a hellhound!"

Nathaniel determined to see Tilly off on her way and brought the tea party to a conclusion as fast as he could. She would be unlikely to achieve much in the way of snooping until tomorrow at the earliest, the last working day of the week and with the possibility of Vere being away from Bath. Maybe she would get a chance to search the dressing room then. He ran his hands through his hair, focusing his thoughts. The chances of finding anything of use were slim. His next move would be to follow up Vere's under-age weaknesses, and there was one woman he was decidedly keen to see again who probably knew all there was to know about Bath brothels.

By late afternoon Nathaniel had positioned Caradoc on guard by the bushes surrounding the gardens in the centre of Queen Square and was in the entrance hall of Coco's building. He had barely an hour before he needed to return home to change for dinner with the Petersons and was relieved when the concierge instantly secured the services of a familiar pasty faced maid to usher him up the stairs to Coco's rooms. As he paced behind her, Nathaniel wondered idly how many clients trod this same worn blue carpet hoping to bargain for Coco's time. The condition of the stairwell deteriorated in direct proportion to its height. By the time they reached Coco's floor it was shabby, with dusty corners and chipped paint, which made the contrast with the interior of her apartment all the more startling. He was shown into a sitting room at once restrained and elegant. The Age of Reason ruled in the salon of Miss Montrechet. No clutter, no riots of stuffed birds or chintz festoons, just smooth gilded surfaces, calm pale hues, cold marble tabletops, a classical statue in one corner and a mahogany Louis XV clock on the mantelpiece. But as he looked more closely at the timepiece he laughed to see that the gilt bronze base sported the figure of a partially clad woman frolicking with two chuckling cherubs in a forest arbor. Suddenly he was aware of her, standing motionless by the window, inspecting him.

"Good afternoon Miss Montrerchet. What a beautiful room you have here."

Coco tripped lightly to him from her vantage point and

planted two chaste kisses on his cheeks.

"Welcome Nathaniel," she said, adjusting her light wool shawl, soft cream and fine as a cobweb, and steering him to take a seat by her on one of her three green and white striped sofas. "I was intrigued to see you walking over the square to see me. So purposeful, so intent! What do you want?" She smiled challengingly, coiling her arms around him and staring into his eyes. "I wondered how long it would take you to return."

Nathaniel took her hands firmly, bringing them down to her waist.

"Coco, pleased as I am to see you, and wonderful as you are looking, I am dashed short of time and I need your help with some rather specialised local information."

She widened her eyes boldly in mock amazement and pursed her lips. "Well?"

"I have spoken with Howard Dill as you suggested. He was most helpful. I now need to speak with some people on the other side of the law. Have you any idea which of the bawdy houses here deal in young girls?"

"Which don't!"

"No, I mean children. Unusual tastes?"

"I am disappointed in you Nathaniel," she said, winding her arms around him once more and whispering in his ear. "So unworldly: so hot in your pursuit of wrongdoers, so vigilant, yet so dismissive of your poor Coco."

She kissed him lingeringly, her lips soft and warm against his. He felt the flutter of her heart, breathed in her gentle scent of lavender, now overlaid with the richness of lily and rose, and took her in his arms. To resist was more than flesh and blood could realistically withstand. More than that, it would not be gallant: it would not be what Lord Byron would have done.

"You taste nice," she said, sitting back suddenly.

"So do you Coco," said Nathaniel. "but I am here on my business, not yours."

"I didn't intend to charge you," she retorted, too quickly.

“Seriously,” said Nathaniel, showing her a kindness by ignoring the weakness, “where should I look for such information?”

“I know where Vere went if that is what you are after.”

He nodded in reply.

“Then go to Green Park West, the house with the pink drapes. It’s run by a couple called Shadwell, Rosie and Joshua. But take care. Joshua doesn’t like to be questioned and he has a couple of men on duty most days. They run some of the Avon Street stews for him, dealing with the rough trade. He is no stranger to violence Nathaniel, but he only allows gentlemen to Green Park.” She laughed shortly. “Gentlemen! A contradiction in terms. You can go there if you want a girl so young she looks like a child, or if you want to be punished.” She paused and he was surprised to read uncompromising disapproval in her face.

“I’ve never worked there, of course,” she continued. “But I’ve heard the stories. You are no parochial yourself Nathaniel, you must know these things. Atrocious deeds are committed in our civilised society which all the King’s forces and all Peel’s policemen care nothing about at all. As well as the work in the houses, children disappear from the slum areas of towns and don’t even make it to the brothels. Poor parents and bad ones sell unwanted children. You must know that there is a white slave trade. They are sent abroad. Some so small they are drugged and sent out in coffins to avoid questions. Some aren’t even for sex. They are tortured to death, Nathaniel, by those who enjoy inflicting pain on the helpless. There’s a cause for you, for the government which seems to prefer to work itself into a fine frenzy about voting or preventing children earning wages in factories or the difficult lives of black slaves on the other side of the world.”

“Do you think the Shadwells or their customers are involved?”

“Why not?”

“What have you heard of Raphael Vere?”

"Nothing specific, but ask a girl called Barbara at the Shadwell's. She's been working in what they call "the nursery". Try her."

Despite his forebodings and the restrictions the event placed on his investigation at the Shadwell's, the evening at the Peterson's turned out to be a surprising and jolly one. It brought good, if puzzling news, and defused the combined effects of his interviews with Tilly and Coco, which had both been distracting in very different ways. Nathaniel had dressed with care for the evening, selecting a bright blue necktie, tying it in his favourite draped knot and matching it with his blue striped waistcoat. An evening round any family hearth was a rare experience for him, and the bonus of a conventionally happy family such as was provided Chez Peterson was rarer still. He brushed his unruly black hair back from his face and grinned broadly. He was rather looking forward to it. The barbed and querulous sessions with the Drakes at their rented rooms in Bristol had not been the same thing at all. Tonight would be for relaxing.

He wore his double-caped greatcoat to guard against the sharp west wind, but was still cold by the time he and Caradoc arrived at Marlborough Buildings. After extended periods with Tom and the Johnty in the kitchen, Nathaniel had felt the terrier might be in danger of overstaying his welcome so he had prised him from the flags by the fire and marched him up the hill and round the back of the Crescent. Again, despite his own blackest forebodings, Caradoc had an unexpectedly excellent evening. Instead of being left "on guard" in the area by the basement kitchen, he had been elevated to the dining room on the insistence of the twins, who had proceeded to fete him flatteringly and relentlessly, placing him under the dining table so he could be fed surreptitiously throughout the evening. As they had led Caradoc away, Nathaniel was delighted to be greeted not only by Captain and Mrs Peterson and Emma, but also by a beaming Anna Grant and Henry Blake.

"I cannot adequately express my relief," insisted Henry later, as they started work on their first course at Mrs Peterson's grand table overlooking the back of the property and the shadowy woods and lawns of the park. Dodging his head round an exuberant table centrepiece of silver gilt nymphs, fluted vases and nodding ferns, he had at length managed to fix Nathaniel with a look of ecstatic relief and proceeded to re-tell his tale.

"I could barely believe it when the officer came and simply said I was free to go. All charges dropped! The body of a man was found in the lower town this very morning," he paused theatrically for effect, "shot to death!" The rest of the party had heard this fact, and a recitation of its significance, a number of times before Nathaniel had arrived and the sensation, for all but Anna, had worn rather thin. She remained enraptured as he continued but the cutlery was very busy at all other place settings. "When the body was inspected bonds from the bank were discovered on his person, from the same issue as those found in my rooms! And," in preparation for this last clinching detail his eyes blazed in triumph, "around his neck on a chain was found Roderick Wilson's gold and diamond ring. Mr Wilson's name was engraved for all to see which indicated the wretch as at least a thief. Thank God the officers finally decided to believe me. As well as Anna's word, others had testified that I had been seen in St James's Square late that fateful night. My visit was far from being the secret I had planned! The dead man was recognised as a bargee, a rent collector and known scoundrel. He had been seen near my rooms in Kingsmead on a number of occasions and it has been decided that he was cunning enough to have tried to disguise his crime by implicating me. It is common knowledge that Mr Wilson and I were the only two clerks in the main office at the New Bank and were known in town."

For Nathaniel, the news was good in so far as that it released him from his duty to investigate the murder for Vere and the

Captain. Henry was free and bumptiously happy, viewing the case as closed: though of course it ought not to be. Nathaniel busied himself in playing the charming guest, congratulating Henry and the efficiency of the constables and responding when necessary to the waves of chatter emanating from the twins. They were both sure they had made a superb impression on the visitor and the exchanges had allowed the solitary Emma time to relax and observe him.

As the banter flowed inconsequentially, she managed to release partially the cruelly tight pins that secured her hair in an intricate bun at the back of her head, whilst leaving the trailing curls at the front. The construction of the extravagant hair-style had been overseen by her mama and radical change would have attracted too much attention. Her fearful anticipation of the evening had created a headache of monstrous proportions and she had been forced to hide in her room to avoid her mother for most of the day. Sadly, it had been impossible to ban her from the final stages of dressing for the evening, and Mama had made herself most tiresome. The hair-dressing, the gown, the choice of jewels and a conversation plan to ensure Emma presented herself congenially to Mr Parry had exercised her considerably. Emma had managed to keep her temper, and practised deep breathing exercises as the remorselessly excitable voice had bleated ever on, as indeed, she suddenly realised it still did.

"Your poor dear mother Anna!" exclaimed Mrs Peterson. "I warned her in my letter that you had very bad news you were preparing to convey concerning your fiancé. What torments she must have endured knowing that he was incarcerated on a murder charge! You must write to her directly to ease her mind."

Anna had been preparing herself for this, her lines were rehearsed and ready, "I decided to spare her the full details Mrs Peterson. I felt it would be too cruel. I simply informed her that there had been an unfortunate death at Henry's place of employment, which was being investigated and he was upset by it."

"Oh," sighed Mrs Peterson, disappointed.

Anna's heart banged unpleasantly, preparing her for another of Mrs Peterson's protracted eruptions, and she glanced over in mute appeal to the Captain.

"Much the best my dear," said the Captain, patting his wife's arm to discourage the voicing of extended dissatisfaction. "Very wise of you, Anna. All over now." He turned to Nathaniel, "Mr Parry, we hope that our little affair has not diverted you too much from your family and other business. I hope your visit to Bristol went well."

"It did indeed," said Nathaniel blandly. "I met my colleague, all very satisfactory."

"I have not been to Bristol for years," declared Emma suddenly. "I enjoyed it so much. So many ships, the masts like forests. So many strange cargoes, the air smelled so rich, so exotic!"

"Would you like to adventure abroad Miss Peterson?" said Nathaniel. "I must confess I feel restless if I stay in one place for too long."

"Oh Mr Parry," simpered Mrs Peterson, who felt Emma's conversational gambit had been unusually promising and provided an opening to play a particularly good, but dangerously high stakes card: hope sprang in the motherly bosom. "Do not say you will be leaving us. You hardly know the company yet and the season is just beginning. Why, a Masked Ball has been announced just this week. It will be at the Upper Rooms on Saturday the 29th. Mr Parry," Mrs Peterson, eyes a-gleam and exerting a vice-like grip on Nathaniel's arm, went for broke, "say you will be of our party!"

On the edge of a regretful refusal, Nathaniel paused, glanced at Emma and almost laughed out loud. She looked horrified, eyes wide in disbelief. Her rich chestnut hair in a glorious profusion of curls, her usual discreet gown replaced by one sweepingly low necked, in apricot satin with a richly laced falling collar, she blushed deeply. She was clearly appalled by her mother's move, but in an instant accepted it with a charming grace and managed to smile at him. He liked her bravery; it was entrancing. Emma Peterson was a very attractive, self-possessed, intelligent woman, different in so many ways from the two other women who had presented themselves to him that day: Tilly, eager for a new shoulder to lean on, another prop for her to coil her beautiful, needy body around and Coco, urgently desirable, dangerous, but her image confused by overlaid visions of the French docks lined with brothels, the worn out, diseased prostitutes lolling at the doors.

"I would be delighted to join your party Mrs Peterson," he said. "And to escort Miss Peterson to the Ball if that would be suitable. I am afraid I must return to London this weekend, but will return after I conclude my business."

Mrs Peterson, almost bursting with delight, had to restrain herself from embracing him and wondered how long it might be before she could bring the newly launched affair to a proper matrimonial conclusion. "We will have the tickets ready and meet you at the Rooms at six on the evening of the 29th! A date to remember! We will be six in our party. Six at six that evening."

"Yes, my dear," said the Captain, hastily. "If it is convenient for you, Mr Parry, we would all be pleased to entertain you. The least we can do. So kind of you to help with our little problems."

The evening continued to pass off well as they worked their way through the fish, meats and desserts. Emma drank more wine than usual and was talkative, feeling that the arrangement for the ball, though grotesquely humiliating at the time, gave her permission to speak to him. It could be seen as a social duty. Anna and Henry were engrossed in each other and the Petersons encouraged the twins to perform on the piano and sing after the meal, loudly commending them and providing cover for her to dally very pleasantly with Nathaniel. They talked of travel and adventure, of London, of sickness and health, of poetry. They warmed to each other as they swopped verses from Keats and clapped enthusiastically as each song ended, encouraging more. They sparred in whispers, duelling with verses from *The Eve of St Agnes*. Emma lost, blushing furiously she pretended she had forgotten the lines, as she was next when the story reached the place where Porphyro stole into Madeline's room. It was too much in mixed company, even if the others were pretending not to hear. She would never have started without the wine.

Finally, as the twins were hoarse they were relieved of their duties, which prompted Anna to make a move to leave. Henry was to escort her to her employer's in St James's Square and the party broke up. Nathaniel took his leave formally, bowing over the ladies' hands, expressing thanks and was out through the door and on the front step in the cold night when the Captain stepped out after him.

"Satisfied with the Wilson business?"

"No sir. I will continue to gather intelligence. In particular I would like to know more of Mr Raphael Vere. I know you are of his circle in Bath and gather you have considerable investments in his bank."

"I have, and am poised to pump more into it. His ventures have been pleasantly remunerative I must say. What's your caveat sir?"

"I think he is under severe strain at present and I would like to know the cause of it. I'll let you know as soon as I make progress."

Caradoc sidled up and Nathaniel held out his hand to his host. "Thank you Captain for a really enjoyable evening. I will return to Bath towards the end of the month."

"In time for the Masked Ball!" said the Captain, raising a bristly eyebrow. "I'd regard it as a personal kindness if you would."

"I intend to."

Emma watched from her window to see Nathaniel and Caradoc walk up Marlborough Buildings to the Royal Crescent, she watched them pause to look at the lights in the vale and saw

Caradoc rush yapping at the shadows thrown by the trees. She watched as they pushed on, round the curve of the buildings and out of sight. She held the curtains tightly, blessing and cursing her mother, hardly daring to believe the possibilities offered to her, on a plate, by that foolish, intolerable woman.

The following evening Nathaniel made very different preparations for his excursion into Bath. He took from his trunk a small bag of mixed coins: shillings, half-crowns and sovereigns, and a frock coat he had not yet worn in the city, a bulky one which did away with need for a greatcoat or his cloak. He tried it on, checking the buttons, all there. It was important, as this was a reversible coat, brown on one side, green on the other, and it would spoil the illusion if it flapped open and displayed the colour hidden within. He had poachers' pockets in the skirts, ready primed with a collapsible top-hat, flatter close-fitting cap, spectacles and white muffler. With the judicious addition of a limp, enough in the way of a disguise for one man to swagger from the upper-town, cut down an alley and emerge for the trek to Green Park as someone different. The makila was selected as a walking stick in preference to the swordstick and Caradoc was relegated to the garden, though Tom, who had been shaping-up as Caradoc's sworn friend and ally by late afternoon, would no doubt order Martha to let him into the kitchen as soon as she returned from her Methodist meeting. Tom and Caradoc had had a tiff earlier, a matter concerning an attack on Tom's knitting, but all now seemed forgiven.

Nathaniel marched off jauntily down Walcot, sporting the top-hat and swinging his makila, practising a few sweeps, adjusting his grip as he went. The street was subdued, with just the odd carter completing his rounds. A ragged boy stood forlornly by the opposite gutter.

"Sweep you a crossin' sir?"

But Nathaniel's way was to the west and he shook his head. He made good time, passing the Saw Close and pushing on to

Kingsmead, the frontier of the lower town. By this stage of his walk the noises of the night had risen to a cacophony around him. Ale houses and inns, garish with gaslight, were rammed with raucous customers, the streets were busy with people dodging the fly carriages which trotted their passengers along the cobbles, rattling and swaying as they picked up speed on the straight. A few sedan chairmen padded like silent ghosts on the pavements in the shadow of the buildings. He side-stepped them and slid into a dingy, deserted alley, safe from the eyes of the street and effected his disguise in seconds. He took off the hat, collapsed it and swapped it for the cap, reversed the coat and donned the conspicuous white muffler and spectacles. He checked that he was unobserved and sidled out, crossing the top of Avon Street. Here the crowds spilling from the assorted drinking dens blocked the pavements and the stench of the slums wreathed around him like a poison gas, gagging in his throat. Lives were lived more on the street in proportion to the unpleasantness of the dwellings, and from here to the river were some of the worst the city could offer. The debris underfoot had become thicker and more noxious, the black mud now glutinous and sucking at his boots. The roaming dogs were more numerous, sharing the detritus with foraging chickens and a rooting, grunting pig, obscenely daubed in filth, a bizarre remnant of rural life, clinging on in the city like an obese ghost of the past. Nathaniel's tapping makila had helped clear the way thus far, but the thickening crowd and its increased volatility had made it unwise to continue flourishing it. Suddenly, to his left, a door flew open and a boisterous knot of drinkers over-spilled from a tavern, shouting wild encouragement to two women who had clearly been fighting for some time and had attracted such partisan support that the landlord had ejected the lot of them.

A blowsy harridan, hair descending in lank rods from a misshapen bun, mouth wide and snarling obscenities was shaping up afresh to her assailant, a handy looking young woman with a rapidly blackening eye and greasy torn bodice.

"Go on moiy love!" bawled a man, jostling others back to allow his pugilist of choice more space. "Land 'er another right 'ook!"

The fat woman obligingly swung her ham of a fist, but as if in slow motion. The handy woman, less drunk and bulky, moved in to block the blow with her left and delivered a powerful punch to the protruding stomach, an open and vast target. Her fist sank in momentarily, but she was clearly experienced and pulled back smartly to miss both the toppling upper body and fountain of vomit which preceded it to the roaring acclamation of the crowd. Nathaniel also dodged, as the back row of spectators billowed towards him. He slowed his gait as he did so and concentrated on developing a pronounced limp, leaning heavily on the makila.

The elegant terrace of Green Park West soon came into view, rearing up out of the dark before the shaved and tree fringed lawn which lay before it across its private road: so close to the river slums, yet it could be miles and worlds away. A patrolling constable nodded to Nathaniel as he made his way to the Shadwell's door. It was more elegant that he had imagined, the drapes Coco had mentioned were a pale dusky pink and grey striped. The house appeared seemly, muted, well appointed, with immaculately clean steps and neat boot scrapers on guard against defilement at each side of the door. He pulled the bell and was ushered into the hall by a comely woman in a green gown, with flaming red lips and stone cold eyes.

"Welcome sir. How may I help you?"

"Thank you Madam. I am visiting your house on a recommendation," he had decided on a recklessly mendacious ploy, as he never intended to darken the doors again. "Mr Raphael Vere suggested I come here for entertainment this evening as I am a visitor to Bath and enjoy exactly the same type of recreations as he does himself. I would particularly like to meet Barbara of whom he speaks so highly. Is that possible Mrs Shadwell? You are Madam Shadwell I presume?"

She took his coat, muffler and cap silently. His makila he retained, still leaning on it and listing to the right as he walked.

"I'm afraid that is impossible sir. And your name is?"

"Mr Jack Drake."

"Well, Mr Drake, Barbara is not available at present. However, Abigail will be delighted to meet you. I assume you know our arrangements here?"

"In terms of?"

"In terms of remuneration, Mr Drake."

"Oh certainly," he lied confidently and well.

After being led upstairs to a salon and plied with drinks and conversation by a bevy of assorted whores, which he rightly guessed was a ruse to increase his bill, he was at length taken to the attic nursery by the girl introducing herself as Abigail. The girl looked about fourteen but was clad in a child's dress with a short skirt falling only to mid-calf. When they reached the nursery she sat him in a chair and placed herself on his lap.

"What would like your little girl to do?" she simpered, head to one side like an inquisitive robin: a practised gesture, arch, pert, and to Nathaniel, surprisingly repellent.

"Abigail, I don't want your usual services. Sit on the bed and listen."

Eyes wide with alarm, but keeping her face compliant, she sat opposite him, hands clenched to small, bony fists.

"I need to speak to Barbara. Babs. Can you manage to bring her in here to speak to me?"

"She's ill sir."

"This is extremely important Abigail." He took the bag of coins from his pocket, judged her price, the time available, Madam Shadwell's obvious suspicions, and knew he had the smallest window of opportunity. He could not afford to offend her sense of worth, so he offered a sovereign.

"Bloody 'ell! Is that for me just for bringing Babs in?"

"Yes. And before you do, tell me how customers pay Madam Shadwell."

"You never been to a knockin' shop mister?" said Abigail, pityingly. "Regulars have a drink with Madam every month or so and settle up. Some gentlemen give us extra for ourselves, but we're not meant to keep it. New customers have to pay on the nail."

"How much is usual for you?"

She eyed him suspiciously but, swayed by his unusual good-looks, blurted out the truth before she had chance to think of anything cleverer. "Depends what we do. For half an hour, just basic, ten shillings." She looked at him hard. "Seein' as you're not a regular, do you understand that if you tell on me to Madam I'll get flayed?"

"Of course I do. Now will you help?"

Abigail paused, her eyes darting as she weighed up the odds. Then she blinked, took the sovereign and left, he heard her walk along the corridor and knock at a door. She returned with a smaller girl who had a swollen face, healing scabs and two purpley-black eyes.

"Sit down Babs," said Nathaniel, motioning to the bed. "Let me guess Raphael Vere visited and left you like this. I've seen other examples of his work."

Babs looked to Abigail briefly for support. "Abi said you know not to breathe a word of what I say outside o' these walls? And you're payin'? Yeah? Right then: it was 'im."

"Babs. Here's a sovereign for you. There's another if you help. What do you remember of Vere's last visit?"

"It was two nights ago. He was wild. Never seen him so afore" Her voice faltered, her accent broadening as she stifled tears. "That night I 'ad to stay alone in my room after 'e went. I've not earned since. Any'ow, I 'eard voices when 'e left, from down the garden, in Mr Shadwell's office. The coach house. And I 'eard a big bang, it was a gunshot sir. Just one, then nothin'. But I looked through the window later and I seen the men carrying out a burden. I'm guessin' it was whoever got shot."

"Do either of you know anything about girls, children,

disappearing, being taken for trade?"

"Not regulars 'ere," offered Abigail. "But you must know it 'appens. Sometimes girls come and stay a night then go off, don't they Babs? Suppose you don't want to ask Mr Shadwell?" She giggled, high pitched and nervous. Even in jest, the thought of questioning Joshua Shadwell made her flesh creep.

As she was speaking Nathaniel had stood up and moved to the window. There were lights in the coach house and he saw Madam Shadwell by the door, starting to make her way back to the house accompanied by two men.

"My time's run out," said Nathaniel tersely. He adjusted the unfamiliar spectacles on his nose and fished out two more coins. "For you girls. Good luck. Now hide them. Babs get back to your room. Abi, to save you from unpleasant questions about what we were doing get me two belts, or sashes, whatever you have. I need to tie you up. Quickly! Tell Madam I over-powered you and made off."

Barbara crept back along the landing and Abigail took two sashes from the drawer. He gagged her swiftly with one and tied her hands to the bedstead with the other.

"Wait 'til you hear the front door close after me then start a disturbance."

He left the nursery door wide open and descended the stairs, just in time to meet Madam Shadwell who was entering the passage from the garden door.

"First rate Madam," he said, pressing a sovereign into her hand. "Must fly. I hope to return very soon."

Immune to the threat in her icy smile, he took his belongings and limped out into the night.

The two henchmen had some pursuit skills, but it was obvious to Nathaniel by the time he reached the end of Green Park that they were on his tail. He decided against the busy route back *via* Kingsmead and deliberately turned towards the quayside. It was likely to be quieter, with fewer partisans to enjoy whatever might be required to rid him of the unwanted attention. He also preferred more space. He slowed down, allowing the two sets of steps to gain on him. They neared, then separated, one to his left, one to his right. He was approaching Broad Quay, close to where Wilson had met his death. There were workshops, alleys, plenty of space to manoeuvre and few people. He turned suddenly.

"Can I help you? You seem eager to catch me up."

They closed in: both powerfully built, though not as tall as Nathaniel, one bull-necked, slow moving, the other quicker, sharp-faced, more of a weasel, the smell of the street on them both. He caught the glimmer of knuckle-dusters in place on their hands to loosen his tongue.

"You didn't pay all yer dues mister. You owe a little in the way of explanation," said the bull-neck on his right, stepping towards him as he spoke. "Callers at Madam's usually come with their sponsors for a first visit. Seems strange don't it, you being alone? Madam doesn't like too much "talkin'" at the house," he leered unpleasantly, enjoying his wit. "Prefers we "talk" elsewhere."

"There is nothing to talk about," replied Nathaniel smoothly. "Mr Vere isn't available to accompany me this evening. Surely his name alone was sufficient introduction!"

As Nathaniel spoke the silent weasel on the left moved in sharply, aiming a right punch at Nathaniel's head. The bulging spiked metal covering his knuckles just nicked Nathaniel's cheek as he stepped back, swinging the makila upwards to deliver a double-handed blow to the man's head, flooring him, insensible, in a second. Simultaneously, bull-neck to the right launched an attack of his own. The makila swung round, again double-handed, delivering a bone-numbing strike to the punching arm. Nathaniel leaned in to bring the heel of the stick down into bull-neck's face. The nose split with a sickening crunch and gushed a fountain of blood as he staggered backwards as if drunk, howling in pain and pawing at his injured face. As he slammed backwards against a workshop door, Nathaniel sprang forward, drew the bladed handle with his right hand, shot up his left elbow below bull-neck's chin and pinioned him. He plunged the deadly makila into the man's exposed belly and bull-neck froze, nose still gushing and eyes pouring. Nathaniel held the blade an agonising quarter-inch into the flesh.

"You want to live?" he demanded, his voice low and menacing. Bull-neck's head nodded, loose like a puppet's. "Keep very, very, still and answer me. Do you know Raphael Vere?"

The man paused, gathering breath, the blade burning in his belly, blood coursing from the face wounds into his mouth. He spat feebly.

"Yes, he's a customer," he gasped. "Seen him often. Owns a bank. Meets with Mr Shadwell in the office. That's all. Take out the blade for Christ's sake."

"I want to know about a dead man with scars on his face, newly marked."

"Mordecai," he said faintly, holding himself rigid. But the swimming eyes in his ravaged face were fighting still, struggling to focus on his assailant, struggling to memorise every feature. He comforted himself, retribution would follow as night followed day. "Works for Mr Shadwell. That's all you bastard. Take it out!"

"That's all I need," said Nathaniel. "Glad to have met you. I didn't want you and your friend skulking behind me all night like two lost dogs."

With that, he pulled out the reddened blade, leaving bull-neck to collapse shuddering and whimpering to the ground. Nathaniel wiped the blade clean on a pocket handkerchief, carefully, unhurriedly, and slid it back into the stick as he slowly backed away. He was pleased to see the weasel now twitching and groaning, to have killed him would have been excessive. At Little Corn Street he turned and disappeared into the shadows, peeling off his muffler, spectacles and cap, stuffing them into his pockets as he went. Glancing behind, he assured himself they were not following, and padded along silently towards the upper-town, weaving round the drunks, the whores, the dogs, the baying cliques of men and lone tramps. As the tide of low life receded and began to be replaced by respectable pedestrians, he became more aware of his ghoulish appearance. He decided on an impulse to make his way to Queen Square. Blood streaked his hands and sleeves and he could feel that the cut on his cheek had opened further. He would need more than an alleyway to render him fit to return to his rooms and, reviewing the possibilities for a port in this particular type of storm, only one name sprang to mind.

Within fifteen minutes he was standing by Coco's building. Lights shone from her room so he flung a stone at the window. She pushed up the sash, ducked her head under it and smiled as she recognised him.

"You don't need to attack my property to get my attention!"

"Coco, if you are alone can I come in?" he called urgently. "I have had a spot of bother and need to clean up." He turned up his face in the halo of gaslight so she could inspect him. "Most of this isn't mine."

She looked down at him appraisingly. "One minute," she said, flitting back into the room and returning with a key. "Catch! And don't make a row on the stairs. I have my reputation to consider."

Chapter 6

Early evening: 14th October, 1831, on the Bath Road.

Joshua Shadwell regretted that he was becoming familiar with the high road between Bath and Bristol. The last five years had seen his visits to Bristol increase in frequency as his business connections with Ravenswood's mercantile empire had grown. Familiarity had not in this case bred contempt, but something far more unpleasant, an unsettling, corrosive fear. It was not wise to be too close to Edwin Ravenswood.

Joshua shifted uneasily in his seat at the unwelcome memory of Ravenswood's displeasure, but was shaken out of his morbid thoughts as the coach swerved sharply into Keynsham high street. He braced himself briefly against the violent lurch, then relaxed and stared morosely at the other passengers occupying inside seats. A drawn, exhausted couple faced him: she with a sleeping child on her lap, both red faced and chill-blained, raw fingers swollen and noses pinched; he, sallow and haunted, his frock coat shiny and eaten by last summer's moths. A sharp stench of urine wafted from the swaddlings of the child as they rattled over a stretch of cobbles, adding to the stink of old clothes and unwashed bodies. Joshua, who was surprisingly fastidious for a man in his profession, shot them a venomous glare and looked away, glancing instead to his right to weigh-up a rich businessman whose well-fed bulk jostled him on every bend. Joshua inhaled the welcome scent of cologne water. The man was olive skinned, the fabric of his coat lustrous and unusual: a foreigner. The port of Bristol brought in many strangers and Bath's spa drew them inland. What else might he be? Card sharp; quack; prospective customer? Joshua's thin lips drew back in a leering smile, alarming the sad mother opposite who had caught his eye and immediately thought better of it, hurriedly busying herself with the child.

The call to visit Ravenswood's residence in Redcliffe had been peremptory and, in view of the events of the previous night, had caused even his hard heart to thump unpleasantly in his chest. The Ravenswood coach had swept up to Green Park Buildings and out had jumped two of Ravenswood's footmen, bold as you please, carrying barely concealed weapons. They had demanded to see him, and Rosie, like a raw girl, had shown them to the office. He had been marched to the coach and driven off, but had not, he noted for the hundredth time, been driven home as readily! He cursed Ravenswood as the coach lurched on a Saltford bend. Shifting for myself once the great man has done with me! He seethed inwardly, his mouth clamped in suppressed fury: then he relaxed, reflected. It could have been very much worse. The idiot Declan had run like a hare after Mordecai was shot, and by noon yesterday was on board the *Blue Dragon*, spilling his guts to Eli Trevellis. Joshua glowered at the thought of how badly it might have gone. By late afternoon he had been climbing the steps to Ravenswood's elegant town house in Redcliffe Parade to offer his explanations.

The house was used as a residence, an office, store and vantage point, as all the life of the wharf could be seen spread out below. The parade ran along the top of the red sandstone cliff, which was itself honeycombed with caves, passages and store-rooms, a number of which could be entered from Ravenswood's basement. At the foot of the cliff was one of the many moorings which stretched down the Floating Harbour from

Redcliffe to Baltic Wharf by the Cumberland Basin. They were all forested with naked masts, swaying lazily, the vessels pulling on their ropes with the gentle swell of passing boats. Drying sails billowed out like clouds above the crowded dock-side with its teeming anthills of men labouring on the ships: repairing, painting, loading. Bales, sacks, drums and packages of every conceivable size and shape waited to be trundled in barrows over the undulating gangplanks and stacked in the bowels of the vessels where they waited to be blown over the seven seas. The smells of the trade goods, the pitch and the brine beckoned to him, overpowering the filth of the city. Men shouted, some sang in a demented chorus with the caged birds on the foredecks. Joshua, as usual, had been intoxicated by the scene, but on this occasion could not enjoy it. He had waited, hanging on the bell pull, a cold sweat breaking out on his back, prickling like a rash.

He had been shown to Ravenswood's headquarters on the first floor, his office *cum* dining room occupying what had been the drawing room of the grand house. The walls were lined with bookcases housing immaculately bound records of transactions, reference books and map collections. The long dining table for meetings and meals occupied the centre of the room and resting against one wall was an elegant bureau, unusually, a volume lay open upon it. Ravenswood's desk faced the window to allow him a view of his ships, the wharf and shipyards and, across the river, the tangled buildings of the Grove, backing onto the elegant Queen Square mansions. Papers rested on the tooled brown leather desk top, set out in severe piles, each sheet meticulously initialled with the master's characteristic flourish. A gold and jewelled paper knife winked cruelly by his right hand. Joshua winced at the memory of the start of the interview. He had been motioned to stand by the desk, a bad sign. Declan had been hauled in to repeat his sorry tale, which he had done, eyes glazed and staring straight ahead, well schooled. But the messenger was not unscathed, the swollen mouth crusting into fresh scabs and blackening eye sockets showed that the first telling of his story had not been a comfortable one.

"So you see," Ravenswood had smiled, eyes ice-cold, as he sat motionless, a predator preparing to strike. "We seem to have a problem, Mr Shadwell. Your employees, who also work indirectly for me, have been sub-contracting their labours profligately. Via your mediation they attempted to perform as assassins on behalf of a certain banker, subsequently broke into locked premises and planted evidence hoping to secure the execution of an innocent clerk. In an unseemly scuffle on Wednesday night, at your premises, this man's accomplice was shot during a brawl with the said banker. This man is now afraid for his life and through the offices of Captain Trevellis has sought my protection." Edwin Ravenswood rested the fingers of both hands on his desk. Joshua noticed with surprise and alarm, that his knuckles were raw.

"Sir," he paused, steadying his breathing. Never in his life had he been so glad to have not just one ace up his sleeve, but what he hoped was a royal flush. "Declan here has nothing to worry about." He tried a reassuring smile in Declan's direction. "If he had stayed long enough he would have been able to help set all to rights. Him and Mordecai have worked for me for years, as well as running the barge they took in rents for me when my men were busy. Generally made themselves useful. Trouble only started when Mr Vere had a personal problem." Joshua felt he had boxed very clever indeed at this point. Any undue indiscretion about Ravenswood's business in front of Declan could have been fatal. "A senior clerk at the bank by the name of Wilson was blackmailing him and tightening the squeeze. I knew you were a customer at Mr Vere's bank sir, so I wanted to smooth his way." Joshua gambled on the fact that Ravenswood did not trouble himself to inspect the details of other New Bank accounts and was ignorant of his growing debts and mortgages, underwritten by Vere. "Mr Vere was rattled sir. His tastes at my house were expensive and, unusual. Also, he was losing more at the gambling and when he was deep in his cups he talked freely about his business. Maybe there was more. Wilson spooked him and he took fright. Wednesday night, after beating my youngest girl cruelly I might add, he came to the office and Declan and Mordecai showed up," he flickered another reassuring glance to Declan. "He set about Mordecai and a pistol discharged."

Allowing the half-truth to settle, he looked at Declan directly, consciously slowing his words, allowing time for them to sink in.

"Then, Declan, for your information, my men dumped Mordecai where the watchmen would pick him up smartly. We searched him, destroyed the papers you two had taken from Wilson's and left a wad of bonds on him to match them hidden at the young clerk's place. I'd kept a few back, for insurance so to speak. Then, when the boys moved him, what should we find! Wilson's ring on a string round his greasy neck! Diamond set and engraved with him and his missus' names clear as day. Keepin' it like a damned sailor's ear-ring for his funeral mebbe! So, that should tie him fair and square for the murder and it'll take the boil off any connection between Mr Vere and your good self, or to me. Mordecai's been taking rents for me in Kingsmead Street for over a twelve month, and what with his face wound from the night with Wilson, he's been easily recognised. Word is he's squarely blamed for planting the bank bonds at the young clerk's."

Ravenswood remained impassive. "Mr Shadwell, Declan here fears Mr Raphael Vere. I am personally disappointed with the performance of our banker friend and am not sorry to inform you that his work in Bath is over. He will be calling to see me later today and will be transferring his attentions to a new business opportunity." He fixed the tormented Declan with a stony stare. "Declan, look at me." The woebegone face turned. "Mr Vere will not be returning to Bath, or indeed to Bristol. Do you understand?" The battered head nodded as Ravenswood turned to Joshua. "Declan will continue to run his barge, he will serve me also in Bristol. He will not undertake any further activities for you, so pay him off. I gather he fled before he was paid. I am gratified to learn that you have been able to neutralise the unnecessary publicity Vere's activities have attracted." Josuah bowed briefly, without lowering his eyes and reluctantly gave Declan two sovereigns. "Declan, go down to the *Blue Dragon*. Report to Captain Trevellis." Ravenswood motioned to Joshua to sit opposite him and poured them both a generous measure of rum as Declan blundered down the stairs, two at a time.

"Now, what more do you have to tell me?" The silence grew as Joshua took a gulp at his drink, mechanically reworking his story, looking for any weak link which needed a bulwark. Ravenswood noted the pause, and continued. "Vere was a loose cannon which had grown increasingly wayward over the last few months. I sent a new operative of mine to Bath over the last few weeks to investigate Vere's gambling and drinking habits which, as you know, had developed to the point of indiscretion. I did not like what I heard, Joshua. I hope you have no hidden habits of which I might disapprove."

"No sir, I have not. And I am glad to hear it was your man prowling round Vere. Some of my informants, the Broad Quay boys, let slip there's a man asking questions. He's made a regular pet of one of the potboys at the Hart."

Ravenswood looked puzzled. "I doubt my man has done so. Is the interrogator they spoke of a foreigner?

"Not as such. Got a Welsh name though. Parry."

Ravenswood's black brows lifted momentarily. "Keep a weather eye on Mr Parry, Joshua. Government man. I will deal with him if necessary, but we have other matters to occupy us today. Who was Vere buying time with at your house?

"Barbara sir. Nursery."

"No loose ends Mr Shadwell. Send her here on the barge. She can go with the next consignment. We'll likely lose one or two before they make the east, she can be, as it were, reserve stock. You must have realised we have held off sailing."

Ravenswood rose and walked to the window to look down on the *Blue Dragon* idling at the wharf. "There's a problem with the victualling. Bloody peasants firing haystacks and fields." His mouth worked in suppressed fury, setting in a harsh line, though his voice was deadly calm. "Melbourne has arrested perpetrators pretty freely but he's weak on sentencing. I would have had their limbs off." He sank briefly into a reverie before continuing. "The Normans had a way with revolts. Are you a historian Mr Shadwell? Are you familiar with our medieval predecessors?" He turned back to Joshua, his face animated at the thought of retribution. "Their methods were similar to those of the tribes of the Middle East. Death itself is too easy. A deterrent is required, to deter others from sin and encourage them to tread the paths of righteousness." The light died in his eyes. "Send the girl to me. Vere will not be telling any tales and neither will she. As for you and your pitiful employee, I will not tolerate any future weakness or failure."

They had been interrupted, much to Joshua's relief, by sounds from the hall. Visitors were being shown up to the office by the maid and the door opened to reveal two figures. Joshua sprung to his feet and made hurried moves to leave. It was some time since he had been in the presence of danger so palpable, and his throat dried in fear. The shorter man, an Asiatic, squarely built with little in the way of a neck and huge hands, radiated evil. His demeanour was coldly hostile, his reptilian eyes darted over Josiah as if sizing him up for the kill, his tongue flickered over his lips. For reassurance Joshua moved to touch his pistol butt through his coat, but froze in the act as the man's eyes tracked his every move, crinkling in silent, derisive glee. The other was also from the east, but looked to be more from the south, more typically Chinese with sleek black hair brushed back from his ivory brow. He looked powerful, vigilant.

Ravenswood was speaking, so Joshua strove to smile. "Mr Kizhe, Mr Lee, may I introduce Mr Joshua Shadwell, he serves our business in Bath, the famous city spa. Mr Lee I know you have spent a few evenings there recently in pursuit of the errant banker Mr Raphael Vere. His career will be curtailed tomorrow. You will wait for him on the *Dragon*, where he will be arriving for a meeting with me very shortly."

Joshua pushed the stiff curtain aside to peer into the dark through the stage-coach window. He was relieved to see that they were passing the Weston toll house. He sighed. Never had he been so pleased to leave Ravenswood's office, though God knows he was never keen to loiter. He almost felt sorry for Vere, but not quite. As he had moved to quit the office, Ravenswood was offering to show the two visitors the under-cliff store rooms. Again, an unfamiliar twinge of pity. As the *Blue Dragon* was not yet ready to sail, the captive girls would still be incarcerated below ground. The infants wouldn't last long after they reached their destination, if they made it that far, but the two others might. And Barbara: she wasn't a bad girl. The men would have to see her off, he hadn't the stomach for it. He dropped the curtain, extinguishing the view, though he continued to gaze, unseeing, as they entered the town.

That same night Arno's Tower was ablaze with light. The Ravenswoods were entertaining, and, as usual, pleasure was intimately bound with business, the mansion stage-set to enthral and overawe. A chain of flambeaux lit the drive, flaring into the night, and culminating in two vast cauldrons of fire on either side of the great doors. The lights caught the stone grotesques, making them leap to life in relief against the inky-black darkness, and as John and Lottie Drake approached in their hired coach, they purposefully avoided catching each other's eye. Both were determined to outdo the other in delight in their new found friends, neither could let themselves admit that the overall effect was alarming rather than welcoming, neither acknowledged the sulphurous whiff of the Inferno. Once inside the formalities proceeded more conventionally and they relaxed, basking in the excessive show of hospitality. Preliminary drinks and tidbits were enjoyed in a salon of hedonistic baroque rather than gothic splendour, though there was a fire crackling fiercely in a cavernous fireplace, relentlessly stoked by one of Ravenswood's legion of servants. Inconsequential conversation drifted harmlessly between them.

Edwin Ravenswood looked breathtakingly handsome to Lottie: so tall, so darkly attractive, especially when compared with her vulpine husband who seemed diminished by Edwin's presence. John's eyes did not light on his wife's to catch the unspoken criticism, but were busy gleaming in delight and envy, swivelling from crystal chandeliers to luscious silk upholstery, and again to towering oils of ancestors perched on benches in pastoral Gainsborough poses beneath leafy trees. Though not Gainsboroughs, and not ancestors, at least not Ravenswoods, thought Lottie shrewdly. Not that she cared over-much, she just hoped John could manage to stop short of obvious sycophancy. He was the government man after all. It was Ravenswood's job to do the wooing. And she would most definitely like to be wooed. She turned to respond to Amanda Ravenswood's unusually polite question about Lizzie. Amanda had no interest of any kind in children, and was playing the chatelaine to perfection, reining in her acid tongue, layering graciousness over her characteristic viciousness. Lottie was amused. Her frequent meetings with Amanda were the high points of the week. They dawdled over tea on at least two mornings and one afternoon, sharpening their conversational talons, shredding the reputations of the rest of Bristol's *bon ton*. How delicious that Amanda was afraid of her husband!

The dinner was served in a magnificent dining hall. The flunkeys were immaculate, a liveried footman behind each place, and the food sublime. However, the jollity so carefully constructed and launched was lost, abruptly shipwrecked, as they were joined by two foreign gentlemen. Lottie sensed the menace in the air and found it thrilling. The older character was a thick-set man reminding her of a sketch she had once seen of an Esquimaux tribesman butchering a whale, his face battered and bitten by the Arctic wind, transfixed by his purpose. The guest, however, was free from furs, scrupulously turned out in evening dress and with the air of a patrician: a tyrannical one. Edwin's manner towards him was careful, studied, at one point almost deferential. She was fascinated. The younger one was clearly subordinate, though held in some respect by the other men. He was attractive and elegantly muscular, but he took no trouble to flirt with her, or even to observe the niceties of polite conversation. Preliminary overtures to Edwin and the older man, a Mr Kizhe, conjured up the expected responses: interest, flattery, encouragement, and gentle sparring, as gentlemen's ripostes should be. The younger one would take considerably more work, which she looked forward to. She consoled herself by observing John, who was acquitting himself surprisingly well with Amanda, offering conversational gambits, admiring the house and the table without misplaced gush. Her observations were interrupted far too soon for her liking as Amanda rose from her chair in response to a piercing glance from her husband. They were obliged to quit the table and withdraw to leave the men to their cigars and spirits. Their skirts whispered, coldly sibilant along the stone floor of the colonnaded landing as they made their way to the drawing room. A triumphant smile played around Lottie's lips as she selected her next barb. "Do tell me more of your experiences in Paris my dear," she said to her friend's retreating back. Amanda was very proud of her time in France, but was furiously disappointed that she had been unable to break into the highest society. "I so loved the evenings John and I spent at Versailles."

As soon as the door was closed behind the ladies, the gentlemen were settled to their port and smokes and then the servants were dismissed, Edwin Ravenswood moved swiftly to business.

"Mr Drake as we have discussed earlier, I am deeply flattered that His Majesty's government has seen fit to honour my company by showing interest in my Far Eastern trade. My vessel, the *Mathilda,* is due to dock within days and the news from her last port is very good. The opium realised 20% more than our maximum forecast. Demand continues to grow in the coastal Chinese cities and our contacts amongst the, shall we say, "privateers" of the China Seas have enabled us to continue using our secure harbours for the foreseeable future. I know how important it is for Britain that this trade continues to flourish. A necessary support of the business is our additional freight, marketed through Mr Kizhe's contacts. We have discussed this briefly, have we not Mr Drake? The additional income raised is not just substantial, but prodigious."

He dwelt on that last word, savoured it and allowed it to rest in the silence that followed, allowing Drake in his greed to swallow it whole. Ravenswood next inclined his head to Kizhe, who acknowledged it with a nod, allowing only his gash of a mouth to offer the faintest ghost of a smile before he replied.

"My employer has been extremely pleased with the females and your service record, though the recent unwelcome delay in sailing will have to be made good during the voyage. Our customers do not like to wait, Mr Ravenswood. I will accompany the *Blue Dragon* on its outward trip at least as far as India, where I have other business." He lifted his massive hand, a meaty bear's paw, and drew deeply on his cigar, breathing out slowly to wreathe himself in aromatic smoke.

"Mr Drake," he said slowly, turning to him, eyes narrowed in scrutiny. "My compliments to your government. I also am gratified to know that our mutual affairs are so strongly supported by the mighty British Empire. Mr Ravenswood tells me that you will convey good news of our opium trade to the noble lords of Whitehall. He also tells me that you will accept our humble thanks, awarded annually I understand, for your continued support?"

John Drake's jaw tightened and he clasped his hands hard to prevent his fingers straying to his neck wound. Lottie had warned him about that, he had never realised before just how often he did it.

"Thank you sir. I am delighted to accept. As you know your opium trade is vital to our Chinese interests and anything we can do to further your successes will be our pleasure."

Even as he spoke the words seemed to stick in his throat. "Anything we can do?" How could he say that? He fixed a rictus smile, and fought to rid his mind of a grinning image of Dr Faustus, selling his soul to the devil, as Kizhe in the role of Mephistopheles was nodding his acceptance and the deal was done. Palmerston would be jovially delighted to hear of the opium runs, the safe havens, the piratical support, and would no doubt be pleased to lend the guns and sabres of the Royal Navy if they ran into serious trouble with the Chinese. Lord Cupid might even understand the trade in prostitutes. But that was not all it was. He felt a stab of pain in his heart as he thought of his Lizzie and the privileged, carefree infants he saw on his walks, dancing over the Downs and clucked after by their nurses. The "additional freight" was human, and to his horror it had become clear that there was no lower age limit for the trade. He had worked with enough perverts in the service to have a clear idea of the range of tastes that unlimited money could cater for. Over a few long alcoholic nights, Ravenswood had drawn him into the web. Yes, he wanted money. Yes, he was furnished with the necessary good news to convey to the Foreign Office and his star would rise. The price had to be paid and the cost would be borne by his savaged conscience.

Drake relaxed his tight smile and reached for his port. "Just one other matter gentlemen. As I have already discussed with Mr Ravenswood, the Office has sent out another gentleman to work with me, a Mr Nathaniel Parry. He is based in Bath with instructions to report on radical agitation, but he has family and contacts there which have developed his interest in Bristol affairs. I have to go to London tomorrow as we both have a meeting in Whitehall next week. Needless to say, I will work to reduce this interest and suggest you reject any advances he might make or any of his attempts to investigate. Let's say he is not amenable to negotiation. His father served before him and he has archaic notions of duty." Drake raised a conspiratorial eyebrow, acknowledged by Ravenswood and Kizhe. Cornelius, silent thus far, appeared to remain implacable, but for the first time that day his inner eye sensed a break in the clouds.

Until Drake's venomous little show, the day had been uniformly depressing for Cornelius Lee and as the table conversation had drifted to a consideration of Ravenswood's extensive wine cellar, he permitted himself a mental review of it. The day had first suffered during extended sessions with Kizhe, checking and re-checking the details of the outward journey to China, and reached its lowest point when he had been obliged to view the clutch of wretched prisoners in Ravenswood's stone vaults. They were quiet enough in their plush cell, drugged and hollow eyed: the infants dozing fretfully, the teenage girls lolling on a sofa under the eye of a powerful woman in a drab apron, assisted by a tight-laced whore with a mane of blonde hair, filing her nails by the fireside. The room had smelled sickly, heavy with perfume and drugs, and his stomach heaved at the memory of it. After Kizhe had inspected the girls to his satisfaction, the men were directed to quit the room via a narrow spiral stair cut into the living rock that wound its way down to the wharf. They had to pick their way slowly as the stairs were dark, steep and irregular. Each carried a flickering candle cupped in their hands to guard the light from the damp blasts of air gusting intermittently from side passages which pierced the wall every ten steps, offering diversions into utter blackness. As they had emerged, blinking, into the raw light of the quay, Kizhe, who was gruffly pleased with the day, had bidden Cornelius farewell before making off into town for a solitary drink.

Cornelius had another duty to perform, and had side-stepped the coiled ropes and paint pots to make his way to the *Blue Dragon*, where he must supervise the meeting with Vere. He had made his way over the gang-plank and into the tarry darkness of the ship to meet Trevellis emerging from the ladder leading to the lower deck, laden with ropes and canvas sheeting. Cornelius had followed him to Trevellis's own cabin, stooping low to keep his head below the spars. He sat in the Captain's chair in the squared-paned bow window and waited. In little more than an hour Raphael Vere had entered the cabin, grotesquely out of place in his silk top hat and lavender gloves, angry not to see Ravenswood and demanding an explanation. Trevellis had shadowed him in, and within seconds he was overpowered and bound. The interview had been predictable. Vere blustered wildly to justify the murder of his senior clerk, all in the worthy cause of protecting the reputation of his valued client and business partner, Mr Ravenswood. Wilson had stolen items from Vere's home which linked directly to sensitive aspects of the Ravenswood shipping interests and so he had to be removed. Furthermore, at the first sign of betrayal, Vere had fearlessly killed the failed assassin and continued to manage the affairs of the bank with the utmost efficiency. He was Bath's puppeteer, his hands pulling all the strings. Furthermore, he had single-handedly shaken off a London investigator, who was now in the palm of his hand. His plump face reddened as he struggled to unburden himself of the tale, and also of Trevellis's vice-like grip. His mouth had become flecked with spittle, his eyes watered with tears of outrage. Unsurprisingly, Trevellis had tired of the performance before Cornelius did, and had dealt Vere a crushing blow to the back of the head. The indignant voice was abruptly silenced and the plump body had crumpled, concertina-like to the ground to be smartly sheathed up in the canvas by Trevellis.

"What are your instructions?" Cornelius had enquired, idly re-arranging the papers on the desk.

“He’s going to board the steam packet to Cork, but ’e might not be there to disembark. It’s powerful rough in the Irish Sea this time of year.”

Cornelius had left Trevellis shouldering his burden, whilst he walked back to Redcliffe Parade to reclaim the horse he had borrowed from Ravenswood’s stables and to make his way back to Arno’s Tower for the dinner party with the man from the Foreign Office.

5 a.m.: 15th October, 1831, Arno’s Tower, Arno’s Vale.

As was his habit, Cornelius dressed for training and slipped out of his room before dawn, silently crossed the terrace, then gathered speed and sprinted through the park to St Anne’s Wood. It was a good start to the day, the starlight was bright, limning the trunks and tangled boughs in silver, silhouetting a dog fox slinking off the path ahead of him. After he crossed the deserted Bath road he slowed his pace and concentrated, wondering if he had sensed a minute change behind him, a different sound. He turned and ran backwards for a step or two but there was nothing new to see or hear: just his soft footfalls and the rustling surge of the wind in the trees. He skirted the old stables and headed off through the wood. He kept up a steady pace until the last few hundred yards when he accelerated and leapt to clear the last huddle of bushes before slowing to a stop in his usual place by the ruined wall and the well. He bowed his head and placed his hands together, focused on his place, his purpose and his soul. Calmly, he breathed deep, and began. Warming his chilling body, he stretched, reached, prepared each limb, arched his neck and stiffened his hands into knife-hard blades, thumbs in and fingers taut, bent slightly inwards. Slowly he moved through the sinuous and deadly dances: rehearsing the ancient battle moves of his art. Some moves he performed agonisingly slowly, precise and perfect, some exploded into a mesmerising flurry of blows against the phantom army: every punch, every kick designed as a final one. Each sequence was practised exactly as he had first been taught, outside in all weather on the dusty square, or in the wooden temple that had once been his home. Twenty years of training had forged Cornelius Lee and his art was his soul: the two indivisible.

After his first hour, he stopped and closed his eyes, to focus on his breathing. In the stillness he immediately sensed another presence, close by in the dell. From his right had come an infinitesimal sound, and soft disturbed wings flapped in the dark. He launched himself into a complex series of forward kicks which moved him across two-thirds of the open space, gathered himself up and soared into the air, somersaulting once, twice, three times to disappear in the shadow of the wall. A dark shape separated itself from the shelter of an oak tree and followed, rounding the wall to an enclosed semi-circle, open to the sky. The burly figure glanced round silently in the pale light, watchful, suspicious, his head turning sharply left and right.

At the moment when he decided that he was quite alone and his quarry had disappeared, Cornelius leaped down from a high perch on the wall behind him. At the soft sound of his landing, the man's surprise was instantly overtaken by instinct: in one smooth circling movement he reached with his right hand for his hidden weapon, drew it ringing from its sheath, and brought the crude blade whistling down to Cornelius's head. Simultaneously, Cornelius had stepped forward, leaning towards his opponent and catching his sword arm in a double-handed cross block below the wrist. Spinning clockwise on his left foot, his right hand gripping his assailant's wrist, he pulled the man down hard, his left hand slamming into the back of the exposed elbow. With a grunt of pain the man loosened his grip on the weapon, which slid away over the damp grass, but with astonishing speed he used the momentum of Cornelius's attack, dropped his left arm to cushion the fall and curled into a double-roll. He was on his feet in seconds, ten feet distant, facing Cornelius. The familiar dead eyes crinkled: "Well, Mr Lee. We seem to have the same plans this morning. A little outdoor training is always congenial at the start of the day."

Cornelius gave a short bow. "Good morning, Mr Kizhe. I was unaware you favoured this place."

"I have been watching you. You have an interesting style, a soft one if I might say so." He glanced round, thinking, surprised at Cornelius's versatility. "It is still early. Would you care to test a few more of your techniques?"

"By all means."

Kizhe shed his heavy cloak and scabbard, rolled his head round, snapped a few punches and dropped into a stance. First they circled each other, assessing each other's height and weight, feeling the ground with their feet, and as they did so, their faces drained of all animation, sinking into the gaze of the warrior: mask-like, unfocused yet all-seeing. Suddenly, Kizhe launched a lightning blow at Cornelius, which was elegantly side-stepped and countered, the return blow stylishly pulled, quarter-inch impact only, just enough to bruise.

Again and again Kizhe rained down swingeing attacks, and every one was used against him. Cornelius had decided on his first meeting with Kizhe that when it came to this, he would spar entirely in defensive mode. He had no wish to injure or kill Kizhe, yet, and had no wish to reveal his spirit to this man. Strategy for Cornelius was The Way, the ultimate craft of the warrior. Every encounter, every moment, was for learning, for reviewing strategic choices: to this there was no beginning and no end. He waited until he sensed his assailant tiring, then chose his moment. He tensed his torso for the impact, allowed Kizhe to catch him with a direct body-blow, stepped back and bowed.

"Shall we walk back together?" he said.

Kizhe allowed his mouth to smile in return.

"You fight well, though I still say your style is a soft one. It seems to have too much of the Buddhist about it!" He gave his harsh bark of a laugh. "You failed to strike me with any power

Mr Lee."

Cornelius smiled in return. "My style is a mixture of many disciplines. This was one," he said quietly.

By the time they approached the house, dawn had broken over the black woods and the sky was barred with iron-grey. A ragged chorus had broken from the bedraggled birds perched on the naked boughs, their wet feathers ineffectually failing to fluff up against the cold.

"It is good to practise with an opponent," said Kizhe, "we should spar again."

"I am sure we will."

Cornelius made his way to the kitchens to search for breakfast but Kizhe made straight for his suite. As soon as he locked the door behind him, he began to peel off his damp clothes before one of the full-length gilt mirrors that Ravenswood provided in such profusion. The satisfaction he had gained by landing the decisive blow on the elusive Mr Lee swiftly evaporated. Stripped naked, he looked carefully at the tight pattern of red bruising on his body. The sight of so many blows, so well placed, so politically pulled, infuriated him. His face darkened to a scowl as he mentally replayed the final moment of their bout. Lee had sustained a punch and retired, but he should have gone down. Kizhe had the unappealing suspicion that he had been played.

He lumbered into the bathroom, and glared balefully at the brimming bath-tub, left steaming and ready by his valet, the mound of warm towels waiting by the fire. He climbed in and reflected: he had learned more than one good lesson this morning. The vulgar luxuries available at Ravenswood's mansion must be rationed, they sapped the strength and must be recognised for what they were. Small doses and regular training would neutralise their influence. He breathed in deeply, allowing his body to sink beneath the surface of the water, and as he rested, shark-like in the depths, he toyed with the thought that there might also be a need to neutralise his new sparring partner.

And on the instant, he surfaced: refreshed and revitalised.

Back in Bath

Later that morning, a female figure disguised in a hooded blue travelling cloak clattered her way along London Street and thence to Walcot. Her dainty pale blue satin shoes were strapped into high wooden pattens which succeeded in raising her feet above the slurry of the roads but slowed her gait to that of an unsteady geisha. As she travelled in the same direction as the crowd of smocked labourers and farmers with their herds and dogs heading for the market, her progress was swifter than it might have been, but it had still taken over half an hour to make the descent from Lansdown Crescent. Fortunately, she found Nathaniel's lodgings easily, closed the gate behind her with some relief and pattered up to the door to beat on the knocker.

"Come in, come in!" shouted a quavering voice. Tilly's face hardened in disappointment.

"Hello Mr Spence," she called, reluctant and sulky, as she entered the hall and made her way to the kitchen.

The rack above the fireplace was laden with steaming sheets, shirts and boiled pudding-cloths, hoisted aloft by the rope secured on the wall. Bread was cooling on wire trays and a pungent meat broth simmered in the cauldron over the fire. Every surface had been scoured, cleanliness being next to godliness, as a wall text reminded her. Old Tom was in his usual seat by the fire, peeling turnips and grinning in toothless delight at the arrival of reinforcements.

"Jus' take a firm 'old of yon Johnty missus. Grab 'im now!"

The rotund baby Johnty had spotted the open door and taken off with surprising speed in a curious shuffling crawl, pulling himself forward on his pudgy hands like a young seal. Tilly made a grab and managed to secure a firm hold on one leg.

"Ye young demon!" cackled Tom. "Jus' look at that missus.

This very week the Johnty 'as taken off! 'E'll need to be tethered now when 'e's out o' they crib. Pick 'im up! I likes to see such spirit in the young but we can't 'ave 'im dashed under a carriage wheel can us? That's it 'old 'im tight. Like a greased eel 'e be! Where wast a-goin' my 'andsome?" He gazed in unfocused delight at his great-grandchild, shaking his head in wonder.

Tilly managed to restrain the Johnty who obligingly settled in her lap, took her velvet cloak in both sticky hands and rubbed his grimy face in it crowing with delight.

"Martha will be in directly missus. Was it Martha you was after?" said Tom, attempting innocence. "Or might it be Mr Parry perchance. Fine young buck 'e is. Back after dawn 'e was this mornin'."

The back door opened, and to Tilly's relief Martha entered with a bowl of bruised apples.

"You're looking better Mrs Vere," she said, examining Tilly's face. "Now these would have been useful last time we met! Did you use rotted apple and rose conserve on the eye? No? Well, you'll know next time. Will you be wanting to speak with Mr Parry?"

As Martha made her way upstairs to fetch Nathaniel, Tilly gave up trying to wrest the handfuls of cloak from Johnty, who was now totally absorbed in testing them, possibly to destruction, and listened half-heartedly to Tom's views on the snail's progress of the bill, livestock prices and the weather. As his eyesight was poor, she was able to read the other texts on the wall as she listened, without giving obvious offence. Finished in cross-stitch and hanging on strings from the picture rail were numerous legends, including: "Whatever thy Hand findeth to do, do it with all thy Might," and, "Order is Heaven's First Law." A small worm wriggled out of the apple nearest to her on the table and she glared at it, annoyed that it reminded her not only of Martha's unappetising concoction for black-eyes, but also of Raphael's treachery.

"Eve and the apple! Arrant lies," she thought crossly. "Adam would have demanded it and wondered why it was not served sooner."

She was distracted by sounds of the party coming downstairs. A woolly black and tan tornado was first to the kitchen, launching itself through the door to land paws and panting head on the Johnty in her lap.

"Oh Caradoc! And Mr Parry! I am pleased to catch you at home. I need to speak with you urgently concerning my husband's business." Tilly had shed her ill-humour on the instant, and concentrated on twinkling prettily, conscious that her pose with the Johnty was not unappealing. As she inspected Nathaniel more closely she noticed the cut on his cheek and continued. "Oh Mr Parry, I see it is your turn today. Have you been in a fight?"

Nathaniel beamed from the door, his Damascus gown tied at the waist over his frilled shirt and trousers. He touched the healing cut gingerly. "Footpads madam, the merest trifle. It is of no account. Down Caradoc! Mrs Vere he is delighted to see you. Shall we talk in the parlour? Mrs Spence, could you kindly bring tea?"

Martha lifted the reluctant baby from Tilly's lap and nodded meaningfully. "Yes Mr Parry, I will be in with it shortly. Will you be needing the rotted apples as well?" But they had already gone.

As they closed the parlour door Tilly gabbled her news, *sotto voce*, grasping Nathaniel's hands between hers as she did so. "Yesterday I got into Raphael's dressing room. I couldn't believe my luck. He was called over to Bristol at short notice. Edwin Ravenswood sent a coach to convey him. He had been expecting a visitor but had to leave anyway and Tanner was instructed to see to him. The maids were busy providing refreshment and I went into Tanner's room. He had left his keys on his desk! I went in and searched Raphael's bureau. Oh Nathaniel, I found some shocking publications. They were disguised under plain covers, but I looked! Such obscenity!"

"Did you bring them?"

"Certainly not!"

"What else?"

"I found a cash-book in the very bottom of a box in the wardrobe and copied out some pages," she said, flushed with her own daring, as she handed him a sheaf of papers from her reticule. He flipped through the pages.

"A great deal in a personal code, needs work to clarify it. But I'd say it looks like your husband had some substantial outgoings of a personal nature Tilly. Also, plenty references to a certain ER." He said, running his eye down the figures rapidly. "And plenty going for "B". Payments from a Mr Shadwell. I know a little about him. Do you know him?"

She shook her head drawing a trembling breath. "And Raphael did not return home last night. Thank God. I don't know how I would have faced him. I think I would have run. I could have come here couldn't I? No one saw me leave today, and I don't want to go home." She edged closer. "And what can the figures from his book do to help me? Can they rid me of him?"

Caradoc put a warning paw on her skirt as Nathaniel heard Martha's tread in the hall and simultaneously disengaged Tilly's hands from his.

"Sit down," he whispered quickly. "Have some tea, then go home and pack. Return to your family for a visit. Leave a note explaining that you are needed. I have to go to London today but will be back soon. Write your family address for me so I know where you are. Now shush." He smiled encouragingly as Martha's ample rear bounced the door open to admit her and the tea tray.

Nathaniel walked Tilly to the door as she left, full of tea, cake and advice from Martha on baking, home remedies and the latest location of her namesake vessel the *Mathilda*, which even as they spoke, was speeding on a fair wind round the north Devonshire coast to the Severn Estuary to return her son to domestic duty in Walcot Street. Tilly scribbled her family address on a scrap of newspaper he had brought from the parlour. She pressed it into his hand and after only the briefest of glances up and down the street, wrapped her arms around Nathaniel and lifted her face to his. "You will help me won't you Nathaniel," she breathed, "don't desert me after all I've done. I need you to support me. I'll wait at my mother's home for a week, until I hear from you." She brushed his lips with hers. "Until next week," she pressed her hand to her lips and blew a parting kiss. Confident now, she turned towards London Street with the light of triumph in her eye. She was too pleased with herself to notice the small figure of a governess hurrying up the street after collecting ribbons and silks for her mistress whilst her charges had extra lessons from a dancing master. Anna's dancing skills were far inferior to her offerings in languages, arithmetic, drawing and music. Additional tuition had been sought and she was relegated, much to her delight, to running errands in town on Saturday mornings. Anna, however, was not too occupied to turn her head on hearing an excited yapping across the road, or to miss Tilly embracing Nathaniel in plain sight on Martha Spence's front path. Anna's main problem now was how, and when, to inform Em that her escort for the Masked Ball was probably not quite as available as she had thought.

On the London Road

Night had fallen, but Nathaniel's coach continued to make good time over Hounslow Heath. He had taken the precaution of keeping his swordstick with him in the coach and held it, at the ready. Though the gibbets and their swaying bodies of hanged highwaymen had been down for over twenty years and there were Peelers and mounted patrols in the more populous areas of the toll road, old habits died hard. The heath, long the most dangerous stretch of road in the country still held its reputation. The odd "high tobyman" was still arrested there for trying his luck, along with the more common footpads and thugs who usually infested town roads but sometimes strayed further afield. The guard was well armed with a blunderbuss, what he called his "new-fangled" pistol, and a sabre for good measure. Admirable as this was, Nathaniel preferred to have his own arrangements. Which, he reflected with pleasure, were shortly to be augmented by a pair of new-fangled pistols of his own. He had inherited a fine pair of Ulrich flint-locks from his father, who had bought them in Stuttgart shortly before he died, from none other than the famous Bernese gunsmith, Franz Ulrich himself. They were pretty little pieces, ultra-compact, like the pocket-size American Derringers, and his London gunsmith had pronounced them easy converts to the new percussion mechanism. They had been sitting in the shop for a week, waiting for him. Owen would have loved to try the new mechanism, which promised virtual immunity from misfires, the curse of the flint-lock. Nathaniel laughed to himself as he conjured up a scene. It would have been on some deserted God-forsaken heath, hour after bone-chilling hour, plugging away at piles of stones, probably in the rain or howling wind, Owen laughing, eyes flashing in delight. His smile was long-lived at the thought of his father, though it carried with it the familiar stab of pain at his loss.

He felt the stagecoach slow down and he looked out to see the lights of the Bell Toll House approach. He bent down to pat Caradoc as he stirred amongst the hay laid down to warm their feet. They would both be glad to arrive at Lambeth for pie and mash, and he was keen to collect his pistols. The week had not been without interest and he was impatient to dispatch the meetings with the noble lords and return to Bath. There was little to report in terms of radical unrest, the reform groups having retreated to their caves, seemingly fully occupied in licking their wounds after the Lords rejection of the Second Reform Bill. Bitterly disappointed, but digging in stoically for a long campaign, they were quiescent and he saw no signs of agitation or incipient riot. The government could perhaps have done with a little more in that department if the Lords were to be frightened out of their resistance to reform by the greater threat of revolution. Drake had kept his business in Bristol jealously to himself and would no doubt be in a position to reassure Palmerston on the health of the opium running business. Nathaniel had decided that Drake's displeasure was a small price to pay, and he would continue to pursue the links between Raphael Vere, Edwin Ravenswood and the unsavoury Shadwells, who seemed to be up to their necks in trading under-aged girls. With regard to the Bath ladies, there was even more to recall him to duty. Tilly's scribbled notes needed closer study and he felt a degree of obligation to her after setting her up to filch evidence from her husband's room. To be honest, it could not be seen as a hardship to have to spend a little more time in Tilly's company. He was also game for the evening at the Masked Ball with the Petersons, the chaste attractions of Miss Emma would act as a distraction and divert him from the charms of the delectable Coco.

Meanwhile, in the heart of the city, Chislett drew the drapes at Brookes's Club in St James's and checked that the Strangers' Room was ready in every particular for Lord Melbourne and his party. He re-positioned the glasses, the favourite port and the biscuits, lit the candles and withdrew as he heard the patrician tread of members on the corridor.

"Good evening Chislett."

"Good evening my Lord."

Melbourne led Palmerston and Drake into the Strangers' Room and took a comfortable armchair by the fire. "Dashed cold what!" he drawled, rubbing his hands and reaching to the flames.

"More exercise needed sir!" said Palmerston flinging himself on to the sofa and pouring himself a drink. "The blood should be agitated daily."

Melbourne pulled a face. His afternoons had in truth been rather less exciting of late, as his boon companion, Caroline

"Norty" Norton, was about to be confined by the birth of her second child. The thought of the ravishing, witty Caroline brought a genial smile to his lips. They had been all but inseparable for over a year, since her ass of a husband had encouraged her to befriend Melbourne in the hope of preferment for himself. Preferment had been obtained to the tune of £1000 per annum, but Norton's greed was unassuaged and she had been allowed to continue her dalliance with the rakish Home Secretary. She was twenty-three years of age to his fifty-two, but the attraction was mutual. Melbourne had a weakness for young women, had adored her grandfather Richard Sheridan, and was entranced to see she had inherited some of his literary genius. His stormy, brilliant, blindingly beautiful Norty distracted him from dwelling on the ancient wreckage of his love life. His wife had finally died over two years ago and his fling with Lady Branden was reduced to exchanging written snippets with her from their latest perusals of French erotica. His sad handicapped boy was out of sight, if not out of mind, and darling Norty really was the spice of life. Dear Richard had understood how essential women were to one's happiness. He absent-mindedly hummed a snatch or two from "Here's to the maiden" from Sheridan's *School for Scandal* before giving up and sighing windily, as he had been doing increasingly often.

"Banish the world-weariness dear boy! Go hunting!" ordered Palmerston.

Melbourne poured himself a port, reflecting ruefully that Palmerston's blood would have been agitated by more than the hunt. When his beloved sister Emily was not orchestrating the action at Almack's Club with her delectable troop of followers, she was still warming Palmerston's bed. At least two of her four children had a look of him.

Drake sat quietly, observing his betters, biding his time. His news was good, so he had no discomforts on that score, but he needed to plant some traps for Parry.

"Well Drake," said Palmerston, smacking his lips noisily.

"Have a port man and bring us up to date. We gather you needed to see us privately before the meeting in the Office on Monday."

"Yes indeed," murmured Drake unctuously. "I have some excellent news my Lords."

As Melbourne kicked the fire lazily, sending renewed showers of sparks racing upwards, and Palmerston basked, arrogant and supine, like a rogue elephant at a watering hole, Drake poured himself a drink and spun his tale. Ravenswood, accomplished, connected and supremely successful was eager to continue helping the government and was as putty in his hand. Drake had details of the privateers of the China Seas who would continue to facilitate the opium trade for Ravenswood and had assurances that Ravenswood would cooperate with other traders to ensure that the Chinese navy continued to fail in all attempts to frustrate business. Drake himself would broker any talks if additional help were to be needed by the traders.

"It is important my Lords, that Mr Ravenswood's business is not impeded and I have one concern on that score." He leaned forward earnestly to add weight to his words. "Mr Parry, sound man as he is, lacks experience. He has become embroiled in some local affairs in Bath which could cause unnecessary publicity for Mr Ravenswood's shipping company and is loathe to approach his findings in a," he allowed himself a superior snigger, "in shall we say, a politic manner."

"Dampen the blighter down Drake. Good man," rumbled Palmerston, reaching for the biscuits. "Gad Melbourne," he declared as he shovelled them down, "we need to move on to dine, haven't eaten since dawn."

Although Melbourne was nodding amiably and making encouraging noises, Drake's treachery had not gone un-noticed and served to intensify Melbourne's existing scorn for that particular bounder. He congratulated himself anew on the appointment of young Parry and looked forward even more to his reports, which with luck would be not only informative, but also extremely impolitic indeed.

Evening: 17th October, 1831.
Carlisle Lane, Lambeth, London.

Two days later, Nathaniel was back in his lodgings in Lambeth with Caradoc, mulling over the day's work as he contemplated the deserted grounds of the Archbishop's Palace which provided his only view. Setting aside the triumphant collection of his pistols from the gunsmith, the visit to London had not been a particularly successful one. He had spent half a day at Whitehall, first waiting by Percy's office, as planned, for a meeting to discuss progress. The amiable Percy had taken his report on Bath and radical activity, scanned it through without comment, and placed it in an overflowing tray on his desk. Nathaniel had then told Percy of his discoveries and suspicions concerning the opium traders of Bristol, the links with the kidnapping of girls and the unsavoury nature of the banker he had been directed to contact as a reliable and promising Whig supporter in Bath. He had produced a detailed report of his findings and to his disappointment, had seen it take the same route as his first offering.

Despite waiting for most of the rest of the day, he had not seen Drake, who apparently had arranged to meet the noble lords separately. He had managed the briefest of exchanges with Lord Palmerston and they had been far from satisfactory. The Foreign Secretary had breezed into Percy's office, glanced perfunctorily at Nathaniel's reports, returning the first one to the tray and beckoned for him to follow. He had been allowed a quarter-hour in His Lordship's office to outline his findings, then been told to keep his eye on the radicals and leave all Bristol business to Drake, who had everything in hand. Lord Melbourne, according to Palmerston, had an urgent appointment and was not available, but would be informed of all Nathaniel's findings in due course. Nathaniel knew he had been out-manoeuvred but, fortunately for his peace of mind, had been spared the indignity of seeing Palmerston carelessly crumple his second report, ball it, and then hoof it unceremoniously into the bin.

"Well Caradoc," said Nathaniel, reaching for a bulky package of mail he had collected at the Office. "It rather looks as though we might be on the Bath coach a little earlier than billed." He spread the correspondence on the table, separated the most inconsequential from the formal and homed in on a communication from his family's solicitor in Wales, which he scanned quickly, his mood lightening with every line. "Not the Bath coach, by the look of it!" he said, leaping up and striding to the window for better light. "We are summoned, my little friend. Pack your bones!"

The solicitor's familiar crabbed hand needed some interpretation, but the gist was that his father's cousin had died, a will was to be read, and it was in his best interests to come to Anglesey to listen to it. It was filthy weather for cross-country coaches, but as yet there was no frost, ice or snow. He flung himself into his writing desk chair and dashed off a letter to the Petersons.

Afternoon: 18th October, 1831, Marlborough Buildings, Bath.

Anna Grant had managed to contain herself until Thursday and her scheduled afternoon tea with Em. Not that she wanted to be the bringer of bad news, but there was such a thing as duty. She set off with a spring in her step from St James's Square and made straight down the hill to the Peterson residence in Marlborough Buildings. She was shown in by a maid, paused briefly by Captain Peterson's study to exchange a few pleasantries with the dear man and then entered the drawing room to let Em settle her into her usual seat.

"You look radiant!" said Em fondly. "You must be so happy now Henry is," she paused, unwilling to dredge up bad memories, "well, out and about let's say, and back at work." She beamed at her friend. "Enid will be up with the tea and the Bath Buns presently. We are still celebrating!"

"Well," said Anna. "To tell you the truth, Henry is more out and about than he should be. The bank has closed for a week as Mr Vere has disappeared!"

"No!"

"Yes!" squeaked Anna. "Not seen since last Friday, and Mrs Vere has gone away."

She bit her lip, the opportunity could not be missed. "Actually Em, I need to say something about Mrs Vere." She struggled momentarily, but decided she would burst if she kept it to herself.

"Em I saw her at Mr Parry's lodgings on Saturday. She was talking to him at the gate. And she kissed him. I'm sorry to say it Em what with you going to the Ball with him. I just thought you should be told."

Emma felt her stomach lurch, but fought to keep her face entirely expressionless. She had thought of little else but the Ball since last Thursday's dinner and Nathaniel's letter from London had been hidden away in her sewing bag as a treasure, kept within reach and re-read a dozen times a day. It had been addressed to her parents but gallantly explained, for her benefit, that he was detained by business matters. He pledged to return at the end of next week, in plenty time for the Masked Ball, which he was looking forward to, eagerly. So he said. She had visited the dressmaker, designed her mask, started making it and even shown off her ideas to the twins. She blenched at the memory of her gales of confident laughter, and felt not only foolish, but acutely ashamed. Anna's tale had dealt her a body blow, but really, how could she have been such a fool? Why else would he have agreed to escort her, but to oblige her family? Why wouldn't he want to kiss Tilly Vere? What man wouldn't? She had to salvage some self-respect.

"You say she kissed him Anna?" said Em. "They are friends you know."

"Oh yes, I know," said Anna. "And it was in public, quite above board."

Enid knocked and brought in the tea. The snatch of

conversation and the strained silence were fascinating surprises. Like a good servant, she could not react, but relayed the scene in detail as soon as she made it back down to the kitchen.

"Miss Emma has gone white as a sheet," she said, sinking her teeth into a bun. "And that Miss Anna looks like she thought she'd won a sweep-stake then realised as she couldn't quite put her hand on the ticket!"

"Why?" asked Cook, looking up suspiciously from her tea. "What were they sayin' when you took in the tray?"

"Somethin' about kissin' and it all bein' in public and above board."

"Who was kissin'?" demanded cook, refusing to be interested before the story showed it had legs, and shapely ones at that.

"Well," reflected Enid, steadily crunching her way through the sugar cubes which infested the base of all authentic Bath buns. "Stands to reason it can't be Mr Henry or Miss Anna would have been bawling. Must be that Mr Parry who came to dinner last week. Miss Emma must be after 'im and 'as been beaten to it."

"Did you see 'im?" said Cook. The tale had taken off and accelerated to an acceptable canter.

"Oh that I did," said Enid, rolling her eyes. "Tall, dark and 'andsome!"

"Now ladies, less of the gossip and more of the service if ye don't mind! Make mine a steaming brew and a couple o' they buns."

"Keep your wig on," grumbled Cook, pouring out the required brew to the footman, who disobligingly removed his wig, deposited it on the table, poured his tea into his saucer and flexed his elbows in preparation for pouring it down his gullet.

Once Anna had gone, Emma had time to come to terms with the news. She was infatuated with a man she did not know. He was a Londoner, well-travelled, an adventurer on foreign service, who quite possibly might never return to Bath after his next visit. He might be in Africa, or India, or Paris, again. She threw herself into her chair and took up her sewing in case her mother came in. Didn't she want to stay at home and not marry for a while? No, she thought to herself, taking out the letter and gazing at his signature again. She did not. She wanted to throw herself into his arms and recite the rest of *The Eve of St Agnes*. And act it out. And run off with him into the storm. She managed a laugh at the ludicrousness of it. How old was she, sixteen? But somehow, just to think of such things made her feel a bit better. One must be pragmatic. He was outrageously handsome. To land a man like that would incur far more in the way of competition than fluffy, beautiful Mrs Vere. Tilly might be a good flirt, but she wasn't clever in other ways. And it had been a kiss bestowed by Tilly, not himself. Emma thrust the letter back into her bag, took up the needle and began to sew. Her breathing steadied and she reached a state of calm. She too had a strategy.

Chapter 7

Early afternoon: Friday 21st October, 1831.
Green Park West, Bath.

"You've no idea what you're talking about woman. Ravenswood has a long arm, and so have all the men working for him. And there are more of them than ever. I saw some Oriental coves at Redcliffe Parade. New men, not his usual gang. Handy lookin' bastards they were."

Joshua Shadwell paused, chewing his lip and glaring at his wife, who sat, cross and exasperated, struggling to out-face him across her table in the front parlour. With a Herculean effort she allowed her face to smile encouragingly.

"Bristol is far enough away," she said, quietly but urgently, unfolding her arms and leaning over, reaching out for his hands. "With Vere and Mordecai dead and Declan in Bristol the link to Bath is broken. He can get his cargo elsewhere. There's hardly a shortage of Bristol trollops willing to sell their children, or a lack of laudanum soaked whores who'd sell their souls for the next bottle. Tell Ravenswood you're out of business. And," she added bitterly, "it's likely to be no more than the truth!"

Joshua shifted in discomfort at the reminder. "It depends what happens to the bank," he said gruffly. "Depends who takes over. I don't know how Vere showed our debts. A lot of our business was private. Anyway, there's nothing happening for now, they're still closed."

"It's not just your debts Joshua! I've warned you about our girls. They don't believe your tale that Babs and Abi are stayin' freely in Bristol and they want to know when they're comin' back. There's a mutiny brewin' and the regulars will play merry hell if the girls aren't workin'."

"There's more where they came from," he said, viciously defiant.

"We've customers booked in today for Babs and Abi. What are we going to do? For sure, you'll find more girls like them, and you might find a Josie, and maybe a Clari, but I doubt it. But Mitzi and Letty?"

The savage lines of his face began to sag, and it gave her the nerve to press her advantage.

"Do you think high-class tarts will work for us if word gets out? They see themselves above the Avon Street service as well you know. You can't treat them like drabs, Joshua! You're out of your depth. You're drowning for Christ's sake! That Ravenswood is evil. Break from him!"

Joshua struggled to absorb the reality of the week. How could his affairs have sunk so low in such a short time? When he had reached home last Friday night, he really thought he had papered over the cracks, smoothed things over and plucked victory out of disaster. The Vere episode had been resolved. Babs would go: sore point, but necessary. Declan was dealt with. Last Saturday, Joshua had risen late to recover from the mental exhaustion of being interviewed by Ravenswood. By the time he had appeared in the breakfast room he had felt quite the debonair businessman, sure of his story and burnished, just a little, with a golden glow of triumph. The colour had been leached out of him in an instant, as if he had been pushed under a cold pump. She had been waiting for him, crouched in her chair like a whipped cur, blurting out her pent-up tale before he'd fully opened the door. His boys had been humiliated, beaten by one rogue punter: Jabez was still in his bed groaning with a belly wound and a shattered beak, whilst Billy was nursing him and his own broken pate. Worse than that, the punter had given Vere's name as his sponsor and asked for Babs. Even though he'd got Abi, Rosie swore the two of them had been conniving with the punter. Rosie's description of him had been unsettling and Joshua smelled a rat, but of far greater importance was the laying-off of his men, and that had only been the start.

"No loose ends." The words of Ravenswood had haunted him. With Jabez and Billy unable to work, he had no one else he could trust with Babs, and after hearing Rosie's tale he knew he had to be rid of Abi as well. It had taken most of the week to negotiate the transfer of the girls with Ravenswood. It had been distasteful. He had taken them to Redcliffe Parade himself in his own coach, pretending they were going to see some special clients. Dosed drinks had laid them out, and he had left hurriedly, guilt-ridden, as they were taken down to the caves by Ravenswood's men. Rosie didn't dare ask too many questions, as she could guess the answers.

"Do you hear me Joshua! Break with him!"

He glared at her, inchoate, impotent rage welling up from his guilty soul. He tore his hands from hers and strode to the window.

"He'd hunt us down. We'd have to sell up. Move away."

Strangely, just saying the words was like catching a rope thrown to him over a void. When he turned back to her the despair in his eyes had died away, smothered by a new light, cunning and feral, a flash of his old self.

"Perhaps we can do it Rosie. That would ditch the debts to the New Bank and get us out of Ravenswood's reach. And well away from these clammering whores," he shot a venomous glare to the rooms above. "What did you say was likely, a mutiny? They can mutiny on their bloody own."

"Leave our home! Run away! No Joshua. Please, no, I love this house." Rosie shouted, shocked and fearful, now that her goading had spurred him too far. "And I won't throw away the business!"

A rapid knocking at the door prevented him from answering or delivering the slap in the mouth she was clearly asking for.

"Come in!" said Rosie, standing to face the angry figure of Clari which now filled the doorway, arms akimbo and spoiling for a fight. Crowding behind her were the other women in a body, faces set hard, standing shoulder to shoulder. Together, as though a dam had burst, they launched a wave of furious complaint at Rosie's head. Joshua dropped into the armchair by the window, struck by how closely Rosie resembled a lighthouse in a stormy sea as it took a battering from the elements. He sank deeper into his chair, mentally retreating to a better place.

The Danby residence, Tilly's family home, Beckington.

Approximately ten miles distant from Joshua Shadwell's discomfort, Tilly Vere was sunk in a slough of dejection of an entirely different type. Rather than feeling pursued, she felt abandoned, a new and most disagreeable emotion. She had endured almost a week at her mother's house and the strain had begun to tell before her bonnet was off. Mama had been of the opinion that Raphael had simply gone on an extended holiday, which was not surprising as Tilly had not made home sufficiently attractive. Without elaborating in any useful way, she had intimated that wives should ensure that all the needs of their husbands were fully catered for, as she had so expertly catered for those of her dear late husband. Tilly had listened and sulked, as her mother had returned to this favourite theme on a daily basis, until Wednesday, when she had ruthlessly acquainted Mama with the sordid details of her husband's sexual preferences. After taking snuff, Mama had proved to be unusually fertile in expedients. Tilly would have to go home, make of it what she could and allow a husband his latitude, as many great women had done before her. By Thursday Tilly had enlarged on Vere's attacks on her person, her fear of more of the same, and her appeal to Nathaniel Parry. This last had been swept aside as a recourse of the flimsiest usage. A lodger in Walcot Street was not promising as a provider and Mama had occupied her waking hours since this last confession in calculating exactly how quickly, and onto whom, she could off-load Tilly.

Meanwhile, Tilly had taken to sitting on the white seat in the orchard at the bottom of her mother's garden, wrapped cocoon-like in a voluminous green and brown cashmere shawl. That Friday afternoon found her there. She had drawn up her feet and rested her head on her knees, listlessly watching energetic blackbirds foraging in the hedge and envying them. The sound of voices caused her to look up and she was surprised to see her mother making swift progress over the lawn accompanied by a maid and a visitor, a portly one, who was beaming a greeting to her, his spectacles flashing opaque in the sun's low rays.

"Mr Dill how very pleasant to see you again," she called.

"Oh madam, the pleasure is all mine. 'If the heart of a man is depressed with cares, the mist is dispelled when a woman appears!' How true! How true! The sight of you dear lady, so beautiful, like a dryad, a spirit of the trees."

"Mr Dill has been to Bath, Mathilda," said her mother meaningfully. "He has called at your home and at the bank. He has some propositions." She could not have dwelled longer on the term, and followed up by smiling coyly at Howard.

"Sir, please do come in for some refreshment. I'm sure you can encourage Mathilda to return to the house, it's far too chill to remain outdoors." She shot a glance at the maid and snapped out an order: "Tea for three in the drawing room. Biscuits and cake." She bestowed a doting smile on Tilly and Howard before following the servant indoors.

Howard Dill extended his hand to Tilly, but instead of relinquishing it after she rose, tucked it instead under his arm. Tears of gratitude flooded her eyes and she turned to give Howard her most shatteringly beautiful smile.

"How very kind of you to visit me Mr Dill."

"Not at all my dear lady. It is always a signal pleasure to see you, but I also need to speak to you of other matters. I need your collaboration. Tanner informed me of your whereabouts." His voice became serious and he slowed to a halt before continuing more urgently. "Mrs Vere, the bank cannot remain closed. As you know I am a major depositor and it is important to me that certain issues are resolved. I propose that we open again under the temporary supervision of young Henry Blake who will recall his subordinates and the other servants of the bank. We will advertise for a senior clerk to replace Mr Wilson. I have contacted Captain Peterson and Dr Parry, the other major depositors living in Bath, and they are in agreement."

She continued to beam at him, so Howard pressed on.

"You may know that we have a significant investment underway at present, as we are arranging the financing of another vessel for Mr Edwin Ravenswood of Bristol. He is also intimately concerned with the bank and much of our corporate investments hinge on his business. My family have known his for generations. You may know of our involvement with Bristol shipping. And you also have interests in the bank, organised by your husband," he smiled benevolently, "of which you might be entirely ignorant dear lady. We need your help in gaining access to relevant papers and there is the trivial matter of some signatures. Will you return to Bath with me? My carriage is at your disposal."

"Mr Dill, I fear for my life if Raphael returns. Things have occurred," she paused, lamely, unsure of how much to say.

Howard Dill wrapped a protective arm around Tilly. "Come in with me, Mrs Vere. May I call you Tilly? I will protect you from all comers, including your husband. Tell me at your leisure what has occurred. You are not alone my dear lady."

As they stood, Tilly entwined in Howard's bear-hug at the edge of the orchard, her mama dropped the curtain she had been peering round, deposited herself on the watered-silk chaise longue and heaved a sigh of utter relief. Howard Dill was a bachelor of enormous resources. His mansion at Norton St Philip was but one of his holdings, which spread as commodiously over the hillside pastures of Mendip as they did over the quays of Bristol. If Vere proved impossible, he might be quite easily replaced, and bettered, in wedlock or out, with this most promising companion.

She reached for her fan, so annoying these sudden rushes of heat in one's middle-age. It had been a sore trial disposing of her numerous daughters, and even the best laid plans could be so easily thwarted after victory seemed entirely secure. She had considered Howard Dill for one of her brood years before, but had always wondered if he liked women at all. She had pegged him, at the very least, as a perpetual bachelor, a dilettante, happy with his books and his enthusiasms. The type who, centuries before, would have been, perhaps, a prosperous Abbot or an ascetic academic immured in his ivory tower. However, confirmed bachelor or not, the acquisition of Mr Dill into her social circle, in any capacity, would be a coup indeed. Perhaps her giddiest daughter would be of some real use after all. The liaison with Vere had been triumphant in its way, but she was not a city person. To shine in one's own parish, on one's own stage! Well, that had to count for more. She leaned over the table which the maid had stacked for tea and chose one of cook's delectable millefruit biscuits: almonds, citrus peel, angelica, crisp and light, no flour, delicious. She was still dispatching it as Howard and Tilly entered.

"Oh come to tea you young people! You must have had so much to talk about. I had quite given you up!"

Late evening: 27th October, 1831.
The White Hart Inn, Stall Street, Bath.

It was the following Thursday before Nathaniel returned to Bath. Night was falling as he made his way back to Walcot from the Hart, Tobias trundling his bags by his side and Caradoc capering and yapping alongside, invigorated at the sight of a friendly face and the smell of familiar streets after the hours of glum jolting in the straw of the coach foot-well.

"You look taller Tobias."

"Good livin' Mr Parry. There've been a few changes over the last couple of weeks. Mrs Spence 'as let me take an attic room in the house. I can pay a bit in rent, but really it's as Old Mr Spence's been laid up in bed. She needed more of a lift with 'im. Also, now I've boots and a set of clothes she says I'm fit to be in her kitchen. And, I do go to the Methody Sunday School now, so as I can learn mi letters. I know half the alphabet already. You can't go unless you've shoes. And I speaks better."

"Yes, I remember you told me that, but it seems odd to me Tobias. Why do you need to be able to afford shoes?"

"Don't know. 'Suppose it shows thrift. Mrs Spence is powerfully keen on thrift."

They arrived to find Mrs Spence and Mary, with the Johnty on her lap, sat in some state round the table in the front parlour. Unfolded before them, lovingly smoothed out to lie flat on the red velvet cloth, was a letter, and before Mary was a glass of Tom's small beer.

"Mr Parry!" exclaimed Mary as he looked round the door to greet them. "We've a letter from Matthew and it's from Bristol! He's going to be home in a couple of days now. They're just sorting the pay and a few jobs on the ship before it's re-fit. We're drinking to his health! Mother has the elderflower. Come and join us for a minute sir if you will." She jumped up to bring over a chair for him, and characteristically swept her own excitement aside. “What news from London sir? We’ve missed your company.”

“I’ll join you with pleasure,” said Nathaniel, taking a seat at the table as Martha sprang up to take another glass from the dresser.

“I can offer you some bread and meat loaf to go with it Mr Parry. And you young Tobias,” she said, the good news getting the better of her judgement. “As it’s an extraordinary occasion, sit ye down with us and have some elderflower cordial. Or indeed the small beer.” As she placed her glasses on the table with a reverent flourish, her lined face shining, sudden unexpected tears coursed down her cheeks. The party looked on, embarrassed to see Martha’s austerity dissolving before their eyes like surface starch. “Oh Mother!” exclaimed Mary. “Are you alright?”

Martha rubbed her cheeks vigorously. “My son is coming home! Thank the Lord! I’ll bring your food.”

“It’s unusual to find you ladies in the parlour,” said Nathaniel to Mary, smoothly filling the silence as Martha hurried out.

“Mr Spence has been poorly and not sleeping at night. He’s been dozing in his box-bed of an evening and we didn’t want to disturb him. He’s on the mend I’m pleased to say, and Tobias has been a saint helping this last week.”

Tobias swelled with pride and held up his glass. “It is my pleasure,” he said grandly, in conscious imitation of Nathaniel.

“Now,” said Martha, fully recovered, sliding her laden tray onto the table and slipping the treasured letter under the toes of the pot shepherd. “Less of the toasting. Our joy is in plain-sight of the Lord and needs no more buttressing in beer. Mr Parry, how was London Town?”

Nathaniel ran his hands through his hair and leaned back in his chair. “Where to start Madam? I spent a few days in London and concluded my business, but travelling to Wales accounted for most of my absence. It wasn’t a planned trip.”

His listeners leaned in, agog. Martha filled his mug with more beer and Nathaniel launched into an edited version of his journeys.

"I received notification that I had inherited some property near Beaumaris, my father's home-town on the Isle of Anglesey, and I had to go immediately to conclude the business."

"The Isle of Anglesey!" said Mary sighing. "It sounds so romantic."

"Oh it is," said Nathaniel laughing. "It is a beautiful place to the far north of Wales, beyond the misty mountains of Snowdonia. There be dragons, Mary! It was a beast of a journey. At times we thought we would never get there at all. It was long and very slow. We took five days from London, most of the time in the teeth of a gale that threatened to blow us away. To spare the horses all the gentlemen passengers walked many a mile once we were off the good roads, even on the flat."

"But 'twas to an island you went? Were they running the ferries in such foul weather?" asked Mary. None of them had ever been to Wales, had not even crossed the Severn. He might as well have spoken of crossing the East China Sea to the Land of the Rising Sun.

"No need for ferries," said Nathaniel, excited by the memory. "We rode over Mr Telford's mighty bridge across the Menai Straits. When your Mr Brunel has finished in Clifton you will have another such closer to hand."

"I'm going to see it," said Tobias. "I shall walk upon it when it's done! When is it to be done?"

"I saw the stones where the foundations will be when I went to Bristol last," said Nathaniel. "But the talk in London was that Brunel has only raised half of the funding at present, so you will have a few years' wait Tobias."

"Did you see your family?" asked Martha, offering Nathaniel the brown brick of meat loaf and a carving knife.

"I saw some distant cousins, and lawyers, Mrs Spence. Many lawyers. Most of my time was spent with lawyers. But it was worth it, as I'm now the proud owner of a property near my old childhood home, though that was sold long ago. And Caradoc had a grand time, didn't you boy?"

Mary reached down to pat Caradoc's wiry back. "Did you love it boy? Did you like the sea then?"

Unusually, Caradoc ignored her and continued his unequal struggle to bolt down an over-generous portion of meat loaf.

" Beaumaris is where he came from. I brought him away with me two years ago, after I had taken my father's body back to Wales. He's my link to the homeland."

Reluctant to say more on the subject, Nathaniel raised his glass. "Ladies, to home-comings! Now we must leave you to enjoy the rest of the evening. Many thanks for the supper Mrs Spence. You are a paragon amongst women."

"Well Mr Parry," said Martha, smoothing her apron in pleasure, "you're welcome I'm sure."

That night Nathaniel lay on his back, watching the stars through his open curtains. The journey to Anglesey had been nostalgic and painfully beautiful, as well as stunningly remunerative. His private means had hitherto stemmed from a legacy left by his late mother, which was substantial but unlikely to last a lifetime. Government pay was erratic, making the new stream of income from property in Wales extremely welcome. Moving between the inn at Beaumaris and the homes of various distant cousins, he and Caradoc had seen much of the island. They had walked the coast round Red Wharf Bay where he had declaimed Byron to his heart's content, in particular a favourite couple of lines about beaches. He recited them again with relish, briefly startling Caradoc.

"There is rapture in the lonely shore,
There is society where none intrudes,
By the deep sea,
And music in its roar."

He grinned with pleasure at the memory of the rolling fields and sitting for hours on the ancient mound of the burial chamber at Bryn Celli Ddu. Later, in the board-hard bed at the inn he had dreamed disturbed dreams, narrated in a torrent of Welsh. He had conjured Druids, oak-groves and Roman slaughters in the cold nights and sung himself hoarse by the sea at daybreak, with no-one but Caradoc to hear as he perfected his rendition of William Williams's *Sea of Glass*.

"*Arglwydd, arwain trwy'r anialwch.*"
Lord, guide me through the wilderness.

He sang again, but quietly, for the pillar of fire, and the pillar of mist and the manna from heaven and resolved to try it out on Martha to see if she knew it. He had not heard her sing it as part of her regular morning repertoire, but his cousins claimed that it was the only Welsh hymn translated to English and sung regularly by English Non-Conformists, especially the Wesleyan Methodists.

He would not, however, try her out with the other accomplishments he had worked up. He had plugged away with the pistols on the headland to perfect his use of the new percussion cap mechanism, at first narrowly missing Caradoc, who had insisted on trying to beat him to the target. The worthy fellow had, perforce, been tied up. Generally speaking, his personal training regime had flourished. He had pounded along the beach before breakfast and managed some boxing and sword-play with the local yeomanry in the evenings. After Caradoc's first misunderstanding over the target shooting, he had also buckled down to some training and had, on occasions, been startlingly obedient.

The return to Bath required him to resume his enquiries and make good on some outstanding promises. In lieu of counting sheep as he tried to fall asleep, he considered his list of obligations. At the start of November he was duty bound to make another report to London on local radicals, though the luke-warm reception of his last efforts had killed his enthusiasm for the assignment. Of greater interest was the case of Wilson's murder. The verdict still rankled and he would like to get to the truth of it, though the likelihood was slim. He had spent a few evenings in Beaumaris dissecting the details of Tilly's notes from Vere's private cash book and it was clear that he was a person of interest. He had been moving large sums, presumably from the bank, to fund his gambling and other recreational interests. Sight of that alone, without any additional evidence on the details of his more unorthodox tastes, would have given Wilson ample material to blackmail his employer. His connections with the Green Park brothel and its possible links to kidnapping muddied the waters further.

He needed to see Captain Peterson to share thoughts on the progress he had made, such as it was. Speaking of which, joining the Peterson party on Saturday and escorting Miss Peterson to the Masked Ball was something else he needed to do. The ball was the day after tomorrow. He made a mental note to ask Martha to prepare his evening wear. He also made a mental note that Emma Peterson had been surprisingly good company at the family dinner: charming and pretty. The ball should be no hardship. More urgently, he needed to know where Vere was, check Tilly was safe, and disentangle himself from her as painlessly as possible. It would probably also be wise to remember not to call on Miss Montrechet again. He fell asleep wearing his Damascus gown and a beatific smile.

He woke to Mary's gentle knocking on his door. "Mr Parry sir, I've got your hot water and there's a letter for you."

Nathaniel repaid Mary the fee she had given the postboy, settled back in bed and broke the seal on the note. It was anonymous, but needed no signature. As he scanned it rapidly it was clear it could be from no-one else but the mysterious Mr Lee. He sat up cross-legged in bed and read it again, carefully.

Dear Mr Parry,

We met some weeks ago in Bristol. You may remember we watched a game of strategy together and we talked. From my connections it is clear that a violent demonstration is likely to be made here in Bristol against the City Recorder, and probably also the Bishop, on Saturday the 29th October. As you will know, the Recorder has made himself notorious, particularly in this City, through his continual attacks on the Reform Bills in the House of Commons. The Bishop has also spoken against it in the Lords. On Saturday the Recorder visits the City and the mob is making ready. I am writing to you as I know you are charged with the reporting of such incidents. I also have some other matters to discuss with you and would appreciate your presence here. From early evening on Friday the 28th October I will be at the inn where we first met.

In the hope that this finds you in time,
From one who aims to serve the light.

Afternoon: Marsh Street, Bristol.

Nathaniel had dug out his reversible frock coat, collapsible top-hat and a long black scarf for the trip to Bristol. Marsh Street was decidedly insalubrious and a degree of anonymity would be politic. In case of trouble, he had settled on taking the makila and the pair of pistols, tucking one into each of his poacher's pockets. He had every intention of returning by Saturday morning at the latest, so toyed with the idea of leaving Caradoc behind, but the loyal creature baulked. He grumbled when Nathaniel ordered him to stay on guard. He growled when reminded of the relevant lines in Byron's Don Juan about the sweetness of hearing the honest deep-mouthed bay of the watch-dog, welcoming the master home. So, it was the man complete with his dog who made his way to the Three Sugar Loaves in the late afternoon.

Marsh Street proved to be very different in daylight hours, with more respectable working women and children in evidence. A few matrons in aprons were chatting in the entrance to an arched alleyway that opened onto the street, arms full of damp linen from the washing lines they had rigged up to zigzag the crooked lane. Some young girls balanced water crocks on their heads, giving them surprising grace as they walked, swaying slowly home from the conduit, laughing together. Chickens pecked in the gutters and a gang of infants chased down the street, pushing each other and shouting wildly.

Nathaniel's purposeful walk, the sight of the makila and the glowering Caradoc, were sufficient to discourage the jostling pack from closing in to beg or pick his pocket. Nathaniel glanced up to the high floors and the attics, down to the areas and the basements. Through the dust-streaked windows he spotted shadowy figures moving in the rooms or pale faces looking out like ghosts. Marsh Street was populated by flocks of poverty stricken tenants, from the sound of them, mainly Irish, who roosted in the gaunt remains of the houses in squalid rented rooms. It was not all housing, the tenements were interspersed with warehouses, mainly for sugar, and drinking dens catering for the dregs of Bristol's drinking public. Most of these seemed deserted, doors closed against the daylight, but in a few hours the wharf rat trade would spill down the street from the quays, unrolling a grimy tide of rackety music and bellowing voices, profanity, vomit and fighting. Amongst the swaying inn signs he finally spotted one sporting the three white triangles of the sugar loaves and pushed his way through the door.

It was dark inside, but a surly barman was on duty talking to a brawny customer in an offensively checked waistcoat and greasy frock coat who lent over the bar towards him, swopping tales with an air of exaggerated confidentiality.

"Brandy and hot water if you please."

The barman moved off reluctantly to get Nathaniel's order.

“Welsh terrier,” grunted the man. “Good little dogs they be. ’Ad one once. Scrappy little fighter ’e was, but characterful if you take mi meanin’.”

“I do sir,” said Nathaniel. “Do you keep a dog now?”

The man gestured to the fireplace, where a hulking Staffordshire lay sleeping, his twitching ears bitten into scallops round the edge like a tea-time doily, skin sleek over tight sculpted muscles.

As it slept, Nathaniel risked a few more moments in the bar.

“I guess the city will be up in arms tomorrow.”

The man hawked and spat with furious precision into the spittoon which squatted on the sawdust floor between them.

“Wetherell won’t know what ’it ’im. Bastard as ’e is. On ’is ’igh ’orse ’e were in London, railin’ against the Bill, a-sayin’ ’e speaks for Bris’l! Booed out o’ the city ’e was at the openin’ of the Assizes, in April that were. Damn him, says Oiy. Our Members are both reformers and the city’s be’ind ’em. We’ll show ’im and the bloody Tory councillors. Do you know Bristol friend?”

“Only been here once before sir,” said Nathaniel. “It seems a great city.”

“It were great,” said the man savagely. “Though we’ve bin a-losin’ out to Liverpool sin’ moiy ould dad were a boy. Dock fees are sky-high ’ere and if the West Indies sugar plantations loses their slaves, as seems most likely Oiy might add, our refinin’ fact’ries will be sunk as deep as the rest o’ the trades. Business is bad ’ere. Men are ’ungered sir! But we’re not standin’ fer it! We’ve ’ad our own Political Union since last year and there’s fightin’ talk there Oiy’ll tell ye. It’s not just Frenchies with the heart to rise up,” he added darkly. “And look at what they done.” He leaned over to Nathaniel, prodding him in the chest to add good measure to his words. “Drummed out their king again didn’t they, an’ this time, pops in another without invitin’ Madame Guillotine! Anyways, even if there’s gore, what’s a riot or a revolution eh! We’ll prob’ly be dead of the cholera before anything else gets us! You know there's been deaths? In Sunderland they were. The Pest from Bengal! It's on its way alright!" He drank deeply, with a macabre satisfaction.

"I've been up-country in Wales," said Nathaniel. "I didn't know."

Nathaniel had liked what he had heard, but sensed customers were starting to trickle in and he needed to keep his eyes open for Cornelius Lee. He turned round to lean on the bar with his elbows and survey the rest of the pub. A few Chinese sailors had entered and were making their way towards the door of the rear bar where he had watched the Wei Ch'i players. Nathaniel made his excuses and followed them. The room was dim and smokey, the fire sulky and reluctant to flare, but he could see that Lee was already seated in the corner, waiting.

"Good evening Mr Lee. I received your note this morning."

"I am pleased to see you," said Cornelius, smiling at Nathaniel and rubbing Caradoc's ears in welcome. The dog had made a bee-line for Cornelius and put his head on the wooden settle next to him.

"I told you of the likely troubles tomorrow to provide a reason for you to travel here. That news is public enough to allow a note, though it had to be an anonymous one." He dropped his voice, motioning Nathaniel to move closer, and glanced round to ensure the sailors at the next table were well out of ear-shot. "There are other matters which I can only speak of. Mr Parry, I know that you and your colleague Mr Drake are here to support the opium shipments of Edwin Ravenswood for the greater good of the British Empire. You know my views on the trade. I want you to know now that my reasons for joining the crew of the *Blue Dragon* are not to assist. I do not wish them well."

"One man against a crew of," Nathaniel paused, calculating swiftly, "would it be about sixty?"

"There are forty men. The *Blue Dragon* is four hundred tons, so it has the usual size of crew for a regular vessel: ten per hundred tons. However, I do have some friends amongst them, maybe ten at most. Four to one: not bad odds as it happens. It could be much worse. The *Blue Dragon* is about a third of the size of a regular East Indiaman but clippers tend to have larger crews than normal, because of their line of business."

Nathaniel nodded. "Ready to fight off unwelcome interest."

"Yes, but I do not intend to fight for the ship Mr Parry. I shall gather intelligence and, as you say in England, keep my powder dry."

"It is rare for a man to cross the world for purely altruistic reasons," said Nathaniel, watching Cornelius closely.

"I agree. My mission has personal motivations. Suffice to say my brother died recently, and miserably, to the great sorrow of our family. He was a hopeless opium addict. His dependence on the drug corrupted him and brought him to his ruin. Truly, he was consumed by the darkness and the opium den he frequented was supplied by none other than Edwin Ravenswood." Cornelius paused briefly, as if closing a door on his secrets. "However, Ravenswood has other interests which I hope you will help me to curtail. On the *Blue Dragon* will be some kidnapped females, two infants and four young girls. They have been especially chosen to be shipped abroad and used as the creatures of an evil man known as the Count. He has English girls taken to the East to be abused in any way he or his associates care to devise. The supply is regular as the girls do not survive long. This is not an isolated instance and Ravenswood is not the only exporter, but if we can save these few, it will be a deed well done. Just before the *Dragon* sails on Sunday they will be moved aboard from caves under Ravenswood's house. The ship is late already and no further delays are possible because of arrangements for the opium collections."

"And you want me to help you release the girls?"

"I want you to effect the release Mr Parry. I cannot do it myself as I cannot risk losing my position on the *Blue Dragon*. I must remain on the ship for the voyage east in order to achieve my own objectives. If you will not help I might have to let them sail. No attempt to bring in help from the watch or other officials will have any chance of success. They will not be able to enter the house against Ravenswood's wishes. He is a man of great power in this city and has the local magistrates, how would you say? In his pocket?"

Nathaniel's eyes searched the impassive face but as before sensed no treachery or threat, just an immense latent power, a compelling force. His mind conjured up, unbidden, a vision of his father, telling his stories in the dark by his bed: tales of eastern warriors and mythical battles, the titanic struggles of the elemental forces of good and evil which would go on throughout all time. He must have smiled, and Cornelius sensed, as well as saw, the relaxation of tension.

"Tomorrow night I dine with Ravenswood at his house. It is in Redcliffe Parade at the top of the red cliff itself. Also there will be a man called Kizhe. He is a very dangerous man, an envoy of the Count himself, sent to pay a courtesy visit to Ravenswood and inspect his business. My friends amongst the Chinese crew have told me that half a dozen of Kizhe's personal guards have been planted amongst them to keep him informed. Kizhe will also sail with the *Blue Dragon*, so tomorrow's dinner is by way of a farewell."

Cornelius paused to take a pencil and notebook from his pocket. He bent over the table in the uncertain light from the fire and the spluttering tallow candles and hurriedly sketched as he continued: "Here's where we are now. Here's the dock. The prisoners are being kept here, in caves below the house in Redcliffe Parade. Ravenswood uses them as cellars. There are dozens of rooms and passages hollowed out in the cliff, some can only be reached from the quay, but many of them are directly below the houses in the Parade and used by the owners. Last time I was in Ravenswood's house I saw the prisoners. I know exactly where they are kept. They are only guarded by two women who drug them if they struggle or complain. A stairway leads down from the caves through the rock to the quayside, just here, where there is often a sailor on guard. I propose a rescue plan for tomorrow evening. It cannot be earlier. If there is sufficient time between the girls' removal and the sailing, Ravenswood will order the kidnapping of more girls. We need a diversion to allow you time to get them out and I have an idea. Ravenswood has another ship at anchor on the quay called the *Mathilda*, docked here. He likes to keep an eye on both vessels from his windows. By tomorrow night the *Mathilda's* crew will have been discharged, so if it were to be set alight there would be no-one to deal with it. He would be drawn down to the quay to rouse the sailors from the *Blue Dragon* to fight the fire. Such a distraction could allow a rescue. We need to have a coach waiting, which could be hired from the stables round the back of the Ostrich."

Cornelius shot a searching glance at Nathaniel as he tore the sketch map from his notebook, crushed it and flung it to the back of the fire. It flared and sighed as he pocketed his belongings. Involving this man had been a calculated gamble which, if he had judged him aright, would be more than justified, and if he had not would have created yet another problem.

"I know the inn," said Nathaniel. "And I also knew of the trade in the children. It's villainous, and in principle I agree that the girls should be released, but I have some affairs to put in place. I really should be in Bath tomorrow." Despite an unwelcome vision of disappointed Petersons, he rose and clapped Cornelius on the back. "Come on let's look at the house where they are held. You say it's close by?"

When they emerged from the Three Sugar Loaves it was full dark and the life of Marsh Street had ignited. Sounds of frenzied fiddling and the stamp of feet blew out on gales of heat from gaping inn doors. Revellers staggered before them, seeking challengers or partners for their random drunken dances, but all instinctively steered clear of the two tall men with their faces muffled against the buffeting noise, the stench and the chill. Cornelius and Nathaniel walked silently down Prince Street towards the harbour and turned left into the Grove, making for the ferry to Recliffe. As they levelled with the Coach and Horses a noisy group left the bar and stepped onto the path in front of them. Four sailors, loudly drunk and keen for everyone to know it, were baiting two women and their slightly-built male escort. They had moved in to surround them, chaffing and pawing at the women, spoiling for a fight. Nathaniel and Cornelius automatically gave the party a wide berth.

"Leave us alone! Let us pass!" shouted a feeble male voice, the delivery agitated and strained. "These ladies need to go home."

"I think they could answer for themselves. Couldn't you moiy 'andsomes!" roared the foremost, rubbing his hands against the cold. "Oiy needs to warm myself and fancies a dance with one o' these shapely pieces 'ere! 'Specially you missus. You've a fine figure on you and you seems a man or two short in your party!"

"A night on the town along of us is what they have a fancy for I'll be bound," chipped in another.

"An' we know just the place don't us lads?" said the boldest sailor, taking one of the women in his arms. "Look! She likes a dance. Don't you missus!" he yelled, twirling her round, at which the woman set up a piercing scream, wriggled an arm free and slapped him full in the face.

As Nathaniel registered that the woman bore a striking resemblance to Mary Spence, Caradoc had already snarled a brief warning and rocketed across the pavement like a black and tan comet, flinging himself at the man and embedding his fangs in his arm. The man went over like a bowling ball, outraged and yelling in pain with Caradoc hanging on like a limpet, whilst the woman, newly released, sprang away to the arms of her companions.

"Get off! Get this mutt off me!" bawled the sailor, rolling on the ground and beating at Caradoc with his free fist, as the man behind him produced a knife and closed in. "Caradoc!" shouted Nathaniel "Here sir!" closely followed by: "Stop! Come here!" to no response whatsoever. As he covered the intervening ground in two strides he tried it again in Welsh, "*Rhoi'r gorau i! Tyrd yma!*"

But Caradoc was lost in the red mist of battle and there was no time for more words. Nathaniel swung the makila up to grip it quarter-staff style in both hands and slammed a blow from the right into the knife-man's middle. As he folded up Caradoc regained control of himself and neatly transferred his attentions to the buckling knife man. The bitten man rose from the ground roaring in fury, to be floored anew by Nathaniel's left-sided follow up, as the female party and timid minder scuttled away into the shadows, the latter calling in desperate gratitude, "I'll rouse the watch! Thank you! Thank you!"

Cornelius had noted the stick work approvingly and was pleased to see that Nathaniel was instinctively aware that there were two more potential assailants. Nathaniel had turned deftly to face them after dropping the second man to the floor. The makila whirled again: right, left, then a crushing blow to the head of the bitten man who had not learned his lesson but, like Lazarus, had risen again. The other three began to pick themselves up ruefully, grumbling but not offering more and Caradoc returned to heel.

"Good man!" said Nathaniel. "*Dyn da*!"

He grinned at Cornelius and made a move to leave. Cornelius nodded, but even as he did so two more burly men sidled out of the bar and decided on the instant to revive the ambitions of the fallen.

"Now lads," hollered a new voice. "What's the game 'ere! Up an' at 'em bully boys!"

Nathaniel dropped back to where Cornelius stood on the quayside. Side by side they had more of a chance against a possible six.

“I’ll take the fore-most,” said Cornelius quickly, as the fresh men ran for them from the door. The first cannon-balled forward to throw a punch at Cornelius’s head, and managed only a wild uncomprehending yell as he found himself up-ended and flying though the air. Cornelius had stepped aside to block and throw his assailant. Head over heels he flew, over the quayside, to crash into the black waters of the dock. The second man, stunned by a blow from Nathaniel blundered towards Cornelius and in seconds had followed the first diver over the side.

In seconds their gasping heads broke the filthy surface. “Help! Help us! Can’t swim! We’re goin’ under!’”

Nathaniel drew a pistol from his coat and motioned to the two men who had escaped the ravages of Caradoc’s teeth and had been advancing for more of a share in the fight. “Pull them out,” he ordered. “Or do you want to test my aim?”

They did not. Nathaniel, Cornelius and Caradoc left them to it, scrabbling for lengths of timber to hold out to the floundering men, who were still cursing and begging, beating the water with their flailing arms.

“You fight well,” said Cornelius, to Nathaniel as he led the way along the quay to the Grove ferry. “Where did you learn?”

“I spent much time with my father and he instructed me,” said Nathaniel. “He was a man of wide experience. He travelled in the east and found there a great deal to admire. From being a child I have enjoyed western style fencing but I also know something of your ways of the sword. And I can still manage a basic conversation in Mandarin. Though it doesn’t match your skill in English. Where did you learn?”

“My mother was born in America.”

Nathaniel stopped in his tracks. “My mother too was American. I should have known. Cornelius can hardly be a popular name in Cathay!”

“And your name is not as common in England as in the United States I guess.”

They smiled to each other across the dark. Two men: both

dark-haired, of almost identical build and age. Nathaniel instinctively held out his hand to Cornelius, who paused momentarily, then took it briefly in his.

"We have some feeling of brotherhood between us, you and I," said Nathaniel. "May I call you Cornelius?"

Cornelius bowed and then stood straight, his hands loose by his sides, watching Nathaniel.

"So, Cornelius, one more question. Your fighting style is unlike that of most Chinese sailors I have seen. Can you tell me where you trained?"

"In China I spent many years at a temple with a master there. I am not a sailor."

"Were you to be a monk?"

Cornelius did not reply, the one question had been answered. They walked in silence to the ferry, he took two ha'pennies from his pocket to pay the ferry-man and they settled on the wooden bench to scan the opposite bank. Redcliffe Wharf lay to the left with its tangle of cranes, barrels and planks, the *Mathilda* and the *Blue Dragon* to the right, rolling gently at anchor at King's Wharf, apart from the other vessels. The *Mathilda* was worn from her long voyage but the *Blue Dragon* was as smart as paint, "Bristol Fashion". Above them was the towering red cliff, topped by the neat palladian terrace of Redcliffe Parade. On landing they took up a vantage point out of sight of the solitary sailor on guard at the entrance to Ravenswood's caves and plotted again how a release could be engineered.

"I know a little about explosives," smiled Cornelius. "It is a simple thing to cause a localised fire on the *Mathilda* and a surprise for the man on the door if he lingers. I can provide these things, and will ensure that Ravenswood and the rest of the dining party are alert and encouraged to intervene. Though I doubt I could stop them. The fear of fire spreading to the *Blue Dragon* after all the delays to her sailing would be insupportable. Do you have other weapons?"

"One more pistol. But my makila is quieter and more

reliable."

"Yes, it is a well made stick. You also have Caradoc. Do not underestimate the power of a fighting dog."

Nathaniel drew the handle from the sheath and the dagger blade glinted in the starlight. "And do not underestimate the Spaniard's stick my friend."

"Come," said Cornelius, "I would like to look at it more closely in the light. We'll make our way through the yard and round the back of the Parade to the mews. We can find the nearest livery and get into the inn by the side-entrance. There we can talk of weapons, and eat, and make decisions about tomorrow."

"I've been here before, with John Drake," said Nathaniel as they entered the bar of the Ostrich. Caradoc made for the inglenook, tail up and well-pleased to see Nathaniel making straight for the bar. He settled amongst the logs, panting in anticipation of a pie and a bowl of beer.

"Not a man to trust far," said Cornelius, taking their pots of cider from Nathaniel. "I know you work with him, but beware, he knows of the trade in girls and is already in the pay of Ravenswood. He will not allow such matters to interfere with the opium runs. Furthermore, I sense he will compromise your reports if it suits him. He is not a man of honour or of loyalty."

"But you are?"

"To death." Cornelius smiled. "As I think are you. Nathaniel, may I now ask you one question? Can you tell me of your business in Bath?"

"As you know I am reporting on radical unrest, if there is any, but I have also become involved in a murder case on behalf of friends. A bank manager by the name of Raphael Vere has disappeared. I am sure he holds the key to the murder of his senior clerk. He is a cruel and unscrupulous husband, and a gambling man of perverted tastes, this I know already, and I suspect he is involved in the traffic you seek to disrupt here."

“I can help you there. Vere should be dead by now. He was to be lost overboard on the Cork steam packet, and you are right, he was deeply involved in the trade. I can also put your mind at rest on the other matter. He bragged to me that he had commissioned the death of his clerk and dispatched the murderer, though I doubt the truth of that. The man was a silken slug used to ordering, not doing. Your colleague Drake seems to me similar, greedy but cleverer, still sharp enough to rise a little further. I am surprised he brought you here. I would not have thought it sufficiently luxurious.”

“He has some interests, apart from himself! He likes boxing and he surprised me by his passion for engineering and for history. He also has a taste for beauty. Perhaps he is not entirely irredeemable. He was fascinated by this place. It was apparently the haunt of notorious pirates.”

“Perhaps his namesake?”

“No, Drake the privateer lived in an earlier time. The pirates of the seventeenth century were here by all accounts. It was Blackbeard’s local, or so Drake said. But I know it must have sea-faring connections. I have often seen an ostrich carved as a figurehead on the prows of ships. It is an African creature but also a sign used by ship owners. I know of one Welsh family, the Probyns who use the ostrich in their arms, but there are others. The Africa trade was important here in the past.”

“To return to my question about Bath, why must you be there tomorrow?”

“I have promised family friends that I will be of their party at a Masked Ball. It seems a trivial matter, but the Captain was a friend of my late father’s and I am to escort his daughter. It would be discourteous to let them down without a word.”

“Then send word! There is still time. There are dozens of coaches daily to Bath from Bristol.”

“Postboy deliveries are erratic. But I have been plotting an idea as an insurance measure. Is the *Mathilda’s* crew still in dock?”

"They are all to be paid off tomorrow before the vessel is moved to the yard for re-fit."

"Excellent. My landlady in Bath has a son on board. If I could catch him with a note to take he could ensure he sees Miss Peterson in person."

Cornelius looked amused. "So it is not just for the estimable father that you are concerned? Tell me, do you lodge in Walcot Street?"

"Yes. How did you know?"

"I have a good memory. I only need to read papers once and remember them well. I have seen the crew rosters for Ravenswood's ships. There was only one Bath man on the sheets I saw. A man called Matthew Spence who lived in Walcot Street."

Nathaniel looked at Cornelius quizzically. "A skill such as yours would come in very useful in my line of work."

"So, Nathaniel," said Cornelius finishing his cider. "Will you play our little game tomorrow?"

"Yes. I will send a message *via* the mail coach and also a personal note *via* Matthew Spence if he is to be found. You dine at six you said? Meet me tomorrow morning with any materials you have and a plan of the caves. I will encourage the *Mathilda* to flare into life a quarter hour after you start and then I will enter the caves. I'll organise a coach, and if the girls are willing to be rescued I will do my best to rescue them."

"It would be better to take them to Bath. They have all come from there through the efforts of a character called Shadwell."

"All of them? Then the links in the chain are clear. I have contacts in Bath who would enjoy a crusade to break it. And I have a few ideas as to where the girls could be taken if no one claims them. There are public institutions in Bath which will take them in. As for tomorrow night, I have some friends I could call on. They might help."

They sat on in silence, gazing into the singing fire and, despite their confident scheming, each considered the foolhardiness of the project and how extremely unlikely it was to succeed. Each ran over alternative possibilities and rejected every one.

The caves in Redcliffe

Theoretically within shouting distance of the fireside of the Ostrich, but embedded deep in the red sandstone cliff, two girls sat close together on a camp bed. They spoke in low whispers, ensuring the two bawds sharing a drink by the door could not hear.

"Babs, you must do as I say," pleaded Abigail, stroking her friend's arm, trying to calm her. "You must not complain or cry out again. Appear happy, smile, say you are looking forward to the trip."

"Oh Abi I'm so a-feared. God save us! An' I've such a pain in my head."

"Shush, you fool, shush," hissed Abi. "They'll drug us again if you start and we must keep clear heads. If we get one chance to get away we'll have to be fit to take it. Do you understand!"

Barbara nodded, her eyes staring in horror, her hands shaking.

"Once we're on the ship it'll be like the press-gang. We'll be gone for years, maybe for ever. From now we'll take turns to sleep so we're always ready. I heard them say we're sailing on Sunday. It's Friday night now. We can do it."

Even as she spoke, Barbara rested her head on Abigail's shoulder and began to slip away.

"So tired Abi. I've such a pain."

Abigail put her arms around Barbara and started to rock them both. Rhythmically to and fro: trying to heal the fear, trying to stay awake. She did not dare sing; must not draw attention to them. She stole a glance over to the door, the two women were laughing softly together, swigging in turn from a bottle and swinging back on their chairs. The little girls were asleep and quiet enough but the babies were sleeping fretfully in a truckle-bed, sometimes calling out, drugged beyond wakefulness, each descended into a nightmare world, a passive infantile hell of their own dreaming. They were comfortable after a fashion, the cave was warmed by a system of hot pipes and a fire, but water dripped down one wall. It was a strange place of limbo, piled with diversions: toys, sweet-meats, clothes to try on. And there were books. Abigail thought she knew most things about men but some of the sketches had sickened her to the core. She had no doubt what their fate would be and she prayed for strength.

"Lord, any chance there might be, any whisper of a chance, I'll take it. I'll get away from here, be a better girl. Help me God if I ever get the chance I'll be different. I'll leave Madam Shadwell's. Oh God, you know Joshua Shadwell betrayed us! Please God strike him down!"

She let her mind run over the betrayal for the hundredth, or the thousandth time. She had lost count. The order to dress in their best, the drive in the best carriage with the prospect of two days in Bristol, the tales of rich clients: all had been excitement and adventure, a welcome change from the routines of Green Park. They had been given a dinner in a smart dining room in Redcliffe Parade. Lots to drink: too much, more than she had ever had. Then the terrible awakening in the red cave: the realisation that they were trapped, the struggling, the shouting, beatings and slapping, foul drinks and unconsciousness. They had been tied at first, until they had promised to obey and be nice. Days had melded into days. She had been hanging onto the snatches of conversation between the guards and had slowly pieced together all she needed to know. They had been sold, their lives thrown down as tribute to the master of this house, a man even Shadwell served. Why had they been chosen? How could he have done this? They'd both been good girls for him and Madam. She had feared him, but life had been better in Green Park than in her squalid home in Avon Street, so she had taken what there was to enjoy and suffered the rest. Perhaps God would answer her prayer and strike him down. But if he didn't, perhaps she, Abigail, would strike instead. Wild schemes of retribution cheered her up and she spent the night devising increasingly brutal punishments for Mr Joshua Shadwell. It was empowering. By dawn her devices had taken on a life of their own and she felt she had something else to live for.

Chapter 8

Late morning: 29th October, 1831, Welsh Back, Bristol.

Nathaniel pushed open the black studded front door of the Llandoger Trow and stepped into the seething welter of King Street, thronged with traders and sailors, loud with the clatter of carts and sounds of the quay which stretched away beyond the gabled press of seventeenth-century houses and inns, down the Floating Harbour to Redcliffe. He paused to whistle a reluctant Caradoc out of the warm bar, and turned to head off towards the Grove ferry. The morning could not have gone better. From first light when the chambermaid at the Ostrich had lingered in his room, game to dawdle away a half-hour, he had been able to edge the rescue plan a little closer to success. The maid was a comely Welsh girl, dark as himself, with hair like black silk and eager to talk.

"Mr Parry is it?" She had said, in her soft Celtic lilt, smiling as she turned from placing his hot water jug on the wash-stand. "Are you a Welshman then sir?"

Then they had talked of Anglesey and her home on the Lleyn Peninsula, which she missed with a passion but did not seem to have ambitions to return to.

"Mud it is here!" she had exclaimed, gesturing down the harbour towards the coast. "Have you seen what they call a beach out 'yer at Weston? Our sand's soft and gold, like sugar it is. And the sea! As clear green as an emerald."

"Like your eyes."

"Oh sir!" She had blushed, very pleased and keen to be helpful. "If you're stayin' you'd like the Wednesday Goose Fair. It's up the harbour and the Welsh traders'll all be there, all the slate men and the coal carriers. Plenty to eat and drink. Their boats and the trows are berthed at the Welsh Back just along the quay," she said pointing now in the opposite direction, past the Grove and up towards Bristol Bridge. "Most of the Welshmen drink at the bottom of King Street in the Ship or the Llandoger."

The information had been more useful than she knew. Before he left and realised its full potential she was more useful still. Paper, pen and ink and sealing wax were magicked up from the bar with his breakfast and within the hour he was out and about. He had found the mail-coach office, left a letter for Captain Peterson and hired a hackney carriage for three days. The driver's only task was to be waiting to hand over the reins in the mews behind Redcliffe Parade by six in the evening. Nathaniel had then found the Llandoger and taken a seat in the bar near the loudest group of Welsh traders he could find. A quarter-hour of listening and a few shared jokes in Welsh had moved him onto the table. Despite the centuries of shared trade, the Bristolians and the Welsh were still not brothers. Canny listening had enabled Nathaniel to isolate a roguish boat owner and a few more drinks had secured the hire of his jolly boat. Nathaniel had spun a fair tale of needing to move some goods at dusk, hinting at illicit trade, hinting too of profits at the expense of a Bristolian rival. A guinea sealed the deal and a couple more were promised if the man met him as planned, at twilight on the Welsh Back.

Nathaniel reflected on the progress. The plan was a good one but it hinged on Cornelius's explosive surprises being small enough to hide on his person and allow the crucial shinning up the anchor cable that he had planned. As he shrugged the thought away and buttoned up his coat against the cold, a deep and mighty bellow of rage sounded from behind the pub in the direction of Queen Square. It was the unmistakeable roar of an enraged crowd about to turn into a mob. He turned on his heel and made his way towards the disturbance. Rounding the corner from King William Avenue he found himself on the edge of a chaos of running fights, swirling in isolated paroxysms of fury within a shifting crowd which covered most of the square. Bystanders had gathered on the periphery of the battles, standing back by the houses, most watching, drawn to the violence and the spectacle, but, as the case of the group of men in front of Nathaniel, some were egging on the combatants, bawling encouragement and suggestions. He moved nearer to the men, moving his hand down the stick of his makila, ready for his next move, as he closed in to speak to them.

"What's caused this?" asked Nathaniel to the man beside him. The thick-set sailor, a quieter man on the edge of the group, had the time and inclination to talk.

"They've chased up here to catch 'old of Wetherell. You a stranger? Well, 'e's the Bris'l Recorder. Chased 'im up 'ere they 'ave. He's 'ad to postpone the openin' of the Assizes and is 'oled up in the Mansion 'ouse over by there." He gestured to the corner mansion of a gracious eighteenth century terrace. Nathaniel glanced around and noted that Queen Square was gracious all round, stately, vast and shady, with trees, gravel walks and an equestrian statue of William III held at a rigid prance in the centre. It seemed more than double the size of Bath's Queen Square and big enough for an army to have mustered in it. The houses were occupied by a mix of residents, businesses and grand municipal offices, but had nothing in the way of civic defences, apart from the scattering of officious looking bludgeon men sporting Council armbands. Armed with wooden staves, they were energetically setting about the livelier demonstrators, breaking heads and beating backs, causing the mood of the crowd to turn ugly.

"Been after 'im from 'is first showin' comin' over Totterdown," continued the sailor. "'Is coach 'as been stoned good and proper. That ain't 'is you're seein' now, over there by the Mansion 'ouse, an' 'e's not farin' so good either by the looks on it."

It was not faring "so good". The coach bore the signs of an enthusiastic pelting and some of the crowd were rocking it, straining to tip it over as they watched.

"Are the troops called out?" enquired Nathaniel.

"Suppose so. Some 'o they Bloody Blues, you know, Light Dragoons, 'ave been quartered in Clifton all the week. They're at the ready and there's Guards about somewheres. Mayor Pinney tried to get three hundred specials but 'e 's short o' decent men. He's made up numbers wi' a hundred or so of these rough buggers. Itchin' for a scrap they are, as you see. Seems to me they're just rilin' everybody up. I'm tellin' you, this ain't lookin' too good. Pinney asked us sailors to 'elp as well, sent word for us all to enrol as specials. 'E knew first sight of Wetherell would rouse people up, but almost to a man we told 'im to be off. Jack Tars are no cat's-paw for the bloody Council. Pinney should 'ave told Wetherell to stay away from Bris'l. 'E's no business 'ere. We're a reformin' city we are and the sooner the bloody Council realises it the bloody better says I!"

"So the Recorder and the Mayor are still in the Mansion House," said Nathaniel, surprised. "Looks like they might have a longer stay than they bargained for."

As crossing the Square was impossible, he and Caradoc retraced their steps, followed the quay round to the Grove and joined the queue for the ferry. Once across and on his way back to the inn he ran over the events in the square in his mind and, just in case the demonstration ran out of control, he made a snap decision to send an interim report to Lord Melbourne. He made his way to the nearest mail-coach office, borrowed writing materials and dispatched a warning note. Within half an hour he was entering the Ostrich again and spotted the familiar figure of Cornelius Lee, sitting as usual with his back to the wall, well placed to see whoever entered or left the inn. Caradoc went straight to him, ready to take exception to a lean, suntanned figure sitting close to Cornelius on the bench. The stranger was unmistakably a sailor back from a long voyage. He appeared exhausted, his demeanour haggard and apprehensive. On the floor by his feet was a travel-stained bag, a rolled hammock and a bird cage in which perched a brilliantly plumaged red and grey parrot. Spread on the table before them were steaming plates of mutton stew, mugs and a jug of beer.

"May I introduce you to Mr Matthew Spence from the *Mathilda*," said Cornelius. "I managed to persuade him to wait until you arrived, but he is anxious to be home."

Caradoc stretched out on the floor under the table, after deciding to accept Matthew but keep a weather eye on the bird. Nathaniel took a seat opposite them and drew a letter from his coat.

"Mr Spence thank you for waiting to hear me. I am lodging at your mother's house in Walcot and knew you'd docked on the *Mathilda*. I would be much obliged if you would take this letter to Bath for me. It is essential that Miss Peterson receives it. I should be at the Assembly Rooms with her this evening but am delayed here. Another lodger at your home, Tobias Caudle, will take it to her once you arrive in Walcot, if you would be so kind as to instruct him to do so." He took two guineas and a sixpence from his pocket. "Please take this. It will help you catch a fast coach and give a few pence to Tobias for his part."

"I will sir," said Matthew slowly. "To tell you the truth our pay is not what we had been promised. Any extra will help. I'll take your letter."

As he reached out for the sealed note Nathaniel noticed the hand Matthew proffered was short of two fingers. Recent wounds by the looks of them, the fingers probably severed by a cable, and the arm bore signs of infected bites. He looked Matthew full in the face and read there the miseries of his voyage. He was a man in shock, still with one foot in his old life, plagued by whatever nightmares he had endured, desperate to be home but unable to imagine his homecoming. Nathaniel postponed his preliminary plan to question Matthew Spence about the cargoes on the *Mathilda.*

"You have a fine family Mr Spence," said Nathaniel. "A sturdy son who will cheer your heart and your mother and your wife are counting down the days and praying for your safe return. They can think of little else."

Matthew's eyes glazed as he stood up clumsily, eager to be gone. "I've never seen him yet sir. Your letter will be delivered, depend upon it. Good day to you gentlemen."

As Matthew made his way out, bundling his luggage through the door and raising an outraged squawk from the parrot as he did so, Cornelius slipped a small sack into Nathaniel's hands. "Here are the charges, half a dozen balls of fire: smoke and firecrackers followed by the flames with a slow-match time delay, but you won't have to place them yourself. Two reliable men have agreed to meet you and lay the charges, you might recognise them from when you watched the Wei Ch'i school. You can keep a look-out for them whilst they are aboard. With my encouragement the results should be enough to draw Ravenswood and Kizhe down to the quay."

"Good, that should improve our chances. Ask your men to be on the Welsh Back near the *Pride of Avon* trow. The skipper's renting his jolly boat to me and we can approach the *Mathilda* from the waterside. I had planned to row over myself, tie up the boat and climb the anchor cable to get aboard, but your men can do that for me with pleasure. Furthermore, there has been an interesting development," said Nathaniel, pulling over an untouched plate of stew. "The potential for riot has grown over the afternoon as the Council's special constables are busy antagonising the demonstrators in Queen Square. I'll go down again later this afternoon to see if it's possible to siphon off a few to Redcliffe. The lock on the grill door to the caves should be easily picked if I get the chance, but I'd also like a sledge-hammer nearby, in case it isn't, and I need to break the stone work. The coach is hired and will be waiting in the mews behind the Parade."

"Good. And now, the route to the cave." Cornelius sketched the stone stairway, its sequence of side tunnels and hollowed out vaults. "You should quit the cliff the same way as you entered, but this is what you look for if you are driven up the steps to the main house. Here's a way out through the kitchens." He paused, deliberating. "Are you taking Caradoc?"

"I was going to leave him with the stableboy until I come with the girls, or without them," answered Nathaniel guardedly. "Why?"

"It might be easier to encourage them to leave with you if you take him. That part of the plan might be difficult. They might be reluctant. Also he could help with the guards. I'll tell the two men who lay the charges to stay on the wharf and wait to help you when you get out of the caves."

The two men drank silently and considered the possibilities. The prospect of transferring brutalised young girls and infants, possibly under fire, was daunting. It was unhelpful to acknowledge it, but, unlike the Vere's of this world, they had between them no experience of under-age females whatsoever. The beer did not last long.

"For good or ill we may not see each other again," said Nathaniel. "You will sail on the *Blue Dragon*, presumably tomorrow?"

Cornelius nodded. "Thank you my friend for agreeing to attempt this and bring some degree of confusion to my enemies. Am I correct to say that it is a typical English toast? In your case: confusion to the French?"

"It was our toast for many years," laughed Nathaniel, "but

we are meant to be allies now."

"As we also are allies?"

"In this case, yes. Confusion to our enemies Mr Cornelius Lee, may they be one and the same."

Afternoon: The Peterson Residence, Marlborough Buildings, Bath.

The atmosphere in the Peterson household had risen to fever pitch over the preceding week, largely whipped up by the twins and Mrs Peterson. Saturday luncheon had been particularly shrill and the Captain had sought refuge in his study immediately after the fruit pudding. Door closed, facing the park, he settled to the newspaper with only the occasional distant shriek and pattering of steps up and down the stairs to disturb him. It wasn't that he was a kill-joy in any way, he reassured himself, he knew he would enjoy the Masked Ball, indeed he had a fondness for charades and disguises. Started in the tropics he recalled, the sailors had always got up a comedy masque of some ilk as they crossed the Equator. Brave shows, damned good! He played Neptune himself pretty frequently. Dashed monster of a grey wig, horsehair beard, tin crown. Liked it. It was the domestic preliminaries he found somewhat tiresome, though the women loved them. Well, Lydia and the twins did, he was not so sure about Emma. Dear Em! Lydia had been investing rather a lot in the prospective company of Mr Nathaniel Parry whom she had as good as engaged to the poor young creature already. The trifling matter of the courtship and proposal had been entirely overlooked. Captain Peterson pursed his lips and then blew out his cheeks speculatively. Couldn't bank on government men being in Place A if national affairs dictated a swift removal to Place B, but he had not breathed a word of his misgivings. Better to let affairs run, the sails were full and they were under way, nothing to be done. Though he did glance at the carriage clock on the mantelpiece. Mid-afternoon and no indication that young

Parry was even in Bath.

On the landing by the school room Ginette and Maddy were moving into the climax of their play. They had set up Papa's gilded Venetian mask on a chair wrapped round with his red cloak and topped with his black tricorn. They were prancing round it with damask curtain cloaks, Ginette in her mother's mask and Maddy in Emma's.

"Now we have the sword fight!" squeaked Maddy. "Get the swords Bad Columbine!"

Ginette ran into the school room and fished out the raspberry canes they had hidden in the cupboard.

"Here catch! *En garde* Good Columbine!" she threw one to her sister as she adjusted the mask which had slipped down her nose.

They lashed at each other happily until they tired of it and flung themselves on the floor.

"I want to be Good Columbine now."

"No," said Maddy instantly, then narrowed her eyes, calculating which reason to offer to achieve the desired effect. She plumped for flattery. "The black mask suits you better."

"But it's the Bad one, I want the Good one. It's got the crystals and feathers and you've had it long enough."

Maddy rolled over, playing for time.

"It was very tedious of Papa to refuse to be Harlequin. Why did he want this beastly mask with the beakey chin? It's so plain!"

"Better than being Pantaloon. He would have looked ridiculous and he does like ridiculous things sometimes." Ginette was fond of the word ridiculous, it was almost as good as her favourite, "hideous", which she used all the time. "He is old enough to be Pantaloon though. But maybe he wanted the full face mask so he can dance with some beautiful ladies and they won't know how old he is."

Both girls set up shrieking laughs and rolled on the floor.

"Funniest thing would be if the doctor wore one of the

plague masks. You know the really, really beakey ones with the pointy, pointy white noses," said Maddy. "He couldn't get near any beauties with that sticking out! Wouldn't it be scary though if he did wear it? Now we've got the new plague coming and we're all going to be dead! Bring out your dead," she growled sonorously, rolling her eyes until only the whites showed. "Bring out your dead!"

"Stop it Maddy," said Ginette. "It's not plague, it's called the Cholera Morbus and it's a fever and only poor people die of it."

"Are you sure?"

"Anything else would be too hideous."

"It would. Now, begin again, I shall be Em and you can be Mr Parry," said Maddy. "Put on the gold beakey mask!"

"No I want Em's mask, you can be Mr Parry." Ginette made a grab for the delicate confection of cream velvet, green silk, crystals and amber feathers. Maddy dodged and set up a yell, so Ginette dived to grab her instead and the two rolled over in a ball of curtaining and cannoned into the chair, which toppled over, sending the grand gilded Bauta mask, the red cloak, and the black tricorn over the banister. Two heads shot over the rail to watch their progress. The red and the black fluttered down to make safe landings, but the gold papier mache did not fare as well and landed with a crack, dividing up smartly into two.

"Hideous," said Ginette.

"Too hideous."

Afternoon: Queen Square , Bristol.

By late afternoon Queen Square in Bristol bore an even closer resemblance to a battle ground, with railings ripped up and flung aside or brandished as spears. Piles of rocks and bricks had appeared ominously in the square, though most ground floor windows had already been smashed and interior shutters had been slammed shut to try to protect the residents and their property. As Nathaniel and Caradoc arrived they felt renewed restlessness in the crowd. There had been a call for the Mayor to show himself.

"Give us the bloody Recorder," bawled a wild voice, cracked from an afternoon of yelling. "We'll murder 'im!" The crowd roared approval and was rewarded by the hunched figure of Mayor Pinney, sidling round the door with an aide who placed a chair on the flags for his Worship to stand on. When he did, there was a slight lull in the noise.

"Serve 'im up to us!" bawled one. "Go on, you can do it!"

The Recorder was not served, but the Riot Act was. Pinney gabbled it out, stuttering over it in his haste to be gone. The howling from the mob grew to a tide of fury and as he ducked indoors a fusillade of bricks and stones broke over the Mansion House front. Armed with spars of wood the mob battered the door down and flowed inside laying waste to the furniture and glass, mirrors and paintings as they surged upstairs in hot pursuit of the fugitive mayor. Nathaniel stayed on the edge of the square, but it was clear that the whole lower floor had been taken by the mob. One man came out laden with fruit and a leg of meat from the kitchens, one rolling a barrel of beer, others lugging crates of wine to the tumultuous approval of the mob.

"They're locked in on the top floor," shouted a man with a roasted chicken under his arm. "Let's smoke 'em out!"

"Smoke 'em out! Aye!" answered the baying crowd and immediately set to shoring up the Mansion House with combustibles, many dragged from inside the house itself.

"Burn it down!"

"Who's got a light here?"

Nathaniel's eye was caught by a movement on the ridge tiles of the roof, a dark figure was scrambling along it and working his way across the terrace. At least one of the mayoral party seemed to be slipping away. He could not follow the unsteady progress further as at that moment a troop of cavalry galloped into the square and scattered the rioters before the Mansion House. They reined in to a majestic stop in a swirl of gravel, peppering any who remained within ten feet. The commanding officer rose in his saddle and shouted up to the barricaded upper windows to tempt the mayor down for parley. The mayor stuck out his head, which stimulated a renewed groaning from the crowd, but his elevation had bolstered his shredded courage.

"Clear the square sir!" he demanded, his voice high pitched as piano wire and close to breaking.

The officer stood his ground, seemingly reluctant to act and started to engage the nearest rioters in conversation, but behind him his men were comprehensively stoned by the mob. Railings and bricks were flying and it was at this moment that Nathaniel noticed a detachment of rioters making off towards Welsh Back. He followed them, dodging the plunging horses' hooves and brickbats in the growing dark. It was getting close to his rendezvous with the skipper and his jolly boat, he had to hurry. Leaping a smashed coach-wheel, he ran across the intervening battle ground and followed the small group of half a dozen to King Street. They were just disappearing into the Llandoger as he caught up with them.

"Lads," he said urgently, suddenly inspired. "The Recorder's escaped and headed off to Redcliffe Parade. There's supporters of his there and Bishop Gray's men. They won't be expecting a rousing yet. We could be first there!"

"Redcliffe Parade, aye there's some stinkin' rich enemies of the people there alright!"

"Aye and the Bloody Blues won't be up there to stop us havin' a fair share. I could 'ave done with a leg or two o' that beef I seen carted out o' the Mansion 'ouse afore the troops come."

"Us'll wet our whistles here and be up directly for a regular soakin' after. Depend on it!" declared the man nearest to the bar. "Now lads a jug o' cider to get us goin'."

Nathaniel disappeared into the night as they refuelled. He skirted the corner of the street and made his way to the shadowy bulk of the trow. Standing on the quayside was the skipper, who pocketed the sovereigns and shot Nathaniel a warning glare. “Right boyo, return this ’ere boat by midnight like we arranged and tie her up tight y’ere.” He seemed reluctant to leave. “Would you be needin’ any ’elp with they Brist’l boys?”

“None at all,” said Nathaniel levelly. “Your boat will be back, tied snug and before the hour. Good night to you.”

Caradoc set up a menacing growl and the skipper glanced from one to the other. Between the two of them they more than convinced him to return to the Llandoger. Nathaniel looked round scouring the harbour-side for a sighting of Cornelius’s men. As he turned back to the little boat, considering his next move, two figures materialised at his side. Dressed entirely in black as Cornelius would have been, they had also black hoods and scarves obscuring their faces. Over their shoulders he spotted ropes and short strung bows, at their waists, short blades. There was no need for words, they bowed and followed him and Caradoc onto the boat, settled into the sculls and pulled away soundlessly into the Float. In a matter of minutes they had pulled level with the *Mathilda*, tied up and taken the sack from Nathaniel. They slipped on black fingerless gloves with viciously spiked palms, and then swarmed nimbly up the cable to land silently on deck.

Nathaniel waited in the tense cold of the jolly boat. From above him on the *Mathilda* he heard, and that only once, the singing whirr of two bowstrings and saw some shining fuses soar up to the rigging. A slight shuffling noise and soft fall as if of a body collapsing on deck, then nothing more. He listened to the distant tide of noise from the square, the confused pounding of hooves, and ragged yells. What he could not understand was the absence of gunfire. But whilst he pondered this fact he had a sudden and unwelcome vision of an enraged Mrs Lydia Peterson, who must by this very moment have realised that her demand for six to convene at six had been denied. It could be a difficult and unpleasant night for Em, and he regretted that.

8 pm: The Assembly Rooms, Bath.

"So we've decided to have the wedding in Spring. We'll wait for better weather won't we Henry? It will have to be St James's as he's taken to it. Admires the vicar no end don't you Henry? He's worshipped there every Sunday without fail, since, well since the incident. Who would have thought just a few weeks ago that our wedding would be possible at all! What with the awful murder, I could quite faint at the thought of it. Couldn't I Henry! Haven't I often said I just felt like fainting away! Of course it's been such a blessing to have him back at work and on his increased salary. He is really indispensable at the bank. The new senior clerk only came on Friday and is quite dependent on you, isn't he Henry?"

Lydia Peterson tried to stop herself grinding her teeth and failed. Even the effort required to maintain a semblance of interest in the subject matter on offer was almost too much for her. She was willing the ineffectual Henry to stem the flow, even to interrupt by offering some feeble responses to the fatuous rhetorical questions. It would have offered some relief. It was clearly too much to ask that he would sweep her off to the dance-floor and not come back. Anna Grant had blossomed into something quite detestable now that Henry had been reinstated. This miraculous re-appointment stemmed originally from the good offices of Mr Howard Dill. Lydia briefly and silently cursed him. Of course, Oliver and Dr Parry had supported it. And it was the right thing, of course. She sighed. It really was insupportable. The Ball had been a disaster and it was nowhere near over. She would by choice have prostrated herself, howled the house down and abandoned the evening, but couldn't, and now to add insult to injury, she had to endure Miss Grant. Oblivious to the ill-wishing, Anna prattled happily on, a buxom meringue in pink and white, with cat mask to match, whiskers a-quiver. The cat has got the cream, reflected Lydia bitterly, but for me, bitter aloes. It had been jinxed from the start. First the girls smashing Oliver's mask so carelessly. The only one they had purchased. How wasteful! Perhaps an omen? Then just as they were to climb into the carriage, Emma looking quite radiant, and her own gown, really, exceptional, Enid running out with the note from the postboy. Damn Mr Nathaniel Parry! Detained in Bristol! Detained forsooth! Nothing should have been permitted to detain him. So sorry, unavoidable, hope to have the pleasure of apologising on his return etc. She would certainly like to see him. Oh yes, she could happily box his ears all night and not tire of it.

"Lovely," boomed Oliver good-naturedly. "Lookin' forward to your nuptials my dear girl. St James's 'ey. Excellent. Yes indeed, and the bank young man? All well?"

"Yes thank you sir, our new clerk, Mr Sanderson, seems to be settling in well. Thank you for helping get everything going again. It was quite a worry." Henry Blake's thin face betrayed the strain of the past weeks, he had lost weight and his eyes glittered unhealthily, but his face had the glow of salvation about it, a wild smile of ecstatic relief usually seen on a drowning man as he catches the life-belt. "But it is odd without Mr Vere sir," he said earnestly. "Is there any news?"

"None whatsoever," said the Captain, pulling his bushy brows together. "Nothing sir. Dashed odd." He glanced round the ballroom fiercely, but his eye softened as he caught sight of Tilly. "Look over yonder! Marvellous to see Mrs Vere. Lovely girl, lovely. Dill's looking after her. Good man. Splendid what!"

Howard was certainly looking after Tilly, and much to her obvious delight. He was shoe-horned into his best dancing suit for the occasion, his characteristically tight shirting up round his ears and finished off with a magnificent magenta neck-cloth. The country dance set currently being called from the dais had obliged him to gallop down the dance-floor with enormous verve, twirling Tilly all the while, and they both seemed to be loving every minute of it. The Captain also enjoyed the spectacle of Tilly capering: her sparkling eyes and flushed pink cheeks, her utterly magnificent bosom straining against her tight-laced evening gown as she gasped for breath and threw back her head, laughing loud and long. Remarkably lovely he thought, remarkable, but he did reflect that this was not the public face of the anxious and bereft wife. She seemed so very glad. Raphael Vere's inexplicable absence was a confounded nuisance as far as business was concerned, but it was obviously pleasing his lady wife. Oliver's kindly face clouded. Nathaniel had not been satisfied by the solution of Wilson's murder and neither was he. Perhaps Vere had something to hide. Howard Dill had sown even more serious seeds of doubt in their meetings the previous week. Vere could very well be shaping up as a monster. Could he have been so wrong in his assessment of the man? For more on that alone he wanted to speak with Nathaniel urgently. He had his own reasons for regretting the absence of the dashing Mr Parry.

Anna and Henry rose to dance and he realised that he would have to gather his wits to solve the most pressing problem caused by Nathaniel's absence that evening, the conspicuous lack of an escort for his daughter. If he did not ask his wife to dance presently there would be trouble of another kind, but he could not yet find it in his heart to abandon Em. The dear girl seemed calm enough, much more so than Lydia who had beaten down hysteria and disappointment just sufficiently to allow her to stay. But there was something rather too silent in Em's demeanour, something too icily correct and accepting. It did not bode well. This was shaping up to be a long night for all of them, a damned long one. He drained his glass of claret, and was in the act of gingerly replacing his fractured mask when Tilly and Howard burst upon their table having spun dangerously out of sequence and abandoned the set.

"Good evening Mrs Peterson, Miss Peterson, Oliver," panted Howard. "May we join you?"

Howard and Tilly's arrival broke the tension and postponed the vexed question of the dancing. "With the greatest of pleasure," said Oliver, who really could not remember when he had been quite so pleased to see the dear fellow.

"I fell into conversation with Mr Casey," said Howard. "Very bad news from Bristol. Have you heard?"

"What's happened?" said Emma sharply.

Her disappointment she had conquered. Long games of strategy must not fall prey to temporary set-backs. Her biggest problem had been how to cope with the reactions of everyone else. To be pitied was a shaming thing: demeaning. She had wondered if a feigned illness would be the only way to draw the sorry enterprise to a halt, and was considering throwing a faint. The Ball that she had been foolish enough to dream about for weeks had turned out to be an endurance test for all of the family. But all of those thoughts evaporated in a second as she heard Howard's words, which brought home to her just how much she loved Nathaniel Parry. The thought of him in danger made her heart lurch and tied her stomach in knots: noose-tight.

"What do you know Mr Dill?"

"Only what Mr Casey has told me dear lady," said Howard, looking closely at Emma. "News came with the mail-coach. A riot has broken out in Queen Square and the troops are out. The mob's after the Recorder for his attacks on the Bill."

"Good God!" exploded the Captain. "If it's anything like Nottingham the destruction will be terrible. Are the Yeomen out?"

"Captain Wilkins hasn't had the call yet but is at the ready. Or so says Casey," added Howard.

"Mr Parry is in Bristol on urgent business!" squawked Mrs Peterson, a ray of light shining up from the abyss of her disappointment. "He is a government man you know. He should be with us this evening but he must do his duty, Mr Dill." She clasped her hands as if in prayer. "He is doing his duty to keep us safe in our beds!"

If Emma had had any emotional energy left she would have saluted this manoeuvre as it signalled a new maternal interpretation of the evening, a triumphant, self-sacrificing and flattering one.

"Here is Mr Casey," said Howard, as Diarmuid cantered into view at the end of the set, whirling his partner round for the return.

"Mr Casey!" shouted Howard. "Mr Casey, do join us when you've time sir!"

Diarmuid grinned widely and made his way over immediately, hauling his dancing partner behind him, seemingly utterly unaware of the stir he caused. Matrons' fans were fluttering at every table with a view of his progress and the young girls were preening, hoping to catch his eye, but when the spectators recognised the identity of his partner the reactions were somewhat different. The matrons hissed behind the fans and the girls' faces fell: it was the gentlemen's turn to preen.

"With pleasure, Mr Dill," called Diarmuid as he closed in on the Petersons' table. "We're just about done in so we are! Ladies and gentlemen may I introduce Miss Colette Montrechet. Coco my dear, Captain and Mrs Peterson, Miss Peterson and Mrs Vere," he smiled wickedly between kissing the ladies' hands. "I believe you know Mr Dill."

As Coco went about her greetings Tilly suffered, she had barely consolidated her recovery after the news of Nathaniel when this new blow fell. Her eyes glinted rock hard as she recognised the enhanced level of threat to her precarious revival. Coco was far too familiar with Howard, and it was apparent that Nathaniel had promised to escort Emma Peterson. The evening had taken an exceedingly disagreeable turn.

Emma, however, was not captivated by the new arrivals and let her attention wander from the party. Her eyes searched out the main door again, as they had done a hundred times that evening. The sea of peacock colours, the gaudy costumes topped by their masked heads continued to revolve, the fiddlers in the gallery sawed away, the fires roared and the heat haze continued to rise, but over the heads, by the door, she caught sight of a tall, muscular figure his gold mask topped by a mane of black hair. She gasped for joy and slipped away from the table, flitted over the polished floor, wove her way through and round the crowd to catch him up.

"Nathaniel!" She caught his arm and he turned.

"Yes madam?"

The realisation of her mistake was like a blow. Her hand flew to her mouth in consternation.

"Oh! I am sorry. So sorry sir. I thought you were someone else."

She recoiled to collide with a couple behind her: his mouth was wrong, his face, his smell, all wrong. Desperate to be out of sight of the stranger she fled, out through the doors and the Octagon, into the card room, behind the door, to take refuge at a neglected table, her heart pounding. She breathed deeply to steady her nerves and put her head in her hands.

"Miss Peterson. Emma?"

She looked up, embarrassed, into the concerned and watchful eyes of Coco Montrechet.

"He would not stay away unless he had no choice. He is a man of honour: he's my friend. You don't need to say anything Emma, no need to explain. It's easy for me to see what's happened."

She solemnly handed Emma her handkerchief to mop up the treacherous tears that had appeared unbidden, soaked the silk base of the mask and trickled down her cheek. Emma pulled off the mask in disgust and mopped her eyes.

"Thank you," she said haltingly. "I thought I saw him, I don't know what possessed me to bolt across here. Quite ridiculous." She looked up at Coco in despair. "I am afraid for him. A riot is an ugly thing. Anything could happen. People die."

"Emma, this is not France. There will be no heads on pikes, so pull yourself together. He is a strong man and a clever one," said Coco smiling. "Now, no point wasting the evening. Come with me; I want you to do me a favour. I need to speak to a lady about some jewellery and I need to abandon Diarmuid for a while."

Coco led Emma back to the ballroom, round the edge of the dancers who were floundering their way to the end of the set, and made a safe landing at the Peterson table. Since they had left the numbers had been boosted by the addition of Dr and Mrs Parry and Diarmuid held sway over them all. The table was captivated and even both the matrons were laughing.

"Diarmuid," said Coco meaningfully, touching his arm, "I must see a friend of mine briefly and Miss Peterson has very kindly agreed to dance with you. Ah! I hear a waltz. Good luck Miss Peterson and thank you."

"You have saved these good people from another tale, Miss Peterson," said Diarmuid bowing and taking her hand. "It's an angel you are, as any man can clearly see."

Lydia Peterson's lips pursed in annoyance.

"Oliver," she hissed in her husband's ear. "Do you realise who that woman was?"

"I don't think I do my dear," he replied, chuckling with indulgent delight at the sight of Emma waltzing away with one of the most eligible men in Bath.

"She was Roderick Wilson's mistress!"

"Was she by George," he said amiably.

"She was, Oliver, and she has manoeuvred our daughter into the arms of her latest beau. He is an Irishman, Oliver. We do not know his family."

"Mrs Peterson," interrupted Dr Parry. "May I have the honour of this dance?"

"Oh Dr Parry," said Lydia, indecisive for just a moment, until the prospect of dancing with one of the richest and most popular men on Sion Hill eclipsed all else. Berating her husband could be postponed, but a close waltz with Charles Parry most definitely could not, so she smiled instead. "With pleasure."

Simultaneously, Tilly took the opportunity to whisk Howard out of harm's way against the imminent return of Coco, leaving

Mrs Parry and Captain Peterson at the table.

"Would you mind terribly staying here with me Captain and talking awhile?" she said. "I'm not terribly keen on being trampled by the herd."

"My thoughts exactly," said Oliver, breathing a sigh of relief. "Allow me to bring you some refreshment, Madam."

He waved over a waiter and they drank a toast together.

"To better times Mrs Parry!"

"Yes indeed. It's sad isn't it Captain. Only last year we had such high hopes. The new government and the new king. So much promise! Dear Earl Grey and his great plans for reform. Now life seems to be plunged in difficulty and quite fraught with danger. Europe seems to be in turmoil and our own people are rising in the towns and the country. They are hungry you know Captain," she said urgently. "Charles has seen people starved to death in the villages. And the terrible news of the cholera morbus! Charles was very dreary about it this morning. It will be here in a matter of months and there is nothing, nothing whatsoever, that can be done about it!"

"We'll lime-wash the walls and isolate the cases. Been done before madam, we'll do it again."

"Yes Captain, but Charles told me that people catch it without being anywhere near other victims and even if they are not in unhealthy air. Miasmas and sufferers are not the only bearers of it."

"Perhaps it is God's punishment for the sins of the world!"

"You don't believe that do you?" said Mrs Parry eying him doubtfully. "Charles sees enough saintly folk dead and villains walking to disprove that old saw!"

"No," said Oliver, "I do not. But I believe in good and evil in this world, and your husband is a good man. Here's to him and his like!"

Early evening: Beneath Redcliffe Parade, Bristol.

Crouched on a double bed in the corner of the cave, face to the red stone wall, Abi held Babs even tighter as tears streamed unheeded down her face. She rocked them both, to and fro, and could not fathom for the life of her why she was doing it, for it could no longer bring calm or sleep. Still she rocked: rocked to keep her sanity, to soothe the pain in her heart and keep her from wailing aloud. After a brief hour of sleep in the early hours Abi had wakened to find Babs stone-cold dead beside her, a trail of vomit down her chin. Poisoned by the drugs, she had suffocated and slipped away. Abi felt sick to her core with pity for the stiffening corpse in her arms, and for herself. Babs had made her escape, no more worries, no good-byes, but what now for herself? She stole a glance over her shoulder, nothing had changed. She still banked on one possible chance to bolt. It would be at the moment they left to get on the boat, and that would be soon. She had kept up the pretence all day. Babs was tired, Babs had finished her food when they weren't looking. Babs was fine.

A small hand grasped her shoulder. "You'll 'ave to put 'er down Abi," whispered Frances, who had slipped over quietly to sit by her. "Tuck 'er up in the corner so as they'll not know." She inclined her head to the doorway. One solitary whore was dozing in her chair, back to the door and feet on the low mantle-shelf of the fireplace. Fortunately for Abi, one of the younger girls had become an ally. Frances, who thought she was probably twelve, and not ten as her mother had insisted when she shovelled her onto the Bristol barge, had the feral survival instincts of a pye-dog. After giving up her initial plan of fighting her way out, those instincts had re-asserted themselves. Playing the game was the only way to avoid further drugging, which was essential if she was to keep sharp. Give or take some aches and pains, she felt she was probably as sharp as she was going to get. Her fellow "ten year old" had proved to be an enemy. Tess either lacked a sense of self preservation or was a born whore. She had fallen in with the guards, especially Tibbs who was scratching herself in the doorway as she snored. Tess had taken to combing her brassy hair for her, creeping around her like an alley-cat and at this very moment was curled up by her feet. Frances had kept well away from both of them, tending the babies if they needed it, but it had to be said her efforts hadn't done much, tonight they were in a poor way. Their eyes didn't look right, swimming in their heads, but they were quiet. The whores had overdone the Godfrey's Cordial, a trick of her own mother's that Frances had seen too many times before. She had grown fond of the infants over the weeks of captivity. She called them Poll and Moll as they didn't seem to have names for themselves. They were twins and delicately beautiful when they had arrived at the caves, fair as two rosebuds with hair blonde as spun gold. Not that they looked so good now, she thought. Their skin was blueish, almost bruised, their faces pinched.

Frances was helping Abi tuck up Babs, when a crazed clattering of feet sounded down the stone stairway. Tibbs's assistant burst through the door and shook her awake.

"Quick, quick! Rouse yersel' there's real trouble 'ere. There's a mob in Queen Square layin' waste an' the troops are out. There's gangs roamin' in the town an' there's some buggers a-comin' down the Parade and smashin' all the glass. The *Mathilda's* a-fire an' the Master's out on the quay with they Chinese! I'm not being trapped down 'ere if there's fire!"

Even as she pulled Tibbs to her feet, they heard the crashing of masonry from the dark pit of the stair-well. The metal grill door slammed open against the rock-side with a hollow clang, followed by the unmistakable sound of running footsteps, and more, a low, growling snarl and the swift scratching of dog's claws as it bounded up the stone steps. As the tarts gawped in horror down the void, Abi and Frances took their chance and sprang from the bed. Wrenching a fire-iron apiece from the companion set on the hearth, they covered the distance between them and their targets in seconds and landed crushing blows on the backs of their heads. Again and again, they swung their arms ’til they ached, mercilessly belabouring their captors with blows hard enough to stun oxen. Tess, startled out of her sleep, set up a wild howling and backed up to flatten herself against the wall in terror. Abi and Frances were oblivious, still beating, beating with all their pent up fear and fury, relentlessly beating, blow on blow until the floor was slick with blood. The women still twitched as Nathaniel and Caradoc reached the doorway, Caradoc leading the way, smelling the captives, the blood and the fear. Tess dodged round them screaming like a banshee as she fled up the stairs, swerving into a narrow side alley, plunging away into the blackness.

“Oh God save us!” said Abi, slowly lowering the bloodied poker as she stared at the tall dark man who had burst into their prison. “Is it Mr Drake?”

“Abi!” Nathaniel stopped in his tracks, his mind racing back to the distant night at Shadwell’s. He smiled in recognition: the alias could still do good service. “Quick now girl. And you,” he shot a warning glance at Frances who still brandished a fire-shovel. “I won’t hurt you. I’ll get you out.” He glanced round the cave, taking in the sleeping infants in the truckle bed, the sprawling bodies by the doorway.

“Now move fast. Lift the babies and follow me.”

Dazed by the speed of events, Abi and Frances moved automatically, wrapping the infants roughly in their bedding as they snatched them up.

“And take those fire-irons. We’ll go the way I came but we might be challenged.”

Suddenly, fresh sounds broke upon them from above and lights shone from the top of the stairs. “Quickly now, down these steps,” commanded Nathaniel. “Follow my light.”

“Stop! Or I’ll shoot you down!”

Nathaniel spun round as a powerful figure in Ravenswood’s livery rounded the turn in the steps, lifting his pistol to fire.

"Drop down!" shouted Nathaniel, pushing back up the steps past the confusion of girls and trailing bedding, simultaneously drawing a pistol and firing into his assailant's body. Even as the man's own weapon fired wide and he slumped over bellowing in pain, a nimble footman wielding a bludgeon leapt over his stricken body to be met head-on by Caradoc. He had leapt at the man's throat, a blur of black and tan, claws and teeth. Nathaniel flung aside his lantern to swap the spent gun for the loaded one as the man yelled out in agony and beat wildly at Caradoc with the bludgeon. Nathaniel levelled the weapon but in the flickering light from the cave there was no clear shot.

"Caradoc! Here! Leave him!"

As the footman and Caradoc fell, struggling in a death roll on the shallow landing before the cave door, Nathaniel leaped forward, stowing the pistol and drawing his makila from his belt to block the flailing bludgeon. Caradoc jumped clear, yelping in pain from the blows as Nathaniel grasped the wooden sheath, drew the dagger and plunged it deep into the heart of his adversary.

He tore out the weapon and rose to his feet. "Follow me!" he said, pushing past the girls to plunge down the dark steps to the waterside. Down they careered after him, hands skinning on the stone as they steadied themselves, round and round the spiral, dreading the sound of pursuit. As they neared the door, lit from without by a red glare, the confused sounds of the quay grew to a crescendo, Nathaniel held up his hand.

"Stop! Go carefully now. Keep close together and don't be alarmed, someone might still be here to help us."

They looked out onto the garish chaos of the Back, edging behind a stack of barrels to put a barrier between them and the crowds of labouring men on the quay. The *Mathilda* was well alight and the crew of the *Blue Dragon* were plying their buckets and pumps to douse it. The air was lit by stark white moon-light and the licking flames, it was full of the acrid smell of the fire and billowing smoke, the yells of the sailors and the crashes of falling spars on the *Mathilda*, all playing out to the distant din of riot from Queen Square. They needed to quit the harbour and work their way round the Bathurst Basin to the mews behind the Parade. One of Cornelius's men was waiting with the coach and the other had offered to stay on the quay. Unsurprisingly Nathaniel could not see him, but took the chance to pause briefly, turning at the sound of an angry voice raised above the tumult. Ravenswood himself, for it could be no other, was standing on a cart directing the fire-fighting operations, his face a mask of fury. Close by him he saw the lone figure of Cornelius, watchful and withdrawn, and over by the fire, his implacable bulk silhouetted against the rage of the flames was Kizhe, his reptilian gaze searing the quay.

As Nathaniel dodged out of sight, turning back to motion Abi and Frances to follow him, the infant in Abi's arms suddenly writhed, made to wriggle free and set up a high-pitched wail. Like lightning Abi clamped a hand over the infant's mouth but fell back against the cliff as the bucking legs caught her in the belly and the flailing head shot back to slam into her face, making her head ring and her eyes pour. Instantly a black figure materialised from the shade of the barrels and in one smooth movement gagged the infant with a cloth.

"He's with us," said Nathaniel tersely to Frances, blocking the raised fire-shovel she had managed to swing up in her free hand.

The man pinioned Poll under one arm and hauled Abi to her feet with the other, propelling her forward towards the Basin. Nathaniel looked round for Caradoc who had limped down the steps to his side and was struggling to raise his tail at the sight of his master. Nathaniel automatically bent down to lift him up and recoiled as his hand slid on the fur, Caradoc's coat was wet with blood. Caradoc allowed himself to be lifted but whimpered piteously, his body wracked by shivering in his pain and shock.

"Is he alright mister?" said Frances, her face showing white as paper in the dark, her thin arms still clinging on to Moll's limp body and her fire-shovel.

Nathaniel could not answer, but managed a quick smile of encouragement. They made what speed they could with their burdens, following Abi and the sailor into the sheltering confusion of the stacked provisions on the quay to be swallowed up by the dark.

Midnight: Marlborough Buildings, Bath.

The short coach journey home had been a better humoured one than the Petersons had dreamed possible. Oliver was content, reflecting on his surprisingly enjoyable talk with Mrs Parry whilst listening with half an ear to Lydia, who was continuing to regale them with a highly satisfied commentary on the dancing. He had been mightily relieved to see Em enjoying herself and would have personally presented Miss Montrechet with a medal for engineering it. After such a night he even felt strong enough for tomorrow's inevitable conversation with Lydia about that particular young woman. Emma herself could not remember a stranger night and, against the odds, it had been a remarkably good one. She recognised that she must really love Nathaniel, as opposed to just saying that she did. The savage pain at the prospect of losing him had taken her breath away. She was also pleased to find she was extremely partial to Mr Diarmuid Casey, who had danced her off her feet. It was more surprising to find she had kindly feelings for Coco, her gratitude for the invitation to dance with Diarmuid eclipsing instinctive pangs of jealousy. They were handed down from the carriage by the footman and were in high good humour waiting for Enid to open the door when a slight figure emerged from the steps leading down to the area and the kitchen.

"Miss Peterson, I've a letter from Mr Nathaniel Parry. I've 'ad to wait Miss and your cook was kind enough to let me sit with 'er. I promised I'd put this in your 'and."

In her bedroom that night she re-read the note from Nathaniel. It was not so much what he said that delighted her as the manner in which it came. He clearly did care for her, or at least cared for what she thought of him. It had been more than a good night. She snuffed out her candle and slipped into her nest of sheets, blankets and eiderdown, turning over the events in her head, looked at them this way and that, but she did not sleep. As the night ebbed away, as they so often did, small insidious worms of doubt intruded, snaking their way into the comfort of her thoughts, laying their sour trails. Before she finally slept, she saw the beautiful elfin oval of Coco's face and heard her lovely voice, strong and sure:

"He's my friend."

One worm of doubt had raised its maggot head, but in the long watches of the night when reason loses its way and small ills cast harsh shadows miles high, one was enough to ruin all.

Coco has his friendship. What else has she of him?

The noose-tight knots regained their grip.

Midnight: The Crown Inn, Keynsham.

The onward journey from the cliff's foot to the coach took on a nightmarish confusion in Abi's memory once she had the leisure to reflect on it. Her knees under her chin, she pressed herself into the depths of the wing-chair before the fire. Poll had damn near knocked her out before the sailor came to help. Perhaps that's why she couldn't recall it straight. She'd almost collapsed with relief when he'd taken Poll, her knees had buckled and the sounds around her had died, but the man had pulled her up, dragged her on, half stumbling, half running over the wharf. As they fled the cold air had seemed to slap her stark-staring awake, her eyes had felt they were bulging out of her head. He'd dodged her round the barrels, up steps, round the corner to the mews, into the coach and somehow, somehow, they had got away. Crammed inside, doors shut, she had had Poll back again on her lap, gagged but kicking like a mule. She'd had to slap her hard. Frances had Moll, who was conscious before the first toll-house, retching and sick. She looked down at the sleeping dog on the hearth and leaned over to smooth his head. He was Caradoc, she knew that now. She checked the bandage round his leg and body, but the red patch seemed no bigger. Mr Drake had had to carry him because of the fight with the footman and then the dog had been rolling in pain on the floor of the coach, whining and crying. So what with the whining and the vomiting and the kicking, she'd had to stick her head out of the window and get Mr Drake to stop. More than that, they needed the privy and Poll and Moll hadn't waited: they reeked to high heaven. They'd got no further than Keynsham, though she knew Mr Drake wanted to get them back to Bath. They'd stopped at the post-house where there was only one room free, so here they were.

She looked over to the big bed with its horsehair mattress and coarse sheets. Frances was lying on the edge, corralling Poll and Moll into the shallow basin in the centre. Later she would have to edge over to the wall and squeeze in there. It wasn't an attractive option, she was tired to the bone but did not want to sleep. Mr Drake had dressed Caradoc's wounds before he'd gone downstairs. There was hot water, clean cloths and supper for them all and he'd left them to their own devices. Somehow she and Frances between them had cleaned down Poll and Moll. Poll had quietened, thank God, worn out after her performances and the two children had spent some time playing with the bread and meat, eating their fill with their fingers, between breaking off and babbling at each other in their peculiar squeaky little voices. She could hardly believe that even part of the ordeal was over. Would Mr Drake tell about the whores and the poker? Would she be hanged? She folded her arms tight, hugging herself in fear, seeing beaten, bleeding heads, seeing Babs white and dead in the bed. Tears ran down her face, blurring the dancing flames and the clouds of wood smoke as they fled up the chimney. She knew where Babs came from, but no-one there would care if she was dead or alive. And no one cared for her. There was no one to tell. Mr Drake had said he had heard they had been kidnapped and would return them all to Bath. She hadn't said anything, but she could never, never return to the Shadwells. At the thought of Joshua Shadwell mouthing his lies she remembered other things, remembered the depth of her despair. After all, there was one good reason for going back to Bath. But after that? Caradoc whined in his sleep, she leaned over to him again, rubbed his wiry head and threw another log on the fire. Tonight she'd sleep in the chair, or better still, stay awake. It occurred to her that it was her turn to be a guard and that idea alone offered some comfort.

Downstairs in the bar Nathaniel stretched out on a settle in the corner, he had no choice but to stay there all night. He'd bring Caradoc down in an hour or two when the bar cleared and check on the girls, who with luck would be asleep, then he'd see it out in the bar until dawn. He'd seen to Caradoc's wounds and been able to leave the infants to Abi and Frances. He had checked out the drinkers and had seen nothing to suggest they had noticed his irregular band enter the inn. The room was crowded and the talk was all of Bristol and the riot. He let the speculation wash over him as he stretched his aching neck and put his feet up on the fender. It could have been worse, he might have perished himself or been captured and failed to save anyone. But such comforts did not banish his regret for Barbara, left entombed in the cave. And the next day would bring its own difficulties.

He pulled his hat over his eyes to discourage conversation and, as usual, ran over his commitments instead of counting sheep. The mood of the older girl, Abi, was uncertain, but he had decided she wasn't a positive danger to the others and would be better left in charge to give her something to do. They were too disorientated to run and seemed to believe he would return them to Bath as he promised: though why the older girls would trust any man surprised him. Probably the absolute lack of a choice had a lot to do with it. He shelved the problem of his first port of call on returning the girls to Bath, deciding to sleep on it and he moved to more predictable outcomes. Good news for Captain Peterson on the investigation front would be followed by fulsome apologies for the Masked Ball debacle. Followed perhaps in turn by an afternoon with Miss Peterson? As the fire collapsed with a sigh and the sounds of the room petered out as the last guests moved off to their beds, sleep suddenly came in stealthy ambush, rapid as the Severn tide. He slid away, down into dark dreams of fire and blood, black-hooded Chinese sailors and Cornelius, in sharp profile against the glare of the *Mathilda*. Then the fire disappeared and there he was in Mrs Spence's parlour with Tilly herself, her head on his shoulder.

"I am so frightened. Please look after me."

Then she was gone, and in his arms was Coco.

Chapter 9

Morning: 30th October, 1831, Redcliffe Parade, Bristol.

"Can you hear it?" demanded Edwin Ravenswood, throwing up the sash window violently and letting in a blast of damp autumn air. Surging in with the draught and filling the stale apartment were the confused yells and crashes of renewed battle in Queen Square. "The God damned *canaille* has roused itself again!"

John Drake looked up wearily from his seat at the dining table, cleared now of the debris of last night's abandoned dinner and waiting for whatever scratch breakfast the servants could muster. Last night had figured with some of the very worst experiences he had endured in the worthy cause of self-advancement. It had been so promising: a farewell dinner celebrating the imminent departure of the *Blue Dragon* and its cargo; and, certainly not before time, one final bout of stilted conversation with the unsettlingly sinister Kizhe and Lee; as a finale, the prospect of cementing his relationship with Ravenswood, job done and a handsome remuneration as good as pocketed. It had started well enough, but the oysters had barely been shucked before the simmering riot across the river had erupted into chaos. His mind wheeled back to the demonic concerto of shattering glass and rending timbers, the howling of the mob, the tattoo of hooves on cobbles as the troops moved in. They had felt safe at first on their high cliff top, the river seeming to provide a *cordon sanitaire* between them and the events across the water. Then, almost simultaneously, came the yell of "Fire!" from the quay and running footfalls drumming on the parade. A splinter group from the square had rampaged towards Ravenswood's house, hurling brickbats systematically against all exposed windows and screaming vengeance on the Recorder, all councillors and all their supporters, whilst below them, inexplicably, the *Mathilda* burst into flame.

Ravenswood had been on his feet in seconds, his chair flying back unheeded, his face furious and terrible. They had been on the parade in minutes: Kizhe wielding the vicious, squat blade that lurked at his belt, in an instant belabouring three men to their knees as Lee effortlessly cut a swathe through the rest of the dozen or so rioters with his bare hands. Drake counted four sprawled on the ground before turning to see Ravenswood mercilessly beating another bloody. He himself had stood, immobile, watching the carnage unfold and feeling strangely removed, until one rioter ricocheted into him from a stunning blow delivered by a footman who had run out with them to the road. Drake had punched the body, jarring his arm and scraping his knuckles, then ducked, but failed to avoid, a right hook. It had caught him squarely, lit up his head with flashing lights and set up a throbbing pain in his jaw, which still pounded dully. He fingered it, letting his fingers stray to the old jagged scar before forcing his hand back down to the table. The fight had petered out quickly with the rioters beating a retreat from the onslaught, those sound of wind and limb gathering up the wounded as they went. He had followed Ravenswood and the others down the stone steps to the quay to join the fire-fight to save the *Mathilda*. The smoke and flames bathed the assorted stores and men on the quayside in a fierce, lurid glaze and the night was clamorous with the fearful thunder of the fire, clanking buckets and alarmed rough cries. Ravenswood had dominated the proceedings: marshalling, admonishing and frequently striking the remnants of the *Blue Dragon* crew who were within reach or hailing distance. They had all been entirely absorbed by the battle on the parade and the fire on the quay until the sickening realisation dawned that the night had an even graver consequence.

Drake shuddered at the memory. Two screaming maids had careered down the steps and broken the news of the catastrophe in the cave. Both infants gone, two girls gone, one girl dead in bed, another stark staring mad and keening like a lunatic, the two tarts on guard, dead, two male servants, dead. More carnage. All that remained of the carefully selected human cargo was the mad grieving girl who was quickly drugged insensible and secured on the *Blue Dragon*. Kizhe's wrath had been truly terrifying. In the aftermath, with the *Mathilda* still smouldering and the *Dragon's* crew hastily reassembled, he had ordered immediate sailing. Captain Trevellis had dealt a surprisingly optimistic card by suggesting that although they should leave at once, they could anchor in North Devon near to his home town where he had contacts with the local poor house. As they were now desperate he could look over the baby-farm there and, if any blonde girls were available, offer to take the infants off their hands. It had been done before but was a hit and miss affair.

"Needs must when the devil drives," Trevellis had said dryly.

Drake remembered Kizhe's face. The Captain had never spoken truer words.

It was a bitter dawn, and the *Blue Dragon* had sailed on the ebb tide, along with Kizhe and the inscrutable Lee, who had borne the reverses with his usual taciturnity. Ravenswood had ordered the removal of the corpses, the boarding up of the windows and the securing of the cave. It had been a gruesome few hours and Drake was dog-tired. Every one of his bones seemed to ache as an accompaniment to his throbbing jaw.

"It is astonishing that they have the energy for more," he said wearily, waving a hand towards the swelling tumult sounding across the river. "Perhaps they are performing in relays."

Ravenswood shot him a look of utter malice. "Their "performances" as you call them need to be curtailed. If I ever find out who targeted my house and my ship I will flay them alive. I lost too many dependable servants in last night's work. Trevellis informed me before they sailed that he had discovered two bodies on the *Mathilda*, charred but recognisable as the watch he had seen on deck in the afternoon. We have lost Elijah and Reuben Berry, they had puncture wounds as if they had been stabbed through the throats, or even shot with arrows. How could that be?"

Drake felt himself wilting under Ravenswood's implacable glare, but decided that to smile politely would be a singularly bad move. He contrived instead to sit, dour and motionless, until Ravenswood marshalled his silent fury, took a seat at the table and resumed his monologue.

"It is very unfortunate that these events occurred at all, and even more regrettable that Mr Kizhe was here to observe them. My contacts with the Count are not my only ones, but they are lucrative. Your share of the proceeds could dwindle Mr Drake, if Trevellis fails to augment the cargo to Kizhe's satisfaction."

Drake smiled thinly as a chasm seemed to open beneath him. Was this a judgement? He had had misgivings about the girls, but had allowed the scheme to run, reeling him into its murky depths where he now seemed in danger of drowning. This was a gloomy thought. He swiftly decided it did not vouch dwelling on and chose instead to throw a life-belt to a far more worthy concern, his self-satisfaction. Had he simply had a lucky escape? He could still claim to have ingratiated himself with Ravenswood and report favourably on the flourishing opium trade, which would satisfy Palmerston. Perhaps he had merely singed his fingers rather than sustained a burn.

"Financial reward is of peripheral concern to me Edwin," he said, with apparent ease. "What is important is the safeguarding of the *Dragon* and the opium trade, which in the view of the government is of principal interest and attracts the goodwill of His Majesty's ministers. You can be assured of full support for that aspect of your business."

Ravenswood did not reply but rose again peremptorily to return to the window and seemed to be absorbed in his study of the opposite river bank. He turned suddenly, "Drake do you have a pistol?"

"Not with me. I never imagined the night would take the turn it did."

"I have a spare brace. Come with me to the square."

Ravenswood's eyes were black pools, his face deathly pale. Drake was struck again by its mask like quality and his memory flashed back to a private discussion he had had in 1819 with Leigh Hunt. Swearing him to secrecy, Hunt had let Drake have sight of a suppressed piece sent from Italy by Shelley, which he was holding back from publication. It was a long poem lampooning the authorities after the so called "Peterloo Massacre" of the crowd at St Peter's Field in Manchester. He had only seen a snatch of it, but it had haunted him for years: "I met murder on the way, he had a mask like Castlereagh." He had seen Castlereagh before his suicide. The man was a positive ray of sunshine next to Ravenswood. Drake adjusted a smirk that threatened to lift the corners of his mouth: it would not do, Ravenswood might strike him down where he stood.

Within the quarter-hour they were equipped with pistols and were on the ferry making their way towards the hubbub of the square. Once they reached the entrance it was as if they had descended into a circle of hell. The square was packed with rioters, now drunk and roistering. Hundreds if not thousands of bottles of the best wines, the best champagnes, the best ports, sherries and rums that the square dwellers could buy had made their way down thousands of greedy throats and were continuing to do so. The revellers staggered, singly and in groups, cursing, brawling and vomiting, oblivious to Riot Acts and troopers, an unstoppable bacchanalian tide. The statue of William III, besieged in the centre, now sported the red cap of liberty and a tricolor. A tipsy reveller hung onto the horse, defiantly chanting snatches of songs, incapable of climbing down. Others fought over bottles or haunches of meat, neither thirsty nor hungry, but frenzied, insatiable and bestial, feasting as if at their last meal, oblivious to the past and the future, the Recorder and the Bill.

Ravenswood smote two men down with his pistol butts, kicking their supine bodies aside as Drake looked round anxiously for an escape route. It was not to be. A dragoon rode over and pulled his horse in savagely by them.

"We need more men like you gentlemen. Go to the Council House and swear in as special constables. The Mayor's sent out an appeal to the churches to get the congregations out. Go on! That way!" He gestured wildly towards Corn Street before spurring his horse away to avoid the shower of stones that the crowd had commenced to rain down on him. Reluctantly Ravenswood abandoned the search for his next victims and took the advice. Drake followed him out of the square. In the side-streets the action was muted, small groups of rioters and dragoons skirmished and a few groups of battered men sat on the ground leaning against the walls. Ravenswood and Drake were able to make their way to join the growing throng outside the Council House. Men of all types were gathering to be sworn in and take the official white linen armband and wooden stave of the Mayor's service: gentlemen, merchants, tradesmen, shop workers, labourers. Drake was reluctant but curious and began to look about him in the queue.

"I'd have thought that the dragoons would have charged before now," he remarked to the man next to him in line.

"And so do we all," he replied. "Are you a stranger, sir? You don't sound like y're from these parts."

"I am from London."

"Then I will tell you something sir. This is a Whig crowd. If you're Tory you won't find many of your fellows along of here. We've Tory Councillors and they've fanned these flames to do the reformers down. Why was the mob not scotched last night? Hey? One sabre charge from the dragoons and they would've been finished."

"No one wants another Peterloo," said a solid man to their right. He lifted his massive head to glower at the speaker. "Would you like to give the order and have women and children run through? There's whole battalions of females and boys in the thick of it in the square and 'ave been since it started there. Would you like the country excoriating you sir! Talk's cheap!"

As the Whig champion rose to the challenge, Drake slipped away to take his place by Ravenswood. Ten more minutes of queuing and they were within earshot of the Mayor's officer who was enlisting the last two men in front of them. Drake gauged one of them to be in his mid-twenties and middle-class, with a cosmopolitan air about him. The other was a substantial gentleman of about forty-five and looked familiar.

"Name?" enquired the officer mechanically. As he looked up, the top half of his body instantly stiffened as if in salute. "Mr Roch sir. Sorry sir."

"Yes officer," said the man urbanely as he took his armband and stick from the officer's assistant. "Nicholas Roch."

"Yon wretches seem to be leavin' the docks be at present sir, but I have had the honour to sign up some of your fellow directors who have volunteered in the public int'rest."

"Good news officer. Excellent."

The man laboriously entered Roch's name on the roster and turned to the younger man.

"And you sir?"

"Brunel. Isambard Kingdom Brunel."

The officer sat back to stare. “You’re the bridge man, then! Glad to make y’r acquaintance sir! Don’t you go a-falling down the gorge now! I’ve a bet on you survivin’. Damned fine odds Oiy might add, beggin’ your pardon for mentionin’ it. Here’s your band, stave and a pair of handcuffs.” He resumed his official tone, taking in Roch as well as Brunel. “Now don’t be shy in using your sticks gentlemen. Lay on with a will and we’ll trounce these ruffians, in quick-sticks you might say,” he added encouragingly.

As the friends turned to move off, Ravenswood impatiently shouldered his way to the desk whilst Drake hung back to step out neatly in front of the young man and capitalise on cornering a celebrity.

“Sir, forgive the intrusion, but I heard your name. You must be Brunel the engineer. Congratulations on winning the bridge competition! I look forward to seeing it completed.”

Brunel was a very short man and seemed a troubled one, particularly after the chaffing at the desk. He pushed back his high top-hat to look at Drake and bowed briefly.

“Thank you sir,” he said. “Though if this foolishness continues we might both have a long wait. We’ve launched the construction project but we need more investors. Riots have a nasty habit of frightening more than just the horses. Investors panic at the first sight of a mob. Are you an investor yourself?”

“No, but I’m lodging at Clifton and have seen where the footings will be started. I might well decide to venture a stake.”

Roch consulted his pocket watch and appeared restless. “Well I’ll be off to the square.”

Brunel grinned wryly to Drake. “Do it quickly my friend, and keep safe.”

He turned to follow Roch and was swallowed up in the crowd, leaving Drake with no further excuse to delay. He reluctantly stepped up to the desk and volunteered his name.

Walcot Street, Bath.

A steady drizzle was falling on the roof of the carriage and a chill had crept into every corner of the cramped interior. Abi sat huddled by the window, rocking herself absently as she looked at the front door of the neat terraced house which had closed behind the man she had thought was Mr Drake and his dog Caradoc. The man had had little to say to any of them since they had quit the Crown. When they had finally fetched up in Bath he had hurriedly charged them to stay put, then disappeared into the house, carrying the wounded dog with him. She hadn't really been surprised when she had heard the old woman at the door call him Mr Parry. New customers at bawdy houses often gave false names. She was not surprised, but unaccountably she had felt an aching sadness in her chest and had struggled to keep back tears which threatened to spill over her cheeks. A boy who looked about twelve had come out to sit on the driver's seat and hold the horses. Should she get out to talk to him? Find out a bit more about "Mr Parry"? Frances was preoccupied with Poll and Moll who were revived after the meals at the inn and were playing an interminable game of peeping round a cloth which Frances was holding up. The pastime had given Abi a break from the three of them and gave time for her to consider her future. The options were not attractive.

"Penny for your thoughts?"

Frances was looking at her, and had probably been doing so for some time. Her sharp eyes bored into Abi like gimlets, raking her thoughts and demanding a response.

"Oh, just thinking what to do next. I've no home now and I've no livin' but I'm never working for the Shadwells again, or anyone else like 'em," she finished fiercely in a hurried flush of anger. The loss of Babs coursed through her afresh like vitriol, making her feel sick, almost dizzy with helpless rage. "I'm stayin' in Bath for a while. I've things to do," she ended abruptly, unsure of everything except a burning need for a visitation of judgement on Shadwell.

"I'm not goin' 'ome neither," said Frances confidently, lifting the toddlers down onto the floor of the coach where they immediately set to wallowing and chuckling to each other in the grubby straw.

"I'm never goin' back to mi ma. I'm goin' to look after Poll and Moll for a bit. See they're alright."

"You can't. You've no money, nor any job, nor any prospects neither, and no place for any of you to sleep."

"Well Mister 'll prob'ly put us all in the poor house for now. I've been in plenty times before. It'll do for a while."

Abi recoiled at the thought, after earning an income and living in what she thought to be some style for a couple of years she could not reconcile herself to being a pauper.

"Not me Frances. I'm older than you. I can get serving work somewhere."

Frances screwed up her nose as she thought. "As you've been on the game and don't want to go for it no more you could go in Ladymead Penitentiary. It's just down the road here, we come by it," she pointed down the street towards town but Abi would not look. "You could stay there for quite a bit for nothing. They'll teach you things about working and things like that," she finished vaguely.

Abi made no answer so Frances tried again.

"There's an asylum for girls up Margaret's Hill. They would take us two, but I'm not goin', Poll and Moll are too little. All three of us could go in the poor house."

"You can't take care of them," said Abi, exasperated she raised her voice as if Frances were deaf. "They're not yours and you're too little."

Frances suddenly swung her hand round and slapped Abi hard on the face.

"Don't you say that!" she shouted. "Stop it!"

Abi gasped with pain and flew at Frances, making a grab for her hair, Poll and Moll, distracted by the violence, set up shrieks by way of a chorus and the coach rocked.

Tobias leaped down from the driver's seat and threw open the door.

"Stop your scrappin' you two! You're making a devil of a din and if Missus Spence hears she'll be out to you and then you'll be sorry."

They sprung back, guilty and stinging.

"Mr Parry told us he brought you all the way from Bristol to help you. You're not goin' to please him carryin' on like fishwives!"

Tobias was a good looking boy, similar to Frances in many ways with his delicate features and blonde hair. She blushed furiously.

"Sorry. Sorry Abi, but you made me mad."

Abi rubbed her face. "Yes. I know," she said, and added grudgingly, "Sorry Frances." She shifted her attention to Tobias. "How do you know Mr Parry then?"

"I work for him," said Tobias, puffed up with a swagger of conceit and stressing his newly learned aitches. "He's from London. Been here a few weeks on and off. Come up for the Season he did. He's lodging here with Mrs Spence."

"Is there room for me?" said Abi. "I could be a chamber maid."

"No. Missus' son's come back from sea and he's not that well. 'Part from him there's Mary his wife and Johnty and old Mr Spence and I lodge here too. Mr Parry's got the big room and a dressing room."

Abi looked crestfallen.

"But if he's taken the trouble to bring you back from whatever coils you was in he'll not leave you on the street. He's a gentleman. He told me not to ask you anything so I won't, but I know the both of you by sight. I come from Little 'Ell myself. I'm Tobias."

"Frances."

"Abigail."

Nathaniel came out to find them shaking hands gravely and, despite his preoccupations and exhaustion, was struck by their beauty. Three handsome children, aged beyond their years by abuse, of one form or another, at the hands of adults. He knew, despite their beatific looks, they were capable of acts of the utmost depravity. "Surely", he reasoned to himself, "they must be retrievable? Aren't we all retrievable? Human nature was a mixture of good and evil and the good must be capable of growing, if only it could be found and cultivated a-right." He was much taken with Robert Owen and his theory of the perfectibility of human nature. Abi was dark and pretty. Tobias and Frances had the fair looks of fallen angels, with Poll and Moll rolling at her feet like cherubim. Tobias seemed a changed creature since his first sighting of him at the Hart. A set of clothes had made an unimaginable difference, and not just to his appearance but to the health of his soul.

Finding billets and occupations for the girls would be a taller order than buying a set of second-hand clothes and would no doubt prove to be wearisome, even more so than the interminable night at the Crown in Keynsham and the crawl back to Bath in the coach. He had not dared whip up the horses for fear of hurting Caradoc more than he already was. Against the odds, after the various skirmishes in Bristol, the terrier seemed to be returning to his old self. The whining misery had ebbed, his eyes were sharp again and he had allowed himself to be settled by the fire to lick his wounds, a task made sweeter by the honey Mary was lavishing on them. Nathaniel shook his head to dispel the memory of the last twelve hours and had the flash of a memory of Cornelius Lee. He would be glad they had won the game. Light versus dark: light four, dark nil. But then he thought of Babs, her body left stiffened on the bed in the cave and the mad screaming child bolting down the tunnel. Dark: two.

He forced a smile. "Out with you girls. Pass Poll and Moll over Frances. "

The toddlers stood uncertainly together on the footpath, as

usual exuding a whiff of stale urine. Martha Spence strode down the path and opened the gate.

"Bring them in Mr Parry. Now then who have we got? Polly and Molly is it? Frances and Abigail? As the Lord said, suffer the little children to come unto me! The first morning service starts presently so we can do no better than to cleanse these mites and take all four of you to the church. The Minister will guide us, and the master of the workhouse will be there with his wife, they'll help us place these wee ones. There's a baby-farm connected with the Walcot workhouse and they can bide there for the meantime." She looked searchingly at Abi and Frances. "And you two girls could go in the casual ward for tonight. We might get a serving place for you, but it will take time."

She added, *sotto voce* to Nathaniel, "Seeing, Mr Parry, as you're determined we can't take the lot of them to the officers of the watch there's nothing more to be done."

"Not advisable to involve the watch at present, Mrs Spence," said Nathaniel. "Thank you for your kind offer to take them to the church."

Even as Frances smiled boldly at Martha, Abi had begun to back away.

"Not for me thank you Madam," she said, her eyes wide like a trapped hare. "I'm grateful sir, but I'll shift for myself."

There were other options. Nathaniel quickly calculated them and settled for the least censorious port for this particular storm.

"Wait Abi! You can help me take the coach to the livery. The horses need stabling, then we can talk."

She wavered, uncertain, but took the lifeline and climbed back in the coach.

"Thank you a thousand times Mrs Spence," said Nathaniel. "Your kindness will not go unrewarded."

Martha smiled, content she was doing the Lord's work, and on the Sabbath! With an infant hand in each of hers, she shepherded Frances before her into the house whilst Tobias hung back to catch a word with Nathaniel.

"I took the message to Miss Peterson last night sir. Matthew gave it me and I took it like you asked. 'Ad to wait hours I did." He put his head on one side, sizing up his chances of an extra sixpence. They were good.

"Lady was right glad to have your note sir."

Nathaniel flicked him a coin. "What was her mood, Tobias?"

"They all came back in rollickin' high spirits after the masquerade Mr Parry. All a-talkin' at once and laughin' fit to bust."

Nathaniel was surprised to feel a pang of regret. What had he expected? Grateful tears? Misery after a wasted evening? He felt oddly discomfited.

"Thank you Tobias, very well done. I'll see you later. I need to come back and clean up before going round to Captain Peterson's. Ask Mary to have some hot water ready in an hour or so."

"Can't see you later sir as I'll be at work at the Hart, but Mary has the Sunday off. Mrs Spence won't have her in work on the Sabbath but she'll let her do the water, seein' as you got filthy whilst you were about good works." He dawdled, unsure whether to speak. "I know them two girls sir. I've seen the little one in Avon Street. The other," he paused, unsure of his audience. "We'll she's a whore sir."

"Not anymore," said Nathaniel. "Thank you for not asking questions Tobias. It would be good to forget you saw them."

"Can't remember anythin' about 'em sir. Oh but Mr Parry, before you go there's one other thing might int'rest you. There was merry 'ell in town last night. Hundreds were millin' round the coach offices hangin' on the news from Bris'l. It got a bit rowdy."

Nathaniel flicked him a second coin and climbed up to the driver's seat.

"I might catch you at the Hart then, I plan to dine there."

Within the half hour Nathaniel and Abi had left the coach and horses at Tasker's livery in Pulteney Mews, the stables Nathaniel had used on his first day, and were rounding the corner of Queen Square to Coco's lodgings. Before leaving the livery he had secured his plans for Monday and taken the opportunity to book out the same pale gold stallion he had ridden before. He would tie it to the hired transport and ride it back from Bristol after he returned the coach and horses. He made desultory attempts to talk to Abigail on the walk from the livery stables but made little progress. She seemed to have retreated into herself and was calculating plans of her own: watchful and ready to bolt if any noose threatened to slip over her head and tighten. After rapping a summons on the door the usual maid let them in and they climbed the stairs together.

As they stood waiting at Coco's door Nathaniel turned to Abi. "Remember, this lady is a friend of mine. She will do you no harm. It was she who first told me about the Shadwells and the trade in girls like you. I'm sure she will help if she can."

He was not. He was not sure at all, and had no real idea of Coco's possible reactions, other than guessing that a visit to the Methodist minister or Walcot poor-house would not be her first thoughts. After some delay, Coco opened the door with a flourish to reveal herself in an apricot silk dressing gown, awash with foaming blonde lace. She took his hands and pulled him over the threshold.

"Nathaniel, where have you been! Neglecting your social duties and skulking about Bristol by all accounts."

She paused to cast an appraising eye over Abi. A pretty child standing awkwardly on the landing, over-dressed in flashy silks, thin coat, indoor shoes, haunted eyes. After her last conversation with Nathaniel whilst scrubbing him free of blood and dirt after the tussle with Shadwell's men, she was sure she knew exactly what type of child young Abigail was.

"Come in Nathaniel darling. And you sweetheart."

She ushered them into her sitting room, its usual restrained calm made hectic by the addition of Diarmuid sporting a loud tartan gown, fiddle in hand, squinting at a sheet of music propped against her clock.

"Would you look who 'tis!" he declared delightedly. "If it isn't the very man! Come over here Nathaniel, I've a new air in this collection before me, and divilish awkward he is to play."

Coco drew Abi over to her. "Come with me to my kitchen *ma chérie*, we'll make some tea."

As they left the room Diarmuid cocked his head in their direction. "Been kidnapping?"

"Quite the reverse. I can't give details and don't want any police interest, but I guess Coco has told you how I found out about the trade. This girl, and another five, had been taken against their will and were going to be shipped as prostitutes to the Far East. They weren't expected to survive long. One was dead when I found them and one ran off, so I brought four of them from Bristol last night and I'm trying to get temporary billets for them in Bath, but I have other business to see to. I was hoping Coco might have some contacts to get this one a servant's job, perhaps in this building or somewhere else in the square?"

"She might well," said Diarmuid speculatively. "I can't say your tale surprises me. I'd heard the like often enough, but I salute you my friend for taking trouble over it. By the by, you might have got out just in time, the mails brought news that the rioters are out again in Bristol. It's worse than yesterday by all accounts. "

Coco returned, closing the door quietly behind her.

"She wants a few minutes to herself. I've given her a drink and some dry slippers. She can keep them." She stretched herself luxuriously over her striped chaise-longe. "You did a good deed for her Nathaniel, I heard what you said to Diarmuid. You can leave her with me for a day or two and I'll see if I can place her. She seems to be in a state of shock but is certain enough she wants to stay in Bath as long as she's well clear of Shadwell's cat-house."

Diarmuid abandoned the fiddle, set to rifling Coco's drinks cabinet and made himself busy pouring whiskey for them all. "To the magnificent escapees! *Slainte*!"

Nathaniel drained the fiery liquid and felt better. The plan was slowly coming together, it might even succeed, and could now be shelved for other matters.

"Coco, were you at the Masked Ball last night?"

"She was the belle of the ball!" interrupted Diarmuid. "And executrix of all affairs! She coupled me with the most charmin' girl I've danced with all week and set more cats amongst the pigeons with all parties than mortal man could keep up with."

Coco purred and held out her glass for more. "Nathaniel, young Miss Emma Peterson was distraught for your safety once she heard of the riots in Bristol. If only she'd known you were breaking and entering, stealing and murdering she could have rested easy!"

Nathaniel shot her a warning glare, which was ignored.

"Your little Abi told me the details over the tea. Nice work," she raised her glass lazily. "*À votre santé*!" She arched her back in a feline stretch; Nathaniel could not look away from her lithe body, and was not meant to. "Emma is a sweet girl," she continued. "I wasn't going to let her languish all night, so I encouraged Diarmuid to take care of her for the evening. They are now the best of friends, aren't you?"

"The very best," said Diarmuid pouring another whiskey. "She handles well in the dancing, light as a will-o'-the-wisp."

"I'm pleased you all had such an agreeable evening, "said Nathaniel laconically.

"You would have loved it," said Coco. "Your divine cousin Dr Parry managed to romance Mrs Peterson out of her temper at your unaccountable absence and Howard's gallant kisses for me almost reduced Tilly Vere to scratching my eyes out."

"Tilly?" said Nathaniel. "With Howard?"

"But of course. She has quite given up on the absent Mr

Vere. Who for my money must be either dead or shipped out to the Far East himself by now."

"So Howard is looking after Tilly," said Nathaniel, surprising himself by the vast relief he felt on learning this. "And," he continued, hardly believing his good luck. "Miss Peterson did not have a wretched evening, which she would not have deserved and would have been entirely my fault." He threw back his head and laughed, for what seemed the first time for days. "Coco, to make my morning complete, say it again, can I really leave Abi with you for a day or so whilst I see to some business? Yes? Capital! I'll see you later. Excellent whiskey Diarmuid."

Nathaniel kissed Coco, shook Diarmuid by the hand and left with a considerably lighter heart.

Washed and brushed up Nathaniel presented himself at the Peterson residence in Marlborough Buildings later that afternoon. He had left Caradoc comfortable and slowly improving by the fireside in the company of Old Tom who was still nursing a hacking cough, the Johnty with a running nose and Matthew who had developed a low fever since his return and was wrapped up in a red flannel blanket. Apart from the addition of the exotic parrot, the kitchen resembled a male hospital ward, with Martha and Mary in lieu of nurses seeing to the needs of the patients. Fresh linen and a sky-blue neckcloth had helped Nathaniel rally, though he still felt his experiences over the last days had roasted him somewhat. He needed to draw away from the fires, take it easy. He might even take the waters: not an appetising thought. Maybe tomorrow.

"Yes sir?" Enid the maid opened the door, her eyes widening.

"Good afternoon. I would like to see the Captain."

"Captain and Madam are out driving sir. Would you like to leave your card?"

"Is Miss Peterson at home perhaps?"

Steps sounded behind Enid. “She is. Thank you Enid, that will be all. Mr Parry, please come in.” Enid pattered off to the kitchen, eager to relay the information to Cook.

Nathaniel and Em faced each other, motionless, in the silent hall. She was smiling to greet him, her thick auburn hair coiling over her shoulder in a rich plait, which snaked down to her waist. Her gown was a luminous pearl silk, sprigged with flowers, her shawl a delicate sage green. He looked at her and saw Botticelli’s Primavera, fresh and radiant, her beauty staggered him.

As always in grand strategy, the first to move is usually at a disadvantage, but Nathaniel was a true Romantic, so he took her hand and kissed it.

“I am so sorry to have failed to be with you last night,” he said, lifting his bright blue eyes to hers and keeping hold of her hand. “I heard you received my note and sincerely hope it helped to redeem my behaviour. Only the gravest emergency kept me from being with you.” He had not really meant to go that far, but the words were out before thoughts could interfere.

“I was frightened for you, Nathaniel, and was so grateful to have your letter. Please do not concern yourself about it. Mama recovered, especially when we heard of the terrible events in Bristol. It was not surprising you were detained. And, I have to say, the evening was not all bad. I made some new friends.”

How long did they have, she wondered? Papa and Mama had driven out, Papa was to visit Mrs Vere and Mama would have more of a drive alone. The twins were sewing in the drawing room upstairs and with continued good luck would remain so. The hall was the only option. She found she was gripping his hand as though her life depended on it: maybe it did.

“So I gather,” he was saying.

“Do you? From whom?”

Wrong move. Instantly she wished she could bite back those words. She really did not want to know if he had seen Coco before calling on her: it would not help her cause but was worse than that, it was a slippery slope to misery.

He let her words hover in the air. No mention of Coco could be allowed to intrude, and it would not be gallant to suggest he had discussed her with Diarmuid.

He fell back on flattery. "I have been told you are a beautiful dancer Em. I regret missing the chance to hold you in my arms."

"Don't miss another one."

She had shocked herself rigid: she could not believe she had said that.

It was the work of a moment. Nathaniel pulled her to him and kissed her, breathing in her scent, burying his face in her neck, whilst above them, muffled shrieks burst from the first floor. Startled, they broke away from each other and looked up directly into the red faces of Ginette and Maddy, frozen in delighted guilt as they hung over the banister rail. Emma surprised herself for the second time.

"Come down directly girls to greet Mr Parry. He has survived the riot in Bristol and come to see us. Come down now!"

Ginette and Maddy trotted downstairs, shame-faced.

"Good afternoon Mr Parry."

Their chorus had lost its edge, they were wrong-footed.

Nathaniel gravely kissed both their hands. "Miss Maddy, Miss Ginette, how delightful to see both of you again."

"How did you remember which one I was?" demanded Maddy.

Since the eyebrows had grown to uniform shape and length he had fallen back on the fact that Maddy always pushed in front of Ginette, but that would not do.

"You move differently. Both equally beautiful, but in your own special ways."

"Do we?"

Em took Nathaniel's arm. "Papa will be at the Vere residence by late afternoon, why not take tea with us then walk up the hill to join him. Maddy and Ginette have a masque of their own they made up to entertain us."

She rang the bell for Enid.

"Go and change girls. I'm sure Mr Parry would love to see your play."

"I can't wait."

The rush of soaring elation in Em's heart threatened to burst it. Perhaps she was becoming a master strategist after all. Should it be mistress? No, that really would not do.

Late afternoon: Lansdown Crescent, the Vere residence.

"So you think Raphael is dead?"

Tilly was animated by a new strength. She had been very busy re-inventing herself and shrugging off the used-up skin of her old life. She had hoped he was dead: the best possible result. Her assets would be substantial, her independence from her mama assured, and just to under-write her triumph, a new safety net had been secured in the comfortable shape of dear Howard. It was extremely important that Raphael was as dead as a coffin nail.

Nathaniel felt sufficiently martyred for all remaining guilt concerning the previous night to be totally expunged. Damned near drowned in tea after viewing and applauding the twins for a good hour and then marching up Lansdown Hill to endure more of the same he was within an ace of completing all duty calls, with just Mrs Peterson remaining to be dealt with in a future bout. Tilly seemed a different creature, basking in Howard's attention and showing no inclination to set about him whatsoever. Despite her exquisite beauty, that had to be a bonus. Even those stunning looks now seemed so unsatisfying after his recent embrace with Em. Tilly's beauty was on a diminutive scale, doll-like, contrived and unreal.

"I'm afraid so Mrs Vere," he said, maintaining the necessary sombre tones. "Though no body has been recovered you must prepare yourself for the worst."

She lowered her eyes and manufactured a small sigh as she grasped Howard's arm.

"Capital, Nathaniel, capital" boomed Captain Peterson. "Dashed unpleasant to hear it though, dashed unpleasant. We must all now look to the future."

"Indeed we must," said Howard unctuously, patting Tilly's hand. "The affairs of the bank have stabilised. Sanderson has proved to be an asset and we intend to move forward with our plans to finance a new vessel for Mr Ravenswood of Bristol. His returns from his other vessels are impressive." He squeezed Tilly's hands now, proprietorially. "Mrs Vere is entirely in agreement with this."

Nathaniel rose to leave. "Well Madam, Gentlemen, I should allow you to complete your discussions in peace. Thank you for your hospitality Mrs Vere."

"There won't be much peace Mr Parry!" said Howard as they rose to take their leave of him. "The centre of Bristol is once more in the hands of the mob, the gaol and toll-houses are on fire and the commanding officer, a certain Lieutenant-Colonel Brereton, has sent the 14th back to Keynsham under Captain Gage! Captain Wilkins has received an order from the magistrates to muster the Yeomanry to help the forces in Bristol. I might join them."

"Oh Howard I beg you not to go!" wailed Tilly, alarmed by an unwelcome vision of her new champion being robbed from her by the Bristol mob.

"I shall go directly into town to see what's a-foot," said Nathaniel.

"Allow me to walk to the door with you," said Captain Peterson. "Do excuse me Howard, Mrs Vere, I will only be a moment."

Once they had quit the house and stood outside together, overlooking the deserted green bowl of fields below, Nathaniel quickly acquainted the Captain with most of the details of the previous night. The omission of Ravenswood's name was a glaring one, but Nathaniel had to play that card close to his chest, in view not only of Palmerston's demands for the opium business to prosper, but also of the urgent needs of the investors in the New Bank.

The Captain nodded slowly. "I respect the necessity for you to keep some aspects of the affair to yourself as persons of note are involved, though the news of the kidnapped girls is grave indeed. You have helped them enormously, admirably I might say, but I have a household of girls of my own and I feel sorry for the young one of working age. Sent to the poor house you say? Perhaps I could offer her a place on my staff? Unblemished character you say previous to her abduction?"

"As far as I know Captain, but what I do know of her is limited. It is generous of you to consider such an offer."

It was very generous, and by saying no more he also chose to be so. Frances might well be unblemished in terms of convictions, but that was probably all. In line with his faith in Owen's theory on the value of nurture overcoming nature, he decided to give her the benefit of the doubt.

"So you're thinking of going back to Bristol? Take care of yourself," said the Captain, giving a bark of a laugh. "Mrs Peterson is very keen to see you in the near future. It would be tiresome if she were disappointed!"

Nathaniel set off down Lansdown Road, jauntily swinging his swordstick and not displeased at the prospect of renewing his acquaintance with Charles Wilkins. He liked the man, and the rest of the fencing club at Morford Street. Despite the leaden exhaustion which had been growing on him after a virtually sleepless night, he felt invigorated and optimistic. Could he settle here? Regular sessions with the Yeoman fencers? Bath buns and balls, walks over the Mendips? Would he miss London? Not really: though he could be there within the day if he did. As he crossed George Street to Milsom Street, its fashionable drapers and toy shops shrouded in blinds for the Sunday observance, he had another thought. Should he do the decent thing and put in an offer for Em? Did he want a wife? She was certainly the type to marry. He felt vaguely discreditable after the kiss in the Peterson hall when the Captain was out. He cheered up at the thought that it would have been more to his discredit if the Captain had been in. He sighed inwardly as he made his way down Union Street. One did not marry the Coco's of this world, and Em's kiss in the hall had been delicious. Lost in contemplating her virtuous delights he was brought up sharp on the edge of a large and potentially volcanic crowd which was seething round a nucleus centred on Pickwick's coach office in the White Hart. Hundreds of people, mostly men and boys and almost all shabby and boisterous, were feeding on news bulletins from the Bristol stage coaches.

"What's happening?" Nathaniel asked of the first respectably dressed man he could find. It was instructive that it had taken a good few minutes to locate him.

"New Gaol's in flames!" he said gleefully. "They done away with the tread-mill and the gallows complete! Prisoners are loosed and there's tales of the crowd moving on the Cathedral. That bugger Grey won't be safe with or without 'is Bishop's hat. They'll teach 'im for goin' agin' the Bill!"

Nathaniel moved away briskly, weaving his way through the crowd to close in on the coach office. He pushed his way to the desk and penned a swift message to Lord Melbourne. From the exponential increase in volume he judged the crowd outside to be shaping up into a mob, a metamorphosis likely to be accelerated as the daylight died. According to Tobias there had been some disturbances last night and the news from Bristol would undoubtedly fuel more. As he re-emerged into Stall Street he could sense that the mood of the men had hardened. Savage faces leered, feeding on Bristol's second-hand anarchy, restlessness flowed like a tide through them, searching for a focus. Ruffians, thieves, the boys of the town: all the refuse of the underclass had risen to the surface and was on the move, looking for a target. Unluckily for Charles Wilkins and the handful of yeomen who accompanied him, they chose that moment to walk round the corner from the White Hart stables in their full uniforms: blue jackets with red fronts and lace, grey trousers with a red stripe and white feathers nodding from their helmets. The mob circled them, blocking the way, isolating them as if in a pit for baiting. Charles motioned to his men to stop trying to move forward and challenged the crowd.

"Out of the way now. We're on the magistrate's business."

"It's our business now," snarled a swarthy man in a fustian jacket and cap directly in front of him. "You're goin' nowhere without explainin' yourself."

The men within earshot bayed their approval, shouting to those behind to spread the word on who had been snared.

"Well Captain, we've 'eard the troop's gathering in Queen Square," said the man, loud enough to entertain the crowd. "Not thinkin' of joinin' 'em were 'ee?"

"I am charged by the magistrates to assist the troops in Bristol. The city is under attack. Homes and businesses are being destroyed and it's our job to protect the citizens. Men, you know me as a reformer. I've every sympathy for the Bill and the feelings of the people of Bristol, but we cannot have the rule of the mob. We must keep the King's Peace. It is our duty!"

His last words were drowned by a barrage of insults. The nearest men shook their fists, some landed half-hearted punches and the crowd began to close in. Nathaniel had seen the way the scene was playing out and had moved swiftly to a position behind the soldiers. They were very close to the front door of the Hart and he had seen Frederick Tooson looking anxiously through the windows, he would be ready to let them in and bar the door behind them.

"Captain Wilkins, this way!" shouted Nathaniel, lifting his stick as a barrier and putting himself between the front line of men who were squaring up and the sanctuary offered behind the iron-clad door of the Hart. Nathaniel glanced at the men warily, ready to draw his blade, but it was not needed. The soldiers did not need a second telling but moved well, and with Frederick's help they were all inside the door in seconds. As it closed fountains of glass exploded into the entrance hall as the mob showered stones at the windows.

"Get those shutters up!" shouted Frederick, red with fury. "Damned vermin! On a Sunday as well! Guttersnipes!"

An auxiliary force of inn servants, including Tobias, burst from the kitchens and spread through the inn to secure the rear and then the upper floors. Nathaniel, Wilkins and his men tackled the front windows which were under the fiercest attack, slamming and barring the wooden shutters, one after another, heads down against the continued showers of glass. An insistent pounding had been set up on the door as a dozen shoulders laid into it, heaving for all they were worth. Fortunately the door seemed to be worth more and held up.

"Mr Bishop sir!" called Frederick to his employer who had emerged, horrified, from his office. "They tried to manhandle Captain Wilkins and his men, they've taken refuge here. Captain needs to muster the Yeomanry and they won't let him pass. They'll do him a mischief if he tries to go out."

"Don't worry Mr Bishop," said Captain Wilkins, making a move to the door. "I won't skulk in here as your inn is brought down around you. I'm going out."

"Not now Charles," said Nathaniel, grasping his arm. "Don't be in a hurry to make yourself the first victim of the Bath Riot. You've a job to do in Bristol."

"You stay put Captain Wilkins. I'll have no killing on my doorstep," said Mr Bishop dourly, before raising his voice with magisterial resolve to bellow upstairs to the servants. "When the shutters are secure get yourselves down here and barricade the doors and windows all round with the settles and benches."

Captain Wilkins dispatched his yeomen to help the inn servants and they all set to hauling furniture against the entrances as the cacophony outside rose to a crescendo. It was heavy, frenzied work. With most windows now broken and the shutters up, the mob took to orchestrated cat-calling and chanting, which grew in volume and menace.

"Have you any weapons, Mr Bishop?" said Captain Wilkins, taking out his pistol and unsheathing his sword.

"I'll open the gun cupboard, but we've only three firearms all told, and they haven't been shot for an age."

At that moment a horrendous rhythmic beating began against every door, front and back.

"They've cudgels!" shouted Tobias, squinting through the shutters on the first floor. "And the bastards are piling up faggots. They're goin' to set fire to us!"

A splintering crash sounded from the front parlour, then repeated heavy blows, sharp now and clear, cheered on by the braying mob.

"They've breeched the parlour!" shouted the Captain, charging through the door to meet them.

"More benches to reinforce," yelled Mr Bishop, grabbing a warming pan from behind the bar as he went.

Nathaniel was ahead of the Captain to meet the first arms and legs that thrust through the smashed shutters. He drew his blade and smote each limb as it presented itself, nicking the flesh to encourage a speedy retreat, as four stocky potboys joined him to shore up the breech with wood, nails and a wardrobe that had been slid downstairs like a ship launching to sea. Nathaniel, no longer tired, felt a professional satisfaction as the front row of assailants pulled back yelping to give way for the next wave. No deaths, no one permanently maimed, easier by far than sparring with the waving curtain at his rooms in Walcot Street.

"Bravo!" shouted Captain Wilkins, pistol-whipping the first head with the butt of his gun, as it thrust through the broken shutter.

As they held the front the side window shutters gave way and two thin youths slid in like eels, laying about them with cudgels, breaking the glass on the paintings, smashing the mirrors, bottles and jugs. Tobias shot in and flailed about him with a metal skillet, landing severe blows to their heads.

"I know you Silas Maynard," he shouted at one youth so all could hear. "It'll be Botany Bay for life if you hurt anyone here. Be off with you whilst you can, you stupid dolt."

Semi-conscious and reeling from the attentions of the skillet, Silas and his accomplice scrambled back out of the smashed shutter, splinters biting into their hands and shards of glass slicing their skin as they went.

"Excellent work Tobias!" shouted Nathaniel as he stopped for breath and the potboys heaved a cupboard into place, covering the shattered window and muffling the din.

"Charles why don't the Yeomen move in here from the Square? They must hear what's a-foot."

"Beg your pardon sir," interrupted Tobias, "but I've seen what's doin' from the first floor, the mob's blocked the end of Stall Street. Only way the Yeomen 'll get here is to ride 'em down and they can't do that without Captain's say so. Also," he said importantly, "I seen a clutch of rioters movin' off to'ard the Abbey. The're goin' to stop any police comin' from Walcot. They can easy do it, there's 'undreds and 'undreds of the buggers sir. And there's somethin' else."

"What for God's sake!" said Mr Bishop, pan at half mast and the light of battle dying in his eye as he surveyed the destruction in the parlour.

"One of 'em is flyin' a red flag sir."

Nathaniel and Charles exchanged grave glances as outside the beating on the shutters sounded ever louder and faster as new men replaced those worn out by the first assault.

Meanwhile, on the landing of the first floor in the corner house of Queen Square, Coco tied her bonnet ribbons and buttoned her grey pelisse methodically. "So you will listen for Abi won't you, Diarmuid darling?"

"Your wish is my command my Lady of Tara," beamed

Diarmuid, flinging down his pen as she spoke to him from his doorway. "The slightest touch on my door and I'll be right there ministering to the need of the young. Don't worry. She'll probably sleep all night and not know you're gone."

"I told her I won't be long. It's quite likely Constance can find a serving job for her, so it's in her interests to wait patiently."

"I'm more concerned about you," said Diarmuid moving to the window and lifting the curtain as he already had done fifty times that night. "There's trouble in town and about a dozen of the Yeoman Cavalry have set up quarters in the square."

"Is there a cab at the stand?"

"Two champing at the bit."

"Then I'll love you and leave you."

Upstairs, Abi crouched at the door listening as Coco's clear voice echoed up the dark stairwell. She slipped back to the dining room where a truckle bed had been rolled out for her to sleep on, and put on her shoes, her coat and the shawl she had purloined from Coco's drawer. The shawl was thin but it would do well. She wrapped it round her face and head to effect a disguise, tapped her right pocket to feel again the hard shape of the small gun she had found in a wardrobe, then the left, feeling gingerly for the slender, curved outline of the knife she had taken from the sideboard. Silent as a ghost she tiptoed down the stairs, past the Irishman's room, and out into the cold night.

"Thank God! There's some officers coming through from Abbey Churchyard!" hollered Tobias from his first floor vantage point. "They're layin' into the lads nearest to them. Oh they're givin' 'em what for!"

"Not a moment too soon," muttered Nathaniel to Charles as the soldiers, potboys and cooks assembled for a crisis meeting in the hall.

"What I need is a diversion," said Charles. "I've made a decision. I'm going out alone to meet the rest of my men. I must complete the muster and ride to Bristol. Mr Bishop, the loan of one of your coachmen's greatcoats if you please. It goes against the grain but I'll cover my uniform and climb out over the roof."

"They need red 'ot pokers up their arses so they do," grumbled the cook.

Even as he finished, every face lit with a wild surmise.

"Are the fires still in?" asked Nathaniel.

"They'll be blown up to do credit to a blacksmith," said the cook in joyous wrath, heading to the kitchen like a man possessed.

"Come on," yelled Tobias. "There's enough fire-irons in this place to arm us all. I'm goin' to the first floor."

They scattered, galloping through the rabbit warren of ancient rooms that lurked behind the elegant exterior of the Hart to search out the ideal poker, tongs, shovel or toasting fork to plunge into the maw of the kitchen fire. Bellows were brought into play expertly by the cook and an ostler who had been caught drinking tea in the kitchen when the battle broke out. Captain Wilkins was waiting impatiently by the skylight when they emerged below him into the hall, with their hands wrapped in wet towels and their weapons of choice before them glowing a rich, satanic red.

"Ready," said Nathaniel. "Captain Wilkins make your move when you hear the front door open. Everyone else, as we open the door, give a battle cry and lay into their legs, we want no maiming of hands or faces from this night's work. When they're on the run, as the cook so rightly said, tan their behinds!"

On the count of three, the iron bound door was flung back and the White Hart battle party howled out of their fastness like furies from hell. Nathaniel and the yeomen led the charge followed by Tobias, Cook and Mr Bishop, with the ostler and assorted potboys bringing up the rear. The surprise visited on the besiegers was total and unmanned them entirely. Their own battle cries melted into wails of terror and a rout began. From his position on the roof Charles Wilkins was gratified to see not only the small band of flailing red weapons making slow and steady progress against the dark mass pitted against them, but also inroads being made on the periphery where an answering halloo came from the fresh throats of dozens of special constables, beating exposed heads with their staves as they swept on towards the Hart.

In the dark, behind a low shrub in the garden of Shadwell's brothel, Abi silently stretched her cramped limbs. She was very cold and had no real plan, apart from staying alive long enough to accomplish her objective. She had taken the spare key from behind the ivy and left the gate undone, but doubted she would survive to pass through it again. At first she thought she might march straight into his office in the stable and confront him, bawl him out and not let him say a word, then shoot him like a rabid dog. On second thoughts she abandoned this. It was a poor idea. Jabez and Billy would more than likely be skulking in their quarters at the back of the stables like guard dogs in kennels. They'd be out and do for her if they heard any disturbance. So she needed to wait, as she kept explaining to herself. He was definitely in there. Candlelight played on the curtains and the lantern was hanging on the outside door to light the path leading to the house. Lights streaked out from behind her, through the chink in the drapes from Clari's room on the second floor and below her the salon was ablaze, but the nursery above was plunged into darkness. It seemed fitting. She and Babs hadn't been replaced quite yet. The distant din from the centre of town ebbed as she waited. The harsh calls, crashes and yells, the staccato clopping of horses' hooves, all seemed to have worn themselves out. It seemed quieter now, but the world was watchful, still a prey to violence, disorder and death, waiting for the next onslaught.

Suddenly the lights in Shadwell's office were extinguished and she heard steps descending the stairs. A dark figure emerged and paused by the lantern, elegant and lean, he fastened up the buttons of his silver-grey frock coat against the chill, seemed to listen to the faint sounds of the distant crowd and sniff the air, then made his way to the path that led to the house. As he approached, she rose silently to her feet, took out Coco's gun and stepped in front of him. He gasped, his hand flying involuntarily to his heart.

"For God's sake! Abi? Is it you?"

She saw him run his hands down his sides, hoping he had left just one weapon concealed, giving him just one chance of killing her where she stood. He had not.

She lifted the small pearl handled gun, straight armed to shoulder height.

"You betrayed us!"

She was alarmed as her voice sounded alien, it trembled and almost died. She saw it gave him hope, he opened his mouth to reason with her.

"You gave us up and Babs is dead. She died in my arms in that rat hole of a cave! You gave us up!"

Strength came to her, but as she squeezed the trigger Shadwell had already lunged at her with a wild yell. The gunshot exploded but the charge went low, missing its mark and embedding itself in his thigh. Her arm kicked back, the gun flicking out of her hand. She snatched the knife from her pocket and slashed wildly at him as they fell together in confusion on the flagged path. Bleeding heavily, Shadwell struggled to capture her hands, forestall the mad cutting blows, but after the first seconds of numbness, pain suddenly leaped into his leg, his vitals, his arms, like a ravening wolf. As he groaned and loosened his grip she wriggled away and crawled out of reach. Moaning in fear, Abi grabbed the gun, scrambled to her feet and made for the garden gate, as behind her Rosie Shadwell reached her husband, screaming his name, and Jabez and Billy's hulking shapes broke out of the stable entrance.

Abi couldn't seem to make her legs move, as in some terrible nightmare she tried to pump them back and forth, but they moved as if under water. Jabez and Billy, seeing Rosie kneeling over Joshua, both turned to pursue Abi. She wrenched the gate open and staggered out into the dark lane where she almost collided with a slight figure in top boots and a riding coat.

"Run Abi, run," a familiar voice, a woman, and a push towards a waiting carriage. The boyish figure whipped out a long pipe and blew it straight into Jabez' face as he rounded the gatepost. A fine orange mist enveloped his head, he clapped his hands to his eyes, loosed a most terrible scream and dropped to his knees. Billy, two steps behind, ploughed into him and was brought up short. He lifted his hands in anticipation to protect his eyes, only to have them brought down again as he sustained a ferocious kick between his legs, opening the way for his own dose of cayenne pepper from the blow pipe. They looked up in their bleary torment into a blunderbuss levelled at them by a man leaning out of a post-chaise, heard a light female voice command the horses and the chaise disappeared into the night.

"Billy," said Jabez, grabbing his comrade's sleeve, his eyes blinded by coursing tears "we was outnumbered. There was three men, do you hear me boy?"

At the upper window, open to the night and all its sounds, Clari continued to stand transfixed by the scene which had unfolded below. The thin girl, her shape and voice so familiar, bringing Shadwell down as he so richly deserved. Then the clincher, that woman's voice: "Run Abi, run!" Clari smiled down on the shrieking Rosie and bellowing Joshua. So Abigail had returned. She pulled down the sash, more satisfied than she had been for many a night.

Chapter 10

Midnight: 30th October, 1831. Queen Square, Bath.

"Pasty sir?"

"By all means," said Nathaniel, wrapping his handkerchief round his hand and selecting one of the burning hot pastries from the tray. He picked it off by the heavy crimping and rested its searing bulk on his knees, where it did additional duty as a hot brick and kept out some of the cold. "You, young man, are a life saver," he said as he combed his pockets for a couple of pence to give to the boy. "Could you rustle up some beer to go with it?"

"Oiy will be back directly," he said, his eyes lazily swivelling over the crowd, his delivery, measured and bordering on the bovine. "Once Oiy've shifted these yer pasties sir."

He had been unlucky in his pasty seller. Grateful and opportunist shopkeepers had been sending out regular squads of boys to ply the yeomen with refreshments as soon as it had become safe to walk from the centre to Queen Square. The Walcot police force and a host of specials had combined to scatter the mob as it was ousted from Stall Street and the former battle grounds were now calm. The horde had fragmented into splinter groups, fleeing the city centre to salve their pride by inflicting piece-meal destruction elsewhere. There had been a cry amongst the boldest to sack other inns owned by Mr Bishop and his partner Mr Cooper, but now their blood was up, any likely target *en route* would be lucky to escape. The square was thick with soldiers, potboys and waiters, traders and other respectable men, carts and horses. Some of the Yeoman Cavalry had lit small fires and some were huddled on camp stools, waiting for the order to ride for Bristol. The siege of the Hart had caused some breaking of ranks and misinformation, some had heard the muster was delayed and had not set out, whilst some had arrived only to go home again. The scene was shambolic, and if Bristol was depending on Bath for an early raising of its siege it was doomed to disappointment. Nathaniel was in the centre of the square, sat on the damp ground and resting his back against Beau Nash's obelisk in the company of Neville Fairfield. They looked up as the familiar figure of Charles Wilkins emerged from the crowd and hurried over to sit by them.

"It will be near to dawn before we can complete the muster," grumbled Wilkins, wrapping his cloak around him and taking a pull of brandy from his hip-flask. "Will you ride with us Nathaniel?"

"I wish I could Charles, but I've got a hired coach and pair from Bristol and they need to be returned before the day's out. They're stabled in Pulteney Mews and I need to settle up for the livery before I leave. The stables open at dawn, but there could be some delay. Perhaps I will see you in Bristol?"

Wilkins nodded despondently after draining half of his brandy. Fairfield looked haggard but he managed a smile. "Take something with a bit more weight than your swordstick! You'll need to be in one piece if we're ever to spar again. Will you be joining us at Morford Street next month?"

"I hope to be in Bath, and in one piece," said Nathaniel, breaking the meat pasty into two so he could pass one to Charles.

"Much obliged," said Captain Wilkins. "I'm famished."

Once the sharp edge of his hunger was dulled, he felt convivial enough to pass round the rest of the brandy but his brow was still furrowed with anxiety. "I hope we are all in one piece come next month. I caught the news from an incoming Welsh coach not ten minutes ago and it's bad. The centre of Bristol is still aflame and they said you could see the glow across the Severn. The Bishop's Palace has fallen now, as well as the Mansion House, Customs and Excise Houses. The warehouses are broken open and the mob's thieving from private homes. This mayhem isn't for the Bill, it's for devilment. It's a damn shame we were held up here, but we'll go as soon as we can. I'll leave it an hour or so, make sure Bath's quiet, then go home to check the mill. My workers are protecting the buildings in shifts, bless their hearts! I'll be back here before dawn."

Nathaniel rose to leave. "So perhaps we will meet in Bristol? Good luck to you gentlemen."

He glanced up at the corner house as he made his way through the horses and scattered camps of men: all was in darkness. Coco and Abi must have retired. Perhaps Diarmuid was out, getting the flavour of the night, maybe he was beating out retribution on some guilty heads as a special constable? Nathaniel felt dazed and his walk slowed almost to a stagger. Delayed exhaustion was flooding his body and without the adrenalin rush of battle for sustenance, it threatened to drown him. He stopped a passing potboy and bought a mug of rough cider. Its acrid burn revived him and he set his course along George Street for Walcot.

His first tap on the door awakened a familiar torrent of barking from Caradoc, but Nathaniel was grieved to note its hoarseness and also that the familiar scrabbling of paws on the flags was slower than it ought to be. Martha was immediately behind Caradoc and opened the door a cautious crack to allow an inspection of the visitor. "Mr Parry! Come in sir!" she said, visibly relaxing and letting the door swing wide. "I feared it might be some scoundrels! Tobias is here and we've heard all about the set-to at the Hart. Come in, come in!" She stuck her head out to check the road up and down. Satisfied she retreated and slammed the door shut behind them.

Nathaniel bent to greet Caradoc, who had defiantly torn off his bandage, but had little strength and was wobbling unsteadily. He swept up the dog and, leaning away from the welcoming licks, he managed to take Martha's hand and plant a swift kiss of his own upon it.

"Thank you Mrs Spence. Thank you from the bottom of my heart for caring for Caradoc, you had more than enough to do with your own family and the girls I inflicted upon you this morning."

Martha was momentarily lost for words, astonished at the rush of pleasure generated by such a piece of gallantry. She could not remember when a gentleman had last kissed her hand. No wonder, she thought, it was the first time. Her husband had done so once or twice, but he had not been a gentleman. A good man: but not a gentleman. She smiled, confused, but managed to mutter, "My pleasure Mr Parry," as she led him into the kitchen.

Mary was pouring beer for Old Tom, who sat looking perkier than Nathaniel had seen him for some time, and also for Matthew, who was on the settle, removed from the fire and without his flannel blanket, but looking gaunt, with the Johnty asleep in his arms. Tobias, clearly in the midst of his tale, or some repetition of it, was leaning with affected nonchalance on the mantelpiece, holding court.

"Mr Parry! Mr Bishop said he was that proud o' me he'll increase my wages. I'm goin' in tomorrow to help him get the parlour straight enough to open. We kept 'em away from the beer and the wines and spirits didn't us sir!"

"You certainly did him proud," agreed Nathaniel, landing himself abruptly on a hard, stiff-backed chair by the kitchen table.

"Oiy 'ave never 'eard the like since Mr Hunt's meetin' in '17," crowed Old Tom. "Though there was no battlin' from the people's side on that occashun." He poked out his head from his shawl, restored to his usual pose of an ancient and scaly tortoise, eyes beady, thin lips parted in anticipation of a morsel. "What's doin' now?"

"The yeomanry will ride to Bristol at dawn," said Nathaniel. "Stall Street and the Square are almost quiet now, the specials are still patrolling."

"They came 'ere for to enrol us but we was too crocked!" said Matthew, shame-faced. "Grandfather too old and me still with the fever. But I have some good news. Arthur Jamieson and Robert Turner came round, a-sportin' their bands and staves and they said there was a press of business down by the barges. One bargee hasn't done a stroke of work for a fortnight gone and he's a man short. I'll go down the quay tomorrow and see if he'll take me on."

Mary's face shone as much with delight as the clammy exhaustion which had enveloped her the whole day in the over-heated sick berth of a kitchen. "Matthew says he won't be goin' to sea for some time now," she said, wiping her forehead on her apron. "Will you Matthew! Maybe he will find regular work in Bath."

Nathaniel accepted a mug of beer from Martha. "Perhaps you need more space here," he said thoughtfully. "I can move out to the Royal York."

An outburst of complaint assured him he could not, and settled the matter.

"You have your room as long as you need it," declared Martha.

"We are snug in Mary's room and need no more," insisted Matthew.

"You are a good tenant," wheezed Tom. "Pays on the nail, 'e do," he continued to himself. "Better food by a long shot since 'e's bin 'ere."

"Tell me Mrs Spence," said Nathaniel, embarrassed. "What happened this morning on your visit to church with Frances and the infants?"

"Well, they're in Walcot Poor-house for the time being," said Martha. "The girl Frances seems a bright little body. She insists she's their cousin and wants to visit them regular. I have asked the Minister if he can help place her in service."

"I might have an earlier offer Mrs Spence. I saw Captain Peterson and he is willing to employ her at Marlborough Buildings."

Martha nodded once and narrowed her eyes. "What about the other girl? Abigail?"

"I took her to a friend's home where she is settled for the night and I have hopes that she will find her a place soon."

"A bad business Mr Parry," said Mary. "The times are perilous. What with all the bother up north, and now with Bath up in arms and Bristol over-run and a-fire. Lord help us, such bloodshed!"

"Bloody hell! Damnation!" squawked the parrot suddenly from the cage in the corner. "God's blood shipmates! Blood and sand! Blood and sand!"

With the righteous battle cry: "Blasphemer!" Martha leaped from her chair, snatched a cloth from the drying rack and flung it over the cage. "That will silence you! You evil, prating bird! I'll wring its neck if this carries on Matthew."

Matthew glowered. "Leave him be Mother, he'll learn. He's an innocent creature brought up in bad ways."

Martha's good humour was put out.

"Mr Parry," appealed Mary. "Don't you believe the creature can be trained?"

"I'm a great believer in the power of the good example," said Nathaniel wearily, "and where could he get a better one than here?" Glancing at the clock on the shelf, he forced himself upright from the chair. "Do excuse me, I need a few hours sleep if I'm to return to Bristol early with the coach and pair." He bent to pick up Caradoc and made for the stairs.

"I'll be about by five sir," said Tobias eagerly. "I'll bring you your water and a bite o'breakfast."

"I shall be up and about in my own kitchen Master Caudle by that hour," said Martha sternly. "Now we all need to retire and pray for God's mercy," she added piously. "There have been calls from the pulpits for a day of repentance for the evil deeds done in this land. We can start with our prayers this very night."

The early hours: 31st October, 1831.
The King's Arms Inn, Malmesbury.

Diarmuid poked the remnants of the fire into life before returning to his unfinished supper at the table. It had been an unusual evening: a rare and reckless one. Coco never ceased to amaze him. He poured another glass of claret and watched the winking firelight play through its richness. He swirled it round the body of the glass, watching it cling and roll slowly down like a translucent receding wave. Malmesbury had proved to be a wise choice. The dark panelled room offered an antique comfort, warmth, a clean bed and plentiful food and drink, even at this god-forsaken hour. The coaching inn was an old but efficient one and he had felt sanguine about leaving his coach and pair in the stables. Despite appearances, Diarmuid Casey was finicky about his personal possessions. He had not always had many and valued those he had acquired. But he did like excitement and a modicum of danger. Squiring Mademoiselle Colette Montrechet round Bath for the last few months had been a joy, all the more delicious for it being unlooked for. "But", he reflected, taking a deep draught of the claret, "all good things must come to an end: just one more trip and the current fandango will be complete."

He picked up the chicken leg and tore at it with his teeth. The Pelican Inn at Gloucester did not sound as commodious as the King's Arms but they need not stay. It should only be a matter of delivering the girl and they could head straight back to Bath: and not before time. His own work had been languishing and he was expected back in London as his lectures in the west had been over for a week and Mr O'Connell had need of him. He would, however, keep his Bath rooms. The bonus of meeting up with Coco again would not be squandered.

The current caper had all gone rather well. By some flash of womanly intuition Coco had known where the girl had gone and what she was up to. They had scooped up the crazed Abigail and whisked her out of Bath avoiding all let and hindrance, putting a good few miles between her and the Shadwells, and with an ounce of luck should settle her in some make-shift employment before noon tomorrow. She could keep her head down until any resulting brouhaha in Bath blew over. He chuckled to himself as he pictured Coco's respectable pose as his relative with her serving maid when they fetched up at the King's Arms. It had been a fortuitous choice. Coaching inns always had advertisements in the stage offices, and although they had not found any vacant positions for her in the forest of notes on the board, a jovial cove travelling from Gloucester over-heard their requests and had given them the break they needed. He had come from the Pelican in St Mary Street, where the landlord had most negligently allowed three chamber maids to slip away over the last week. His bad luck should soon become their doxy's salvation.

His thoughts were interrupted by a soft creak as the communicating door opened to admit Coco. "How now fair cousin!" said Diarmuid amiably.

Coco sat down with him and poured herself a drink. "*Slainte*! So far so good. She is grateful for the chance of work in Gloucester and has fallen asleep. There should be no more escape bids tonight."

"Congratulations to you my dear one," said Diarmuid. "You're a woman of great resource and I keep discovering more. Where will it end? I have to know! With any tale I am a regular terror and always read the last page first, so indulge me and confess all now!" He watched her, teasing, yet as always with her, he was not in full control. He felt the thrill of the chase:

would he ever manage to uncover all of her charming deceits? Would the firelight help him do it, the exhilaration of the past danger, the undoubted romance of the night? For Coco to rise, dance, sing him a song, throw off her clothes and tumble into bed with him was commonplace: it was her secrets he lusted after, as they had, to date, been unattainable. The fire collapsed, singing, in the hearth and he rose to throw on another log. It could be a time for confidences.

"What exactly would you like me to confess darling?" said Coco, entertained by his interest.

"I've known you for a good many years, so I have," said Diarmuid slowly. "I've seen you charm men, women and the birds out of the trees. I've seen you plenty times before in men's riding gear, and I've seen you drive a pair, but I've never seen you fighting, my girl! Let's start with that. Where did that particular skill originate might I ask?"

"I've not had a sheltered life Diarmuid."

"Neither have many women, but they still can't fight. Go on, tell me more!"

Coco put her head to one side, weighing up the merits of divulging some tantalising half-truths against spinning a few outright lies. "You know I was orphaned. I had older brothers and we fended for ourselves after our mother eventually died. I spent some formative years in *arrondisements* which were far from genteel, Diarmuid! I was also in Marseilles," her face clouded and closed, he really didn't need to know that, but she continued: without the names, without the gothic tales of misery. "I learned savate," she smiled, appearing pleased with herself. "Have you heard of it? No? Such a sheltered life *cherie*! It is a good way to defend yourself if you need to. I will train you! You will be a force to be reckoned with."

"What did you do to their eyes? What was in the pipe?"

"Just pepper. Cayenne. Most effective and better if you target it. So remember, don't throw it, shoot it directly. A man I knew had so many treasures from the East. He had a beautiful collection of lacquered boxes holding different concoctions of stinging pepper. They were used as weapons. Some had mouthpieces for blowing a cloud at his enemies. Small blowpipes work just as well. Just one charge has very desirable effects."

"As I saw," said Diarmuid, watching her intently. "Fortunately those are not the only desirable effects you have Coco."

She smiled, her eyes opaque, watchful, and leaned over to kiss him.

Mid-morning: Bristol.

As Nathaniel passed the Wells fork in the Bath road, and descended the incline to follow the south bank of the river to Redcliffe, he could hear the ominous rushing of distant flames and taste the smoke in his mouth. Black clouds edged in an angry red billowed up from the direction of Queen Square and he could hear the distant tumult of battle, briefly outmatched by a thunderous crash and confused cries as another building collapsed, reluctantly giving up the ghost after two days of torment. Isolated groups of ragged men were dodging the traffic and fleeing from the centre, some laden with booty, who would rue their greed when the troops began their sweeps of the arterial roads and the surrounding fields. For now they staggered on unmolested, most rolling drunk, blackened and wounded. One man ran crazily at the horses' heads brandishing what looked like a communion goblet.

"I got silver matey! Give us a sovereign! Give us ten shillings then!"

Nathaniel whipped the horses on and the man fell cursing into the road. He drove alongside the mud banks of the Avon, pleased that the buildings on the south side of the river seemed whole enough. Some had shattered glass, many had boarded up their ground floors, but the flames had not spread here. Nathaniel hurried on to Redcliffe and was relieved to find the livery was also intact. He bullied a reluctant groom from the office where he lurked behind make-shift barricades, settled his debt and after bargaining for water and a rub-down for the stallion, decided to try to ride into the city over Bristol Bridge to see the action for himself, then make his way to Drake's rooms in Clifton.

He made slow progress along the Welsh Back to Queen Square, as he had to pick his way as if over a battlefield. With the whip left behind at the stables, he drew his makila from his belt and held it with the reins, ready for service. Fires were still flaring from King Street and in the square beyond, but it occurred to him that without the intermittent drizzle the furious destruction would have been even wider spread. Wailing cries rent the air, groups of women knelt by some of the ruined houses, rocking and praying, hands clasped in desperation, eyes closed on the desolation before them, prayers unanswered. Charred bodies lay like rough-barked tree trunks where they had fallen or crawled to as they made their escapes from the infernos, some were impaled on railings after losing their footing on higher floors, other corpses were dismembered or disfigured by gaping wounds, cut by sabres after falling victim to earlier charges from the roaming cavalry detachments. Groups of dragoons continued to search the streets, Gloucester men and other Wiltshire cavalry detachments, men of the Somerset yeomanry including some familiar faces from Captain Wilkins's troop, all clattered past to mop up remaining cells of rioters still bent on plunder, or simply too befuddled with drink and lethargy to escape. Loosed pigs grunted as they rooted in the corpses, chickens picked at abandoned caches of food and dogs howled for their masters. His horse stumbled on pavements forced up into ridges by the burning in the vaults below and shied away from shimmering rivers of molten lead which snaked down walls from the melting roofs, enamelling them with a demonic sheen. Nathaniel unwound his neck-cloth and wrapped it round his face to protect it from the searing heat and choking smoke: the overwhelming stench of liquor, rum and brandy, burning, blood, and death.

With reckless daring, given the heavy military presence, some rioters were still trying to sell their booty on the streets. Feather beds for a shilling, gold and silver plate, furnishings and bedding, all on offer from ragamuffins stuffed out like bolsters, wearing so many layers of waistcoats and topcoats in the heat that they resembled nothing so much as three-bird Christmas roasts. Occasional gangs of young boys still rampaged wielding burning brands, though they scattered as they caught sight of any of the avenging detachments of troops, their reluctance to miss any last opportunity for pillage outmatched by a feral sense of self-preservation.

Sickened by the sights, Nathaniel decided to skirt the square, make for the drawbridge at the far end of St Augustine's Reach and thence to the Cathedral precinct. The destruction there had blazed a trail as far as the Bishop's Palace where fires still burned, though the precinct itself seemed quiet. The Cathedral doors hung open and a rearguard, all weary and soot smeared, some bandaged and bloody, stared out like sleepwalkers as they heard fresh hooves approach, then fell back to their miserable task of clearing debris and sorting the spoil. The ground was littered with torn pages of manuscripts, which lifted occasionally to swirl in the fitful gusts, briefly revivified, to die again amongst the charred books, hassocks and abandoned flags as the wind dropped. Nathaniel pushed on through Clifton Wood towards Drake's rooms in Cornwallis Crescent, relieved to see fewer signs of the depredations as he climbed higher, though the streets were eerily quiet for a Monday morning, the houses closed and barred.

He rode round to the stables and left his mount with a groom. Drake's horse was missing, which was not a good sign, but he was resolved to go in, Drake or no. The horse needed more of a rest and he might at least learn something of Drake's movements, even if he were missing. He was shown to the drawing room to meet Lottie, but did not find her alone.

Amanda Ravenswood and Lottie Drake had spent an increasingly fractious morning in each other's company. Normally they drank tea, wine, Bristol sherry or gin, depending on the company or lack of it, and divided their time between Lottie's drawing room, the Assembly Rooms and walking the crescents and the Downs. They gossiped, they dissected the reputations of the rest of Clifton's finest, they competed and they generally enjoyed, but today had been very different. In fact it had been uniquely unpleasant. Amanda had arrived, sulky and cross, after being driven from Arno's Tower to Redcliffe Parade, as planned, only to find it empty of all but the most menial of servants. Edwin had not waited to entertain her for luncheon, as arranged, but had instead gone to town, determined to enrol as a special constable according to the gibbering maid who had come out to speak to her. Only a boorish under-footman was available to help her coachman with the horses and the house had an uneasy, neglected air. There had been some calamitous misadventure that no-one seemed willing to speak of. The *Mathilda* was a smouldering ruin and apparently some servants had been killed, there were certainly no arrangements made for her reception whatsoever. Unaccountably, and despite the rumoured sabre charge at dawn from assorted dragoons, she had still seen some marauding gangs of the lower classes roaming the streets as she had been driven to Clifton. Three days of mayhem. She pursed her lips peevishly. What on earth was the military for if it could not keep order?

The arrival of a visitor offered a promising diversion, as Lottie's anxiety over the whereabouts of her husband had become tedious well over an hour before. Amanda had no fears for Edwin's safety whatsoever, in fact, apart from her annoyance about luncheon his extended absence was something of a bonus. His mood of late had been alarming, and at times of any type of difficulty he tended to vent his frustration on her in a variety of ways. Most of which were unpleasant. She had been looking forward to the departure of the Chinese visitors and the *Blue*

Dragon, which had clearly occurred, but otherwise the day had fallen far short of her expectations. A visitor, any visitor, would have relieved the ennui, but this one was diversion indeed. She extended her hand to greet a tall, powerfully built young man in his mid-twenties, a good decade her junior, with thick black hair swept back from his face, sparkling bright blue eyes and something else, there was a dynamic energy about him which she found compellingly attractive. It was a life-force of a different quality from Edwin's, who was also tall, darkly handsome and undoubtedly energetic. This man, this Nathaniel Parry, had a wholesome appeal. He even smelled of the open air. With a pang of discomfort she compared it unfavourably with the spiced unguents and scents that Edwin had favoured of late. She felt a physical response as Nathaniel took her hand, a charge of passion, which even as it rose within her was almost instantly extinguished by a cold flush of fear. How could she even think it? Edwin had an uncanny ability to read her thoughts. Even an attraction to another man would be seen as a betrayal. She withdrew her hand abruptly. Edwin was a monster, but, she reminded herself, as she had so often before, he was wealthy and devoted to her, the two attributes necessary for her to remain with him. But even as she rehearsed the familiar mantra of justification, another voice, whispering and insistent, corrected her. "He is wealthy, the prime and only attribute necessary". It had often surprised her, despite her vanity, that she had not found him to have a mistress or other occasional women.

"Any day, any time," whispered the voice, "it could happen. It may already have done so, and you are powerless."

Nathaniel was settled on a high backed chair with a glass of sherry, opposite the two women who perched on a striped sofa, their fashionably padded sleeves and full skirts competing for space, their jewels vying. He could see the similarities between Charlotte Drake and Ravenswood's wife, both enjoying their riches, both brittle and haughty. They were beautiful, in a harsher, more studiedly elegant manner than the fluffy Tilly, though they were decked out in a similar style, the extravagant leg o'mutton sleeves, the plunging necklines, the yards of lace and ribbons. He had a fleeting vision of Coco, she would not have poised herself like these two harpies, ready to pounce and dissect him, but would have stretched herself out languorously, invitingly, kicking off her shoes. He smiled at the thought of her and her generosity of spirit. Neither of the two society women would have wasted one moment's thought on such a pitiful creature as the child-whore Abigail.

"Well Mr Parry," said Lottie, the anxiety in her voice overlaid by the sharpness of frustration and a growing anger. "Do you have news of my husband? He went to dinner with Mr Ravenswood last night and we gather they have gone to join the special constables. What possessed him I cannot imagine!"

"I have come here to ask you the same question Mrs Drake. I need to discuss business with him and hoped to find him here."

"They will probably return to Redcliffe Parade after they have finished performing as constables. We have a house there," said Amanda, watching Nathaniel stonily. "Tell me Mr Parry, what exactly is going on in town?"

"It is in ruins," said Nathaniel shortly. "It still burns and the mobs are not entirely banished, though the military have the upper hand. I would advise you ladies to stay indoors. Where is your main residence Madam?"

"Arno's Vale," said Amanda. "I have my coach waiting. The driver will take me home later. I shall try Redcliffe Parade on my way and see if Edwin has returned. I know he will not quit the city as a ship of ours has been damaged and we have some trouble at the Redliffe house. I gather the mob attacked it, we are some servants short."

Nathaniel watched her closely, relieved to hear that his deeds had been palmed off on the mob. It was a good moment to try to disengage Drake from Bristol as they were both due to make their reports to the noble lords within days and, unlike their last trip, he was determined to keep Drake with him for the journey as the long hours on the road could be put to good use.

"Mrs Drake you might be wise to remove to Bath. I gather your husband's business with Mr Ravenswood will conclude shortly and it will be safer there. There was some trouble last night but it is trivial in comparison to the events here. Mr Drake and I need to travel to London urgently and it would be wise to go to Bath before he leaves."

Lottie reviewed her situation. The adventure in Bristol had soured. Amanda was far less diverting than she had been and the city was too volatile to vouch keeping Lizzie there any longer. It was all too tiresome and she was ready for a change.

"The Bath Season is well under way is it not?" she said, fixing Nathaniel with a cold interrogatory stare. "I read there was to be a Reform Soiree at the Assembly Rooms on November 5th. We are rather tired of random bonfires but a little *feu d'artifice*, a little sparkle, might not go amiss. It seems the Whig campaign still has life in it despite the Lords' judgement, and provided the miserable populace will conclude its roistering and allow ordinary life to continue, the evening might well be an interesting one."

"I would like to go," said Amanda, feeling suddenly unwilling to lose her new companion. "Charlotte, you could ask John to encourage Edwin to attend."

"Well ladies," said Nathaniel, rising to leave. "Thank you for your hospitality. I think my best move will be to go to Redcliffe Parade and wait for the gentlemen to return."

After he had been seen out, Amanda said. "He never asked for the number of our house. He seems a resourceful man. And he is rather handsome."

"Is he? I suppose so," said Lottie absently, turning down her mouth in disapproval. "He's a subordinate of John's. He might well be right though. I might insist we go to Bath." And, she thought to herself, she might do well to encourage Amanda to insist that she and her husband follow suit. She had not quite abandoned her designs on Edwin Ravenswood, and the waltz was the most convenient invention imaginable, providing as it did an unrivalled opportunity to be close, very close indeed, with other women's husbands. Her anxiety for John had become tedious and she allowed herself to move on to far more stimulating possibilities. Assuming a smile she liked to think looked brave yet vulnerable, she picked up the sherry decanter and poured two generous measures into the empty blue glasses.

Nathaniel rode back through the shattered town, easily avoiding trouble. The dragoons had grown in number and there were literally thousands of special constables seeking out rioters and looters, dispensing brutal summary justice before hauling them off to the magistrates. He made his way to Ravenswood's residence in Redcliffe Parade, tied his horse to the railings and climbed the steps to the front door. Additional make-shift shutters had been attached both to the door itself and to all the windows on the front of the house, though the piles of broken glass in the area and on the side of the steps showed that these had come too late to forestall the first wave of vandalism he had generated in the Llandoger. He was admitted to the house and shown into a dining room on the first floor where he found Ravenswood standing by the window, deep in conversation with Drake. It was Nathaniel's first sighting of him since the hectic night on the wharf and as the ship owner turned to shake his hand, he was struck by the brooding menace of the man. He was of a similar height to Nathaniel and black-headed like him, though of Drake's age. Ravenswood's eyes were dead pools, allowing no emotion or expression, his hands, though immaculately manicured, were bruised and swollen.

"Mr Parry, what can I do for you?"

"I have need to speak with Mr Drake on matters of business sir. I came here after visiting Cornwallis Crescent. The ladies directed me here."

Drake flinched at the mention of his wife. "How is Lottie? How's Lizzie? Has the Crescent escaped harm? I have been too occupied to return!"

"They are safe in Clifton as the mob spread no further than the cathedral precinct, but I did suggest Mrs Drake might be more comfortable in Bath."

Nathaniel sensed an unpleasant tension between the men, and he had no desire to prolong his stay. His dealings with Drake needed privacy.

"Mr Drake, as our meeting in London is imminent and we have much to discuss, perhaps you might change your usual plans and travel with me?"

Drake brightened visibly. "Oh yes indeed Parry. We must return urgently, given the circumstances. I will come to Bath tomorrow, with my family, and you and I will leave directly for London. I gather the situation in Bath is better than here!"

"Well, don't head for the Hart. There was some disturbance in the city but the York House is untouched."

"Capital," said Drake unevenly. Even the unattractive prospect of hours of cross-questioning by Parry was preferable to one extra day, or one extra minute with Ravenswood. After the disastrous night and endless day in the town battling with looters he was exhausted. He felt filthy, his mouth gritty and sour. An early removal to London would also reduce the time spent explaining himself to Lottie, which was another important aspect to be borne in mind. "Well Ravenswood," he continued. "I thank you for your hospitality. It was unfortunate that all did not fare as well as it might."

"You had a ship ready to sail I gather," said Nathaniel innocently. "Not the one lying at anchor I hope."

"No, not that one," said Ravenswood, with an unpleasant smile. "No doubt we will meet again at some point Mr Parry."

"No doubt sir," said Nathaniel bowing, and intending to postpone that threat if he were ever allowed the choice. Turning to Drake he said, "Tomorrow morning then, at the Royal York," turned on his heel and left.

Evening: Queen Square, Bath.

That evening, Nathaniel and Caradoc were standing in the twilight on the landing by Coco's door: Nathaniel convincing himself that he was glad to hear Diarmuid's voice as he waited. After dealing with Drake he had spent plenty of time soul-searching on his ride back from Redcliffe. He knew it was far from wise to spend more time alone with Coco, but needed to find out how her good deed for Abigail had gone. Coco opened the door with her customary flourish, arms wide in welcome like a burlesque dancer emerging from a stage curtain.

"A man and his dog! Come in, come in! Take a seat Nathaniel, darling. We have settled your little girl in Gloucester. She is waiting on tables in the Pelican and vows she will stay put. You could visit her if you like."

"Why should she not stay put?"

Coco screwed up her nose at Diarmuid who was fastening himself into a greatcoat and seemed ready to leave.

"Stay for the tale Diarmuid. Sit down Nathaniel, your little miss was up to mischief last night."

"Coco, she is not my miss," complained Nathaniel mildly, but took a seat whilst Caradoc made a bee-line for Diarmuid, who seemed a more likely ticket to the outdoors. Caradoc had spent too long cooped up after the exploit in Bristol and sensed the call at Coco's could be a long one.

Coco briefly explained how they had rescued Abigail after her failed assassination attempt on Shadwell and spirited her away by coach, whilst Diarmuid embroidered Coco's role, shamelessly flattering her, as they both watched the effect on Nathaniel. His obvious admiration for her entertained both of them, good-natured sybarites that they were.

"So you see, Nathaniel, our beautiful Coco is a force to be reckoned with: a force of nature sure she is. Cross her at your peril sir!"

Nathaniel was tired of the jokes. Evenings with the pair were rather like consuming absinthe, the green drink of Maison Pernod Fils: *la fee verte*, the lethal green fairy. The first sips were magical, but the wormwood inexorably rose to eclipse the magic as the long night wore on. A little went a very long way.

"You have worked wonders," he said, rising to leave.

"Walked on water," chimed in Diarmuid. "Your debts are off the scale and you will be in our thrall for ever!"

Nathaniel managed to raise a laugh. "That may be the case, but I must leave you for now. I'm truly grateful that you gave the girl a chance to redeem herself. Are you in Bath much longer, Diarmuid? I'm away to London tomorrow but will return shortly. I gather there is a Reform Soiree and speaking of redemption, I need to redeem myself with Miss Peterson."

"We will be there," said Coco. "But I expect you to dance with me Nathaniel. Diarmuid will abandon me for your Miss Peterson as soon as he sets eyes on her."

Unaccountably vexed at the chaffing, Nathaniel needed the walk to Marlborough Buildings to clear his head. He did not know exactly what he would say to Em, but knew he needed to see her. He felt a physical ache of loneliness and wanted to slide into the warmth of her embrace, and that of the whole Peterson household if they would allow it, they could do him sterling service as an emollient bath. He felt he needed to cleanse his spirit in their familial nest. He had not been used to such a retreat but had started to value it. He would not mind seeing the twins, or even Mrs Peterson, and in that respect his luck was in, if it could by any stretch of the imagination be called that. Enid informed him that the only senior Peterson available was that very lady.

Nathaniel was shown into the drawing room to greet Mrs Lydia Peterson, who was standing by the fireplace wearing a gown of pale blue silk moiré and an expression that could only be described as forbidding. "Well, at last, Mr Parry," she said acidly.

"Mrs Peterson, how glad I am to see you!" Nathaniel turned

on the tattered remnants of his charm: ate humble pie for his lamentable failure to attend the Masked Ball; enquired after her health and that of the Captain; the fortunes of the twins; the situations of Miss Anna Grant and Mr Henry Blake; the progress of Miss Grant and Mr Blake's wedding plans; and of course, he wondered where Miss Peterson might be. The chill in Mrs Peterson's demeanour lifted, reluctantly, and by degrees. This was a game he played well and he was rarely resisted.

"We realised of course that you were unavoidably delayed by the unfortunate occurrences in Bristol. A place I always regard as demonstrating the most shameless vulgarity I might say. It seems to me to be the fount of all evil-doing in this part of the world." She smiled thinly, he could almost hear the ice break. "We did appreciate your letters of apology. And I know that some poor girls were saved, Mr Parry. I fully appreciate the need for discretion, my husband has explained that matters of national importance are involved. Quite heroic, I can see that now." She had not seen it at all a mere hour ago and had remonstrated volubly as Oliver and Emma had prepared to go to the poor-house to appoint one of them as a kitchen domestic. "Even as we speak the Captain and Emma are in Walcot, negotiating employment for a child, I believe by the name of Frances."

There was no point in staying longer. Catching Em alone today was going to be impossible. Better delay it until he returned from London.

"I gather there is a Reform Soiree at the Rooms on the 5th November." He hurried on despite a new ice-age tightening its grip on Mrs Peterson's features. "I intend to return and attend, hoping to redeem myself somewhat and escort Miss Peterson."

"Perhaps it would be wise not to make too firm a declaration Mr Parry," said Mrs Peterson, surprising and also profoundly depressing him, by arranging her face in a poignantly rueful smile.

1st November, 1831, the Bath-London Road.

The coach journey to London was a sore trial for John Drake. Parry made it abundantly clear before the first change of horses that he knew as much as he, Drake, knew of Ravenswood's opium runs, the illicit trade in females and the nefarious methods employed to obtain the same. He also knew of the calamity in the caves, and worse than all of this, he knew of Drake's complicity in all aspects of the venture and his connivance in the suppression of Parry's reports to Melbourne. To add insult to injury, these painful home truths were imparted in gruesome discomfort on the roof of the coach to ensure privacy, and on their return to the inside seats, after a change of horses, he had to endure Parry's cavalier exchanges with the other passengers and the attentions of the dog Caradoc, who had taken an entirely unwarranted interest in him. It was a trying and miserable day.

Nathaniel's spirits had risen with every mile they covered. He managed to let Drake know that his plotting was discovered without divulging the identity of the informant. Cornelius Lee remained anonymous as Nathaniel's confederate. He was free to deliver whatever retribution of his own he wished to visit on the heads of the crew of the *Blue Dragon*, the shadowy Count, or even, in the fullness of time, Ravenswood himself. Though, reflected Nathaniel, it would probably take more than Lee, talented as he was, to bring down such a well-connected scourge as Edwin Ravenswood. Drake's experiences with him must have been severe indeed, as he seemed entirely unmanned by them. There was no trace of the greedy, swaggering braggart, the bumptious and callous superior, just the empty shell that had housed him. Drake had even tormented himself, in the long silences between bouts of home-truths, with the suggestion that Ravenswood had abandoned him so utterly that he had himself taken Nathaniel into his confidence and revealed all. By the time they reached Reading, Nathaniel had even been moved to sympathy and encouraged Drake to relive his more positive experiences as special constable. The chance meeting with Mr Brunel was expanded upon and enlarged, to become glorious, recasting Drake from casual conversationalist to Brunel's confidante and friend, his brush with a looter would have given the Bow Street men a run for their money. By the time they rattled over the London cobbles Drake had retrieved some semblance of self-esteem and it was not a moment too soon for his emergence from the pit, as the meeting with Melbourne and Palmerston was scheduled for the following day.

Morning: 2nd November, 1831, Carlisle Lane, Lambeth, London.

Nathaniel had had a good sleep at his lodgings in Carlisle Lane. Fortunately his letter had arrived in time and the housekeeper had been able to make herself busy on his behalf. He had been greeted with a dust and bug free apartment, a bowl of clean water and an aired bed: nothing not to like. Apart from the silence. He had risen this All Souls Day with no morning chorus from Martha, no chirruping from the Johnty or Mary's soft steps on the landing. No crashes as Tobias careered down the stairs, no wheezing cackle from Old Tom. Caradoc too seemed to feel bereft and was reluctant to be left, but eventually saw the sense of it. Nathaniel stoked the fire, bade him good-day and stepped outside in his three-caped greatcoat, glanced up and down the deserted road, then swung his swordstick full-circle and tapped off smartly towards Westminster Bridge. November had come with a vengeance and there was a vicious east wind cutting up the Thames estuary from the North Sea. He missed the wild west wind, the softer breath of Autumn, Shelley's enchanter scattering the ghostly leaves. But there was no time left to dwell on his loss; he pulled his hat down hard and hurried on to Whitehall. He was heading for Downing Street, the current head-quarters of both the Home and Foreign Offices and as such official lair of both the noble lords.

Melbourne lounged, rather than sat, opposite Nathaniel and Drake, but there was nothing relaxed in his mood. He appeared testy and eyed them bleakly across his desk. Percy was busy arranging their various reports before him so Melbourne could remind himself of them at a glance. Nathaniel noted that one was distinctly more battered than the others, creased and curling at the edges: it was one of his. Percy caught his eye and risked flashing a conspiratorial grin in his direction. The two employees sat in silence as Melbourne ran his eyes over the reports again, eye-lids half closed, but one tapping finger on the desk signalling his displeasure. Melbourne tapped with increasing resolve: tap, tap, tap, remorseless as a clock, until Drake could bear it no longer.

"My Lord, I hope you were pleased with my," he paused unwillingly, "that is, our reports from the south-west. My Lord Palmerston has expressed his pleasure in the links I have forged with Mr Ravenswood, the Bristol ship owner. He will be a reliable source of information on the status of the opium trade to China and is a man of powerful influence in the area. He is a loyal Whig supporter."

Melbourne glared balefully. "Valuable as that link may prove to be Mr Drake, we must focus our attention on your other duties in the area. Parry's early reports of the trouble fomenting in Bristol were of particular utility. And," he added in a theatrical undertone, "his cautionary comments regarding Ravenswood's enterprises did not go unappreciated."

Drake felt the sweat trickle down his back and he tugged at his neckcloth for relief.

Melbourne continued: "The rash of violent outbreaks since the Lords rejected the Bill has been greatly disturbing and it was only by the swiftest action on the part of local magistrates that it was contained. The disgraceful scenes in Bristol show that action was in that case far from swift. The commanding officer

Brereton and the Mayor are being questioned for their lamentable failure to order an immediate cavalry charge on Saturday the 29th, as soon as the Mansion House was attacked. Arrests are likely." He sighed as if exhausted already by the prospect. "Brereton's was potentially a capital crime. Capital crime damn it!" He seemed suddenly animated, and repeated the charge fiercely, the energy of it rousing him to lean menacingly over the desk, before slumping back. "Law and order, gentlemen, law and order: it relies on swift and efficient action from our Justices of the Peace. The yeomen cavalry are our backstops. Come the day when there are police forces in all towns and counties we will be better informed and better able to control the mobs. That day is a long way off and will no doubt bring with it problems and annoyances all of its own." He waved a weary hand towards the pile of reports. "Bristol is now over-run with detachments from every county of the south-west. And there's the Welsh brigade from Cardiff. We've even sent damned frigates to patrol the Severn!"

Melbourne ruminated for a while, then, seemingly satisfied he looked up, and Nathaniel decided to build a few bridges.

"Mr Drake is probably too modest to tell you my Lord, but he enlisted as special constable in Bristol whilst I was engaged in my work in Bath."

He sat, impassive, as Melbourne grunted a few enquiries and Drake bleated a few words in response. It would not do any harm to offer a life-belt to the drowning man. It would act as a reassurance that Nathaniel was unlikely to inform on him and pave the way for future work, converting Drake from an active enemy to a more humble and congenial colleague.

"Well then, the immediate dangers seem to be over. What!" continued Melbourne, "But I require you both to return to the West Country to keep a weather eye open. I gather that one of our up and coming supporters has disappeared. A Mr Vere of the New Bank? I had considered appointing him to the magistrates' bench. It would appear that the existing bench has at least a quorum of imbeciles singularly ill-equipped to deal with the ferocity of the populace. Lord Palmerston is keen for Mr Ravenswood to be appointed and I intend to appoint my other close contact, a Captain Peterson, who has kept me informed throughout. Excellent man. Speaks highly of you Parry."

Nathaniel could not disguise his surprise. "Captain Peterson? Your contact in Bath?" To see Parry wrong-footed gave Drake another crumb of comfort. He hadn't seen that bloody man so comprehensively baffled since he'd met him. It wasn't much, but on a barren day such as this it did a little to raise his game.

Evening: 5th November, 1831. The Assembly Rooms, Bath.

The Rooms were full to bursting with Bath's *beau monde* and a fair sprinkling of eminent Bristolians, briefly escaping the ruins of their own city for a Reformers' fund-raiser. A string quartet was performing the country sets, lathered in sweat with the effort, faces like the morning sun, armpits chaffed and raw as they sawed away in their embroidered livery. The dance floor beneath the sparkling chandeliers was thronged with lines of dancers, some puffing down the lines, some prancing, some quite lost a full four beats behind and scrambling to catch up. There was an air of defiance in the revelry and a sense of triumph. Though the Bill was not yet through, the victory of law and order over the dark forces of riotous revolt was something to celebrate. On this Bonfire Night, unlike other reforming cities, Bath had not resorted to burning effigies of the Lords and Bishops in the place of Guy Fawkes. The city had bandaged its wounds and was, by and large, open for business. They were ready for the next bout.

Captain and Mrs Peterson, Anna Grant and Henry Blake, Tilly Vere and Howard Dill, Dr Parry and, a very rare sighting indeed, Mrs Parry, made up one set and were cutting reasonable figures in the *Sir Roger de Coverley*, the grand finale of the country dances.

Further down the floor, Coco and Diarmuid were stepping out with a group of younger dancers, two giggling girls in their first season, two raw-boned young men from the country set and an aspiring politician and his wife down to see Diarmuid and accompany him to London after the week-end revels. "Bi'Jaysus," whispered Diarmuid in Coco's ear as they met again after the furious section of strip the willow. "These two young bloods are fox hunting men and cutting a fine dash. It's goin' to do for me! Drinks at the next halt!"

"Drinks it is!" shouted Coco as they capered down the line.

"What ho!" hallooed one of the young men as he tore by. "Don't mind if we do! What!"

At a table in the corner sat a quartet in close conversation. One man seemed sunk in thought, the other paying relaxed attention to a handsome, brittle woman in her late thirties. His wife seemed tense, attempting to break into the conversation between her husband and her friend but not quite managing to do so. The exchanges did not go unremarked. Both women were decked out in sumptuous gowns of the latest fashion, eclipsing the boldest of Bath's beauties, including the sparkling Tilly Vere. Their finery, and in particular their flashing jewels had drawn much attention, including a sharp glance from Coco who had made it her business to scrutinise the pair as she sped by.

"Perhaps we should dance, Mr Ravenswood," said the handsome woman, her hauteur exchanged for a beguiling smile. "I seem to have some dances free."

"Perhaps we should," he answered. "But not a country romp, surely Mrs Drake."

"Oh no Mr Ravenswood, I think they are finishing, perhaps a waltz?"

"And Mr Drake shall dance with me," said Amanda, her eyes glittering with fury as she turned to him. "Let us not sit idly on our hands sir."

Away from the hurly-burly, Emma Peterson had taken refuge in the ladies' cloakroom. She stood before a mirror, expressionless. Nathaniel had not yet arrived and she was summoning the courage to return to the ballroom. She had spent a trying afternoon in Anna's company listening to wedding plans, to tales of the progress of the trousseau, which was formidable, and to monologues on the excellence of Henry Blake. She was certain she could take no more of the same. She had exhausted most avenues of conversation with Dr and Mrs Parry, her mother having forbidden her to touch on the subject of the rapid advance of the cholera, as well as any mention of the peculiar circumstances of the arrival of their new kitchen maid. Not that she would have discussed Nathaniel's business in public. She felt herself flush at the thought of his name and leaned closer to the mirror. She would not cry, but did she look as though she had? She had had another note from him it was true, telling her of his rooms in Lambeth and his walks by the Thames. It rested in her reticule even now, but she prevented herself from taking it out. Her new found self-assurance was in grave danger of shipwreck. Like Shelley. After their game with *The Eve of St Agnes* she had prepared by re-reading more Keats, more Byron and much more Shelley. Poor shipwrecked Shelley. She recited to herself:

"And the sunlight clasps the earth, and the moonbeams kiss the sea; What are all these kissing's worth, If thou kiss not me?"

And one tear slowly welled up to roll down her cheek.

Off Cape Finisterre, aboard the *Blue Dragon*.

Cornelius had been able to ensure that his four principal allies amongst the crew shared his small cabin with him. He had his two most trusted friends, the sailors who had fired the *Mathilda* and covered Nathaniel's escape from Redcliffe as well as two others, both regular players in the Three Sugar Loaves, men who had proved their worth. The *Blue Dragon* had floated on the ebb tide, down the Avon to the Severn Estuary without mishap. Luckily for them all, given the mood of Ravenswood and also of Kizhe, both pilot and tide were ready to see them out when Ravenswood issued his commands. Delay would have been painful for everyone concerned. Also to his surprise, Trevellis's ploy had managed to succeed and assuage Kizhe's temper. They had anchored off North Devon as planned and the Captain had secured the purchase of four blonde paupers from a secluded rural poor-house, all under ten years of age. They had been added to the cache in the secure cabin to travel with the other child brought from Redcliffe Parade. There had been no noise from the cabin, which boded ill, but Cornelius was powerless to relieve their condition. A hulking woman with suspiciously muscled forearms was in charge of them, all guarded by two of Kizhe's most loyal men.

Kizhe himself had been allocated a superior cabin near Trevellis, protected by a couple of his men and it was only at mealtimes that Cornelius had guaranteed access to it. That particular night, both of them, Kizhe's henchmen and the Captain were at supper in Kizhe's cabin.

"We will anchor at Lisbon," said Kizhe, his sharp eyes piercing Trevellis as he tore a knuckle of ham apart with a snap. "I need to see a Portuguese trader for a few more girls. The transatlantic trade still runs well there. A few more exotic birds will spice the dish." He laughed shortly, a harsh snort, briefly displaying his discoloured teeth. "After Madeira, we'll aim for Guinea. More exotic still!"

"I don't have the instructions from Mr Ravenswood for extra ports," said Trevellis gruffly, too sure of himself to notice the deadly glint in Kizhe's eye. In seconds Kizhe had lunged from his seat, drawn the short ugly weapon he habitually carried at his hip and pinned Trevellis to the back of his chair, the dull blade with its vicious hook rammed against his throat, the chair leaning back crazily, Trevellis's feet dangling clear of the floor.

"I am giving you instructions Captain," he said, quietly and slowly in the paralysed silence of the cabin. "I assure you that I take full responsibility for this," he tightened his grip making Trevellis flinch, "shall we say, this "deviation" from your preferred route. Mr Ravenswood's arrangements fell short of the Count's requirements. That was a pity," as he continued a thin trickle of blood began to seep from Trevellis's neck as the hook bit into it. "A great pity: but it will be remedied. The requirements will be fulfilled. The extra ports will be added to the journey. I remind you Captain that I have not only my own group of men on board, but a sizeable portion of the rest of the crew is also more than ready to follow my instructions. Those loyal to me will not go unrewarded. I advise you to do likewise. Do you understand me Captain?"

As Trevellis managed a strangled assent, Cornelius could only assume that the performance had been as much for his benefit as the Captain's. He let his mind roam back to the start of his assignment in the Autumn of 1830, when through his timely ambush of the crew sent from Canton, he and his men had managed to replace them and travel to England on the *Blue Dragon*. The following summer had been profitably spent embedding himself into Ravenswood's operation, but the arrival of Kizhe had made his position precarious. Since the shooting of the poacher and their fight in the wood, but especially after the discovery of the sailors with arrow wounds on the *Mathilda*, he had known that Kizhe mistrusted him. He must warn his men as Kizhe could move against them at any time, but probably would not do so yet. The meal concluded raggedly, Trevellis slinking off to his cabin leaving Kizhe and his men to finish the food. Cornelius found he had little appetite.

Alone in his own cabin after supper, Kizhe stripped off his shirt and carefully wiped his hachiwari: the helmet breaker. The squat blade with its hook was his signature weapon. Just to hold it gave him a savage, elemental pleasure. He returned it to its ornate sheath and flung himself into his hammock, holding the case up to the swinging light of his lantern and running his blunt fingers over the scroll work. He remembered every moment of the night when he first took it for his own. The dark Tokyo streets, the shrill whistles, the running feet of the police. Many of them carried a hachiwari for street fighting and to combat swordsmen, but few could match this beauty. It had battered his back and his skull as the policeman beat him to the ground, it had bruised his body and fractured his arm, but he had broken that man's neck. He laughed at the memory. Snap! Like a ham knuckle-bone! Perhaps some other necks would need to be snapped. He scowled at the thought of the rat-like Trevellis and the blundering crew, but also at the thought of Cornelius Lee. As planned, three men had sailed from China to Bristol with the *Blue Dragon*, transporting the payment from the opium and paying off Ravenswood. Three men had been expected and three had appeared, as had the sealed money chest but there was something unusual about Lee. He wasn't the usual type of envoy sent by the opium bosses in Canton: crude, venal men with men's normal appetites, men after Kizhe's own heart. Lee was abstemious, zealous: there was something strange. Kizhe paused, scouring his memory. Yes, the soft fighting style, deceptively useful, there had been something of the monk about Lee: a whiff of incense. Kizhe's scowl relaxed and he snorted out a harsh bark of pleasure at his own wit. He was resolved that any remaining mysteries would be unravelled before much longer. Enquiries would be started as soon as they put into Madras, and if his suspicions were aroused before that time, well, so much the worse for Lee. He put the helmet breaker beneath his pillow, and like the other dark creatures of the deep he drifted away, at one with the treacherous rolling of the sea.

Martha Spence's house, Walcot St, Bath.

Nathaniel had spent considerable time preparing for the evening. He had decided on the blue neck-cloth, tied in his favourite draped Byronic knot, and his blue and white striped waistcoat. Mary had starched his shirt and Tobias had brushed his evening coat. He left Caradoc sleeping in the kitchen and after closing the door behind him, stood for a moment, undecided, on the path. Tonight he would make a decision about Em, but not quite yet. Instead of going straight up Lansdown to Alfred Street he detoured along the London Road, walking behind the houses near the river. The sky was periodically lit with squibs and he caught sight of fires burning in back gardens. Some families were out together, arcs of children squealed round fathers as they lit their small stores of fireworks against the garden fences. Some children stood like statues, silent and mesmerised by the fizz of spinning Catherine Wheels, others danced and screamed with delight as the bangers and crackers exploded. He raked the bushes with his stick as he walked, deep in thought. When he reached Grosvenor, he turned left to regain the highway. He had out-paced the pedestrians of the town and the road had become solitary. As he turned to make his way back, the odd private coach rattled by, with powdered couples making for the Rooms. He overtook two old people, strolling on the pavement, arm in arm and bundled in shawls. "Nothing in the world is single," he quoted to himself. "All things by a law divine, in another's being mingle. Why not I with thine?"

He felt pretty sure she was game for mingling. The embrace in the hall in Marlborough Buildings had been surprisingly warm, he could feel it still. But making an offer was a step further. He needed to see her. Still feeling troubled, he hurried on, but still arrived late for the soiree. The Rooms were brilliantly lit and crowded, as if society was flaunting its confidence, facing down the darkness that prowled still in the haunts of the destitute, the starving villages and the miserable city slums. Those who could afford to celebrate were resolved to do so. He made his way down the grand entrance hall of the Rooms and almost reached the entrance to the ballroom when he was waylaid by a group of revellers catching a breath of air outside the press of the dance floor.

"Mr Parry! Well met!"

Nathaniel paused reluctantly at the greeting and found himself surrounded by a group led by Neville Fairfield, his right arm muffled in a sling.

"What happened!" exclaimed Nathaniel.

"Injured in Bristol so I had to come back. Sword arm don't you know!" said Fairfield ruefully. "Thirty-six hours in the saddle we had Parry. The Captain and the rest of the troop are still under orders. Should be there mi'self."

Before he could extricate himself he had to extend pleasantries to Mrs Fairfield, to Mrs Cruttwell and all the others in the party, even before Neville began to enlarge on the deeds of the yeomen in Bristol. It all took some considerable time before he could make his way to the ballroom. He arrived at a lull in the dancing and immediately he caught sight of Coco's graceful back, instantly recognisable, and Diarmuid, talking and laughing as usual, and as usual not just to Coco, but also to a crush of young women, with their men ranged behind them, doomed to play second, third and fourth fiddles until Mr Casey had done. Nathaniel made to beat a retreat, but Diarmuid hailed him.

"If it isn't himself! Colette my dear, it is himself Mr Nathaniel Parry and just as we'd given him up for dead!"

As Nathaniel walked unwillingly towards the group he saw Em approaching. She looked pale and beautiful, in a fitted gown of cream muslin, her hair piled up with a diamond clasp, shining strands curling to her shoulders.

"Em! Miss Peterson!" he said. "I am so pleased to see you."

"Miss Peterson has come to claim me Nathaniel," said Diarmuid. "I had the divil of a job tracking her down and we are promised for this dance."

"Nathaniel you will dance with me," said Coco smiling.

From a safe seat by Howard, Tilly watched the crowds of dancers closely. She had already spotted a man she had known from her youth. John Drake had gone up in the world since their early fumbles at Frome Assemblies. But of more immediate interest, she had not missed the warmth of Nathaniel's smile as he saw Emma Peterson, nor the frisson between the two of them, Mr Casey, and his detestable partner. Earlier that Autumn she had herself kept an optimistic eye on Mr Casey but had given up when she realised the parlous state of his finances. She watched the two couples waltz out of view and turned to Howard.

"Mr Parry is much struck by Miss Peterson don't you think? But he dances with Miss Montrechet, and there is definitely something between the two of them. I can sense it."

Even as she said it she regretted it. A far-away look came into Howard's eyes.

"Ah yes my dear, Miss Montrechet." He caught sight again of Coco's whirling skirts, and Nathaniel's head close to hers as they talked. "There is most definitely something, but it need not interfere with Miss Peterson's plans."

As the music stopped Nathaniel disengaged himself from Coco's embrace, took her by the arm and steered her towards Diarmuid and Em.

"Thank you Mr Casey," Em was saying, as Diarmuid bowed low over her hand and kissed it tenderly.

"Like a will-o'-the-wisp you are to be sure," he said smiling into her eyes. "Didn't I tell you before Parry. She dances like a fairy so she does."

"Yes you did," said Nathaniel shortly. "Miss Peterson, may I have the next dance."

And even as Diarmuid complained that he had booked that dance as well, Nathaniel took her in his arms and they moved swiftly out of reach.

"Did you get my note Em?" said Nathaniel smiling, breathing in her scent and tightening his hold on her waist.

"Yes, thank you. I have them all. How long can you stay in Bath, Nathaniel?"

"Certainly a few days. I need to speak to your father."

At the light leaping in her eyes he bit back his next words. He had been going to say he had some business to discuss after his meeting with Melbourne. Instead he held her even closer.

"Em, I'm sorry."

"For what?"

"For not being here."

"You are here now, Nathaniel."

"Em we have only known each other for a month, but I've missed you whilst I've been away. Do you think you could be happy with me?"

"I have been reading Shelley," she said suddenly. "He had more of love than Keats, and I want more of it, Nathaniel. I have loved you from the first time I saw you. You must know what he said: "As the sun clasps the earth and the moonbeams kiss the sea," she faltered, unable to go on.

But Nathaniel could, putting his lips to her ear he whispered, "What are all these kissings worth, if thou kiss not me!"

Epilogue: One year later

Late afternoon: 5th November, 1832.
Brooks's Club, St James's Street, London.

"Gad! Deuced fine this 1811!" Lord Melbourne stuck his legs out to rest them on the raised fender. Heels together, he clapped his feet smartly, three times on the trot, as coda to his enjoyment. He was ensconced in the depths of a wing-backed chair, drying out from the brief drenching he had sustained whilst moving from his coach to the club's front porch. A passing post-chaise, furiously driven by a young blood, had dashed through a deep puddle and splattered most of its contents onto his trousers. Opposite him on the other side of a low table and with his back to the main door, sat Palmerston, deep in thought, lower lip at the jut. He swallowed a mouthful of the port absentmindedly.

"Tell me if Charles comes in. I need a word."

"Doubt if you'll be in luck," said Melbourne, amused. "Poor fellow looked damned seedy earlier today. Wouldn't surprise me if he threw over the whole damned business and retired to Howick to immure himself in his library."

Palmerston narrowed his eyes, "And then who else but your good self could possibly be in line to step into Number 10?"

"Well my dear fellow," said Melbourne, lazily. "Quite so, *noblesse oblige* what!"

Palmerston was acutely aware that Lord Grey could abandon his post at any moment making his brother-in-law in waiting even more valuable to him than he already was. As the most senior Whig he was clearly the Prime Minister in waiting. After the titanic struggle with the Lords had ended in crowning success with the passage of the Reform Act in June, Charles had seemed to wilt before their eyes. Job done and his place in history secured, he had faded and most days appeared as a wizened old man. The death of his favourite grandson and continuing tussles with his son-in-law had contributed to his decline. It was a matter of time, maybe a few years, or a few months, before his final retirement. Palmerston knew he must alert Melbourne to the growing threat to the Chinese trade.

"I have had a disturbing communication."

Melbourne smiled amiably. Palmerston pressed on: irritated.

"The harbours which Drake assured me would be continuously useful for opium shipments have been blockaded by Chinese troops. By some means the Emperor's forces in Canton have been made aware of the route and have taken steps to close it. Ravenswood's interests in the opium growing in India continue unmolested, but his little wheeze for landing the goods discreetly will not be running so smoothly in the future. He might have to take his chances with the ships running Company opium," He dropped his gaze and glowered into the fire. "There might come a day in the near future when the Emperor will need to be taught a lesson."

Melbourne allowed himself a sustained sigh. The prospect of expending time and energy on such an adventure was not enticing.

"My dear fellow, things might not be so bad. You know that our intelligence gathering is, well, rather hit and miss. You may not have the full story, or even a quarter of it. You're better off reading *The Times* than listening to our own people. Damned reliable those *Times* fellows. Dashed well informed." He allowed that to sink in, then continued. "We need to be alert to domestic matters Pam. Speaking of the press, it was drawn to my attention by Percy that *The Poor Man's Guardian* has seen fit to fulminate against the Act and is stirring up the lower classes for all it's worth. Which won't be much if I've anything to do with it! They're after lowering the bar on the household value for the townsmen's vote. Damned ink's barely dry on the dashed Act! Furthermore, I need hardly remind you that the day of fasting and humiliation for the cholera, demanded so vociferously by the Church, made no appreciable difference. The air, even here in London, remains foetid despite all efforts and apparently panic is setting in. Even the hackney cabs are damned near ruined as people fear using public facilities!" From the glazed expression he sensed a faltering in Palmerston's resolve and pressed his initiative home. "And quite apart from existing trials, the Factory and Education Bills must command our attention at present, not to mention the Slavery Bill. They must all be pushed through next session well before we finish our review of the Poor Law. Root and branch reform we've promised! Election promises my dear fellow. The rate payers will not stick such high poor rates for much longer. Damned stratospheric!" He looked slyly at Palmerston. "It will be another generation in the wilderness for the Whigs if we don't deliver the goods on our watch. Younger men's careers might founder on the back benches 'til they're put out to grass."

Palmerston shrugged his shoulders. "Yes, yes. I know. First things first. The China trade is inconvenienced but has not as yet entered a critical phase. We will bide our time." Temporarily out-manoeuvred he rose abruptly and shot his cuffs. "Now my dear fellow, are you in form for gaming? I told Russell we'd be at the tables before we dine."

Nathaniel's lodgings in Carlisle Lane, Lambeth.

Across the Thames in Carlisle Lane, a tall young man was seated by the fireplace in his top floor rooms. A wiry black and tan Welsh terrier was lying spread-eagled by the log box and, apart from the wind rattling the window-frame and the juddering lick of the flames, all that could be heard was the steady ticking of the clock on the mantel. Nathaniel Parry searched his pockets and placed two letters on the table. The one from Em had been read and re-read. He now had a collection and would add this latest one. Perhaps tomorrow he could leave for Bath. The Season had started there and his work had reached a pause: it was a good time to go. Occasional bangs and cracks outside reminded him of the day. It was twelve months to the night since he had proposed to Em. The Captain's relations with Lord Melbourne had been a surprise. He did not know if he had been manipulated, but did not really care. Byron, he decided, had a few things right. "Each kiss a heart-quake" he liked that, he'd grown attached to Em's kisses and looked forward to some more. But was Byron right about a man's love being different from a woman's, being a thing apart from the rest of his life? Perhaps, in part. He laughed and felt happy. The future seemed bright.

He took out the second letter which he had read once, clandestinely, at Whitehall where it had been delivered some weeks before and had been sitting waiting for him on Percy's desk. He had been lucky it had been scooped up by Percy, which had allowed it to remain unread before his return. Guarded though it was in tone and content, it could have been more illuminating than it intended to be if Drake had managed to cast his eyes over it. It was worn and marked from its long journey, heavily creased, the ink faded. It announced in neat italic script that it had travelled from the British Residency of Singapore, in the sub-division of Bengal, and after the first polite salutations, had much of interest to tell.

"I am well set up in lodgings by the harbour," wrote his correspondent, *"which are serviceable despite being as sweltering and airless as you can imagine, as our latitude is virtually on the equator. I hope this news of my voyage reaches you at your London office as now, with my task complete, my thoughts frequently return to you. I want to tell you the tale of the journey we spoke of before I set sail. Also, I am curious to know how you fare. In particular I would like to hear of the undertakings you made last Autumn and trust they met with success. For my part, you will be interested to know that after leaving Bristol we added to our cargo in Devon, in Lisbon and Guinea, much to our visitor's satisfaction, and all rounded the Cape safely. We spent some time in Bombay, where significant transactions were made, before we followed the coast and rounded the extreme south of India. Our visitor disembarked in Madras but I will ensure my path crosses his again. Depend upon it. Despite heavy seas in the Gulf of Bengal and the Malacca Straits and some episodes of disturbance and discomfort aboard ship, the cargo remained in fair shape and we made landfall here in Singapore. The town had grown since I last saw it ten years before and is a thriving entrepot. No signs remain of the Dutch masters and the British reign supreme. From here we journeyed on up the Gulf of Tonkin until we reached our designated harbour. All survived and the cargo was disembarked. I did not continue north with the cargo, but left my men to fulfil that task and went alone to Canton where I reported to my employer. I have now returned to lodgings here in Singapore, awaiting my passage back to Europe where I have further business to attend.*

So, my friend, my mission met with some success, as did yours, though the works of evil men still thrive and spread, as you say in England, like the green bay tree.

Until we meet again, I have the honour to be,

Your most humble servant, CL."

Nathaniel smiled to himself: “And I yours Cornelius Lee: and I yours. May our paths also cross again, and in happier times.”

He pocketed the letters and stood up, turning to look out at the darkening sky. The patchy clouds, wreathed with smoke from Guy Fawkes’ fires, blurring and haloing the harsh white moonlight, were suddenly pierced with gold. A fizz of sparks shot up; high, wild and bright, followed by a battery of multi-coloured geysers of rich red, green, blue and silver, flying up in a fiery rainbow. He felt a surge of elation, grabbed his greatcoat and swordstick, roused Caradoc with a call of: “Mutton-chops and beer sir!” and within the minute they were down the stairs and out into the gaudy night.

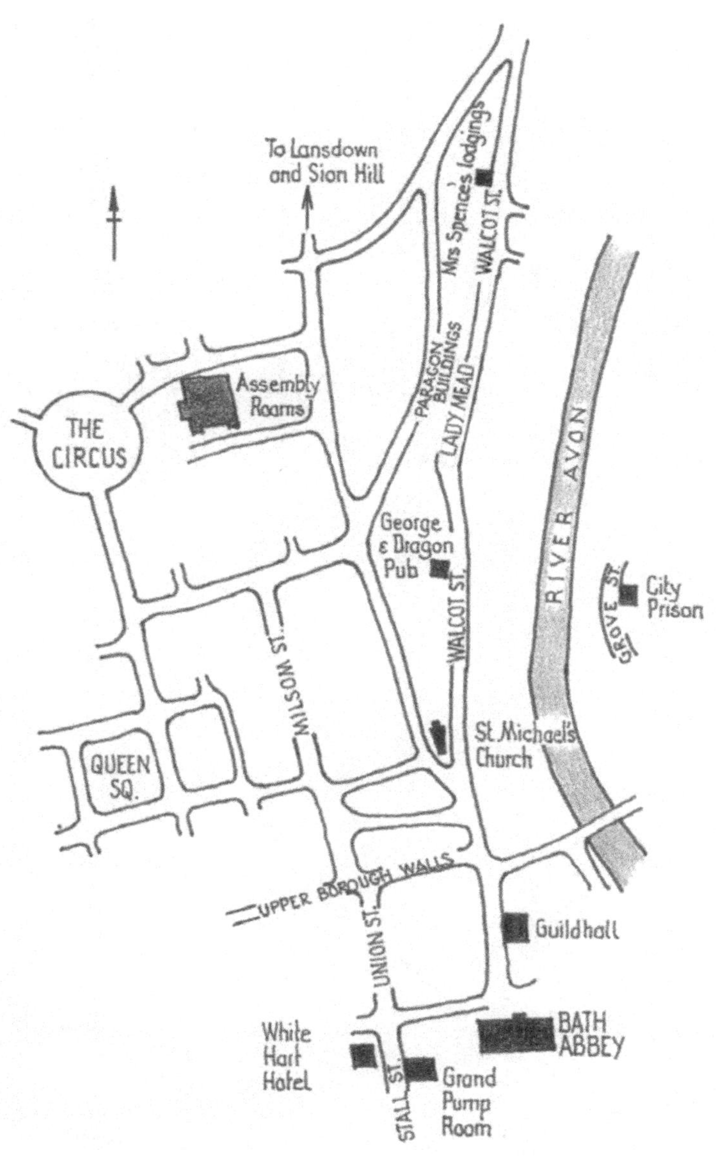

The Upper Town, Bath

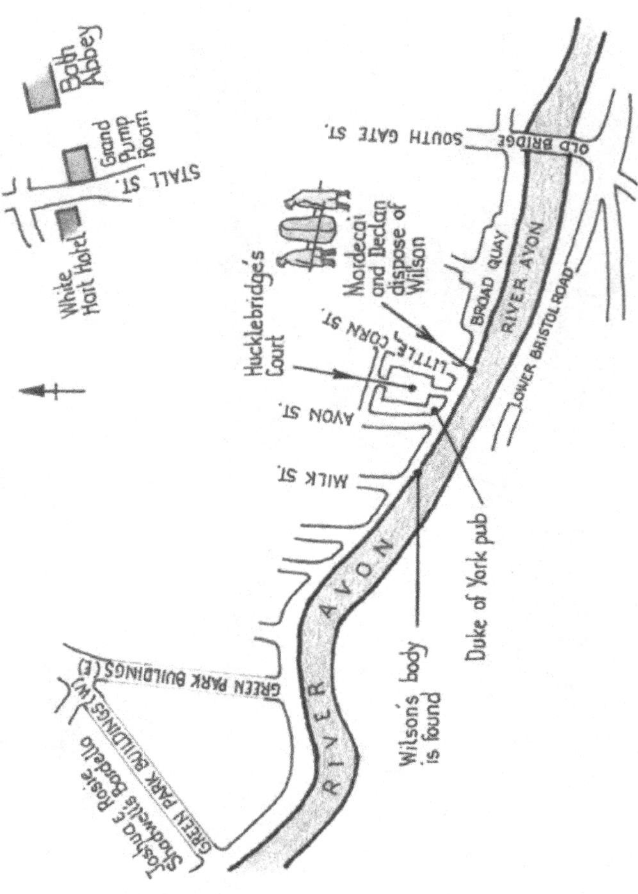

The Quays, Bath

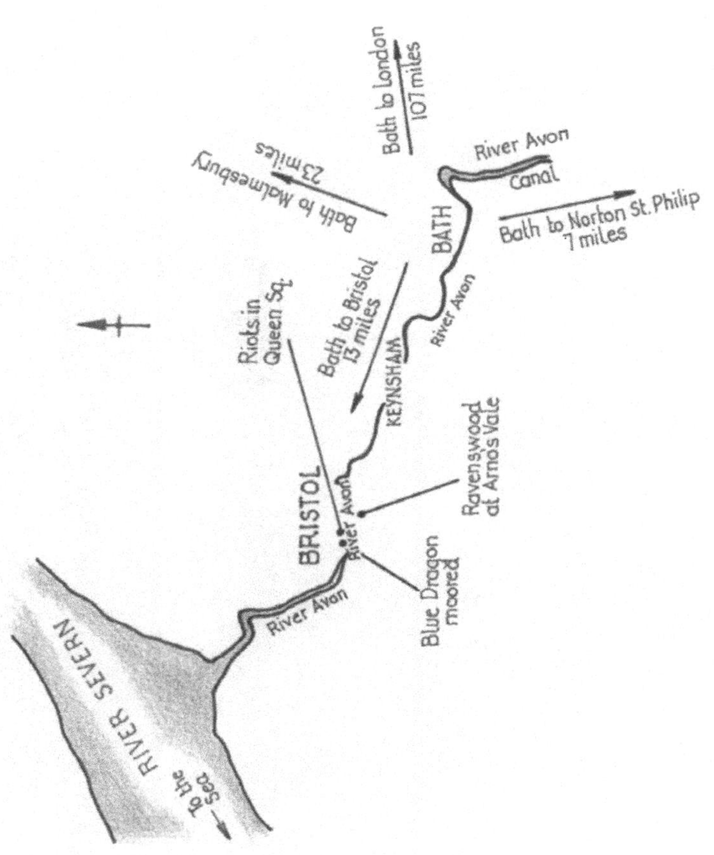

Bristol and Bath

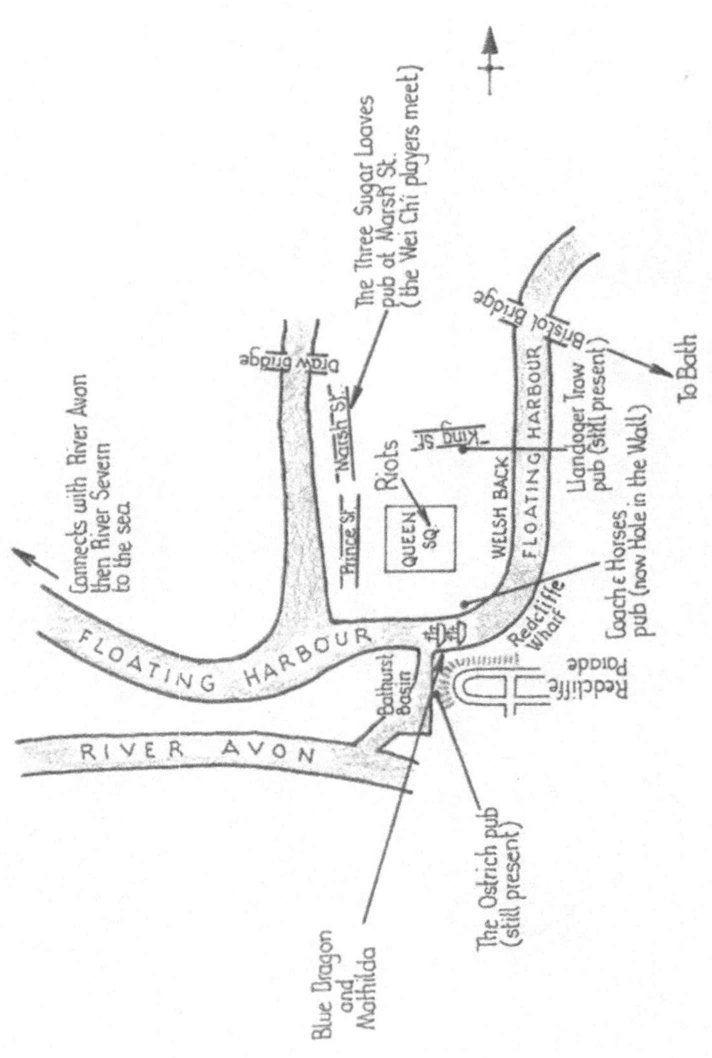

The Centre of Bristol

Voters and Political Parties in 1831

Voting qualifications

Approximately 10% of adult males in England and Wales were entitled to vote before the Reform Act of 1832. These men made up less than 3 % of the total population, yet even they were often unable to use their vote. Only about one third of the constituencies were contested in an "election" and open ballots were the rule. Having to declare a vote in public allowed the intimidation of voters by landlords and employers. As the right to vote was often connected to property ownership, owners of multiple properties could vote more than once.

Rural (county) constituencies had different voting qualifications from urban (borough) constituencies. All county seats observed the same rules. Adult males owning land valued at two pounds or more for the land tax were allowed to vote.

Whigs and Tories

The two main political parties in 1831 were called the Whigs and the Tories. The party system was not as rigid as it is in the 21st century. Individuals moved more frequently between parties and approximately 60 MPs remained independent of both these groups. The party names date from the 17th century when the party more loyal to the wishes of the monarch were insulted by being called Tories. This Irish term suggested that they were encouraging the King in his support of Catholics, despite their own loyalty to the Church of England. Those who were more critical of the King became known as Whigs, a term referring to rebellious Scots.

Authors' Note

Although this book is a work of fiction, the disorder which took place in Bristol and Bath in 1831 was all too real. The events in Bristol were notorious on a national scale as the worst of the Reform Bill riots that broke out after the rejection of the Bill in the House of Lords. Apart from Lords Melbourne and Palmerston, Doctor Parry and Captain Wilkins, all major characters are fictional, though many peripheral characters have the names of real Bath personalities of the time e.g. Mr Bishop and Mr Cooper were the landlords of the Hart, Mr Tasker ran the livery in Pulteney Mews and General Palmer was Bath's reforming MP. Also fictional is the idea that there was an organised and covert plan between the Home and Foreign Secretaries to develop surveillance during the 1831-2 Reform Bill crisis. However, as activities of that nature were not scrupulously documented we allowed our imaginations to speculate.

Whilst there was a brisk and illegal opium trade, on a triangular route from England to India to collect the drug, and then on to China for sale through brokers, the activities described in Bristol are wholly fictional. This being the case, it was very pleasing to discover that the clipper *Sea Witch* (1846) had a dragon figurehead similar to that described on the bow of Ravenswood's ship, the *Blue Dragon*. The first opium clipper was the *Red Rover*, launched in 1829 to beat the north-east monsoon and establish three opium runs per year instead of the usual one. In the 1830s the clippers came to dominate the trade. The first vessels in this class, built for speed with "rakish masts" set at an angle and sharp streamlining, were the Baltimore Clippers first used in the late 1770s during the American War of Independence. Clippers alarmed other vessels, as they were the chosen craft of privateers and pirates. Sadly, kidnapping and the trade in young girls flourished at the time. The campaign against it only gathered pace in the 1880s when it resulted in the raising of the age of consent to sixteen years.

Although the doings of the noble lords are more widely known, as both of them survived long enough in politics to become Prime Minister, the Bath characters, Dr Parry and Mr Charles Wilkins, are not familiar even in Bath. Dr Caleb Parry and his famous son William Edward were real Bath characters, as was Caleb's eldest son Dr Charles Parry. Charles and his wife lived in Bath at the time of the novel, though their characters have been imagined. Charles's gregarious nature was developed from evidence that he and William Edward grew up in an enterprising family. Caleb Parry was nationally important as a physician, and occupied his leisure time with music, painting, literature and experimental sheep farming. William Edward was a successful Arctic explorer and Charles was well known for his medical and history writing. He was active in Bath society and established an organisation to provide jobs for the unemployed. Charles Wilkins can be seen in the local newspaper reports to be not only a rich and successful mill owner, but also a kind employer. His exploits with the local Yeomanry can also be discovered in the news and letters sections of the local newspapers. Unlikely as it may seem, he really did escape in disguise over the roof of the Hart during the riot and the staff fought off the besieging mob with red-hot pokers. The regular fencing training in Bath is an invention, though Nathaniel's reference to the London club is accurate. The Bath Season of 1831 ran regular balls and the Reform Soirees were popular, though not necessarily on the nights designated in the story.

All the inns and habitations referred to, apart from Arno's Tower, were actual locations, some of which survive. Arno's Vale was a popular place for the *nouveau riche* of Bristol to build their mansions at this time, the most notable being Mount Pleasant, which is the present Arno's Court Hotel. The black stables remain beyond the Bath Road, as does the holy well of St Anne, though in a park as opposed to a wood. Detail concerning the weapons is also accurate. Nathaniel's swordstick with spring loaded quillons forming a hand-guard was based on nineteenth century examples, though his version has a special Japanese blade. The makila, a Basque walking stick, is still manufactured. In the nineteenth century it was common for one variety of makila to have a short concealed blade. The hachiwari referred to in the story is believed to be the forerunner of the jutte weapon, and was used by the Japanese police when they were unable to carry swords as they were not members of the Samurai class. Coco's use of a pepper spray was also a technique borrowed from the Japanese police of the Edo period (1603-1868). A policeman would have a small lacquered box called a gantsubushi which had a mouth-piece and pipe for directing the flow of cayenne pepper into the eyes of individuals resisting arrest. Expertise in Savate, French kick-boxing, was current in the early 1830s. This allowed Coco to have experience of this style of fighting. The fighting skills demonstrated by Cornelius reflect the well-respected Chinese martial styles, often taught in secret, which underpinned and influenced further developments of martial arts and weaponry on the island of Okinawa in Japan.

Acknowledgements

Accurate details concerning the locations, the political situation, the characters of the politicians, events in the Bristol Riots, and the disturbances in Bath have been researched by Alex over many years and adapted for the purposes of the narrative. The staff of Bath and Bristol Reference Libraries and Colin Johnston and his staff at Bath Record Office were extremely helpful, as was Graham Snell, Secretary of Brooks's Club in London, who was most kind in sharing his expert knowledge of the history of the Club. We extend our grateful thanks to them all. We would also like to take the opportunity to thank our friends and family: Jane and Malcolm Thick for the time they have taken to read draft chapters and advise us of any historical infelicities they discovered. Any remaining errors rest with the authors. Thanks also to Sarah Sawyer, Richard Hill and

James and Claire Kolaczkowski for their time spent in reading the draft chapters, for their comments and their encouragement. Thanks also to Stan Kolaczkowski, for his advice on martial arts, plotting and presentation, and also to Max Schonbach who assisted with the preparation of the illustrations and maps, and drew the swordstick on the cover. We also thank Ana María Espiñeira Luksić for preparation of the rest of the cover art, and Hilary Strickland for the cover layout. Finally, we appreciate the patience of Bob's wife Marina during the preparation of this work

Watch out for Nathaniel's second adventure:
Napoleon's Gold - The Wages of Sin.

Bath, January 2016
Dr Alex Kolaczkowski
Professor Robert Hayes

10012016

The Authors

The nominal author of the book, Alex E. Robertson, is a pen name, incorporating the names of the creators of the work. The text was written by Dr Alex Kolaczkowski, based on an original idea from Robert Hayes, who is also the research collaborator, producer and editor of the project.

Dr Alex Kolaczkowski has taught history at schools in Bath and Bristol, as well as in Wiltshire, Oxfordshire and Surrey. Her B.Ed degree was awarded by the University of Bristol and her Ph.D by the University of Bath. A dedicated teacher, passionate about all aspects of her subject, she took her pupils on frequent field trips, making ancient, medieval, early modern and modern topics alike come vividly to life. Bath and Bristol are cities very well known to her having lived, studied and worked in both of them. Her expertise in Bath history stemmed from her years spent researching the city as a case-study for her doctoral topic on the development of municipal socialism and the civic ideal in the nineteenth century. By invitation from the Dictionary of National Biography she provided the entry for Sir Jerom Murch who was Mayor of Bath on seven occasions, and wrote a paper on aspects of Bath Non-Conformism for the Unitarian Journal. These research activities helped provide her specialist background knowledge of the period and places in which the novel is set.

Professor Robert Hayes is a full-time academic at the University of Alberta in Canada. Apart from his distinguished research and teaching in chemical engineering, he is a calculating thinker with an interest in mystery and intrigue within a historical context. As a PhD student at the University of Bath in the early 1980s, he developed an interest in the game of Go (which originated as Wei Ch'i in China), often travelling to Bristol to play at the Go Club in Hotwells, and later was a founder member of the Bath Go Club at the Crown Inn, Bathwick Street. During the 1990s he was a frequent visitor to Bath and Bristol. In addition to his passion for historical mysteries, he is a lover of fine wines, single malt whisky, and of course whiskey.

Brief introduction to the use of local dialect

In some sections of the story, to convey the atmosphere of the region, conversations with people native to the area are expressed in a phonetic version of a south-west English accent. There are many different varieties of this gentle rural accent, and the version used in this novel is typical of the accent which could still frequently be heard in Bath well into the twentieth century.

You will notice that the accent tends to exclude letters at the beginning and ends of words, to shorten words, and alter grammar. In the nineteenth century it was normal for the lower classes in all areas to exclude the "h" at the start of words, and if they wished to sound very polite to include an "h" at the beginning of words where there was no such letter. To help the reader, we have provided more detailed explanations of selected phrases as they first feature in the story.

This will help visitors, particularly those from abroad, to identify and appreciate the local accent, which can still be heard occasionally today.

	Phonetic version	**Meaning**
Prologue		
p. 2	I'd take 'er home	I would take her home
	I can't see 'er fittin' in	I cannot see her fitting in
	Exac'ly	Exactly
	Come wi'me mi'dear	Come with me my dear
Chap.1		
p. 30	Oiy could 'elp	I could help
p. 31	'is beard	his beard
	y'r lodgings	your lodgings
p. 33	mi' and	my hand
	Thank'ee sir	Thank you sir
	The Dragon ain't far	The Dragon is not far
	Not that she's a drinker mind	She does not drink heavily you understand

p. 33	She be not	She is not
p. 34	then we was thronged	then we were crowded
	rollickin' times	exciting times
	beatin'	beating
	Oiy don't start 'til breakfast	I don't start until breakfast
p. 35	til 'e's on 'is feet	until he is able to work again
p. 36	givin' us warning	giving us warning
	not just them as	not just those who
	who 'mongst us	who amongst us
	Oiy 'ave	I have
	Oiy pays	I pay
	somewheres	somewhere
	Them as pays	Those who pay
	see 'ow it goes	see how it goes
	what was to 'appen	what was to happen.
	'Nat-chu-ral roights' we 'ave	'Natural rights' we have
	the workin' and the fightin'	the working and the fighting
	they Frenchey wars	the French wars
	Oiy vote 'cos moiy 'ouse	I vote because my house
	'cos 'e lives	because he lives
	Ye 'ave representation	You have representation
	ye'll 'ave more	you will have more
	mi'self	my self
	Majisty	Majesty
	more 'an	more than
	ye're a mouthin'	you are expressing
	sentimints	beliefs
	No one's a mouthin' loike a Yankee as I 'ear	No one is speaking like an American that I can hear.

p. 36	ye're a patriot through an' through	you are entirely a patriot
p. 37	I'm not sayin' as I want	I am not saying that I want
	Tis a mighty	It is a mighty
	They great cities	The great cities
	'E never give	He never gave
	'oo did?	who did?
p. 40	Bastard was 'eavy	The bastard was heavy
p. 41	Get 'im out	Get him out
p. 42	Ye've skewered 'im	You have stabbed him
	done 'imself in	committed suicide

Chap.2

p. 51	She straight away upped and said	She immediately said
	afore she leaves	before she leaves
	'as bin found	has been found
	saw 'im a-floatin' 'ead down	saw him floating with his head down
p. 52	is norm'ly	are normally
p. 53	go a-tramplin' the babe	treading on the baby
	'ee do get sore underfoot	annoyingly he is often under your feet
p. 54	Ye young besom	You young rascal (a besom was a broom made of rough twigs)
p. 62	Frenchies a-winding up	the French annoying
p. 63	Poles hammer and tongs at the Ruskies.	the Polish people attacking the Russians
	Find a good 'orse sir?	Did you find a good horse sir?
	go amok at the weekends.	become violent at the weekends

	H'immigrants	Immigrants
	When mi ma was	When my mother was
	Little 'Ell	Little Hell
p. 64	Oiy ain't never bin	I have never been
p. 65	loike a new pin	like a new pin (shining and clean)

Chap.3

p. 80	Come ye over	Come here
	take a seat along o'me	sit next to me
	ye didn't!	you did not!
	Don't ye be a worritin' y'self	Do not worry yourself
	are a-wantin' it	are wanting it
p. 80	were a-cryin' out	were demanding
p. 81	were agin' it	were against it
	All they wild talkers	All of the aggressive speakers
	and a-wearin' they damned	and wearing the damned
	thought 'e talked sense	thought he spoke sensibly
p. 82	Critters you never	Creatures you never
	'Twas ever the same!	It was always the same.
	Do'ee know	Do you know
	to improve they selves?	to improve themselves?
p. 88	Oiy gat somethin'	I have something
	Two of 'em 'eard a racket	Two of them heard loud noises
	Lot of runnin' an' roarin'	There was a lot of running and shouting

Chap. 4

p. 137	Per'aps	Perhaps

Chap. 5

p. 147	Plough boys most of 'em	Most of them are plough boys
	Slavers y'know	They were involved in the slave trade you know
p. 148	Got a mind o' its own!	It has got a mind of its own!
	You all roight wit' other end	Are you alright with the other end
	Ooh arr	Oh yes
	Oiy got 'er 'oisted perfect 'ere!	I have hoisted it perfectly!
p. 149	Ye young demon!	You young demon!
p. 150	mi'boys from Little 'Ell	my boys from Little Hell
p. 153	Oiy would welcome it like a brother mi'self	I myself would welcome it like a brother
	Thirsty work conversin' with this young sprig 'ere	I feel thirsty after talking with this young child
	Just a'fore ye go to be closeted in the parlour	Just before you go for a secret conversation in the parlour
	folk a'goin' down the street	people going down the street
p. 167	Sweep you a crossin' sir?	Shall I sweep the road so that you may cross sir?
p. 169	Go on moiy love!	Go on my love!
	Land 'er another right 'ook!	Hit her again with your right fist!
p. 171	outside o'these walls? And you're payin'?	outside of these walls? And you are paying?
	Any'ow, I 'eard voices when 'e left	Anyway, I heard voices when he left
p. 172	regulars 'ere	regular customers here

Chap. 6

p. 180	his funeral mebbe!	his funeral maybe!
p. 194	Yon	yonder (over there)
	Jus' look at that missus	Just look at that madam
p. 195	when 'e's out o' they crib.	when he is out of his cradle.
	'e be!	he is.
	Where wast a-goin' my 'andsome?	Where were you going my handsome child?
	young buck	lively young man

Chap. 7

p. 215	Methody	Methodist
p. 217	But 'twas to	But it was to
p. 223	'Ad one once.	I once owned one.
	if you take mi' meanin'	if you understand my meaning
	a-sayin 'e speaks for Bris'l!	saying that he speaks on behalf of Bristol!
	Though we've bin a-losin' out to Liverpool sin' moiy ould dad were a boy	We have been losing trade to Liverpool since my old dad was a boy
	men are 'ungered	men are hungry
p. 229	Up an' at 'em bully boys!	Up and attack them my fine boys!

Chap. 8

p. 241	Been after 'im from 'is first showin' comin' over Totterdown	They have followed him since he first appeared from Totterdown
	but 'e's short o' decent men.	he has not enough good men.
	itchin' for a scrap	wanting a fight
	rilin' everybody	annoying everyone

p. 241	Jack Tars are no cat's paw	Sailors will not be used
p. 248	Serve 'im up to us!	Present him to us!
	Aye!	Yes!
p. 249	I could 'ave done with a leg or two o' that beef	I wanted a leg or two of that beef
	Us'll wet our whistles here	We will have a drink here
p. 250	y'ere (Welsh accent)	Here
p. 259	You'll 'ave to put 'er down Abi	You will have to put her down Abi
p. 260	Rouse yersel'	Rouse yourself
	smashin'	smashing

Chap. 9

p. 275	Leavin' the docks be	Leaving the docks unmolested
p. 276	Glad to make y'r acquaintance sir!	Glad to meet you sir!
p. 278	I'm not goin' 'ome neither	I am not going home either
	Well Mister 'll prob'ly	The man will probably
p. 279	Come up for the season he did	He came up for the Bath season
	No. Missus' son's come back.	No. The lady's son has returned
p. 282	in rollickin' high spirits	in extremely high spirits
	Hundreds were millin' round	Hundreds were milling (crowding) round
p. 293	Not thinkin' of joinin' 'em were 'ee?	You were not thinking of joining them were you?
p. 296	Rioters movin' off to'ard the Abbey	rioters moving off towards the Abbey
p. 297	givin' 'em what for	attacking them fiercely

Chap. 10

p. 305	Oiy ’ave never ’eard the like	I have never heard anything like it
p. 306	on that occashun	on that occasion